A Garland Series

Foundations of the Novel

Representative Early

Eighteenth-Century Fiction

A collection of 100 rare titles
reprinted in photo-facsimile in 71 volumes

Foundations of the Novel

compiled and edited by

Michael F. Shugrue

Secretary for English for the M.L.A.

with New Introductions for each volume by

Michael Shugrue, *City College of C.U.N.Y.*
Malcolm J. Bosse, *City College of C.U.N.Y.*
William Graves, *N.Y. Institute of Technology*

The
Life, Adventures, and Pyracies of the Famous Captain Singleton

by
Daniel Defoe

with a new introduction
for the Garland Edition by
Malcolm J. Bosse

Garland Publishing, Inc., New York & London

1972

Library of Congress Cataloging in Publication Data

Defoe, Daniel, 1616?-1731.
    The life, adventures, and pyracies of the famous
Captain Singleton.

    (Foundations of the novel)
    Facsim. reprint of the 1720 ed.
    I. Title. II. Series.
PZ3.D362Lh2 [PR3404]   823'.5   70-170544
ISBN 0-8240-0545-7

Printed in the United States of America

Introduction

The remarkable evocation of setting which distinguishes Captain Singleton *is proof of Defoe's extensive knowledge of geography, his firm grasp of contemporary accounts of exploration, and his singular ability to create an imaginary world of sensuous accuracy from second-hand information. To write narratives about places that he had never seen, Defoe "took hints from Hakluyt's* Voyages, *from Dampier's* New Voyage *round the World, from Robert Knox's* Historical Relation *of Ceylon, and from other contemporary travel books."* [1] *It is likely that Defoe read the works of Bartholomew Sharp, Lionel Wafer, Thomas Phillips, Edward Cooke, and Woodes Rogers, and might well have personally known some of these adventurers; for his creation of an African setting, he probably used the accounts of the former Guinea trader Mr. Freeman, Governor Dalby Thomas, and the ship's surgeon John Atkins.* [2] *Defoe's sure handling of the materials at hand resulted in a narrative pulsing with the kind of factual detail that makes of his fiction at its best a prime source of felt life during the eighteenth century.*

It is typical of Defoe that he wastes no time getting into the story; in the initial three pages the boy Singleton is kidnapped on the street, sold by a beggar-woman to a gypsy, raised as a ward of a parish,

INTRODUCTION

and sent to sea at age twelve. Soon he is captured by Turkish pirates, rescued by sailors from Portugal, and after a two-year stay in that country, sails for the East Indies. By his own account young Singleton is a rogue who steals from the ship's captain and harbors the desire to kill his master. Nearly hanged for his part in an attempted mutiny, Singleton is set ashore with four companions on the coast of Madagascar. A score of other sailors from the ship join them and the ensuing narrative relates their efforts to survive on the island. Much is made of the metal ornaments hammered out by the cutler for use as barter with the natives; trade on whatever level of sophistication was always a matter of fascination for Defoe. The European castaways wander around the island and rebuild an abandoned Dutch boat, but the story moves along sluggishly until Defoe discovers a strong narrative thread. He finds it in the idea of an overland journey through Africa. The lagging pace quickens and the detail becomes telling when the group of wanderers decide to embark on this dangerous enterprise. In their encounters with African natives, the Europeans prove resourceful but brutal, and it is a measure of Defoe's belief in the concept of the Noble Savage that those Africans who have had close contact with Western civilization through traders are far more deceitful and murderous than their brothers in the interior.

During the hazardous trip Singleton becomes the leader of the group by virtue of his fearlessness and ingenuity. He is a cold pragmatist whose lack of

INTRODUCTION

compassion is exceeded only by his talent for survival. When they find a wounded native, Singleton makes a decision based purely on expediency:

> *... he was by both these Wounds quite disabled, so that we were once going to turn him away, and let him die; and if we had, he would have died indeed in a few Days more: But as I found the Man had some Respect shew'd him, it presently occurred to my Thoughts, that we might bring him to be useful to us... (p. 75).*

During the arduous march through lands teeming with leopards, elephants, crocodiles, and snakes, the travelers avoid catastrophe because of their modern weaponry and their European belief in reason rather than in magic. Defoe spends as much time on details of food and shelter as he does on hunting wild animals and fighting African tribesmen; indeed, he is the novelist of logistics. The headlong pace of the narrative slows for the introduction of a new theme: European exploitation of the wealth of new lands. The marchers meet an English merchant who has been living with the natives and who persuades Singleton and his companions to stop awhile in order to dig for gold. Having loaded themselves down with gold and elephant tusks, the adventurers finally reach a Dutch settlement, where they divide the spoils and immediately go separate ways. Though they have shared untold hardships for two years, their parting is described without sentiment. In Defoe's fictional world there is no time for a nostalgic look backward.

INTRODUCTION

Once Singleton has spent his fortune in England, he sets out again, this time for the West Indies where, by his boastful admission, he quickly takes to piracy:

> *I that was, as I have hinted before, an original Thief, and a Pyrate even by Inclination before, was now in my Element, and never undertook any Thing in my Life with more particular Satisfaction (p. 182).*

In the ensuing pages Defoe's passion for logistics is indulged through a specific enumeration of the kind and quantity of supplies taken on board the pirate ships lying at Tobago, the type of cargoes of traders running the islands, the value of booty taken by Singleton and his companions. The result is a dense, believable account of life among freebooters who flourished in the Indies during the late seventeenth and early eighteenth centuries.

Singleton's abilities bring him high command, although his piratical activities encourage the growth of a callousness so pervasive that at times it leads to cruelty. He denies that his men have committed certain atrocities, but calmly admits that "more was done than it is fit to speak of here" (p. 188). In this portion of the novel events pile up rapidly, and there are chases and sea battles in which Singleton proves himself an able, courageous, and imaginative leader. Defoe stresses the enterprise of such captains who organize together for mutual protection and gain. From the Indies the scene shifts to the East African coast and Madagascar where

8

INTRODUCTION

the pirates continue to plunder and sail restlessly in search of new conquests. Defoe draws a portrait of men whose love of gold is less urgent than their need for adventure. This lust for novelty takes Singleton and his men into the Pacific as far as the Philippines, before they trace their way back to the Indian Ocean and Ceylon. Friend William, a Quaker surgeon, becomes the center of the narrative as he outwits a Ceylonese king and rescues a Dutch slave. William displays further resourcefulness by succeeding in trade negotiations with English merchants in India. He serves Singleton loyally and bravely as a kind of man Friday; he is, moreover, a Christian humanist and healer who ultimately persuades his captain that a life of piracy leads nowhere. When Singleton contemplates suicide while in the throes of repentance, William convinces him that the idea of taking one's life is the "Devil's Notion" (p. 332) and therefore must be ignored.

Returning to England by way of Venice, they agree to remain together for life. The chastened Singleton marries William's widowed sister and the story ends rapidly on a note of domestic peace. It is significant that Singleton conceals his true identity from his countrymen in order to escape punishment for his sins. Defoe's heroes are rarely men who indulge in empty gestures of honor; to the end they follow the dictates of self-preservation.

In this novel Defoe has managed the difficult creative task of portraying a callous rogue who is also admirable. Singleton's ability to survive his trials without complaint

9

INTRODUCTION

has the effect at times of casting him in a heroic mold. Like many of the men and women in Defoe's fiction who succeed in a harsh world, Singleton makes up in energy, boldness, and zest for life what he lacks in sensitivity. As a whole and especially in those pages describing the march through Africa, Captain Singleton *stands as a powerful eighteenth-century testament to the ability of men of courage to endure.*[3]

Malcolm J. Bosse

NOTES

[1] *James Sutherland,* Defoe *(1950), p. 234.*

[2] *John Robert Moore,* Daniel Defoe: Citizen of the Modern World *(1958), pp. 265, 276.*

[3] *Pagination skips from p. 224 to p. 209 and thereafter continues accurately from p. 209. Consequently, the book is sixteen pages longer than the pagination indicates.*

THE
LIFE,
ADVENTURES,
AND
PYRACIES,

Of the Famous

Captain *SINGLETON:*

Containing an ACCOUNT of his being set on Shore in the Island of *Madagascar,* his Settlement there, with a Description of the Place and Inhabitants: Of his Passage from thence, in a Paraguay, to the main Land of *Africa,* with an Account of the Customs and Manners of the People: His great Deliverances from the barbarous Natives and wild Beasts: Of his meeting with an *Englishman,* a Citizen of *London,* among the *Indians,* the great Riches he acquired, and his Voyage Home to *England:* As also Captain *Singleton*'s Return to Sea, with an Account of his many Adventures and Pyracies with the famous Captain *Avery* and others.

LONDON: Printed for *J. Brotherton,* at the *Black Bull* in *Cornhill, J. Graves* in St. *James's Street, A. Dodd,* at the *Peacock* without *Temple bar,* and *T. Warner,* at the *Black Boy* in *Pater-Noster-Row.* 1720.

THE
ADVENTURES
AND
PYRACIES, &c.

A S it is ufual for great Perfons whofe Lives have been remarkable, and whofe Actions deferve Recording to Pofterity, to infift much upon their Originals, give full Accounts of their Families, and the Hiftories of their Anceftors: So, that I may be methodical, I fhall do the fame, tho' I can look but a very little Way into my Pedigree as you will fee prefently.

If I may believe the Woman, whom I was taught to call Mother, I was a little Boy, of about two Years old, very well drefs'd, had a Nurfery Maid to tend me, who took me out

B   on

on a fine Summer's Evening into the Fields towards *Iflington*, as fhe pretended, to give the
Child fome Air, a little Girl being with her of
Twelve or Fourteen Years old, that lived in the
Neighbourhood. The Maid, whether by Appointment or otherwife, meets with a Fellow,
her Sweet-heart, as I fuppofe; he carries her
into a Publick-Houfe, to give her a Pot and a
Cake; and while they were toying in the Houfe,
the Girl plays about with me in her Hand in
the Garden, and at the Door, fometimes in Sight,
fometimes out of Sight, thinking no Harm.

At this Juncture comes by one of thofe Sort
of People, who, it feems, made it their Bufinefs
to Spirit away little Children. This was a Hellifh Trade in thofe Days, and chiefly practifed
where they found little Children very well dreft,
or for bigger Children, to fell them to the
Plantations.

The Woman pretending to take me up in her
Arms and kifs me, and play with me, draws
the Girl a good Way from the Houfe, till at
laft fhe makes a fine Story to the Girl, and
bids her go back to the Maid, and tell her where
fhe was with the Child; that a Gentlewoman
had taken a Fancy to the Child, and was kiffing
of it, but fhe fhould not be frighted, or to that
Purpofe; for they were but juft there; and fo
while the Girl went, fhe carries me quite away.

From this time it feems I was difpofed of to
a Beggar-Woman that wanted a pretty little
Child to fet out her Cafe, and after that to
a Gypfey, under whofe Government I continued
till I was about Six Years old; and this Woman,
tho' I was continually dragged about with her,
from one Part of the Country to another, yet
never

never let me want for any thing, and I called
her Mother; tho' she told me at last, she was
not my Mother, but that she bought me for
Twelve Shillings of another Woman, who told
her how she came by me, and told her that my
Name was *Bob S'ngleton*, not *Robert*, but plain *Bob*;
for it seems they never knew by what Name I
was Christen'd.

It is in vain to reflect here, what a terrible
Fright the careless Hussy was in, that lost me;
what Treatment she received from my justly
enraged Father and Mother, and the Horror
these must be in at the Thoughts of their Child
being thus carry'd away; for as I never knew
any thing of the Matter, but just what I have
related, nor who my Father and Mother were;
so it would make but a needless Digression to talk
of it here.

My good *Gypsey Mother*, for some of her wor-
thy Actions *no doubt*, happened in Process of Time
to be hang'd; and as this fell out something too
soon for me to be perfected in the Strolling
Trade, the Parish where I was left, which for my
Life I can't remember, took some Care of me to
be sure; for the first thing I can remember of my
self afterwards, was, that I went to a Parish-
School, and the Minister of the Parish used to
talk to me to be a good Boy; and that tho' I was
but a poor Boy, if I minded my Book, and served God, I might make a good Man.

I believe I was frequently removed from one
Town to another, perhaps as the Parishes dispu-
ted my supposed Mother's last Settlement. Whether I was so shifted by Passes, or otherwise, I
know not; but the Town where I last was kept,
whatever its Name was, must be not far off from

B 2   the

the Sea Side; for a Mafter of a Ship who took a Fancy to me, was the firft that brought me to a Place not far from *Southampton*, which I afterwards knew to be *Buffelton*, and there I tended the Carpenters, and fuch People as were employ'd in Building a Ship for him; and when it was done, tho' I was not above Twelve Years old, he carried me to Sea with him, on a Voyage to *Newfoundland*.

I lived well enough, and pleafed my Mafter fo well, that he called me his own Boy; and I would have called him Father, but he would not allow it, for he had Children of his own. I went three or four Voyages with him, and grew a great fturdy Boy, when coming Home again from the Banks of *Newfoundland*, we were taken by an *Algerine* Rover, or Man of War; which, if my Account ftands right, was about the Year 1695, for you may be fure I kept no Journal.

I was not much concerned at the Difafter, tho' I faw my Mafter, after having been wounded by a Splinter in the Head during the Engagement, very barbaroufly ufed by the *Turks*; *I fay*, I was not much concerned, till upon fome unlucky thing I faid, which, as I remember, was about abufing my Mafter, they took me and beat me moft unmercifully with a flat Stick on the Soles of my Feet, fo that I could neither go or ftand for feveral Days together.

But my good Fortune was my Friend upon this Occafion; for as they were failing away with our Ship in Tow as a Prize, fteering for the Streights, and in Sight of the Bay of *Cadiz*, the *Turkifh* Rover was attack'd by two great *Portuguefe* Men of War, and taken and carried into *Lisbon*.

As

As I was not much concerned at my Captivity, not indeed underſtanding the Conſequences of it, if it had continued; ſo I was not ſuitably ſenſible of my Deliverance: Nor indeed was it ſo much a Deliverance to me, as it would otherwiſe ha' been; for my Maſter, who was the only Friend I had in the World, died at *Lisbon* of his Wounds; and I being then almoſt reduced to my primitive State, *viz.* of Starving, had this Addition to it, that it was in a foreign Country too, where I knew no body, and could not ſpeak a Word of their Language. However, I fared better here than I had Reaſon to expect; for when all the reſt of our Men had their Liberty to go where they would, I that knew not whither to go, ſtaid in the Ship for ſeveral Days, till at length one of the Lieutenants ſeeing me, enquired what that young *Engliſh* Dog did there, and why they did not turn him on Shore?

I heard him, and partly underſtood what he meant, tho' not what he ſaid, and began then to be in a terrible Fright; for I knew not where to get a Bit of Bread; when the Pilot of the Ship, an old Seaman, ſeeing me look very dull, came to me, and ſpeaking broken *Engliſh* to me, told me, I muſt be gone. Whither muſt I go (ſaid I?) Where you will, (ſaid he), Home to your own Country, if you will. How muſt I go thither (ſaid I?) Why have you no Friend (ſaid he?) No, (ſaid I) not in the World, but that Dog, pointing to the Ship's Dog, (who having ſtole a Piece of Meat juſt before, had brought it cloſe by me, and I had taken it from him, and eat it) for he has been a good Friend, and brought me my Dinner.

Well,

Well, well, says he, *you must have your Dinner;
Will you go with me?* Yes, says I, *with all my Heart.*
In short, the old Pilot took me Home with him,
and used me tolerably well, tho' I fared hard
enough, and I lived with him about two Years,
during which time he was solliciting his Busineſs,
and at length got to be Master or Pilot under
Don Garcia de Pimentesia de Carravallas, Captain of
a *Portugueſe* Gallion, or Carrack, which was bound
to *Goa* in the *Eaſt-Indies*; and immediately having gotten his Commiſſion, put me on Board
to look after his Cabbin, in which he had stored himself with Abundance of Liquors, Suc-
cades, Sugar, Spices, and other things for his
Accommodation in the Voyage, and laid in afterwards a conſiderable Quantity of *European*
Goods, fine Lace, and Linnen; and alſo Bays,
Woollen, Cloath, Stuffs, &c. under the Pretence
of his Clothes.

I was too young in the Trade to keep any
Journal of this Voyage, tho' my Master, who
was for a *Portugueſe* a pretty good Artiſt, prompted
me to it: But my not underſtanding the Language, was one Hindrance; at leaſt, it ſerved
me for an Excuſe. However, after ſome time
I began to look into his Charts and Books; and
as I could write a tolerable Hand, underſtood
ſome *Latin,* and began to have a Smattering of
the *Portugueſe* Tongue; ſo I began to get a little
ſuperficial Knowledge of Navigation, but not
ſuch as was likely to be ſufficient to carry me
thro' a Life of Adventure, as mine was to be.
In ſhort, I learnt ſeveral material Things in this
Voyage among the *Portugueſe:* I learnt particularly to be an errant Thief and a bad Sailor;
and I think I may ſay they are the beſt Maſters

fters for Teaching both thefe, of any Nation in the World.

We made our Way for the *Eaft-Indies*, by the Coaft of *Brafil*; not that it is in the Courfe of Sailing the Way thither; but our Captain, either on his own Account, or by the Direction of the Merchants, went thither firft, where at *All Saints Bay*, or as they call it in *Portugal*, the *Rio de Todos los Santos*, we delivered near an Hundred Ton of Goods, and took in a confiderable Quantity of Gold, with fome Chefts of Sugar, and Seventy or Eighty great Rolls of Tobacco, every Roll weighing at leaft 100 Weight.

Here being lodged on Shore by my Mafter's Order, I had the Charge of the Captain's Bufinefs, he having feen me very diligent for my own Mafter; and in Requital for his miftaken Confidence, I found Means to fecure, that is to fay, to fteal about twenty Moydores out of the Gold that was Shipt on Board by the Merchants, and this was my firft Adventure.

We had a tolerable Voyage from hence to the Cape *de bona Speranza*; and I was reputed as a mighty diligent Servant to my Mafter, and very faithful (I was diligent indeed, but I was very far from honeft; however, they thought me honeft, which by the Way, was their very great Miftake) upon this very Miftake, the Captain took a particular Liking to me, and employ'd me frequently on his own Occafions; and on the other Hand, in Recompence for my Officious Diligence, I received feveral particular Favours from him; particularly, I was by the Captain's Command, made a kind of a Steward under the Ship's Steward, for fuch Provifions as the Captain de-

manded

manded for his own Table. He had another Steward for his private Stores besides, but my Office concerned only what the Captain called for of the Ship's Stores, for his private Use.

However, by this Means I had Opportunity particularly to take Care of my Master's Man, and to furnish my self with sufficient Provisions to make me live much better than the other People in the Ship; for the Captain seldom ordered any thing out of the Ship's Stores, as above, but I snipt some of it for my own Share. We arrived at *Goa* in the *East-Indies*, in about seven Months, from *Lisbon*, and remained there eight more; during which Time I had indeed nothing to do, my Master being generally on Shore, but to learn every thing that is wicked among the *Portuguese*, a Nation the most perfidious and the most debauch'd, the most insolent and cruel, of any that pretend to call themselves Christians, in the World.

Thieving, Lying, Swearing, Forswearing, join'd to the most abominable Lewdness, was the stated Practice of the Ship's Crew; *adding to it*, that with the most unsufferable Boasts of their new Courage, they were generally speaking the most compleat Cowards that I ever met with; and the Consequence of their Cowardice was evident upon many Occasions. However, there was here and there one among them that was not so bad as the rest; and as my Lot fell among them, it made me have the most contemptible Thoughts of the rest, as indeed they deserved.

I was exactly fitted for their Society indeed; for I had no Sense of Virtue or Religion upon me.

me. I had never heard much of either, except what a good old Parſon had ſaid to me when I was a Child of about Eight or Nine Years old; nay, I was preparing, and growing up apace, to be as wicked as any Body could be, or perhaps ever was. Fate certainly thus directed my Beginning, knowing that I had Work which I had to do in the World, which nothing but one hardened againſt all Senſe of Honeſty or Religion, could go thro'; and yet even in this State of Original Wickedneſs, I entertained ſuch a ſettled Abhorrence of the abandon'd Vileneſs of the *Portugueſe*, that I could not but hate them moſt heartily from the Beginning, and all my Life afterwards. They were ſo brutiſhly wicked, ſo baſe and perfidious, not only to Strangers, but to one another; ſo meanly ſubmiſſive when ſubjected; ſo inſolent, or barbarous and tyrannical when ſuperiour, that I thought there was ſomething in them that ſhock'd my very Nature. Add to this, that 'tis natural to an *Engliſhman* to hate a Coward, it all joined together to make the Devil and a *Portugueſe* equally my Averſion.

However, according to the *Engliſh* Proverb, *He that is Shipp'd with the Devil muſt ſail with the Devil*; I was among them, and I manag'd my ſelf as well as I could. My Maſter had conſented that I ſhould aſſiſt the Captain in the Office as above; but as I underſtood afterwards, that the Captain allowed my Maſter Half a Moydore a Month for my Service, and that he had my Name upon the Ship's Books alſo, I expected that when the Ship came to be paid four Months Wages at the *Indies*, as they it ſeems always do, my Maſter would let me have ſometing for my ſelf.

But

But I was wrong in my Man, for he was none of that Kind: He had taken me up as in Diſtreſs, and his Buſineſs was to keep me ſo, and make his Market of me as well as he could; which I began to think of after a different Manner than I did at firſt; for at firſt I thought he had entertained me in meer Charity, upon ſeeing my diſtreſt Circumſtances, but did not doubt, but when he put me on Board the Ship, I ſhould have ſome Wages for my Service.

But he thought, it ſeems, quite otherwiſe; and when I procured one to ſpeak to him about it when the Ship was paid at *Goa*, he flew into the greateſt Rage imaginable, and called me *Engliſh* Dog, young Heretick, and threaten'd to put me into the Inquiſition. Indeed of all the Names the Four and Twenty Letters could make up, he ſhould not have called me Heretick; for as I knew nothing about Religion, neither *Proteſtant* from *Papiſt*, or either of them from a *Mahometan*, I could never be a Heretick. However, it paſs'd but a little, but as young as I was, I had been carried into the Inquiſition; and there, if they had ask'd me, if I was a *Proteſtant* or a *Catholick*, I ſhould have ſaid Yes to that which came firſt. If it had been the *Proteſtant* they had ask'd firſt, it had certainly made a Martyr of me for I did not know what.

But the very Prieſt they carried with them, or Chaplain of the Ship, as we call him, ſaved me; for ſeeing me a Boy entirely ignorant of Religion, and ready to do or ſay any thing they bid me, he ask'd me ſome Queſtions about it, which he found I anſwered ſo very ſimply, that he took it upon him to tell them, he would anſwer for my being a good Catholick; and he hoped he ſhould
be

be the Means of faving my Soul; and he pleafed himfelf, that it was to be a Work of Merit to him; fo he made me as good a *Papift* as any of them in about a Week's Time.

I then told him my Cafe about my Mafter how, it is true, he had taken me up in a mife-rable Cafe, on Board a Man of War at *Lisbon*; and I was indebted to him for bringing me on Board this Ship; that if I had been left at *Lisbon*, I might have ftarv'd, and the like: And therefore I was willing to ferve him; but that I hop'd he would give me fome little Confidera-tion for my Service, or let me know how long he expected I fhould ferve him for nothing.

It was all one; neither the Prieft or any one elfe could prevail with him, but that I was not his Servant but his Slave; that he took me in the *Algerine*; and that I was a *Turk*, only preten-ded to be an *Englifh* Boy, to get my Liberty, and he would carry me to the Inquifition as a *Turk*.

This frighted me out of my Wits; for I had no body to vouch for me what I was, or from whence I came; but the good *Padre Antonio*, for that was his Name, cleared me of that Part by a Way I did not underftand: For he came to me one Morning with two Sailors, and told me they muft fearch me, to bear Witnefs that I was not a *Turk*. I was amazed at them, and frighted; and did not underftand them; nor could I imagine what they intended to do to me. However, ftripping me, they were foon fatisfy'd; and Fa-ther *Anthony* bad me be eafy, for they could all Witnefs that I was no *Turk*. So I efcaped that Part of my Mafter's Cruelty.

And now I refolved from that time to run away from him if I could; but there was no
doing

doing of it there; for there were not Ships of any Nation in the World in that Port, except two or three Perfian Veffels from Ormus; fo that if I had offer'd to go away from him, he would have had me feized on Shore, and brought on Board by Force. So that I had no Remedy but Patience, and this he brought to an End too as foon as he could; for after this he began to ufe me ill, and not only to ftraiten my Provifions, but to beat and torture me in a barbarous Manner for every Trifle; fo that in a Word my Life began to be very miferable.

The Violence of this Ufage of me, and the Impoffibility of my Efcape from his Hands, fet my Head a-working npon all Sorts of Mifchief; and in particular, I refolved, after ftudying all other Ways to deliver my felf, and finding all ineffectual; I fay, I refolved to murther him. With this Hellifh Refolution in my Head, I fpent whole Nights and Days contriving how to put it in Execution, . the Devil prompting me very warmly to the Fact. I was indeed entirely at a Lofs for the Means; for I had neither Gun or Sword, nor any Weapon to affault him with. Poifon I had my Thoughts much upon, but knew not where to get any; or if I might have got it, I did not know the Country Word for it, or by what Name to ask for it.

In this Manner I quitted the Fact intentionally a Hundred and a Hundred Times; but Providence, either for his fake, or for mine, always fruftrated my Defigns, and I could never bring it to pafs; fo I was obliged to continue in his Chains till the Ship, having taken in her Loading, fet Sail for Portugal.

I can

I can fay nothing here to the Manner of our Voyage; for as I faid, I kept no Journal; but this I can give an Account of, that having been once as high as the *Cape of Good Hope*, as we call it; or *Cabo de bona Speranza*, as they call it, we were driven back again by a violent Storm from the W. S. W. which held us fix Days and Nights, a great Way to the Eaftward; and after that ftanding afore the Wind for feveral Days more, we at laft came to an Anchor on the Coaft of *Madagafcar*.

The Storm had been fo violent, that the Ship had received a great deal of Damage, and it required fome time to repair her; fo ftanding in nearer the Shore, the Pilot, *My Mafter*, brought the Ship into a very good Harbour, where we rid in Twenty fix Fathom Water, about Half a Mile from the Shore.

While the Ship rode here, there happen'd a moft defperate Mutiny among the Men, upon Account of fome Deficiency in their Allowance, which came to that Height, that they threaten'd the Captain to fet him on Shore, and go back with the Ship to *Goa*. I wifh'd they would, with all my Heart, for I was full of Mifchief in my Head, and ready enough to do any. So, tho' I was but a Boy, as they called me, yet I prompted the Mifchief all I could, and embarked in it fo openly, that I efcap'd very little being hang'd in the firft and moft early Part of my Life; for the Captain had fome Notice, that there was a Defign laid by fome of the Company to murther him; and having partly by Money and Promifes, and partly by Threatning and Torture, brought two Fellows to confefs the Particulars, and the Names of the Perfons con-

cerned,

cerned, they were prefently apprehended, till one accufing another, no lefs than fixteen Men were feized, and put into Irons, whereof I was one.

The Captain, who was made defperate by his Danger, refolving to clear the Ship of his Enemies, try'd us all, and we were all condemned to die. The Manner of his Procefs I was too young to take Notice of; but the Purfer and one of the Gunners were hang'd immediately, and I expected it with the reft. I do not remember any great Concern I was under about it, only that I cry'd very much; for I knew little then of this World, and nothing at all of the next.

However, the Captain contented himfelf with executing thefe two; and fome of the reft, upon their hmble Submiffion, and Promife of future good Behaviour, were pardoned; but five were ordered to be fet on Shore on the Ifland, and left there, of which I was one. My Mafter ufed all his Intereft with the Captain to have me excufed, but could not obtain it; for fomebody having told him that I was one of them, who was fingled out to have killed him, when my Mafter defired I might not be fet on Shore, the Captain told him, I fhould ftay on Board if he defired it, but then I fhould be hang'd; fo he might chufe for me which he thought beft: The Captain, it feems, was particularly provok'd at my being concerned in the Treachery, becaufe of his having been fo kind to me, and of his having fingled me me out to ferve him, as I have faid above; and this perhaps obliged him to give my Mafter fuch a rough Choice, either to fet me on Shore, or to have me hang'd on Board: And had my Mafter indeed known

what

what good Will I had for him, he would not
ha' been long in chusing for me; for I had certainly determined to do him a Mischief the
first Opportunity I had had for it. This was
therefore a good Providence for me, to keep
me from dipping my Hands in Blood, and it
made me more tender afterwards in Matters of
Blood, than I believe I should otherwise have
been. But as to my being one of them that was
to kill the Captain, that I was wrong'd in, for I
was not the Person; but it was really one of them
that were pardoned, he having the good Luck
not to have that Part discovered.

I was now to enter upon a Part of indepen-
dent Life, a thing I was indeed very ill prepared
to manage; for I was perfectly loose and dissolute
in my Behaviour, bold and wicked while I was
under Government, and now perfectly unfit to be
trusted with Liberty; for I was as ripe for any
Villainy, as a young Fellow that had no solid
Thought ever placed in his Mind could be supposed to be. Education, as you have heard, I had
none; and all the little Scenes of Life I had
pass'd thro', had been full of Dangers and desperate Circumstances; but I was either so
young, or so stupid, that I escaped the Grief and
Anxiety of them, for want of having a Sense of
their Tendency and Consequences.

This thoughtless, unconcern'd Temper had
one Felicity indeed in it; that it made me daring
and ready for doing any Mischief, and kept off
the Sorrow which otherwise ought to have attended me when I fell into any Mischief; that this
Stupidity was instead of a Happiness to me, for
it left my Thoughts free to act upon Means of
Escape and Deliverance in my Distress, however

ever great it might be; whereas my Companions in the Mifery, were fo funk by their Fear and Grief, that they abandoned themfelves to the Mifery of their Condition, and gave over all Thought but of their perifhing and ftarving, being devoured by wild Beafts, murthered, and perhaps eaten by *Cannibals, and the like.*

I was but a young Fellow abont 17 or 18; but hearing what was to be my Fate, I received it with no Appearance of Difcouragement; but I asked what my Mafter faid to it, and being told that he had ufed his utmoft Intereft to fave me, but the Captain had anfwered I fhould either go on Shore or be hanged on Board, which he pleafed; I then gave over all Hope of being received again: I was not very thankful in my Thoughts to my Mafter for his folliciting the Captain for me, becaufe I knew that what he did was not in Kindnefs to me, fo much as in Kindnefs to himfelf; I mean to preferve the Wages which he got for me, which amounted to above fix Dollars a Month, including what the Captain allowed him for my particular Service to him.

When I underftood that my Mafter was fo apparently kind, I asked if I might not be admitted to fpeak with him, and they told me I might, if my Mafter would come down to me, but I could not be allowed to come up to him; fo then I defired my Mafter might be fpoke to to come to me, and he accordingly came to me; I fell on my Knees to him, and begg'd he would forgive me what I had done to difpleafe him; and indeed the Refolution I had taken to murther him, lay with fome Horrour upon my Mind juft at that Time, fo that I was once

once juft a-going to confefs it, and beg him to forgive me, but I kept it in: He told me he had done all he could to obtain my Pardon of the Captain, but could not; and he knew no Way for me but to have Patience, and fubmit to my Fate; and if they came to fpeak with any Ship of their Nation at the Cape, he would endeavour to have them ftand in, and fetch us off again if we might be found.

Then I begg'd I might have my Clothes on Shore with me. He told me he was afraid I fhould have little Need of Clothes, for he did not fee how we could long fubfift on the Ifland, and that he had been told that the Inhabitants were *Cannibals* or *Men-eaters* (tho' he had no Reafon for that Suggeftion) and we fhould not be able to live among them. I told him I was not fo afraid of that, as I was of ftarving for want of Victuals; and as for the Inhabitants being *Cannibals*, I believed we fhould be more likely to eat them, than they us, if we could but get at them: But I was mightily concerned, I faid, we fhould have no Weapons with us to defend our felves, and I begg'd nothing now, but that he would give me a Gun and a Sword, with a little Powder and Shot.

He fmiled and faid, they would fignify nothing to us, for it was impoffible for us to pretend to preferve our Lives among fuch a populous and defperate Nation as the People of the Ifland were. I told him, that however it would do us this Good, for we fhould not be devoured or deftroy'd immediately; fo I begged hard for the Gun. At laft he told me, he did not know whether the Captain would give him Leave to give me a Gun, and if not, he durft not do it; but

C   he

he promifed to ufe his Intereft to obtain it forme, which he did, and the next Day he fent me a Gun, with fome Ammunition, but told me, the Captain would not fuffer the Ammunition to be given us, till we were fet all on Shore, and till he was juft going to fet Sail. He alfo fent me the few Clothes I had in the Ship, which indeed were not many.

Two Days after this we were all carried on Shore together; the reft of my Fellow-Criminals hearing I had a Gun, and fome Powder and Shot, follicited for Liberty to carry the like with them, which was alfo granted them; and thus we were fet on Shore to fhift for our felves.

At our firft coming into the Ifland, we were terrified exceedingly with the Sight of the barbarous People; whofe Figure was made more terrible to us than really it was, by the Report we had of them from the Seamen; but when we came to converfe with them a while, we found they were not *Cannibals*, as was reported, or fuch as would fall immediately upon us and eat us up; but they came and fat down by us, and wondered much at our Clothes and Arms, and made Signs to give us fome Victuals, fuch as they had, which was only Roots and Plants dug out of the Ground, for the prefent, but they brought us Fowls and Flefh afterwards in good Plenty.

This encouraged the other four Men that were with me very much, for they were quite dejected before; but now they began to be very familiar with them, and made Signs, that if they would ufe us kindly, we would ftay and live with them; which they feemed glad of, tho' they knew little of the Neceffity we were under

to

to do fo, or how much we were afraid of them.

However, upon other Thoughts, we refolved that we would only ftay in that Part fo long as the Ship rid in the Bay, and then making them believe we were gone with the Ship, we would go and place our felves, if poffible, where there were no Inhabitants to be feen, and fo live as we could, or perhaps watch for a Ship that might be driven upon the Coaft, as we were.

The Ship continued a Fortnight in the Road repairing fome Damage which had been done her in the late Storm, and taking in Wood and Water; and during this time the Boat coming often on Shore, the Men brought us feveral Refrefhments, and the Natives believing we only belong'd to the Ship, were civil enough. We lived in a kind of a Tent on the Shore, or rather a Hut, which we made with the Boughs of Trees, and fometimes in the Night retired to a Wood a little out of their Way, to let them think we were gone on board the Ship. However, we found them barbarous, treacherous, and villainous enough in their Nature, only civil for Fear, and therefore concluded we fhould foon fall into their Hands when the Ship was gone.

The Senfe of this wrought upon my Fellow-Sufferers even to Diftraction; and one of them, being a Carpenter, in his mad Fit, fwam off to the Ship in the Night, tho' fhe lay then a League to Sea, and made fuch pitiful Moan to be taken in, that the Captain was prevailed with at laft to take him in, tho' they let him lye fwimming three Hours in the Water before he confented to it.

Upon

Upon this, and his humble Submiffion, the Captain received him, and, in a word, the Importunity of this Man (who for fome time petition'd to be taken in, tho' they hanged him as foon as they had him) was fuch as could not be refifted; for, after he had fwam fo long about the Ship, he was not able to have reached the Shore again; and the Captain faw evidently that the Man muft be taken on Board, or fuffered to drown, and the whole Ship's Company offering to be bound for him for his good Behaviour, the Captain at laft yielded, and he was taken up, but almoft dead with his being fo long in the Water.

When this Man was got in, he never left Importuning the Captain and all the reft of the Officers in Behalf of us that were behind, but to the very laft Day the Captain was inexorable; when, at the time their Preparations were making to fail, and Orders given to hoift the Boats into the Ship, all the Seamen in a Body came up to the Rail of the Quarter-Deck, where the Captain was walking with fome of his Officers, and appointing the Boatfwain to fpeak for them, he went up, and falling on his Knees to the Captain, begged of him in the humbleft manner poffible, to receive the four Men on Board again, offering to anfwer for their Fidelity, or to have them kept in Chains till they came to *Lisbon*, and there to be delivered up to Juftice, rather than, as they faid, to have them left to be murthered by Savages, or devoured by wild Beafts. It was a great while e'er the Captain took any Notice of them, but when he did he ordered the Boatfwain to be feized, and
threat-

threatned to bring him to the Capſtern for
ſpeaking for them.

Upon this Severity, one of the Seamen, bolder
than the reſt, but ſtill with all poſſible Reſpect
to the Captain, beſought his Honour, as he called him, that he would give Leave to ſome more
of them to go on Shore, and die with their
Companions, or, if poſſible, to aſſiſt them to
reſiſt the Barbarians. The Captain, rather provoked than cow'd with this, came to the Barricado
of the Quarter-Deck, and ſpeaking very prudently to the Men, (for, had he ſpoken roughly,
two Thirds of them would have left the Ship,
if not all of them) he told them, it was for their
Safety as well as his own, that he had been obliged to that Severity; that Mutiny on board a
Ship was the ſame thing as Treaſon in the King's
Palace, and he could not anſwer it to his Owners
and Employers to truſt the Ship and Goods Committed to his Charge, with Men who had entertained Thoughts of the worſt and blackeſt Nature; that he wiſhed heartily that it had been
any where elſe that they had been ſet on Shore,
where they might have been in leſs Hazard
from the Savages; that if he had deſigned they
ſhould be deſtroyed, he could as well have executed them on board as the other two; that he
wiſhed it had been in ſome other Part of the
World, where he might have delivered them
up to the Civil Juſtice, or might have left them
among Chriſtians; but that it was better their
Lives were put in Hazard, than his Life, and the
Safety of the Ship; and that tho' he did not
know that he had deſerved ſo ill of any of them,
as that they ſhould leave the Ship, rather than
do their Duty; yet if any of them were reſolved

to do fo unlefs he would confent to take a Gang of
Traytors on board, who, as he had proved before them all, had confpired to murther him,
he would not hinder them, nor, for the prefent,
would he refent their Importunity; but if there
was no body left in the Ship but himfelf, he
would never confent to take them on board.

This Difcourfe was delivered fo well, was in
it felf fo reafonable, was managed with fo much
Temper, yet fo boldly concluded with a Nega-
tive, that the greateft Part of the Men were fatisfied for the prefent: However, as it put the
Men into Juncto's and Cabals, and they were not
compofed for fome Hours; the Wind alfo flacken-
ing towards Night, the Captain ordered not to
weigh till next Morning.

The fame Night 23 of the Men, among whom
was the Gunner's Mate, the Surgeon's Affiftant,
and two Carpenters, applying to the Chief Mate,
told him, that as the Captain had given them
Leave to go on Shore to their Comerades, they
begged, that he would fpeak to the Captain not
to take it ill that they were defirous to go and
die with their Companions; and that they
thought they could do no lefs in fuch an Extremity, than go to them; becaufe if there was
any way to fave their Lives, it was by adding
to their Numbers, and making them ftrong
enough to affift one another in defending themfelves againft the Savages, till perhaps they might
one time or other find Means to make their
Efcape, and get to their own Country again.

The Mate told them in fo many Words, that
he durft not fpeak to the Captain upon any fuch
Defign, and was very forry they had no more
Refpect for him, than to defire him to go of
fuch

ſuch an Errand ; but if they were reſolved upon ſuch an Enterprize, he would adviſe them to
take the Long-Boat in the Morning betimes, and
go off, ſeeing the Captain had given them Leave,
and leave a civil Letter behind them to the
Captain, and to deſire him to ſend his Men on
Shore for the Boat, which ſhould be delivered
very honeſtly, and he promiſed to keep their
Counſel ſo long.

Accordingly an Hour before Day, thoſe 23
Men, with every Man a Fire-lock and Cutlaſs,
with ſome Piſtols, three Halbards or Half-Pikes,
and good Store of Powder and Ball, without any
Proviſion but about Half an Hundred of Bread,
but with all their Cheſts and Clothes, Tools,
Inſtruments, Books, &c. embarked themſelves ſo
ſilently, that the Captain got no Notice of it till
they were gotten half the Way on Shore.

As ſoon as the Captain heard of it, he called
for the Gunner's Mate, *the Chief Gunner being at that
time ſick in his Cabbin,* and ordered to fire at them ;
but, to his great Mortification, the Gunner's
Mate was one of the Number, and was gone with
them ; and indeed it was by his Means they
got ſo many Arms, and ſo much Ammunition.
When the Captain found how it was, and that
there was no Help for it, he began to be a little
appeaſed, made light of it, and called up the
Men, ſpoke kindly to them, and told them he
was very well ſatisfied in the Fidelity and Ability of thoſe that were now left ; and that he
would give to them, for their Encouragement,
to be divided among them, the Wages which was
due to the Men that were gone ; and that it was a
great Satisfaction to him that the Ship was freed

from

from such a mutinous Rabble, who had not the least Reason for their Discontent.

The Men seemed very well satisfied, and particularly the Promise of the Wages of those that were gone, went a great way with them. After this the Letter which was left by the Men was given to the Captain, by his Boy, with whom, it seems, the Men had left it. The Letter was much to the same Purpose of what they had said to the Mate, and which he declined to say for them; only that at the End of their Letter they told the Captain, that as they had no dishonest Design, so they had taken nothing away with them which was not their own, except some Arms and Ammunition, such as were absolutely necessary to them, as well for their Defence against the Savages, as to kill Fowls or Beasts for their Food, that they might not perish; and as there were considerable Sums due to them for Wages, they hoped he would allow the Arms and Ammunition upon their Accounts. They told him, that as to the Ship's Long-Boat which they had taken to bring them on Shore, they knew it was necessary to him, and they were very willing to restore it to him; and if he pleased to send for it, it should be very honestly delivered to his Men, and not the least Injury offered to any of those who came for it, nor the least Perswasion or Invitation made use of to any of them to stay with them; and at the Bottom of the Letter they very humbly besought him, that for their Defence, and for the Safety of their Lives he would be pleased to send them a Barrel of Powder, and some Ammunition, and give them Leave to keep the Mast

and

and Sail of the Boat, that if it was poſſible for
them to make themſelves a Boat of any kind,
they might ſhift off to Sea to ſave themſelves in
ſuch Part of the World as their Fate ſhould direct them to.

Upon this the Captain, who had won much
upon the reſt of his Men by what he had ſaid
to them, and was very eaſy as to the General
Peace ; (for it was very true, that the moſt mutinous of the Men were gone) came out to the
Quarter-Deck, and calling the Men together,
let them know the Subſtance of the Letter ; and
told the Men, that however they had not deſerved ſuch Civility from him, yet he was not
willing to expoſe them more than they were willing to expoſe themſelves, he was inclined to
ſend them ſome Ammunition ; and as they had
deſired but one Barrel of Powder, he would ſend
them two Barrels, and Shot, or Lead, and
Moulds to make Shot in proportion: and, to
let them ſee that he was civiller to them than
they deſerved, he ordered a Cask of Arrack,
and a great Bag of Bread to be ſent them for
Subſiſtence, till they ſhould be able to furniſh
themſelves.

The reſt of the Men applauded the Captain's
Generoſity, and every one of them ſent us
ſome thing or other ; and about three in the Afternoon the Pinnace came on Shore, and brought
us all theſe things, which we were very glad
of, and returned the Long-Boat accordingly ;
and as to the Men that came with the Pinnace,
as the Captain had ſingled out ſuch Men as he
knew would not come over to us, ſo they had
poſitive Orders not to bring any one of us on
board again, upon Pain of Death ; and indeed
both

both were fo true to our Points, that we neither asked them to ftay, nor they us to go.

We were now a good Troop, being in all 27 Men, very well armed and provided with every thing but Victuals; we had two Carpenters among us, a Gunner, and, which was worth all the reft, a Surgeon or Doctor, that is to fay, he was an Affiftant to a Surgeon at *Goa*, and was entertained as Supernumerary with us: The Carpenters had brought all their Tools, the Doctor all his Inftruments and Medicines, and indeed we had a great deal of Baggage, that is to fay, in the whole, for *fome of us* had little more than the Clothes on our Backs, of whom I was one; but I had one thing which none of them had *viz.* I had the 22 Moydores of Gold, which I ftole at the *Brafils*, and two Pieces of Eight. The two Peices of Eight I fhewed, and one Moydore, but no more; and none of them ever fufpected that I had any more Money in the World, having been known to be only a poor Boy taken up in Charity, as you have heard, and ufed like a Slave, and in the worft Manner of a Slave, by my cruel Mafter the Pilot.

It will be eafy to imagine we four, that were left at firft, were joyful, nay, even furprized with Joy, at the coming of the reft, tho' at firft we were frighted, and thought they came to fetch us back to hang us; but they took ways quickly to fatisfy us that they were in the fame Condition with us, only with this additional Circumftance, that theirs was voluntarily, and ours by Force.

The firft Piece of News they told us after the fhort Hiftory of their coming away, was, that our Companion was on board, but how he got

thither

thither we could not imagine; for he had given us the Slip, and we never imagined he could swim so well as to venture off to the Ship, which lay at so great a Distance; nay, we did not so much as know that he could swim at all, and not thinking any thing of what really happen'd, we thought that he must have wandered into the Woods, and was devoured, or was fallen into the Hands of the Natives and was murthered; and these Thoughts filled us with Fears enough, and of several kinds, about its being some time or other our Lot to fall into their Hands also.

But hearing how he had with much Difficulty been received on board the Ship again, and pardon'd, we were much better satisfied than before.

Being now, as I have said, a confiderable Number of us, and in Condition to defend our selves, the first thing we did was to give every one his Hand, that we would not separate from one another upon any Occasion whatsoever, but that we would live and die together; that we would kill no Food, but that we would distribute it in publick; and that we would be in all things guided by the Majority, and not insist upon our own Resolutions in any thing, if the Majority were against it; that we would appoint a Captain among us to be our Governour or Leader during Pleasure; that while he was in Office, we would obey him without Reserve, on Pain of Death; and that every one should take Turn, but the Captain was not to act in any particular thing without Advice of the rest, and by the Majority.

Having establifhed these Rules, we resolved to enter into some Measures for our Food, and for

conver-

conversing with the Inhabitants or Natives of the Island, for our Supply; as for Food, they were at first very useful to us, but we soon grew weary of them, being an ignorant, ravenous, brutish sort of People, even worse than the Natives of any other Country that we had seen; and we soon found that the principal Part of our Subsistance was to be had by our Guns, shooting of Deer and other Creatures, and Fowls of all other Sorts, of which there is Abundance.

We found the Natives did not disturb or concern themselves much about us; nor did they enquire, or perhaps know whether we stay'd among them or not, much less that our Ship was gone quite away, and had cast us off, as was our Case; for the next Morning after we had sent back the Long-Boat, the Ship stood away to the South-East, and in four Hours time was out of our Sight.

The next Day two of us went out into the Country one Way, and two another, to see what kind of a Land we were in; and we soon found the Country was very pleasant and fruitful, and a convenient Place enough to live in; but as before, inhabited by a Parcel of Creatures scarce human, or capable of being made sociable on any Account whatsoever.

We found the Place full of Cattle and Provisions; but whether we might venture to take them where we could find them, or not, we did not know; and tho' we were under a Necessity to get Provisions, yet we were loath to bring down a whole Nation of Devils upon us at once, and therefore some of our Company agreed to try to speak with some of the Country, if we could, that we might see what Course was to be taken

taken with them. Eleven of our Men went of this Errand, well armed, and furnifhed for Defence. They brought Word, that they had feen fome of the Natives, who appeared very civil to them, but very fhy and afraid, feeing their Guns; for it was eafy to perceive, that the Natives knew what their Guns were, and what Ufe they were of.

They made Signs to the Natives for fome Food, and they went and fetched feveral Herbs and Roots, and fome Milk; but it was evident they did not defign to give it away, but to fell, making Signs to know what our Men would give them.

Our Men were perplexed at this, for tney had nothing to Barter; however, one of the Men pulled out a Knife and fhewed them, and they were fo fond of it, that they were ready to go together by the Ears for the Knife: The Seaman feeing that, was willing to make a good Market of his Knife, and keeping them chaffering about it a good while, fome offered him Roots, and others Milk; at laft one offered him a Goat for it, which he took. Then another of our Men fhewed them another Knife, but they had nothing good enough for that; whereupon one of them made Signs that he would go and fetch fomething; fo our Men ftay'd three Hours for their Return, when they came back and brought him a fmall fized, thick, fhort Cow, very fat, and good Meat, and gave him for his Knife.

This was a good Market, but our Misfortune was we had no Merchandize; for our Knives were as needful to us as to them, and but that we were in Diftrefs for Food, and muft of Neceffity

ceffity have fome, thefe Men would not have parted with their Knives.

However, in a little time more we found that the Woods were full of living Creatures which we might kill for our Food, and that without giving Offence to them; fo that our Men went daily out a Hunting, and never failed to kill fomething or other; for as to the Natives, we had no Goods to Barter; and for Money, all the Stock among us would not have fubfifted us long; however, we called a general Council to fee what Money we had, and to bring it all together, that it might go as far as poffible; and when it came to my Turn, I pulled out a Moydore and the two Dollars I fpoke of before.

This Moydore I ventured to fhew, that they might not defpife me too much for adding too little to the Store, and that they might not pretend to fearch me; and they were very civil to me upon the Prefumption that I had been fo faithful to them as not to conceal any thing from them.

But our Money did us little Service, for the People neither knew the Value or the Ufe of it, nor could they juftly rate the Gold in Proportion with the Silver; fo that all our Money, which was not much when it was all put together, would go but a little way with us, that is to fay, to buy us Provifions.

Our next Confideration was to get away from this curfed Place, and whether to go; when my Opinion came to be afked, I told them I would leave that all to them, and I told them I had rather they would let me go into the Woods to get them fome Provifions, than confult with me, me, for I would agree to whatever they did; but they would not agree to that, for they would not confent that any of us fhould go into the Woods alone; for tho' we had yet feen no Lions or Tygers in the Woods, we were affured there were many in the Ifland, befides other Creatures as dangerous, and, perhaps worfe, as we afterwards found by our own Experience.

We had many Adventures in the Woods for our Provifions, and often met with wild and terrible Beafts, which we could not call by their Names, but as they were like us feeking their Prey, but were themfelves good for nothing, fo we difturbed them as little as poffible.

Our Confultations concerning our Efcape from this Place, which as I have faid, we were now upon, ended in this only, that as we had two Carpenters among us, and that they had Tools almoft of all Sorts with them, we fhould try to build us a Boat to go off to Sea with, and that then perhaps we might find our way back to *Goa*, or land on fome more proper Place to make our Efcape. The Counfels of this Affembly were not of great Moment, yet as they feem to be introductory of many more remarkable Adventures which happened under my Conduct hereabouts many Years after, I think this Miniature of my future Enterprizes may not be unpleafant to relate.

To the Building of a Boat I made no Objection, and away they went to work immediately; but as they went on, great Difficulties occurred, fuch as want of Saws to cut out Plank; Nails, Bolts, and Spikes, to faften the Timbers, Hemp, Pitch and Tar, to Caulk and Pay her Seams, *and the like:* At length one of the Com-

pany

pany propofed, that inftead of building a Bark or Sloop, or Shalloup, or whatever they would call it, which they found was fo difficult, they fhould rather make a large *Periagua*, or Canoe, which might be done with great Eafe.

It was prefently objected, that we could never make a Canoe large enough to pafs the great Ocean, which we were to go over, to get to the Coaft of *Malabar*, that it not only would not bear the Sea, but it would never bear the Burthen; for we were not only Twenty feven Men of us, but had a great deal of Luggage with us, and muft, for our Provifion, take in a great deal more.

I never propofed to fpeak in their General Confultations before; but finding they were at fome Lofs about what kind of Veffel they fhould make, and how to make it; and what would be fit for our Ufe, and what not; I told them I found they were at a full Stop in their Counfels of every kind; that it was true we could never pretend to go over to *Goa*, or the Coaft of *Malabar* in a Canoe, which tho' we could all get into it, and that it would bear the Sea well enough, yet would not hold our Provifions, and efpecially we could not put frefh Water enough into it for the Voyage; and to make fuch an Adventure would be nothing but meer running into certain Deftruction, and yet that neverthelefs I was for making a Canoe.

They anfwered, that they underftood all I had faid before well enough, but what I meant by telling them firft how dangerous and impoffible it was to make our Efcape in a Canoe, and yet then to advife making a Canoe, that they could not underftand.

To

To this I anfwer'd, that I conceiv'd our Bufinefs was not to attempt our Efcape in a Canoe,
but that as there were other Veffels at Sea befides our Ship, and that there were few Nations
that lived on the Sea-Shore that were fo barbarous, but that they went to Sea in fome Boats
or other, our Bufinefs was to cruife along the
Coaft of the Ifland, which was very long, and
to feize upon the firft we could get that was better than our own, and fo from that to another,
till perhaps we might at laft get a good Ship
to carry us whither ever we pleafed to go.

Excellent Advice, fays one of them, admirable Advice, fays another. Yes, yes, fays the
third, which was the Gunner, the *Englifh* Dog
has given excellent Advice; but it is juft the
way to bring us all to the Gallows; the Rogue
has given Devilifh Advice, indeed, to go a
Thieving, till from a little Veffel we come to a
great Ship, and fo we fhall turn downright
Pyrates, the End of which is to be hanged.

You may call us Pyrates, fays another, if you
will, and if we fall into bad Hands, we may be
ufed like Pyrates; but I care not for that, I'll
be a Pyrate, or any thing, nay, I'll be hang'd
for a Pyrate, rather than ftarve here; and therefore I think the Advice is very good; and fo
they cry'd all, Let us have a Canoe. The Gunner over-ruled by the reft, fubmitted; but as
we broke up the Councii, he came to me, takes
me by the Hand, and looking into the Palm of
my Hand, and into my Face too, very gravely,
My Lad, *fays he,* thou art born to do a World
of Mifchief; thou haft commenced Pyrate very
young, but have a Care of the Gallows, young

D   Man;

Man; have a Care, I fay, for thou wilt be an eminent Thief.

I laugh'd at him, and told him, I did not know what I might come to hereafter; but as our Cafe was now, I fhould make no Scruple to take the firft Ship I came at, to get our Liberty: I only wifh'd we could fee one, and come at her. Juft while we were talking, one of our Men that was at the Door of our Hutt, told us, that the Carpenter, who, it feems, was upon a Hill at a Diftance, cried out, *a Sail, a Sail.*

We all turn'd out immediately; but tho' it was very clear Weather, we could fee nothing; but the Carpenter continuing to holloo to us, *a Sail, a Sail,* away we run up the Hill, and there we faw a Ship plainly; but it was at a very great Diftance, too far for us to make any Signal to her. However, we made a Fire upon the Hill, with all the Wood we could get together, and made as much Smoke as poffible. The Wind was down, and it was almoft calm; but as we thought by a Perfpective Glafs which the Gunner had in his Pocket, her Sails were full, and fhe ftood away large with the Wind at E. N. E. taking no Notice of our Signal, but making for the Cape *de bona Speranza*; fo we had no Comfort from her.

We went therefore immediately to Work about our intended Canoe, and having fingled out a very large Tree to our Mind, we fell to Work with her; and having three good Axes among us, we got it down, but it was four Days time firft, tho' we worked very hard too. I do not remember what Wood it was, or exactly what Dimenfions; but I remember that it was a very large one, and we were as much encouraged when we launched

ched

ched it, and found it swam upright and steady,
as we would have been at another time, if we
had a good Man of War at our Command.

She was so very large, that she carried us all
very easily, and would have carried two or
three Ton of Baggage with us; so that we began
to consult about going to Sea directly to *Goa*; but
many other Considerations check'd that Thought,
especially when we came to look nearer into it;
such as Want of Provisions, and no Casks for fresh
Water; no Compass to steer by; no Shelter from
the Breach of the high Sea, which would certainly founder us; no Defence from the Heat of
the Weather, and the like; so that they all came
readily into my Project, to cruise about where
we were, and see what might offer.

Accordingly, to gratify our Fancy, we went
one Day all out to Sea in her together, and we
were in a very fair Way to have had enough of
it; for when she had us all on Board, and that
we were gotten about Half a League to Sea, there
happening to be a pretty high Swell of the Sea,
tho' little or no Wind, yet she wallow'd so in
the Sea, that we all of us thought she would
at last wallow her self Bottom up; so we set
all to Work to get her in nearer the Shore, and
giving her fresh Way in the Sea, she swam more
steady, and with some hard Work we got her
under the Land again.

We were now at a great Loss; the Natives
were civil enough to us, and came often to discourse with us; one time they brought one whom
they shew'd Respect to as a King, with them,
and they set up a long Pole between them and
us, with a great Tossel of Hair hanging, not on
the Top, but something above the Middle of it,

adorn'd

adorn'd with little Chains, Shells, Bits of Brafs,
and the like ; and this we underftood afterwards
was a Token of Amity and Friendfhip, and they
brought down to us Victuals in Abundance, Cattel, Fowls, Herbs, Roots, but we were in the
utmoft Confufion on our Side ; for we had nothing to buy with, or exchange for ; and as to
giving us things for nothing, they had no Notion of that again. As to our Money, it was
meer Trafh to them, they had no Value for it ;
fo that we were in a fair Way to be ftarved.
Had we had but fome Toys and Trinckets, Brafs
Chains, Baubles, Glafs Beads, or in a Word, the
verieft Trifles that a Ship Loading would not have
been worth the Freight, we might have bought
Cattel and Provifions enough for an Army, or
to Victual a Fleet of Men of War, but for Gold
or Silver we could get nothing.

Upon this we were in a ftrange Confternation. I was but a young Fellow, but I was for
falling upon them with our Fire Arms; and
taking all the Cattel from them, and fend them
to the Devil to ftop their Hunger, rather than
be ftarved our felves; but I did not confider
that this might have brought Ten Thoufand of
them down upon us the next Day; and tho'
we might have killed a vaft Number of them,
and perhaps have frighted the reft, yet their
own Defperation, and our fmall Number, would
have animated them fo, that one time or other
they would have deftroy'd us all.

In the Middle of our Confultation, one of
our Men who had been a kind of a Cutler, or
Worker in Iron, ftarted up, and ask'd the Carpenter, if among all his Tools he could not help
him to a File. Yes, fays the Carpenter, I can,
but

but it is a fmall one. The fmaller the better,
fays the other. Upon this he goes to Work,
and firft by heating a Piece of an old broken
Chiffel in the Fire, and then with the Help of
his File, he made himfelf feveral Kinds of Tools
for his Work ; and then he takes three or four
Pieces of Eight, and beats them out with a Hammer upon a Stone, till they were very broad and
thin, then he cut them out into the Shape of
Birds and Beafts ; he made little Chains of them
for Bracelets and Necklaces, and turn'd them into fo many Devices, of his own Head, that it is
hardly to be expreft.

When he had for about a Fortnight exercifed
his Head and Hands at this Work, we try'd the
Effect of his Ingenuity ; and having another Meeting with the Natives, were furprized to fee the
Folly of the poor People. For a little Bit of
Silver cut out in the Shape of a Bird, we had
two Cows; and, which was our Lofs, if it had
been in Brafs, it had been ft ll of more Value.
For one of the Bracelets made of Chain-work,
we had as much Provifion of feveral Sorts, as
would fairly have been worth in *England*, Fifteen
or Sixteen Pounds ; and fo of all the reft. Thus,
that which when it was in Coin was not worth
Six-pence to us, when thus converted into Toys
and Trifles, was worth an Hundred Times its
real Value, and purchafed for us any thing we
had Occafion for.

In this Condition, we lived upwards of a Year,
but all of us began to be very much tir'd of it, and
whatever came of it, refolv'd to attempt an Efcape.
We had furnifhed our felves with no lefs than
three very good Canoes ; and as the *Monfoones*,
or Trade-Winds, generally affect that Country,

D 3   blowing

blowing in moſt Parts of this Iſland one ſix Months
of a Year one Way, and the other ſix Months
another Way, we concluded we might be able
to bear the Sea well enough. But always when
we came to look nearer into it, the Want of
freſh Water was the thing that put us off from
ſuch an Adventure, for it is a prodigious Length,
and what no Man on Earth could be able to
perform without Water to drink.

　Being thus prevailed upon by our own Reaſon to ſet the Thoughts of that Voyage aſide,
we had then but two things before us; one was,
to put to Sea the other Way, _viz_. Weſt, and go
away for the _Cape of Good Hope_, where firſt or
laſt we ſhould meet with ſome of our own Country Ships, or elſe to put for the main Land of
Africa, and either travel by Land, or ſail along
the Coaſt towards the Red Sea, where we ſhould
firſt or laſt find a Ship of ſome Nation or other,
that would take us up, or perhaps we might take
them up; which, by the bye, was the thing that
always run in my Head.

　It was our ingenious Cutler, whom ever after
we called _Silver-Smith_, that propoſed this; but
the Gunner told him, that he had been in the
Red Sea, in a _Malabar_ Sloop, and he knew this,
that if we went into the Red Sea, we ſhould
either be killed by the wild _Arabs_, or taken and
made Slaves of by the _Turks_; and therefore he
was not for going that Way.

　Upon this I took Occaſion to put in my Vote
again. _Why_, ſaid I, _do we talk of being killed by the_
Arabs, _or made Slaves of by the_ Turks? _Are we not
able to board almoſt any Veſſel we ſhall meet with in
thoſe Seas; and inſtead of their taking us, we to take
them?_ Well done, _Pyrate_, ſaid the Gunner, he
that

that had look'd in my Hand, and told me I
ſhould come to the Gallows; *I'll ſay that for
him*, ſays he, *he always looks the ſame Way. But I
think o' my Conſcience*, 'tis *our only Way now.* Don't
tell me, *ſays I,* of being a Pyrate, *we muſt be Pyrates,
or any thing, to get fairly out of this curſed Place.*

In a Word, they concluded all by my Advice,
that our Buſineſs was to cruize for any thing
we could ſee. Why then, *ſaid I* to them, our
firſt Buſineſs is to ſee, if the People upon this
Iſland have no Navigation, and what Boats they
uſe; and if they have any better or bigger than
ours, let us take one of them. Firſt indeed all
our Aim was to get, if poſſible, a Boat with a
Deck and a Sail; for then we might have ſaved
our Proviſions, which otherwiſe we could not.

We had, to our great good Fortune, one Sailor
among us, who had been Aſſiſtant to the Cook,
he told us, that he would find a Way how to
preſerve our Beef, without Cask or Pickle; and
this he did effectually by curing it in the Sun,
with the Help of Salt-Petre, of which there
was great Plenty in the Iſland; ſo that before
we found any Method for our Eſcape, we had
dry'd the Fleſh of ſix or ſeven Cows and Bullocks, and ten or twelve Goats, and it reliſhed ſo
well, that we never gave our ſelves the Trouble to boil it when we eat it, but either broiled
it, or eat it dry: But our main Difficulty about
freſh Water ſtill remained; for we had no Veſſel to put any into, much leſs to keep any for
our going to Sea.

But our firſt Voyage being only to coaſt the
Iſland, we reſolved to venture, whatever the
Hazard or Conſequence of it might be; and in
order to preſerve as much freſh Water as we

D 4   could,

could, our Carpenter made a Well thwart the
Middle of one of our Canoes, which he feparated from the other Parts of the Canoe, fo as to
make it tight to hold the Water, and cover'd
fo as we might ftep upon it; and this was fo
large, that it held near a Hogfhead of Water
very well. I cannot better defcribe this Well,
than by the fame Kind which the fmall Fifher-
Boats in *England* have to preferve their Fifh alive
in; only, that this, inftead of having Holes to
let the Salt Water in, was made found every
Way to keep it out; and it was the firft Invention, I believe, of its Kind, for fuch an Ufe:
But Neceffity is a Spur to Ingenuity, and the
Mother of Invention.

It wanted but a little Confultation to refolve
now upon our Voyage. The firft Defign was only
to coaft it round the Ifland, as well to fee if we
could feize upon any Veffel fit to embark our felves
in, as alfo to take hold of any Opportunity which
might prefent for our paffing over to the Main;
and therefore our Refolution was to go on the
Infide, or Weft Shore of the Ifland, where at
leaft at one Point, the Land ftretching a great
Way to the North-Weft, the Diftance is not
extraordinary great from the Ifland to the Coaft
of *Africk*.

Such a Voyage, and with fuch a defperate
Crew, I believe was never made; for it is certain we took the worft Side of the Ifland to look
for any Shipping, efpecially for Shipping of other
Nations, this being quite out of the Way: However, we put to Sea, after taking all our Provifions and Ammunition, Bag and Baggage on Board;
we had made both Maft and Sail for our two
large Periagua's, and the other we paddl'd along

as

as well as we could; but when a Gale fprung up, we took her in Tow.

We fail'd merrily forward for feveral Days, meeting with nothing to interrupt us. We faw feveral of the Natives in fmall Canoes, catching Fifh, and fometimes we endeavoured to come near enough to fpeak with them, but they were always fhye, and afraid of us, making in for the Shore, as foon as we attempted it; till one of our Company remember'd the Signal of Friendfhip which the Natives made us from the South Part of the Ifland, *viz.* of fetting up a long Pole, and put us in Mind, that perhaps it was the fame thing to them as a Flag of Truce was to us: So we refolved to try it; and accordingly the next time we faw any of their Fifhing Boats at Sea, we put up a Pole in our Canoe that had no Sail, and rowed towards them. As foon as they faw the Pole, they ftaid for us, and as we came nearer, paddl'd towards us. When they came to us, they fhewed themfelves very much pleafed, and gave us fome large Fifh, of which we did not know the Names, bnt they were very good. It was our Misfortune ftill, that we had nothing to give them in Return; but our Artift, of whom I fpoke before, gave them two little thin Plates of Silver, beaten, as I faid before, out of a Piece of Eight; they were cut in a Diamond Square, longer one way than t'other, and a Hole punch'd at one of the longeft Corners. This they were fo fond of, that they made us ftay till they had caft their Lines and Nets again, and gave us as many Fifh as we cared to have.

All this while we had our Eyes upon their Boats, view'd them very narrowly, and examined whether any of them were fit for our Turn;

but

but they were poor forry things; their Sail was made of a large Matt, only one that was of a Piece of Cotton Stuff, fit for little, and their Ropes were twifted Flags, of no Strength; fo we concluded we were better as we were, and let them alone. We went forward to the North, keeping the Coaft clofe on Board for twelve Days together; and having the Wind at Eaft, and E. S. E. we made very frefh Way. We faw no Towns on the Shore, but often faw fome Hutts by the Water Side, upon the Rocks, and always Abundance of People about them, who we could perceive run together to ftare at us.

It was as odd a Voyage as ever Men went: We were a little Fleet of three Ships, and an Army of between Twenty and Thirty as dangerous Fellows as ever they had among them; and had they known what we were they would have compounded to give us every thing we defired, to be rid of us.

On the other Hand, we were as miferable as Nature could well make us to be; for we were upon *a* Voyage and *no* Voyage, we were bound *fome* where and *no* where; for tho' we knew what we intended to do, we did really not know what we were doing: We went forward and forward by a Northerly Courfe; and as we advanced, the Heat increafed, which began to be intolerable to us who were upon the Water, without any Covering from Heat or Wet; befides we were now in the Month of *October*, or thereabouts, in a Southern Latitude, and as we went every Day nearer the Sun, the Sun came alfo every Day nearer to us, till at laft we found our felves in the Latitude of 20 Degrees, and having paft the Tropick about five or fix Days before that,

in

in a few Days more the Sun would be in the Zenith, juſt over our Heads.

Upon theſe Conſiderations we reſolved to ſeek for a good Place to go on Shore again, and pitch our Tents till the Heat of the Weather abated. We had by this time meaſured Half the Length of the Iſland, and were come to that Part where the Shore tending away to the North-Weſt, promiſed fair to make our Paſſage over to the main Land of *Africk*, much ſhorter than we expeſted. But notwithſtanding that, we had good Reaſon to believe it was about 120 Leagues.

So, the Heats conſider'd, we reſolved to take Harbour; beſides, our Proviſions were exhauſted, and we had not many Days Store left. Accordingly, putting in for the Shore early in the Morning, as we uſually did once in three or four Days, for freſh Water, we ſat down and conſidered, whether we ſhould go on, or take up our Standing there; but upon ſeveral Conſiderations too long to repeat here, we did not like the Place, ſo we reſolved to go on for a few Days longer.

After Sailing on N. W. by N. with a freſh Gale at S. E. about ſix Days, we found at a great Diſtance, a large Promontory, or Cape of Land, puſhing out a long Way into the Sea; and as we were exceeding fond of ſeeing what was beyond the Cape, we reſolved to double it before we took into Harbour; ſo we kept on our Way, the Gale continuing, and yet it was four Days more before we reach'd the Cape. But it is not poſſible to expreſs the Diſcouragement and Melancholy that ſeized us all when we came thither; for when we made the Head Land of the Cape, we were ſurprized to ſee the Shore

fall

fall away on the other Side, as much as it had advanced on this Side, and a great deal more; and that, in fhort, if we would adventure over to the Shore of *Africk*, it muft be from hence; for that if we went further, the Breadth of the Sea ftill increafed, and to what Breadth it might increafe, we knew not.

While we mufed upon this Difcovery, we were furprized with very bad Weather, and efpecially violent Rains, with Thunder and Lightning moft unufually terrible to us. In this Pickle we run for the Shore, and getting under the Lee of the Cape, run our Frigates into a little Creek, where we faw the Land overgrown with Trees, and made all the Hafte poffible to get on Shore, being exceeding wet, and fatigued with the Heat, the Thunder, Lightning and Rain.

Here we thought our Cafe was very deplorable indeed, and therefore our Artift, of whom I have fpoken fo often, fet up a great Crofs of Wood on the Hill, which was within a Mile of the Head Land, with thefe Words, but in the *Portuguefe* Language,

Point Defperation. Jefus have Mercy!

We fet to work immediately to build us fome Hutts, and fo get our Clothes dry'd, and tho' I was young, and had no Skill in fuch Things, yet I fhall never forget the little City we built, for it was no lefs; and we fortify'd it accordingly; and the Idea is fo frefh in my Thought, that I cannot but give a fhort Defcription of it.

Our Camp was on the South Side of a little Creek on the Sea, and under the Shelter of a fteep Hill, which lay, tho' on the other Side of the Creek, yet within a Quarter of a Mile of us N. W. by N. and very happily intercepted the

Heat

Heat of the Sun all the after Part of the Day.
The Spot we pitched on had a little fresh Water,
Brook, or a Stream running into the Creek by
us, and we saw Cattle feeding in the Plains and
and low Ground, East and to the South of us a
great Way.

Here we set up twelve little Hutts, like Soldiers Tents, but made of the Boughs of Trees
stuck into the Ground, and bound together on
the Top with Withes, and such other things
as we could get; the Creek was our Defence on
the North, a little Brook on the West, and
the South and East Sides we fortify'd with a
Bank, which entirely covered our Hutts; and
being drawn oblique from the North West to
the South East, made our City a Triangle.
Behind the Bank, or Line, our Hutts stood, having three other Hutts behind them at a good
Distance. In one of these, which was a little one,
and stood further off, we put our Gun-powder,
and nothing else, for fear of Danger; in the
other, which was bigger, we drest our Victuals,
and put all our Necessaries; and in the third,
which was biggest of all, we eat our Dinners,
called our Councils, and sat and diverted our
selves with such Conversation as we had one
with another, which was but indifferent truly at
that time.

Our Correspondence with the Natives was absolutely necessary, and our Artist, the Cutler,
having made Abundance of those little Diamond
cut Squares of Silver, with these we made Shift
to Traffick with the black People for what we
wanted; for indeed they were pleased wonderfully with them: And thus we got Plenty of
Provisions. At first, and in particular, we got

about

about fifty Head of Black Cattel and Goats, and
our Cook's Mate took care to cure them, and dry
them, falt and preferve them for our grand
Supply; nor. was this hard to do, the Salt and
Salt-Petre being very good, and the Sun exceffively hot; and here we lived about four
Months.

The Southern Solftice was over, and the Sun
gone back towards the *Equinoctial*, when we confidered of our next Adventure, which was to go
over the Sea of *Zanquebar*, as the *Portuguefe*
call it, and to land, if poffible, upon the Continent of *Africa*.

We talked with many of the Natives about
it, fuch as we could make our felves intelligible
to; but all that we could learn from them was,
that there was a great Land of Lions beyond
the Sea, but that it was a great Way off; we
knew as well as they that it was a long Way, but
our People differed mightily about it: Some
faid it was 150 Leagues, others not above
100. One of our Men that had a Map of the
World fhewed us by his Scale, that it was
not above 80 Leagues. Some faid there were
Iflands all the Way to touch at; fome that there
were no Iflands at all: For my Part, I knew
nothing of this Matter one way or another, but
heard it all without Concern, whether it was
near or far off; however, this we learned from
an old Man who was blind, and led about by a
Boy, that if we ftay'd till the End of *Auguft*, we
fhould be fure of the Wind to be fair, and the
Sea fmooth all the Voyage.

This was fome Encouragement, but ftaying
again was very unwelcome News to us, becaufe
that then the Sun would be returning again
to'

to the South, which was what our Men were
very unwilling to. At laſt we called a Council of
our whole Body; their Debates were too tedious to take Notice of, only to note, that when it
came to *Captain Bob*, (for ſo they called me ever
ſince I had taken State upon me before one of
their great Princes) truly I was on no Side,
it was not one Farthing Matter to me, I told
them, whether we went or ſtayed, I had no home,
and all the World was alike to me; ſo I left it
entirely to them to determine.

In a Word, they ſaw plainly there was nothing
to be done where we were, without Shipping;
that if our Buſineſs indeed was only to eat and
drink, we could not find a better Place in the
World; but if our Buſineſs was to get away, and
get home into our own Country, we could not
find a Worſe.

I confeſs, I liked the Country wonderfully,
and even then had ſtrange Notions of coming
again to live there; and I uſed to ſay to them
very often, that if I had but a Ship of 20 Guns,
and a Sloop, and both well Manned, I would not
deſire a better Place in the World to make my
ſelf as rich as a King.

But to return to the Conſultations they were
in about going : Upon the whole, it was reſolved
to venture over for the Main; and venture we
did, madly enough, indeed; for it was the
wrong time of the Year to undertake ſuch
a Voyage in that Country; for, as the Winds
hang Eaſterly all the Months from *September*
to *March*, ſo they generally hang Weſterly all
the reſt of the Year, and blew right in our
Teeth, ſo that as ſoon as we had, with a kind
of a Land Breeze, ſtretched over about 15 or 20

Leagues, and, as I may say, just enough to lose our selves, we found the Wind set in a steady fresh Gale or Breeze from the Sea, at West W. S. W. or S. W. by W. and never further from the West; so that, in a Word we could make nothing of it.

On the other Hand, the Vessel, such as we had would not lye close upon a Wind; if so, we might have stretched away N. N. W. and have met with a great many Islands in our Way, as we found afterwards; but we could make nothing of it, tho' we tried, and by the trying had almost undone us all; for, stretching away to the North, as near the Wind as we could, we had forgotten the Shape and Position of the Island of *Madagascar* it self; how that we came off at the Head of a Promontory or Point of Land that lies about the Middle of the Island, and that stretches out West a great way into the Sea; and that now being run a Matter of 40 Leagues to the North, the Shore of the Island fell off again above 200 Miles to the East, so that we were by this Time in the wide Ocean, between the Island and the Main, and almost 100 Leagues from both.

Indeed as the Winds blew fresh at West, as before, we had a smooth Sea, and we found it pretty good going before it, and so taking our smallest Canoe in Tow, we stood in for the Shore with all the Sail we could make. This was a terrible Adventure; for if the least Gust of Wind had come, we had been all lost, our Canoes being deep, and in no Condition to make Way in a high Sea.

This Voyage, however, held us eleven Days in all, and at length having spent most of our

Provi-

Provisions, and every Drop of Water we had, we spied Land, to our great Joy, tho' at the Distance of ten or eleven Leagues, and as under the Land, the Wind came off like a Land Breeze, and blew hard against us, we were two Days more before we reached the Shore, having all that while excessive hot Weather, and not a Drop of Water, or any other Liquor, except some Cordial Waters, which one of our Company had a little of left in a Case of Bottles.

This gave us a Taste of what we should have done, if we had ventured forward with a scant Wind and uncertain Weather, and gave us a Surfeit of our Design for the Main, at least 'till we might have some better Vessels under us; so we went on Shore again, and pitched our Camp, as before, in as convenient Manner as we could, fortifying our selves against any Surprize; but the Natives here were exceeding courteous, and much civiller than on the South Part of the Island; and tho' we could not understand what they said, or they us, yet we found Means to make them understand that we were Sea-faring Men, and Strangers; and that we were in Distress for want of Provisions.

The first Proof we had of their Kindness was, that, as soon as they saw us come on Shore, and begin to make our Habitation, one of their Captains or Kings, for we knew not what to call them, came down with five or six Men and some Women, and brought us five Goats and two young fat Steers, and gave them to us for nothing; and when we went to offer them any thing, the Captain, or the King, would not let any of them touch it, or take any thing of us. About two Hours after came another King or Captain, with forty or fifty Men after him; we began to be afraid of him, and laid Hands upon our Weapons; but he perceiving it, caused two Men to go before him carrying two long Poles in their Hands, which they held upright, as high as they could, which we prefently perceiv'd was a Signal of Peace, and these two Poles they set up afterwards sticking them up in the Ground; and when the King and his Men came to these two Poles, they stuck all their Lances up in the Ground, and came on unarmed, leaving their Lances, as also their Bows and Arrows behind them.

This was to satisfy us, that they were come as Friends, and we were very glad to see it; for we had no Mind to quarrel with them, if we could help it. The Captain of this Gang seeing some of our Men making up their Hutts, and that they did it but bunglingly, he becken'd to some of his Men to go and help us. Immediately 15 or 16 of them came and mingled among us, and went to Work for us; and, indeed, they were better Workmen than we were, for they run up three or four Hutts for us in a Moment, and much handfomer done than ours.

After this they sent us Milk, Plantanes, Pumpkins, and Abundance of Roots and Greens that were very good, and then took their Leave, and would not take any thing from us that we had. One of our Men offer'd the King or Captain of these Men a Dram, which he drank, and was mightily pleased with it, and held out his Hand for another, which we gave him; and, in a Word, after this, he hardly failed coming to us two or three times a Week, always bringing
us

us something or other, and one time sent us seven Head of Black Cattle, some of which we cured and dried as before.

And here I cannot but remember one thing which afterwards stood us in great stead, *viz.* that the Flesh of their Goats and their Beef also, but especially the former, when we had dried and cured it, looked red, and eat hard and firm, as dry'd Beef in *Holland*; they were so pleased with it, and it was such a Dainty to them, that at any time after they would Trade with us for it, not knowing, or so much as imagining, what it was; so that for Ten or Twelve Pound Weight of smoked dry'd Beef, they would give us a whole Bullock, or Cow, or any thing else we could desire.

Here we observed two Things that were very material to us, even essentially so; first, we found they had a great deal of Earthen-Ware here, which they make use of many ways, as we did: Particularly they had long deep Earthen Pots, which they used to sink into the Ground to keep the Water which they drank cool and pleasant; and the other was, that they had larger Canoes than their Neighbours had.

By this we were prompted to enquire if they had no larger Vessels than those we saw there; or if any other of the Inhabitants had not such. They signified presently, that they had no larger Boats than that they shewed us; but that on the other Side of the Island they had larger Boats, and that with Decks upon them, and large Sails; and this made us resolve to Coast round the whole Island to see them; so we prepared and victualled our Canoe for the Voyage, and, in a Word, went to Sea for the third time.

It

It coft us a Month or fix Weeks time to perform this Voyage, in which time we went on
Shore feveral times for Water and Provifions, and
found the Natives always very free and courteous; but we were furprized one Morning early,
being at the Extremity of the Northermoft Part of
the Ifland, when one of our Men cried out *a Sail,
a Sail*: We prefently faw a Veffel a great Way
out at Sea; but after we had looked at it with
our Perfpective Glaffes, and endeavoured all we
could to make out what it was, we could not
tell what to think of it; for it was neither Ship,
Ketch, Gally, Galliot, or like any thing that
we had ever feen before: All that we could
make of it was, that it went from us ftanding
out to Sea. In a Word, we foon loft Sight of it,
for we were in no Condition to chafe any thing,
and we never faw it again, but by all we could
perceive of it, from what we faw of fuch things
afterwards, it was fome *Arabian* Veffel which
had been trading to the Coaft of *Mofambique*, or
Zanguebar, the fame Place where we afterwards
went, as you fhall hear.

I kept no Journal of this Voyage, nor indeed
did I all this while underftand any thing of Navigation, more than the common Bufinefs of a
Fore-maft Man; fo I can fay nothing to the La-
titudes or Diftances of any Places we were at,
how long we were going, or how far we failed
in a Day; but this I remember, that being now
come round the Ifland, we failed up the Eaftern
Shore due South, as we had done down the Weftern Shore due North before.

Nor do I remember that the Natives differed
much from one another, either in Stature or
Complexion, or in their Manners, their Habits
their

their Weapons, or indeed in any thing; and yet
we could not perceive that they had any Intelligence one with another; but they were extremely kind and civil to us on this Side, as well as
on the other.

We continued our Voyage South for many
Weeks, tho' with several Intervals of going on
Shore to get Provisions and Water. At length,
coming round a Point of Land which lay about
a League farther than ordinary into the Sea, we
were agreeably surprized with a Sight, which,
no doubt, had been as disagreeable to those concern'd, as it was pleasant to us. This was the
Wreck of an *European* Ship, which had been cast
away upon the Rocks, which in that Place run a
great Way into the Sea.

We could see plainly at Low Water, a great
deal of the Ship lay dry; even at High Water,
she was not entirely covered; and that at most
she did not lye above a League from the Shore.
It will easily be believ'd, that our Curiosity led
us, the Wind and Weather also permitting, to go
directly to her, which we did without any Difficulty, and presently found that it was a *Dutch*-
built Ship, and that she could not have been very
long in that Condition, a great deal of the upper
Work of her Stern remaining firm, with the
Mizen Mast standing. Her Stern seem'd to be
jaum'd in between two Ridges of the Rock,
and so remained fast, all the Fore-part of the Ship
having been beaten to Pieces.

We could see nothing to be gotten out of
the Wreck that was worth our while; but we
resolv'd to go on Shore, and stay sometime thereabouts, to see if perhaps we might get any Light
into the Story of her, and we were not without

Hopes

Hopes that we might hear fomething more particular about her Men, and perhaps find fome of
them on Shore there, in the fame Condition that
we were in, and fo might encreafe our Company.

It was a very pleafant Sight to us, when coming on Shore, we faw all the Marks and Tokens of a Ship-Carpenter's Yard; as a Launch
Block and Craddles, Scaffolds and Planks, and
Pieces of Planks, the Remains of the Building a
Ship or Veffel; and, in a Word, a great many
things that fairly invited us to go about the
fame Work, and we foon came to underftand, that
the Men belonging to the Ship that was loft, had
faved themfelves on Shore, perhaps in their Boat,
and had built themfelves a Bark or Sloop, and fo
were gone to Sea again; and enquiring of the
Natives which Way they went, they pointed to
the South and South-Weft, by which we could
eafily underftand that they were gone away to the
Cape of Good Hope.

No body will imagine we could be fo dull as not
to gather from hence, that we might take the
fame Method for our Efcapes; fo we refolved firft
in general, that we would try, if poffible, to
build us a Boat of one Kind or other, and go
to Sea as our Fate fhould direct.

In order to this, our firft Work was to have
the two Carpenters fearch about to fee what Materials the *Dutchmen* had left behind them that
might be of Ufe; and in particular, they found
one that was very ufeful, and which I was much employ'd about, and that was a Pitch-Kettle, and a
little Pitch in it.

When we came to fet clofe to this Work, we
found it very laborious and difficult, having but

few

few Tools, no Iron Work, no Cordage, no Sails; so that, in short, whatever we built, we were oblig'd to be our own Smiths, Rope-Makers, Sail-Makers, and indeed to practise twenty Trades that we knew little or nothing of: However, Necessity was the Spur to Invention, and we did many things which before we thought impracticable, that is to say, in our Circumstances.

After our two Carpenters had resolved upon the Dimensions of what they would build, they set us all to Work, to go off in our Boats, and split up the Wreck of the old Ship, and to bring away every thing we could; and particularly, that, if possible, we should bring away the Mizen Mast, which was left standing, which with much Difficulty we effected, after above twenty Days Labour of fourteen of our Men.

At the same time we got out a great deal of Iron-Work; as Bolts, Spikes, Nails, &c. all which our Artist, of whom I have spoken already, who was now grown a very dexterous Smith, made us Nails and Hinges for our Rudder, and Spikes such as we wanted.

But we wanted an Anchor, and if we had had an Anchor, we could not have made a Cable; so we contented our selves with making some Ropes with the Help of the Natives, of such Stuff as they made their Matts of, and with these we made such a kind of cable or *Tow Line*, as was sufficient to fasten our Vessel to the Shore, which we contented our selves with for that time.

To be short, we spent four Months here, and work'd very hard too; at the End of which time we launch'd our Frigate, which, in a few Words, had many Defects, but yet, all things

consiconfidered, it was as well as we could expect it to be.

In fhort, it was a kind of a Sloop, of the Burthen of near 18 or 20 Ton, and had we had Mafts and Sails; ftanding, and running Rigging, as is ufual in fuch Cafes, and other Conveniences, the Veffel might have carry'd us wherever we could have had a Mind to go; but of all the Materials we wanted, this was the worft, *viz.* that we had no Tar or Pitch to pay the Seams, and fecure the Bottom; and tho' we did what we could with Tallow and Oil, to make a Mixture to fupply that Part, yet we could not bring it to anfwer our End fully; and when we launch'd her into the Water, fhe was fo leaky, and took in the Water fo faft, that we thought all our Labour had been loft, for we had much ado to make her fwim; and as for Pumps, we had none, nor had we any Means to make one.

But at length one of the Natives, a black *Negro-man,* fhewed us a Tree, the Wood of which being put into the Fire, fends forth a Liquid that is as glutinous, and almoft as ftrong as Tar, and of which, by boiling, we made a Sort of Stuff which ferv'd us for Pitch, and this anfwered our End effectually; for we perfectly made our Veffel found and tight, fo that we wanted no Pitch or Tar at all. This Secret has ftood me in ftead upon many Occafions fince that time, in the fame Place.

Our Veffel being thus finifhed, out of the Mizen Maft of the Ship, we made a very good Maft to her, and fitted our Sails to it as well as we could; then we made a Rudder and Tiller; and, in a Word, every thing that our prefent

Neceffi-

Neceſſity called upon us for ; and having victu-
ailed her, and put as much freſh Water on Board
as we thought we wanted, or as we knew how
to ſtow (for we were yet without Casks) we put
to Sea with a fair Wind.

We had ſpent near another Year in theſe
Rambles, and in this Piece of Work ; for it was
now, as our Men ſaid, about the Beginning of
our *February*, and the Sun went from us apace,
which was much to our Satisfaction, for the
Heats were exceeding violent. The Wind, as
I ſaid, was fair, for as I have ſince learnt, the
Winds generally ſpring up to the Eaſtward, as
the Sun goes from them to the North.

Our Debate now was, which Way we ſhould
go, and never were Men ſo irreſolute ; ſome were
for going to the Eaſt, and ſtretching away directly for the Coaſt of *Malabar* ; but others who
conſidered more ſeriouſly the Length of that Voyage, ſhook their Heads at the Propoſal, knowing
very well, that neither our Proviſions, eſpecially
of Water; or our Veſſel, were equal to ſuch a
Run as that is, of near 2000 Miles, without
any Land to touch at in the Way.

Theſe Men too had all along had a great
Mind to a Voyage for the main Land of *Africk*,
where they ſaid we ſhould have a fair Caſt for
our Lives, and might be ſure to make our ſelves
rich which Way ſoever we went, if we were but
able t o make our Way through, whether by Sea
or by Land.

Beſides, as the Caſe ſtood with us, we had
not much Choice for our Way ; for if we had
reſolv'd for the Eaſt, we were at the wrong Seaſon of the Year, and muſt have ſtaid till *April* or
May before we had gone to Sea. At length, as
we

we had the Wind at S. E. and E. S. E. and fine promising Weather, we came all into the first Proposal, and resolved for the Coast of *Africa*; nor were we long in disputing as to our Coasting the Island, which we were upon; for we were now on the wrong Side of the Island for the Voyage we intended; So we stood away to the North, and having rounded the Cape, we hall'd away Southward under the Lee of the Island, thinking to reach the West Point of Land, which, as I observed before, runs out so far towards the Coast of *Africa*, as would have shorten'd our Run almost 100 Leagues. But when we had failed about thirty Leagues, we found the Winds variable under the Shore, and right against us; so we concluded to stand over directly, for then we had the Wind fair, and our Vessel was but very ill fitted to lye near the Wind, or any Way indeed but just afore it.

Having resolv'd upon it therefore, we put in to the Shore, to furnish our selves again with fresh Water and other Provisions, and about the latter End of *March*, with more Courage than Discretion, more Resolution than Judgment, we launch'd for the main Coast of *Africa*.

As for me, I had no Anxieties about it; so that we had but a View of reaching some Land or other, I cared not what or where it was to be, having at this time no Views of what was before me, nor much Thought of what might, or might not befal me; but with as little Consideration as any one can be supposed to have at my Age, I consented to every thing that was proposed, however hazardous the thing it self, however improbable the Success.

The

The Voyage, as it was undertaken with a great deal of Ignorance and Defperation, fo really it was not carry'd on with much Refolution or Judgment; for we knew no more of the Courfe we were to fteer, than this, that it was any where about the Weft, within two or three Points N. or S. and as we had no Compafs with us, but a little Brafs Pocket Compafs, which one of our Men had more by Accident than otherwife, fo we could not be very exact in our Courfe.

However, as it pleafed God that the Wind continued fair at S. E. and by E. we found that N. W. by W. which was right afore it, was as good a Courfe for us as any we could go, and thus we went on.

The Voyage was much longer than we expected; our Veffel alfo, which had no Sail that was proportion'd to her, made but very little Way in the Sea, and fail'd heavily. We had indeed no great Adventures happen'd in this Voyage, being out of the Way of every thing that could offer to divert us; and as for feeing any Veffel, we had not the leaft Occafion to hail any thing in all the Voyage; for we faw not one Veffel fmall or great, the Sea we were upon being entirely out of the way of all Commerce; for the People of *Madagafcar* knew no more of the Shores of *Africa* than we did, only that there was a Country of Lions, as they call *it, that Way.*

We had been eight or nine Days under Sail, with a fair Wind, when, to our great Joy one of our Men cry'd out, *Land.* We had great Reafon to be glad of the Difcovery; for we had not Water enough left for above two or three

Days

Days more, tho' at a short Allowance. However, tho' it was early in the Morning when we discover'd it, we made it near Night before we reach'd it, the Wind slackening almost to a Calm, and our Ship being, as I said, a very dull Sailer.

We were sadly baulk'd upon our coming to the Land, when we found, that instead of the main Land of *Africk*, it was only a little Island, with no Inhabitants upon it, at least, none that we could find; nor any Cattel, except a few Goats, of which we killed three only. However, they served us for fresh Meat, and we found very good Water; and it was fifteen Days more before we reach'd the Main, which, however, at last we arriv'd at; and which was most essential to us, we came to it just as all our Provisions were spent. Indeed we may say they were spent first; for we had but a Pint of Water a Day to each Man for the last two Days. But to our great Joy, we saw the Land, tho' at a great Distance, the Evening before, and by a pleasant Gale in the Night, were, by Morning, within two Leagues of the Shore.

We never scrupled going ashore at the first Place we came at, tho' had we had Patience, we might have found a very fine River a little farther North. However, we kept our Frigate on Float by the Help of two great Poles which we fasten'd into the Ground to *More* her, like Piles; and the little weak Ropes, which, as I said, we had made of Matting, served us well enough to make the Vessel fast.

As soon as we had viewed the Country a little, got fresh Water, and furnished our selves with some Victuals, which we found very scarce here, we went onboard again with our Stores. All we got for
Provi-

Provifion, was fome Fowls that we killed, and a
kind of wild Buffloe, or Bull, very fmall, but good
Meat: I fay, having got thefe things on Board,
we refolved to fail on along the Coaft, which lay
away N. N. E. till we found fome Creek or River
that we might run up into the Country, or fome
Town or People; for we had Reafon enough to
know the Place was inhabited, becaufe we feveral times faw Fires in the Night, and Smoke in
the Day, every way at a Diftance from us.

At length we came to a very large Bay, and in
it feveral little Creeks or Rivers emptying themfelves into the Sea, and we run boldly into the
firft Creek we came at; where feeing fome Hutts
and wild People about them, on the Shore, we run
our Veffel into a little Cove on the North Side
of the Creek, and held up a long Pole with a
white Bit of Cloath on it, for a Signal of Peace
to them. We found they underftood us prefently, for they came flocking to us both Men,
Women, and Children, moft of them of both
Sexes ftark naked. At firft they ftood wondering
and ftaring at us, as if we had been Monfters,
and as if they had been frighted; but we found
they inclined to be familiar with us afterwards.
The firft thing we did to try them, was, we
held up our Hands to our Mouths, as if we were
to drink, fignifying that we wanted Water. This
they underftood prefently, and three of their
Women and two Boys ran away up the Land, and
came back in about Half a Quarter of an Hour,
with feveral Pots made of Earth pretty enough,
and bak'd, I fuppofe, in the Sun; thefe they
brought us full of Water, and fet them down
near the Sea-fhore, and there left them, going

ing back a little, that we might fetch them, which we did.

Sometime after this, they brought us Roots and Herbs, and some Fruits which I cannot remember, and gave us; but as we had nothing to give them, we found them not so free as the People in *Madagascar* were. However, our Cutler went to Work, and as he had saved some Iron out of the Wreck of the Ship, he made Abundance of Toys, Birds, Dogs, Pins, Hooks, and Rings, and we helped to file them, and make them bright for him; and when we gave them some of these, they brought us all the Sorts of Provisions they had, such as Goats, Hogs, and Cows, and we got Victuals enough.

We were now landed upon the Continent of *Africa*, the most desolate, desart, and unhospitable Country in the World, even *Greenland* and *Nova Zembla* it self not excepted; with this Difference only, that even the worst Part of it we found inhabited; tho' taking the Nature and Quality of some of the Inhabitants, it might have been much better to us if there had been none.

And, to add to the Exclamation I am making on the Nature of the Place, it was here, that we took one of the rashest and wildest, and most desperate Resolutions that ever was taken by Man, or any Number of Men, in the World; this was, to travel over Land through the Heart of the Country, from the Coast of *Mozambique*, on the East-Ocean to the Coast of *Angola* or *Guinea*, on the Western or *Atlantick* Ocean, a Continent of Land of at least 1800 Miles; in which Journey we had excessive Heats to support, unpassable Desarts to go over, no Carriages, Camels

or

or Beasts of any kind to carry our Baggage,
innumerable Numbers of wild and ravenous
Beasts to encounter with, such as Lions, Leopards, Tigers, Lizards, and Elephants; we had
the Equinoctial Line to pass under, and consequently were in the very Center of the Torrid Zone; we had Nations of Savages to encounter with, barbarous and brutish to the last
Degree, Hunger and Thirst to struggle with;
and, in one Word, Terrors enough to have
daunted the stoutest Hearts that ever were placed
in Cases of Flesh and Blood.

Yet, fearless of all these, we resolved to adventure, and accordingly made such Preparation
for our Journey, as the Place we were in
would allow us, and such as our little Experience
of the Country seem'd to dictate to us.

It had been some time already that we had
been used to tread bare-footed upon the Rocks,
the Gravel, the Grass and the Sand on the Shore;
but as we found the worst thing for our Feet
was, the walking or travelling on the dry burning Sands, within the Country; so we provided
our selves with a sort of Shoes made of the Skins
of Wild Beasts, with the Hair inward, and being
dryed in the Sun, the Out-side were thick and
hard, and would last a great while. In short,
as I called them, so I think the Term very proper still, we made us Gloves for our Feet,
and we found them very convenient and very
comfortable.

We conversed with some of the Natives of
the Country who were friendly enough. What
Tongue they spoke, I do not yet pretend to
know. We talked as far as we could make them
understand us, not only about our Provisions,
but

but also about our Undertaking ; and ask'd them what Country lay that Way, pointing West with our Hands. They told us but little to our Purpose, only we thought by all their Discourse, that there were People to be found of one Sort or other every where ; that there were many great Rivers, many Lions and Tygers, Elephants, and furious wild Cats (which in the End we found to be Civet Cats) and the like.

When we ask'd them, if any one had ever travelled that Way, they told us Yes, some had gone to where the Sun sleeps, meaning to the West ; but they could not tell us who they were. When we ask'd for some to guide us, they shrunk up their Shoulders as *Frenchmen* do when they are afraid to undertake a thing. When we ask'd them about the Lions and wild Creatures they laught, and let us know they would do us no Hurt, and directed us to a good way indeed to deal with them, and that was to make some Fire, which would always fright them away, and so indeed we found it.

Upon these Encouragements we resolved upon our Journey, and many Considerations put us upon it, which, had the thing it self been practicable, we were not so much to blame for, as it might otherwise be supposed ; I'll name some of them, not to make the Account too tedious.

First, We were perfectly destitute of Means to work about our own Deliverance any other way ; we were on shore in a Place perfectly remote from all *European* Navigation ; so that we could never think of being relieved, and fetch'd off by any of our own Country-men in that Part of the World. Secondly, If we had adventured to have sailed on along the Coast of

Mozam-

Mozambique, and the defolate Shores of *Africa* to
the North, till we came to the Red Sea, all we
could hope for there, was to be taken by the
Arabs, and be fold for Slaves to the *Turks*, which
to all of us was little better than Death. We
could not build any thing of a Veffel that
would carry us over the great *Arabian* Sea
to *India*, nor could we reach the Cape *de Bona
Speranza*, the Winds being too variable, and the
Sea in that Latitude too tempestuous; but we all
knew, if we could crofs this Continent of Land,
we might reach fome of the great Rivers that
run into the *Atlantick* Ocean, and that on the
Banks of any of thofe Rivers we might
there build us Canoes which would carry us
down, if it were Thoufands of Miles; fo that
we could want nothing but Food, of which we
were affured we might kill fufficient with our
Guns: And, to add to the Satisfaction of our
Deliverance, we concluded we might every one
of us get a Quantity of Gold, wh ch, if we came
fafe, would infinitely recompence us for our Toil.

I cannot fay, that in all our Confultations I
ever began to enter into the Weight and Merit
of any Enterprize we went upon till now. My
View before was, as I thought, very good, *viz.*
that we fhould get into the *Arabian* Gulph,
or the Mouth of the Red Sea, and waiting for
fome Veffel paffing, or repaffing there, of which
there is Plenty, have feized upon the firft
we came at, by Force, and not only have
enriched our felves with her Cargo, but have
carried our felves to what Part of the World we
had pleafed: But when they came to talk to
me of a March of 2 or 3000 Miles on Foot, of
Wandering in Defarts, among Lions and Tygers,

F   I con-

I confefs my Blood run chill, and I ufed all the Arguments I could to perfwade them againft it.

But they were all pofitive, and I might as well have held my Tongue; fo I fubmitted, and told them, I would keep to our firft Law, to be governed by the Majority, and we refolved upon our Journey. The firft thing we did, was to take an Obfervation, and fee whereabouts in the World we were, which we did, and found we were in the Latitude of 12 Degrees, 35 Minutes South of the Line. The next thing was to look on the Charts, and fee the Coaft of the Country we aimed at, which we found to be from 8 to 11 Degrees South Latitude, if we went for the Coaft of *Angola*, or in 12 to 19 Degrees North Latitude, if we made for the River *Niger*, and the Coaft of *Guiney*.

Our Aim was for the Coaft of *Angola*, which by the Charts we had, lying very near the fame Latitude we were then in, our Courfe thither was due Weft; and as we were affured we fhould meet with Rivers, we doubted not, but that by their Help we might eafe our Journey, efpecially if we could find Means to crofs the great Lake, or Inland Sea, which the Natives call *Coalmucoa*, out of which it is faid the River *Nile* has its Source or Beginning; but we reckoned without our Hoft, as you will fee in the Sequel of our Story.

The next thing we had to confider was, how to carry our Baggage, which we were firft of all determined not to travel without; neither indeed was it poffible for us to do fo, for even our Ammunition which was abfolutely neceffary to us, and on which our Subfiftence, I mean for Food, as well as our Safety; and particularly our Defence

againft

against wild Beafts, and wild Men depended: I fay,
even our Ammunition was a Load too heavy for
us to carry in a Country where the Heat were
fuch, that we fhould be Load enough for our felves.

We enquired in the Country, and found there
was no Beaft of Burthen known among them;
that is to fay, neither Horfes or Mules or Affes,
Camels or Dromedaries; the only Creature they
had, was a kind of Buffloe, or tame Bull, fuch a
one as we had killed; and that fome of thefe they
had brought fo to their Hand, that they taught
them to go and come with their Voices, as they
called them to them, or fent them from them;
that they made them carry Burthens, and particularly, that they would fwim over Rivers
and Lakes upon them, the Creatures fwimming
very high and ftrong in the Water.

But we underftood nothing of the Management or Guiding fuch a Creature, or how to bind
a Burthen upon them; and this laft Part of
our Confultation puzzled us extremely: At laft
I propofed a Method for them, which after
fome Confideration, they found very convenient; and this was to quarrel with fome of the
Negro Natives, take ten or twelve of them
Prifoners, and binding them as Slaves, caufe
them to travel with us, and make them carry our Baggage; which I alledged would be
convenient and ufeful many ways, as well to
fhew us the Way, as to converfe with other
Natives for us.

This Counfel was not accepted at firft, but
the Natives foon gave them Reafon to approve
it; and alfo gave them an Opportunity to put
it in Practice; for as our little Traffick with
the Natives was hitherto upon the Faith of
their firft Kindnefs, we found fome Knavery

among

among them at laſt; for having bought ſome
Cattel of them for our Toys, which, as I ſaid,
our Cutler had contrived, one of our Men
differing with his Chapman, truly they huff'd
him in their Manner, and keeping the things
he had offered them for the Cattel, made their
Fellows drive away the Cattel before his
Face, and laugh at him; our Man crying out
loud of this Violence, and calling to ſome of us,
who were not far off, the Negro he was dealing
with threw a Lance at him, which came ſo
true, that if he had not with great Agility
jumped aſide, and held up his Hand alſo to
turn the Lance as it came, it had ſtruck through
his Body, and, as it was, it wounded him in
the Arm; at which the Man enraged took up
his Fuzee, and ſhot the Negro through the
Heart.

The others that were near him, and all thoſe
that were with us at a Diſtance, were ſo tèr-
ribly frighted; firſt, at the Flaſh of Fire; ſe-
condly, at the Noiſe: And thirdly, at ſeeing their Countryman killed, that they ſtood
like Men ſtupid and amazed, at firſt, for ſome
time: But after they were a little recovered
from their Fright, one of them, at a good Diſtance from us, ſet up a ſudden ſcreaming Noiſe,
which, it ſeems, is the Noiſe they make when
they go to Fight; and all the reſt underſtanding
what he meant, anſwered him, and run together to the Place where he was, and we not
knowing what it meant, ſtood ſtill looking upon
one another like a Parcel of Fools.

But we were preſently undeceived, for in
two or three Minutes more we heard the ſcreaming roaring Noiſe go on from one Place to a-
nother, through all their little Towns; nay,
even

even over the Creek to the other Side; and, on a sudden we saw a naked Multitude running from all Parts to the Place where the firft Man began it, as to a Rendezvous; and, in lefs than an Hour, I believe there was near 500 of them gotten together, armed fome with Bows and Arrows, but moft with Lances, with which they throw, at a good Diftance, fo nicely, that they will ftrike a Bird flying.

We had but a very little time for Confultation, for the Multitude was encreafing every Moment; and I verily believe, if we had ftay'd long, they would have been 10000 together in a little time. We had nothing to do therefore, but to fly to our Ship or Bark, where indeed we could have defended our felves very well, or to advance and try what a Volley or two of fmall Shot would do for us.

We refolved immediately upon the latter, depending upon it, that the Fire and Terror of our Shot would foon put them to Flight; fo we drew up all in a Line, and marched boldly up to them; they ftood ready to meet us, depending, I fuppofe, to deftroy us all with their Lances; but before we came near enongh for them to throw their Lances, we halted, and ftanding at a good Diftance from one another, to ftretch our Line as far as we could, we gave them a Salute with our Shot, which befides what we wounded that we knew not of, knocked fixteen of them down upon the Spot, and three more were fo lamed, that they fell about 20 or 30 Yards from them.

As foon as we had fired, they fet up the horrideft Yell, or Howling, partly raifed by thofe that were wounded, and partly by thofe that

piti-

pitied and condoled the Bodies they faw lye dead, that I never heard any thing like it before or fince.

We ftood Stock ftill after we had fired, to load our Guns again, and finding they did not ftir from the Place, we fired among them again; we killed about nine of them at the fecond Fire; but as they did not ftand fo thick as before, all our Men did not fire, feven of us being ordered to referve our Charge, and to advance as foon as the other had fired, while the reft loaded again ; of which I fhall fpeak again prefently.

As foon as we had fired the fecond Volley we fhouted as loud as we could, and the feven Men advanced upon them, and, coming about 20 Yards nearer, fired again, and thofe that were behind having loaded again, with all Expedition, follow'd but when they faw us advance, they run fcreaming away as if they were bewitched.

When we came up to the Field of Battle, we faw a great Number of Bodies lying upon the Ground, many more than we could fuppofe were killed or wounded, nay more than we had Bullets in our Pieces when we fired; and we could not tell what to make of it; but at length, we found how it was _viz._ that they were frighted out of all manner of Senfe; nay, I do believe feveral of thofe that were really dead, were frighted to Death, and had no Wound about them.

Of thofe that were thus frighted, as I have faid, feveral of them, as they recovered themfelves, came and worfhipped us (taking us for Gods or Devils, I know not which, nor did it much matter to us) fome kneeling, fome throwing themfelves flat on the Ground, made a Thoufand antick Geftures, but all with Tokens of the moft

pro-

profound Submiffion. It prefently came into my Head, that we might now by the Law of Arms take as many Prifoners as we would, and make them travel with us, and carry our Baggage: As foon as I propofed it, our Men were all of my Mind; and accordingly we fecured about 60 lufty young Fellows, and let them know they muft go with us; which they feemed very willing to do: But the next Queftion we had among our felves, was, how we fhould do to truft them, for we found the People not like thofe of *Madagafar*, but fierce, revengful and treacherous, for which Reafon we were fure, that we fhould have no Service from them but that of meer Slaves, no Subjection that would continue any longer than the Fear of us was upon them, nor any Labour but by Violence.

Before I go any farther, I muft hint to the Reader, that from this time forward I began to enter a little more ferioufly into the Circum-ftance I was in, and concern'd my felf more in the Conduct of our Affairs; for, tho' my Come-rades were all older Men, yet I began to find them void of Counfel, or, as I now call it, Prefence of Mind, when, they came to the Execution of a thing. The firft Occafion I took to obferve this, was in their late Engagement with the Natives, when, tho' they had taken a good Refolution to attack them, and fire upon them, yet when they had fired the firft time, and found that the Negroes did not run as they expected, their Hearts began to fail, and I am perfwaded if their Bark had been near Hand, they would every Man have run away.

Upon this Occafion, I began to take upon me a little to hearten them up, and to call upon

them

them to load again, and give them another Volley, telling them that I would engage, if they would be ruled by me, I'd make the Negroes run fast enough. I found this heartned them, and therefore, when they fired a second time, I desired them to reserve some of their Shot to an Attempt by it self, as I mentioned above.

Having fired a second time, I was indeed forced to command, as I may call it. Now, *Seigniors*, said I, let us give them a Chear; so I open'd my Throat, and shouted three times, as our *English* Sailors do on like Occasions; and now follow me, said I to the seven that had not fired, and *I'll warrant you we will make Work with them*; and so it proved indeed: For as soon as they saw us coming, away they run as above.

From this Day forward they would call me nothing but *Seignior Capitanio*; but I told them, I would not be called *Seignior*. Well then, said the Gunner, who spoke good *English*, you shall be called Captain *Bob*, and so they gave me my Title ever after.

Nothing is more certain of the *Portuguese* than this, take them nationally or personally; if they are animated and hearten'd up by any body to go before, and encourage them by Example, they will behave well enough; but if they have nothing but their own Measures to follow, they sink immediately: These Men had certainly fled from a Parcel of naked Savages, tho' even by flying they could not have saved their Lives, if I had not shouted and halloo'd, and made rather Sport with the thing, than a Fight, to keep up their Courage.

Nor was there less need of it upon several Occasions hereafter; and I do confess, I have often

ten wonder'd how a Number of Men, who, when they came to the Extremity, were so ill supported by their own Spirits, had at first Courage to propose, and to undertake the most desperate and impracticable Attempt that ever Men went about in the World.

There were indeed two or three indefatigable Men among them, by whose Courage and Industry all the rest were upheld; and indeed those two or three were the Managers of them from the Beginning; that was the Gunner, and that Cutler whom I call the Artist; and the third, who was pretty well, tho' not like either of them, was one of the Carpenters. These indeed were the Life and Soul of all the rest, and it was to their Courage that all the rest ow'd the Resolution they shewd upon any Occasion. But when those saw me take a little upon me, as above, they embraced me, and treated me with particular Affection ever after.

This Gunner was an excellent Mathematician, a good Scholar, and a compleat Sailor; and it was in conversing intimately with him, that I learnt afterwards the Grounds of what Knowledge I have since had in all the Sciences useful for Navigation, and particularly in the Geographical Part of Knowledge.

Even in our Conversation, finding me eager to understand and learn, he laid the Foundation of a general Knowledge of things in my Mind, gave me just Ideas of the Form of the Earth and of the Sea, the Situation of Countries, the Course of Rivers, the Doctrine of the Spheres, the Motion of the Stars; and, in a Word, taught me a kind of System of Astronomy, which I afterwards improv'd.

In

In especial Manner, he filled my Head with aspiring Thoughts, and with an earnest Desire after learning every thing that could be taught me; convincing me, that nothing could qualify me for great Undertakings, but a Degree of Learning superior to what was usual in the Race of Seamen; he told me, that to be ignorant, was to be certain of a mean Station in the World, but that Knowledge was the first Step to Preferment. He was always flattering me with my Capacity to Learn; and tho' that fed my Pride, yet on the other Hand, as I had a secret Ambition which just at that time fed it self in my Mind, it prompted in me an insatiable Thirst after Learning in general, and I resolved, if ever I came back to *Europe*, and had any thing left to purchase it, I would make my self Master of all the Parts of Learning needful to the making of me a compleat Sailor; but I was not so just to my self afterwards, as to do it when I had an Opportunity.

But to return to our Business; the Gunner, when he saw the Service I had done in the Fight, and heard my Proposal for keeping a Number of Prisoners for our March, and for carrying our Baggage, turns to me before them all, Captain *Bob, says he*, I think you must be our Leader, for all the Success of this Enterprize is owing to you. *No, no, said I,* do not compliment me, you shall be our *Seignior Capitanio*, you shall be *General*, I am too young for it; so in short, we all agreed he should be our Leader; but he would not accept of it alone, but would have me join'd with him, and all the rest agreeing, I was oblig'd to comply.

The

The firſt Piece of Service they put me upon in this new Command, was as difficult as
any they could think of, and that was to manage the Priſoners; which however I chearfully
undertook, as you ſhall hear preſently : But the
immediate Conſultation was yet of more Conſequence; and that was, *Firſt*, Which Way we
ſhould go, and *Secondly*, How to furniſh our ſelves
for the Voyage with Proviſions.

There was among the Priſoners one tall, well-
ſhap'd, handſom Fellow, to whom the reſt ſeem'd
to pay great Reſpect, and who, as we underſtood
afterwards, was the Son of one their Kings, his
Father was, it ſeems, killed at our firſt Volley,
and he wounded with a Shot in his Arm, and
with another juſt on one of his Hips or Haunches. The Shot in his Haunch being in a fleſhy
Part, bled much, and he was half dead with
the Loſs of Blood. As to the Shot in his Arm,
it had broke his Wriſt, and he was by both
theſe Wounds quite diſabled, ſo that we were once
going to turn him away, and let him die; and
if we had, he would have died indeed in a few
Days more : But as I fouud the Man had ſome
Reſpect ſhew'd him, it preſently occurred to my
Thoughts, that we might bring him to be uſeful
to us, and perhaps make him a kind of Commander over them. So I cauſed our Surgeon to
take him in Hand, and gave the poor Wretch
good Words, that is to ſay, I ſpoke to him as well
as I could by Signs, to make him underſtand that
we would make him well again.

This created a new Awe in their Minds of us,
believing that as we could kill at a Diſtance by
ſomething inviſible to them (for ſo our Shot was
to be ſure) ſo we could make them well again
too.

too. Upon this the young Prince (for ſo we called him afterwards) called ſix or ſeven of the Savages to him, and ſaid ſomething to them; what it was we knew not, but immediately all the ſeven came to me, and kneel'd down to me, holding up their Hands, and making Signs of Entreaty, pointing to the Place where one of thoſe lay whom we had killed.

It was a long time before I or any of us could underſtand them; but one of them run and lifted up a dead Man, pointing to his Wound, which was in his Eye, for he was ſhot into the Head at one of his Eyes. Then another pointed to the Surgeon, and at laſt we found it out, that the Meaning was, that he ſhould heal the Prince's Father too, who was dead, being ſhot thro' the Head, as above.

We preſently took the Hint, and would not ſay we could not do it, but let them know, the Men that were kill'd were thoſe that had firſt fallen upon us, and provoked us, and we would by no Means make them alive again; and that if any other did ſo, we would kill them too, and never let them live any more: But that if he (the Prince) would be willing to go with us, and do as we ſhould direct him, we would not let him dye, and would make his Arm well. Upon this he bid his Men go and fetch a long Stick or Staff, and lay on the Ground. When they brought it, we ſaw it was an Arrow; he took it with his left Hand, (for his other was lame with the Wound) and pointing up at the Sun, broke the Arrow in two, and ſet the Point againſt his Breaſt, and then gave it to me. This was as I underſtood afterwards, wiſhing the Sun, whom they worſhip, might ſhoot him into the Breaſt with an Arrow,

if

if ever he failed to be my Friend; and giving
the Point of the Arrow to me, was to be a Testi-
mony, that I was the Man he had sworn to; and
never was Christian more punctual to an Oath,
than he was to this, for he was a sworn Servant
to us for many a weary Month after that.

When I brought him to the Surgeon, he immediately dress'd the Wound in his Haunch or
Bottock, and found the Bullet had only graz'd
upon the Flesh, and pass'd, as it were, by it,
but it was not lodg'd in the Part; so that it was
soon healed and well again: But as to his Arm,
he found one of the Bones broken, which are in
the Fore-part from the Wrist to the Elbow; and
this he set, and splinter'd it up, and bound his
Arm in a Sling, hanging it about his Neck, and
making Signs to him that he should not stir it;
which he was so strict an Observer of, that he set
him down, and never mov'd one Way or other,
but as the Surgeon gave him Leave.

I took a great deal of Pains to acquaint this
Negroe what we intended to do, and what Use
we intended to make of his Men; and particularly, to teach him the Meaning of what we said:
Especially to teach him some Words, such as *Yes*
and *No*, and what they meant, and to innure him
to our Way of Talking, and he was very willing
and apt to learn any thing I taught him.

It was easy to let him see, that we intended
to carry our Provision with us from the first Day;
but he made Signs to us to tell us we need not,
for that we should find Provisions enough every
where for fourty Days. It was very difficult for
us to understand how he express'd Forty; for he
knew no Figures, but some Words they used to
one another that they understood it by. At last,

one

one of the Negroes, by his Order, laid fourty little Stones one by another, to fhew us how many Days we fhould travel, and find Provifions fufficient.

Then I fhew'd him our Baggage, which was very heavy, particularly our Powder and Shot, Lead, Iron, Carpenters Tools, Seamens Inftruments, Cafes of Bottles, and other Lumber. He took fome of the things up in his Hand to fee the Weight, and fhook his Head at them; fo I told our People, they muft refolve to divide their Things into fmall Parcels, and make them portable; and accordingly they did fo, by which means we were fain to leave all our Chefts behind us, which were Eleven in Number.

Then he made Signs to us, that he would procure fome Buffloes, or young Bulls, *as I called them*, to carry things for us, and made Signs too, that if we were weary, we might be carry'd too; but that we flighted, only were willing to have the Creatures, becaufe at laft, when they could ferve us no farther for Carriage, we might eat them all up if we had any Occafion for them.

I then carry'd him to our Bark, and fhewed him what things we had there; he feem'd amaz'd at the Sight of our Bark, having never feen any thing of that Kind before, for their Boats are moft wretched things, fuch as I never faw before, having no Head or Stern, and being made only of the Skins of Goats fewed together with dried Guts of Goats and Sheep, and done over with a kind of flimy Stuff like Rofin and Oil, but of a moft naufeous, odious Smell, and they are poor miferable things for Boats, the worft that any Part of the World ever faw; a Canoe is an excellent Contrivance compared to them.

But

But to return to our Boat: We carried our new Prince into it, and help'd him over the Side, becaufe of his Lamenefs. We made Signs to him, that his Men muft carry our Goods for us, and fhewed him what we had ; he anfwer'd, *Ce Seignior*, or, *Tes Sir*, (for we had taught him that Word, and the Meaning of it) and taking up a Bundle, he made Signs to us, that when his Arm was well, he would carry fome for us.

I made Signs again, to tell him, that if he would make his Men carry them, we wou'd not let him carry any thing. We had fecured all the Prifoners in a narrow Place, where we had bound them with Matt Cords, and fet up Stakes like a Palifado round them; fo when we carry'd the Prince on Shore, we went with him to them, and made Signs to him, to ask them if they were willing to go with us to the Country of Lions. Accordingly he made a long Speech to them, and we could underftand by it, that he told them, if they were willing, they muft fay, *Ce Seignior*, telling them what it fignify'd. They immediately anfwered, *Ce Seignior*, and clapt their Hands, looking up to the Sun, which the Prince fignify'd to us, was Swearing to be faithful. But as foon as they had faid fo, one of them made a long Speech to the Prince, and in it, we perceived by his Geftures, which were very antick, that they defired fomething from us, and that they were in great Concern about it. So I ask'd him as well as I could, what it was they defired of us; he told us by Signs, that they defired we fhould clap our Hands to the Sun (that was to fwear) that we would not kill them, that we would give them *Chiaruck*, that is to fay, Bread, would not ftarve them, and would not let the Lions eat them.

them. I told him we would promise all that; then he pointed to the Sun, and clapt his Hands, signing to me, that I should do so too, which I did; at which all the Prisoners fell flat on the Ground, and rising up again, made the oddest, wildest Cries that ever I heard.

I think it was the first time in my Life that ever any religious Thought affected me; but I could not refrain some Reflections, and almost Tears, in considering how happy it was, that I was not born among such Creatures as these, and was not so stupidly ignorant and barbarous: But this soon went off again, and I was not troubled again with any Qualms of that Sort for a long time after.

When this Ceremony was over, our Concern was to get some Provisions, as well for the present Subsistence of our Prisoners, as our selves; and making Signs to our Prince, that we were thinking upon that Subject, he made Signs to me, that if I would let one of the Prisoners go to his Town, he should bring Provisions, and should bring some Beasts to carry our Baggage. I seemed loath to trust him, and supposing that he would run away, he made great Signs of Fidelity, and with his own Hands tied a Rope about his Neck, offering me one End of it, intimating, that I should hang him, if the Man did not come again. So I consented, and he gave him Abundance of Instructions, and sent him away, pointing to the Light of the Sun, which it seems was to tell him, at what time he must be back.

The Fellow run as if he was mad, and held it till he was quite out of Sight, by which I supposed he had a great Way to go. The next Morning, about two Hours before the Time
appoin-

appointed, the Black Prince, for so I always called him, beckoning with his Hand to me, and hollooing after his Manner, desired me to come to him, which I did, when pointing to a little Hill about two Miles off, I saw plainly a little Drove of Cattel, and several People with them; those he told me by Signs were the Man he had sent, and several more with him, and Cattel for us.

Accordingly by the time appointed, he came quite to our Hutts, and brought with him a great many Cowys, oung Runts, about 16 Goats, and, four young Bulls, taught to carry Burthens.

This was a Supply of Provisions sufficient; as for Bread we were obliged to shift with some Roots which we had made use of before. We then began to consider of making some large Bags like the Soldiers Knapsacks, for their Men to carry our Baggage in, and to make it easy to them; and the Goats being killed, I ordered the Skins to be spread in the Sun, and they were as dry in two Days as could be desired; so we found means to make such little Bags as we wanted, and began to divide our Baggage into them : When the Black Prince found what they were for, and how easy they were of Carriage when we put them on, he smiled a little, and sent away the Man again to fetch Skins, and he brought two Natives more with him, all loaded with Skins better cured than ours, and of other kinds, such as we could not tell what Names to give them.

These two Men brought the Black Prince two Lances of the sort they use in their Fights, but finer than ordinary, being made of black smooth Wood, as fine as Ebony, and headed at the Point with the End of a long Tooth of some Creature,

G

we

we could not tell of what Creature; the Head was fo firm put on, and the Tooth fo ftrong, tho' no bigger than my Thumb, and fharp at the End, that I never faw any thing like it in any Place in the World.

The Prince would not take them till I gave him Leave, but made Signs that they fhould give them to me; however I gave him Leave to take them himfelf, for I faw evident Signs of an honourable juft Principle in him.

We now prepared for our March, when the Prince coming to me, and pointing towards the feveral Quarters of the World, made Signs to know, which way we intended to go; and when I fhewed him pointing to the Weft, he prefently let me know, there was a great River a little further to the North, which was able to carry our Bark many Leagues into the Country due Weft. I prefently took the Hint, and enquired for the Mouth of the River, which I underftood by him was above a Day's March, and by our Eftimation we found it about feven Leagues further; I take this to be the great River marked by our Chart-Makers at the Northmoft Part of the Coaft of *Mozambique*, and called there *Quilloa*.

Confulting thus with our felves, we refolved to take the Prince, and as many of the Prifoners as we could ftow in our Frigate, and go about by the Bay into the River; and that eight of us with our Arms fhould march by Land, to meet them on the River-fide; for the Prince carrying us to a rifing Ground, had fhew'd us the River very plain a great Way up the Country, and in one Place it was not above fix Miles to it.

It

It was my Lot to march by Land, and be
Captain of the whole Carravan: I had eight of
our own Men with me, and Seven and Thirty
of our Prifoners, without any Baggage, for all
our Luggage was yet on board. We drove the
young Bulls with us; nothing was ever fo
tame, fo willing to work, or carry any thing.
The Negroes would ride upon them four at a
Time, and they would go very willingly; they
would eat out of our Hand, lick our Feet, and
were as tractable as a Dog.

We drove with us fix or feven Cows for
Food; but our Negroes knew nothing of curing
the Flefh by falting and drying it, till we
fhew'd them the Way, and then they were
mighty willing to do fo as long as we had any
Salt to do it with, and to carry Salt a great
Way too, after we found we fhould have no more.

It was an eafy March to the River Side for us
that went by Land, and we came thither in a
Piece of a Day, being as above not above fix *Englifh*
Miles; whereas it was no lefs than five Days
before they came to us by Water, the Wind in
the Bay having failed them, and the Way, by
Reafon of a great Turn or Reach in the River
being above fifty Miles about.

We fpent this time in a thing which the
two Strangers, which brought the Prince the
two Lances, put into the Head of the Prifoners;
(*viz.*) to make Bottles of the Goats-Skins to carry
frefh Water in, which it feems they knew we
fhould come to want; and the Men, did it fo dex-
teroufly, having dried Skins fetched them by
thofe two Men, that before our Veffel came up,
they had every Man a Pouch like a Bladder, to
carry frefh Water in, hanging over their Shoulder

by

by a Thong made of other Skins, about three In-
ches broad, like the Sling of a Fuzee.

Our Prince, to affure us of the Fidelity of the
Men in this March, had ordered them to be
tied two and two by the Wrift, as we handcuff
Prifoners in *England*; and made them fo fenfible
of the Reafonablenefs of it, that he made them
do it themfelves, appointing four of them, to
bind the reft; but we found them fo honeft, and particularly fo obedient to him, that after we were
gotten a little further off of their own Country,
we fet them all at Liberty, tho' when he came
to us, he would have them tied again, and they
continued fo for a good while.

All the Country on the Bank of the River was
a high Land, no marfhy fwampy Ground in it,
the Verdure good, and Abundance of Cattel feeding upon it, wherever we went, or which
Way foever we look'd; there was not much
Wood indeed, at leaft not near us, but further up
we faw Oak, Cedar, and Pine Trees, fome of which
were very large.

The River was a fair open Channel about as
broad as the *Thames* below *Gravefend*, and a
ftrong Tide of Flood, which we found held us
about 60 Miles, the Channel deep; nor did we
find any Want of Water for a great Way. In
fhort, we went merrily up the River with the
Flood, and the Wind blowing ftill frefh at E. and
E. N. E, we ftemm'd the Ebb eafily alfo, efpecially
while the River continued broad and deep; but
when we came paft the Swelling of the Tide,
and had the natural Current of the River to go
againft, we found it too ftrong for us, and began
to think of quitting our Bark; but the Prince
would by no means agree to that, for finding we
had

had on board pretty good Store of Roping made
of Matts and Flags, which I defcribed before,
he ordered all the Prifoners which were on fhore,
to come and take hold of thofe Ropes, and tow
us along by the Shore Side; and as we hoifted
our Sail too, to eafe them, the Men run along
with us at a very great Rate.

In this Manner the River carry'd us up by our
Computation near 200 Miles, and then it narrow-
ed apace, and was not above as broad as the *Thames*
is at *Windfor,* or thereabouts; and after another
Day, we came to a great Water-fall or Cataract,
enough to fright us, for I believe the whole
Body of Water fell at once perpendicularly down
a Precipice, above fixty Foot high, which made
a Noife enough to deprive men of their Hearing,
and we heard it above Ten Miles before we came
to it.

Here we were at a full Stop, and now our Prifoners went firft on Shore; they had worked very
hard, and very chearfully, relieving one another,
thofe that were weary being taken into the Bark.
Had we had Canoes, or any Boats which might
have been carried by Mens Strength, we might
have gone 200 Miles more up this River in fmall
Boats, but our great Boat could go no farther.

All this Way the Country looked green and
pleafant, and was full of Cattel, and fome People we faw, tho' not many; but this we obferv'd
now, that the People did no more underftand our
Prifoners here, than we could underftand them;
being it feems of different Nations, and of different Speech. We had yet feen no wild Beafts, or at
leaft none that came very near us; except two
Days before we came at the Water-fall, when we
faw three of the moft beautiful Leopards that ever

were

were feen, ftanding upon the Bank of the River
on the North-fide, our Prifoners being all on the
other Side of the Water. Our Gunner efpy'd
them firft, and ran to fetch his Gun, putting a
Ball extraordinary in it; and coming to me,
now Captain *Bob*; fays he, where's your Prince,
fo I called him out, now, fays he, tell your
Men not to be afraid, tell them they fhall fee
that Thing in his Hand, fpeak in Fire to one
of thofe Beafts, and make it kill it felf.

The poor Negroes looked as if they had
been all going to be killed, notwithftanding
what their Prince faid to them, and ftood ftaring to expect the Iffue, when on a fudden the
Gunner fired; and as he was a very good Marks-
Man, he fhot the Creature with two Sluggs juft
in the Head. As foon as the Leopard felt her
felf ftruck, fhe rear'd up on her two hind Legs
bolt upright, and throwing her Fore-Paws about
in the Air, fell backward, growling and ftruggling, and immediately died; the other two
frighted with the Fire and the Noife, fled, and
were out of Sight in an Inftant.

But the two frighted Leopards were not in
half the Confternation that our Prifoners were;
four or five of them fell down as if they had
been fhot, feveral others fell on their Knees, and
lifted up their Hands to us; whether to wor-
fhip us, or pray us not to kill them, we did
not know ; but we made Signs to their Prince
to encourage them, which he did, but it was
with much ado that he brought them to their
Senfe; nay, the Prince, notwithftanding all that
was faid to prepare him for it, yet when the
Piece went off, he gave a Start as if he would
have leap'd into the River.

When

When we faw the Creature killed, I had a great Mind to have the Skin of her, and made Signs to the Prince, that he fhould fend fome of his Men over to take the Skin off As fcen as he fpoke but a Word, four of them that offered themfelves were untied, and immediately they jump'd into the River, and fwam over, and went to work with him: The Prince having a Knife that we gave him, made four wooden Knives fo clever, as I never faw any thing like them in my Life, and in lefs than an Hour's time, they brought me the Skin of the Leopard, which was a monftrous great one, for it was from the Ears to the Tail about feven Foot, and near five Foot Broad on the Back, and moft admirably fpotted all over ; the Skin of this Leopard I brought to *London* many Years after.

We were now all upon a Level, as to our travelling ; being unfhipp'd, for our Bark would fwim no farther, and fhe was too heavy to carry on our Backs ; but as we found the Courfe of the River went a great Way farther, we confulted our Carpenters, whether we could not pull the Bark in Pieces, and make us three or four fmall Boats to go on with. They told us, we might do fo, but it would be very long a-doing ; and, that when we ha   e, we had neither Pitch or Tar to make   m found, to keep the Water out, or Nails to faften the Plank ; but one of them toldus, that as foon as he could come at any large Tree, near the River he would make us a Canoe or two in a Quarter of the Time, and which would ferve us as well for all the Ufes we could have any Occafion for as a Boat ; and fuch, that if we came to any Water-falls, we might take them up, and carry them for a Mile or two by Land, upon our Shoulders.

Upon

Upon this we gave over the Thoughts of our Frigate, and hauling her into a little Cove, or Inlet, where a small Brook came into the main River, we laid her up for those that came next, and marched forward. We spent indeed two Days dividing our Baggage, and loading our tame Buffloes and our Negroes: Our Powder and Shot, which was the thing we were most careful of, we ordered thus: First the Powder we divided into little Leather Bags, that is to say, Bags of dried Skins with the Hair inward, that the Powder might not grow damp; and then we put those Bags into other Bags made of Bullocks Skins, very thick a nd hard, with the Hair outward, that no Wet might come in; and this succeeded so well, that in the greatest Rains we had, whereof some were very violent and very long, we always kept our Powder dry. Besides these Bags which held our chief Magazine, we divided to every one a Quarter of a Pound of Powder, and Half a Pound of Shot to carry always about us; which as it was enough for our present Use, so we were willing to have no Weight to carry more than was absolutely necessary, because of the Heat.

We kept still on the Bank of the River, and for that Reason had very little Communication with the People of the Country; for, having also our Bark stored with Plenty of Provisions, we had had no Occasion to look abroad for a Supply; but now we came to march on Foot, we were obliged often to seek out for Food. The first Place we came to on the River that gave us any Stop, was a little Negro Town, containing about 50 Hutts, and there appeared about 400 People, for they all came out to see us,

and

and wonder at us. When our Negroes appea-
peared, the Inhabitants began to fly to Arms,
thinking there had been Enemies coming upon
them; but our Negroes, tho' they could not
speak their Language, made Signs to them, that
they had no Weapons, and were tied two and two
together, as Captives; that there were People
behind who came from the Sun, and that could
kill them all, and make them alive again, if they
pleased; but that they would do them no Hurt,
and came with Peace. As soon as they understood
this, they laid down their Lances, and Bows and
Arrows, and came and stuck twelve large Stakes
in the Ground, as a Token of Peace, bowing
themselves to us in Token of Submission. But as
soon as they saw white Men with Beards, that
is to say, Mustachoes, they run screaming away
as in a Fright.

We kept at a Distance from them, not to be
too familiar; and when we did appear, it was
but two or three of us at a time. But our Prisoners made them understand, that we required
some Provisions of them; so they brought us
some black Cattel, for they have Abundance of
Cows and Buffloes all over that Side of the
Country, as also great Numbers of Deer. Our
Cutler, who had now a great Stock of things of
his Handy-work, gave them some little Knick
Knacks, as Plates of Silver and of Iron, cut Diamond Fashion, and cut into Hearts and into Rings,
and they were mightily pleased. They also
brought several Sorts of Fruits and Roots, which
we did not understand, but our Negroes fed heartily on them, and after we had seen them eat
them, we did so too.

Having

Having ftock'd our felves here with Flefh and
Roots as much as we could well carry, we divided the Burthens among our Negroes, appointing
about 30 to 40 Pound Weight to a Man, which
we thought indeed was Load enough in a hot
Country ; and the Negroes did not at all repine
at it, but would fometimes help one another
when they began to be weary, which did happen
now and then, tho' not often : Befides, as moft of
their Luggage was our Provifion, it lighten'd every Day like *Æfop*'s Basket of Bread, till we came
to get a Recruit. Note, when we loaded them,
we untied their Hands, and tied them two and
two together by one Foot. The third Day of our
March from this Place, our chief Carpenter defired us to halt, and fet up fome Hutts, for he
had found out fome Trees that he liked, and
refolved to make us fome Canoes ; for as he told
me, he knew we fhould have Marching enough on
Foot after we left the River, and he was refolved
to go no farther by Land than needs muft.

We had no fooner given Order for our little
Camp, and given Leave to our Negroes to lay
down their Loads, but they fell to Work to build
our Hutts ; and tho' they were tied, as above,
yet they did it fo nimbly, as furprized us. Here
we fet fome of the Negroes quite at Liberty,
that is to fay, without tying them, having the
Prince's Word pafs'd for their Fidelity ; and fome
of thefe were ordered to help the Carpenters,
which they did very handily, with a little Direction, and others were fent to fee whether they
could get any Provifion near Hand ; but inftead
of Provifions, three of them came in with two
Bows and Arrows, and five Lances. They could
not eafily make us underftand how they came by
them,

them, only that they had furprized fome Negroe
Women, who were in fome Hutts, the Men being from Home, and they had found the Lances
and Bows in the Hutts or Houfes, the Women
and Children flying away at the Sight of them,
as from Robbers. We feem'd very argry at them,
and made the Prince ask them, if they had not
kill'd any of the Women or Children, making
them believe, that if they had kill'd any Body,
we would make them kill themfelves too; but
they protefted their Innocence, fo we excufed
them. Then they brought us the Bows and Arrows and Lances; but at a Motion of their black
Prince, we gave them back the Bows and Arrows,
and gave them Leave to go out to fee what they
could kill for Food; and here we gave them the
Law of Arms, *viz.* That if any Men appeared to
affault them, or fhoot at them, or offer any Violence to them, they might kill them; but that
they fhould not offer to kill or hurt any that
offer'd them Peace, or laid down their Weapons,
nor any Women or Children, upon any Occafion
whatfoever. Thefe were our Articles of War.

Thefe two Fellows had not been gone out above
three or four Hours, but one of them came running to us without his Bow and Arrows, hallooing
and hooping a great while before he came at us,
Okoamo, Okoamo, which it feems was, *Help, Help.*
The reft of the Negroes rofe up in a Hurry,
and by Two's, as they could, run forward toward
their Fellows to know what the Matter was. As
for me, I did not underftand it, nor any of our
People; the Prince look'd as if fomething unlucky
had fallen out, and fome of our Men took up
their Arms, to be ready on Occafion. But the
Negroes foon difcover'd the Thing; for we faw
four

four of them prefently after coming along with a great Load of Meat upon their Backs. The Cafe was, that the firft two who went out with their Bows and Arrows, meeting with a great Herd of Deer in the Plain, had been fo nimble as to fhoot three of them ; and then one of them came running to us for Help, to fetch them away. This was the firft Venifon we had met with upon all our March, and we feafted upon it very plentifully ; and this was the firft time we began to prevail with our Prince to eat his Meat dreft our Way; after which, his Men were prevailed with by his Example, but before that, they eat moft of the Flefh they had quite raw.

We wifh'd now we had brought fome Bows and Arrows out with us, which we might have done ; and we began to have fo much Confidence in our Negroes, and to be fo familiar with them, that we oftentimes let them go, or the greateft Part of them, unty'd, being well affured they would not leave us, and that they did not know what Courfe to take without us; but one thing we refolved not to truft them with, and that was the Charging our Guns; but they always believed our Guns had fome heavenly Power in them, that they would fend forth Fire and Smoke, and fpeak with a dreadful Noife, and kill at a Diftance whenever we bid them.

In about eight Days we finifhed three Canoes, and in them we embarked our white Men and our Baggage, with our Prince, and fome of the Prifoners. We alfo found it needful to keep fome of our felves always on Shore, not only to manage the Negroes, but to defend them from Enemies and wild Beafts. Abundance of little Incidents happened upon this March, which it is

not

not poffible to crowd into this Account; particularly, we faw more wild Beafts now than we
did before, fome Elephants, and two or three
Lions; none of which Kinds we had feen any of
before; and we found our Negroes were more
afraid of them a great deal than we were; principally becaufe they had no Bows and Arrows,
or Lances, which were the particular Weapons
they were bred up to the Exercife of.

But we cured them of their Fears, by being
always ready with our Fire-Arms. However, as
we were willing to be fparing of our Powder,
and the Killing any of the Creatures now was no
Advantage to us, feeing their Skins were too heavy for us to carry, and their Flefh not good to
eat, we refolved therefore to keep fome of our
Pieces uncharg'd, and only prim'd, and caufing
them to flafh in the Pan, the Beafts, even the
Lions themfelves, would always ftart, and fly
back when they faw it, and immediately march off.

We paft Abundance of Inhabitants upon this
upper Part of the River, and with this Obfervation, that almoft every ten Miles we came to,
a feveral Nation, and every feveral Nation had
a different Speech, or elfe their Speech had differing Dialects, fo that they did not underftand
one another. They all abounded in Cattel, efpecially on the River Side; and the eighth Day of
this fecond Navigation, we met with a little Negroe Town, where they had growing a Sort of
Corn like Rice, which eat very fweet; and as we
got fome of it of the People, we made very good
Cakes of Bread of it, and making a Fire, bak'd
them on the Ground, after the Fire was fwept
away very well; fo that hitherto we had no
Want of Provifions of any kind we could defire.

Our Negroes towing our Canoes, we travelled at a confiderable Rate, and by our own Account, could not go lefs than 20 or 25 *Englifh*
Miles a Day, and the River continuing to be much
at the fame Breadth, and very deep all the Way,
till on the tenth Day we came to another Ca-
tarað; for a Ridge of high Hills croffing the whole
Channel of the River, the Water came tumbling
down the Rocks from one Stage to another in
a ftrange Manner : So that it was a continued
Link of Catarads from one to another, in the
Manner of a Caskade ; only, that the Falls were
fometimes a Quarter of a Mile from one another,
and the Noife confufed and frightful.

We thought our Voyaging was at a full Stop
now ; but three of us, with a Couple of our
Negroes, mounting the Hills another Way, to
view the Courfe of the River, we found a fair
Channel again after about half a Mile's March, and
that it was like to hold us a good Way farther.
So we fet all Hands to Work, unloaded our Cargo, and hauled our Canoes on Shore, to fee if
we could carry them.

Upon Examination, we found that they were
very heavy ; but our Carpenters fpending but
one Day's Work one them, hew'd away fo much
of the Timber from their Outfides, as reduced
them very much, and yet they were as fit to
fwim as before. When this was done, ten Men
with Poles took up one of the Canoes, and made
nothing to carry it. So we ordered twenty Men
to each Canoe, that one Ten might relieve another ; and thus we carried all our Canoes, and
launch'd them into the Water again, and then
fetch'd our Luggage, and loaded it all again
into the Canoes, and all in an Afternoon ; and
the

the next Morning early we mov'd forward a-
gain. When we had towed about four Days
more, our Gunner, who was our Pilot, begun to
obferve that we did not keep our right Courfe fo
exactly as we ought, the River winding away a
little towards the North, and gave us Notice
of it accordingly. However, we were not willing to lofe the Advantage of Water-Carriage, at
leaft not till we were forced to it; fo we jogg'd on,
and the River ferved us about Threefcore Miles
further; but then we found it grew very fmall
and fhallow, having pafs'd the Mouths of feveral little Brooks or Rivulets which come into it,
and at Length it became but a Brook it felf.

We tow'd up as far as ever our Boats would
fwim, and we went two Days the further, having been about twelve Days in this laft Part
of the River, by Lightning the Boats, and taking
our Luggage out, which we made the Negroes
carry, being willing to eafe our felves as long
as we could; but at the End of thefe two Days,
in fhort, there was not Water enough to fwim
a *London* Wherry.

We now fet forward wholly by Land, and
without any Expectation of more Water Carriage. All our Concern for more Water, was to
be fure to have a Supply for our Drinking; and
therefore upon every Hill that we came near,
we clamber'd up to the higheft Part, to fee the
Country before us, and to make the beft Judgment we could which way to go to keep the low-
eft Grounds, and as near fome Stream of Water
as we could.

The Country held verdant, well grown with
Trees, and fpread with Rivers and Brooks, and
tolerably well with Inhabitants, for about thirty
Days

Days March. After our leaving the Canoes, during which time things went pretty well with us; we did not tye our felves down when to march, and when to halt, but order'd thofe things as our Convenience, and the Health and Eafe of our People, as well our Servants, as our felves, required.

About the Middle of this March, we came into a low and plain Country, in which we perceived a greater Number of Inhabitants than in any other Country we had gone thro'; but that which was worfe for us, we found them a fierce, barbarous, treacherous People, and who at firft look'd upon us as Robbers, and gathered themfelves in Numbers to attack us.

Our Men were terrified at them at firft, and began to difcover an unufual Fear; and even our black Prince feemed in a great deal of Confufion : But I fmiled at him, and fhewing him fome of our Guns, I asked him, if he thought that which killed the fpotted Cat, (for fo they called the Leopard in their Language) could not make a Thoufand of thofe naked Creatures die at one Blow? Then he laugh'd, and faid Yes, he believ'd it would. Well then, faid I, tell your Men not to be afraid of thefe People, for we fhall foon give them a Tafte of what we can do, if they pretend to meddle with us. However, we confidered we were in the Middle of a vaft Country, and we knew not what Numbers of People and Nations we might be furrounded with; and above all, we knew not how much we might ftand in Need of the Friendfhip of thefe that we were now among; fo that we ordered the Negroes to try all the Methods they could, to make them Friends.

Accor-

Accordingly, the two Men who had gotten Bows and Arrows, and two more to whom we gave the Prince's two fine Lances, went foremoft with five more having long Poles in their Hands; and after them ten of our Men advanced toward the Negro Town that was next to us, and we all ftood ready to fuccour them if there fhould be Occafion.

When they came pretty near their Houfes, our Negroes halloo'd in their fcreaming Way, and called to them as loud as they could ; upon their calling, fome of the Men came out, and anfwer'd, and immediately after the whole Town, Men Women and Children appeared : Our Negroes with their long Poles went forward a little, and ftuck them all in the Ground, and left them, which in their Country was a Signal of Peace, but the other did not underftand the Meaning of that. Then the two Men with Bows, laid down their Bows and Arrows, went forward unarmed, and made Signs of Peace to them, which at laft the other began to underftand; fo two of their Men laid down their Bows and Arrows, and came towards them: Our Men made all the Signs of Friendfhip to them that they could think of, putting their Hands up to their Mouths, as a Sign that they wanted Provifions to eat, and the other pretended to be pleafed and friendly, and went back to their Fellows, and talk'd with them a while, and they came forward again, and made Signs that they would bring fome Provifions to them before the Sun fet ; and fo our Men came back again very well fatisfied for that time.

But an Hour before Sun-fet our Men went to them again, juft in the fame Pofture as before,

H
and

and they came according to their Appointment, and brought Deers Flesh, Roots, and the same kind of Corn like Rice, *which I mentioned above,* and our Negroes being furnish'd with such Toys as our Cutler had contrived, gave them some of them, which they seem'd infinitely pleas'd with and promis'd to bring more Provisions the next Day.

Accordingly, the next Day they came again, but our Men perceived they were more in Number by a great many than before; however, having sent out ten Men with Fire-Arms to stand ready, and our whole Army being in View also, we were not much surprized; nor was the Treachery of the Enemy so cunningly ordered as in other Cases; for they might have surrounded our Negroes, which, were but nine, under a Shew of Peace; but when they saw our Men advance almost as far as the Place where they were the Day before, the Rogues snatch'd up their Bows and Arrows, and come running upon our Men like so many Furies, at which our ten Men called to the Negroes to come back to them, which they did with Speed enough at the first Word, and stood all behind our Men. As they fled, the other advanced, and let fly near a 100 of their Arrows at them, by which two of our Negroes were wounded, and one we thought had been killed. When they came to the five Poles that our Men had stuck in the Ground, they stood still a while, and gathering about the Poles, looked at them, and handled them as wondering at what they meant. We then who were drawn up behind all, sent one of our Number to our ten Men, to bid them fire among them, while they stood so thick, and to

put

put fome fmall Shot into their Guns, befides the ordinary Charge, and to tell them, that we would be up with them immediately.

Accordingly they made ready, but by that time they were ready to fire, the Black Army had left their wondering about the Poles, and began to ftir as if they would come on, tho' feeing more Men ftand at fome Diftance behind our Negroes, they could not tell what to make of us; but if they did not underftand us before, they underftood us lefs afterwards, for as foon as ever our Men found them begin to move forward, they fired among the thickeft of them, being about the Diftance of 120 Yards, as near as we could guefs.

It is impoffible to exprefs the Fright, the Screaming and Yelling of thofe Wretches upon this firft Volley; we killed fix of them, and wounded 11 or 12, I mean as we knew of; for, as they ftood thick, and the fmall Shot, as we called it, fcattered among them, we had Reafon to believe we wounded more that ftood farther off; for our fmall Shot was made of Bits of Lead, and Bits of Iron, Heads of Nails, and fuch things as our diligent Artificer the Cutler help'd us to.

As to thofe that were killed and wounded, the other frighted Creatures were under the greateft Amazement in the World, to think what fhould hurt them; for they could fee nothing but Holes made in their Bodies they knew not how. Then the Fire and the Noife amazed all their Women and Children, and frighted them out of their Wits, that they ran ftaring and howling about like mad Creatures.

However, all this did not make them fly, which was what we wanted; nor did we find

any

any of them die as it were with Fear, as at firſt, ſo we reſolved upon a ſecond Volley, and then to advance as we did before. Whereupon our reſerved Men advancing, we reſolved to fire only three Men at a time, and move forward like an Army firing in Platoons; ſo being all in Line we fired firſt three on the Right, then three on the Left, and ſo on; and every time we killed or wounded ſome of them; but ſtill they did not fly, and yet they were ſo frighted, that they uſed none of their Bows and Arrows, or of their Lances; and we thought their Numbers encreaſed upon our Hands; particularly we thought ſo by the Noiſe; ſo I called to our Men to halt, and bid them pour in one whole Volley, and then ſhout, as we did in our firſt Fight, and ſo run in upon them, and knock them down with our Muſquets.

But they were too wiſe for that too, for as ſoon as we had fired a whole Volley, and ſhouted, they all run away, Men, Women, and Children, ſo faſt, that in a few Moments we could not ſee one Creature of them, except ſome that were wounded and lame, who lay wallowing and ſcreaming here and there upon the Ground, as they happen'd to fall.

Upon this we came up to the Field of Battle, where we found we had killed 37 of them, among which were three Women, and had wounded about 64 among which were two Women; by wounded I mean, ſuch as were ſo maimed, as not to be able to go away, and thoſe our Negroes killed afterwards in a cowardly manner in cold Blood, for which we were very angry, and threatned to make them go to them if they did ſo again.

There

There was no great Spoil to be got, for they were all ftark naked as they came into the World, Men and Women together; fome of them having Feathers ftuck in their Hair, and others a kind of Bracelets about their Necks, but nothing elfe; but our Negroes got a Booty here which we were very glad of, and this was the Bows and Arrows of the vanquifhed, of which they found more than they knew what to do with, belonging to the killed and wounded Men; thefe we ordered them to pick up, and they were very ufeful to us afterwards. After the Fight, and our Negroes had gotten Bows and Arrows, we fent them out in Parties to fee what they could get, and they got fome Provifions; but, which was better than all the reft, they brought us four more young Bulls, or Buffloes, that had been brought up to Labour, and to carry Burthens: They knew them, it feems, by the Burthens they had carry'd having galled their Backs; for, they have no Saddles to cover them with in that Country.

Thofe Creatures not only eafed our Negroes, but gave us an Opportunity to carry more Provifions, and our Negroes loaded them very hard at this Place, with Flefh and Roots, fuch as we wanted very much afterwards.

In this Town we found a very little young Leopard, about two Spans high; it was exceeding tame, and purr'd like a Cat when we ftroked it with our Hands, being, as I fuppofe, bred up among the Negroes like a Houfe-Dog. It was our Black Prince, it feems, who making his Tour among the abandoned Houfes or Hutts, found this Creature there, and making much of him, and giving

H 3   a Bit

a Bit or two of Flesh to him, the Creature followed him like a Dog; of which more hereafter.

Among the Negroes that were killed in this Battle, there was one who had a little thin Bit or Plate of Gold, about as big as a Six-Pence, which hung by a little Bit of a twisted Gutt, upon his Forehead, by which we supposed he was a Man of some Eminence among them; but that was not all, for this Bit of Gold put us upon searching very narrowly, if there was not more of it to be had thereabouts, but we found none at all.

From this Part of the Country we went on for about 15 Days, and then found our selves obliged to march up a high Ridge of Mountains frightful to behold, and the first of the Kind that we met with ; and having no Guide but our little Pocket Compass, we had no Advantage of Information as to which was the best, or the worst Way, but were obliged to chuse by what we saw, and shift as well as we could. We met with several Nations of wild and naked People in the plain Country, before we came to those Hills, and we found them much more tractable and friendly than those Devils we had been forc'd to fight with ; and tho' we could learn little from these People, yet we understood by the Signs they made, that there was a vast Desart beyond those Hills, and, *as our Negroes called them*, much Lion, much spotted Cat (so they called the Leopard) and they sign'd to us also, that we must carry Water with us. At the last of these Nations we furnished our selves with as much Provision as we could possibly carry, not knowing what we had to suffer, or what Length we had to go ; and to make our Way as familiar to us as possible, I proposed, that of
the

the laft Inhabitants we could find, we fhould make
fome Prifoners, and carry them with us for
Guides over the Defart, and to affift us in carrying Provifion, and perhaps in getting it too.
The Advice was too neceffary to be flighted;
fo finding by our dumb Signs to the Inhabitants,
that there were fome People that dwelt at the
Foot of the Mountains, on the other Side, before we came to the Defart it felf, we refolved
to furnifh our felves with Guides, by fair Means
or foul.

Here, by a moderate Computation, we concluded our felves 700 Miles from the Sea Coaft
where we began. Our Black Prince was this Day
fet free from the Sling his Arm hung in, our Surgeon having perfectly reftored it, and he thewed
it to his own Countrymen quite well, which
made them greatly wonder. Alfo our two Negroes began to recover, and their Wounds to heal
apace, for our Surgeon was very skilful in ma-
naging their Cure.

Having with infinite Labour mounted thefe
Hills, and coming to a View of the Country beyond them, it was indeed enough to aftonifh as
ftout a Heart as ever was created. It was a vaft
howling Wildernefs, not a Tree, a River, or a
Green thing to be feen, for as far as the Eye
could look; nothing but a fcalding Sand, which,
as the Wind blew, drove about in Clouds, enough
to overwhelm Man and Beaft; nor could we fee
any End of it, either before us, which was
our Way, or to the right Hand or left: So that
truly our Men began to be difcouraged, and
talk of going back again; nor could we indeed
think of venturing over fuch a horrid Place as

that

that before us, in which we faw nothing but prefent Death.

I was as much affected with the Sight as any
of them, but for all that I could not bear the
Thoughts of going back again. I told them we had
march'd 700 Miles of our Way, and it would be
worfe than Death to think of going back again;
and that if they thought the Defart was not paffa-
ble, I thought we fhould rather change our Courfe,
and travel South till we came to the *Cape of Good
Hope*, or North to the Country that lay along the
Nile, where perhaps we might find fome Way
or other over to the Weft Sea; for fure all *Africa*
was not a Defart.

Our Gunner, who, as I faid before, was our
Guide as to the Situation of Places, told us, that
he could not tell what to fay to going for the
Cape; for it was a monftrous Length, being from
the Place where we now were, not lefs than
1500 Miles, and by his Account, we were come
now a third Part of the Way to the Coaft of *Angola*,
where we fhould meet with the Weftern Ocean,
and find Ways enough for our Efcape Home. On
the other Hand, he affured us, and fhewed us a
Map of it, that if we went Northward, the Weftern Shore of *Africk* went out into the Sea above a
Thoufand Miles Weft; fo that we fhould have fo
much, and more Land, to travel afterwards;
which Land might, for ought we knew, be as
wild, barren, and defart, as this: And therefore,
upon the whole, he propofed that we fhould attempt this Defart, and perhaps we fhould not find
it fo long as we feared; and however, he propofed that we fhould fee how far our Provifions
would carry us, and in particular, our Water;
and that we fhould venture no farther than Half
fo

fo far as our Water would laft; and if we found
no End of the Defart, we might come fafely back
again.

This Advice was fo reafonable, that we all
approved of it; and accordingly we calculated,
that we were able to carry Provifions for 42
Days, but that we could not carry Water for
above 20 Days, tho' we were to fuppofe it to
ftink too before that time expired. So that we
concluded, that if we did not come at fome Water in ten Days time, we would return, but if we
found a Supply of Water, we could then travel
21 Days; and if we faw no End of the Wildernefs in that time, we would return alfo.

With this Regulation of our Meafures, we defcended the Mountains, and it was the fecond
Day before we quite reached the Plain, where
however, to make us amends, we found a fine
little Rivulet of very good Water, Abundance
of Deer, a fort of Creature like a Hare, but not
fo nimble, and whofe Flefh we found very agreeable; but we were deceived in our Intelligence,
for we found no People; fo we got no more Prifoners to affift us in carrying our Baggage.

The infinite Number of Deer and other Creatures
which we faw here, we found was occafioned by
the Neighbourhood of the Waft or Defart, from
whence they retired hither for Food and Refrefhment. We ftored our felves here with Flefh and
Roots of divers Kinds, which our Negroes underftood better than we, and which ferved us for
Bread; and with as much Water as, (by the Allowance of a Quart a Day to a Man for our Negroes, and three Pints a Day a Man for our felves,
and three Quarts a Day each, for our Buffloes)
would ferve us 20 Days: And thus loaden for a
long

long miſerable March,, we ſet forward, being
all found in Health, and very chearful, but not
alike ſtrong for ſo great a Fatigue; and which
was our Grievance, were without a Guide.

In the very firſt Entrance of the Waſt, we
were exceedingly diſcouraged; for we found the
Sand ſo deep, and it ſcalded our Feet ſo much with
the Heat, that after we had, as I may call it, wa-
ded rather than walk'd thro' it, about ſeven or
eight Miles, we were all heartily tired and faint;
even the very Negroes lay down and panted, like
Creatures that had been puſh'd beyond their
Strength.

Here we found the Difference of Lodging greatly injurious to us; for (as before) we always made
us Hutts to ſleep under, which cover'd us from
the Night Air, which is particularly unwholeſom
in thoſe hot Countries: But we had here no Shelter, no Lodging after ſo hard a March; for here
were no Trees, no not a Shrub near us: And
which was ſtill more frightful, towards Night we
began to hear the Wolves howl, the Lions bel-
low, and a great many wild Aſſes braying, and
other ugly Noiſes which we did not underſtand.

Upon this we reflected upon our own Indiſcre-
tion, that had not at leaſt brought Poles or Stakes
in our Hands, with which we might have, as it
were palliſadoed our ſelves in for the Night;
and ſo we might have ſlept ſecure, whatever
other Inconveniences we ſuffer'd. However, we
found a Way at laſt to relieve our ſelves a little.
For firſt we ſet up the Lances and Bows we
had, and endeavoured to bring the Tops of them
as near to one another as we could, and ſo hung
our Coats on the Top of them, which made us
a kind of a ſorry Tent; the Leopard's Skin, and
a few

a few other Skins we had put together, made us
a tolerable Covering, and thus we lay down to
Sleep, and flept very heartily too for the firft
Night, fetting however a good Watch, being two
of our own Men with their Fuzees, whom we re-
liev'd in an Hour at firft, and two Hours afterwards; and it was very well we did this; for
they found the Wildernefs fwarm'd with raging
Creatures of all Kinds, fome of which came directly up to the very Enclofure of our Tent. But
our Centinels were ordered not to alarm us with
Firing in the Night, but to flafh in the Pan at
them, which they did, and found it effectual; for
the Creatures went off always as foon as they faw
it, perhaps with fome Noife or Howling, and
purfued fuch other Game as they were upon.

If we were tired with the Day's Travel, we
were all as much tired with the Night's Lodging:
But our Black Prince told us in the Morning, he
would give us fome Counfel, and indeed it was
very good Counfel. He told us we fhould all be
kill'd if we went on this Journey, and thro' this
Defart, without fome Covering for us at Night;
fo he advifed us to march back again to a little
River Side where we lay the Night before, and
ftay there till we could make us Houfes, as he
called them, to carry with us to lodge in every
Night. As he began a little to underftand our
Speech, and we very well to underftand his Signs,
we eafily knew what he meant, and that we
fhould there make Matts; (for we remembered
that we faw a great deal of Matting, or Bafs
there that the Natives make Matts of) I fay,
that we fhould make large Matts there for Covering our Hutts or Tents to lodge in at Night.

We

We all approv'd this Advice, and immediately refolved to go back that one Day's Journey, refolving, tho' we carried lefs Provifions, we would carry Matts with us to cover us in the Night. Some of the nimbleft of us got back to the River with more Eafe than we had travell'd it out the Day before; but as we were not in Hafte, the reft made a Halt, encamp'd another Night, and came to us the next Day.

In our Return of this Day's Journey, our Men that made two Days of it, met with a very furprizing thing, that gave them fome Reafon to be careful how they parted Company again. The Cafe was this. The fecond Day in the Morning, before they had gone Half a Mile, looking behind them, they faw a vaft Cloud of Sand or Duft rife in the Air, as we fee fometimes in the Roads in Summer, when it is very dufty, and a large Drove of Cattel are coming, only very much greater; and they could eafily perceive that it came after them, and that it came on fafter than they went from it. The Cloud of Sand was fo great, that they could not fee what it was that raifed it, and concluded, that it was fome Army of Enemies that purfued them; but then confidering that they came from the vaft uninhabited Wildernefs, they knew, it was impoffible any Nation or People that Way fhould have Intelligence of them, or of the Way of their March: And therefore, if it was an Army, it muft be of fuch as they were, travelling that Way by Accident. On the other Hand, as they knew that there were no Horfes in the Country, and that they came on fo faft, they concluded, that it muft be fome vaft Collection of wild Beafts, perhaps making to the Hill Country for Food or
Water,

Water, and that they fhould be all devoured or
trampled under Foot by their Multitude.

Upon this Thought, they very prudently obferved which Way the Cloud feem'd to point,
and they turned a little out of their Way to
the North, fuppofing it might pafs by them.
When they were about a Quarter of a Mile, they
halted to fee what it might be. One of the Negroes, a nimbler Fellow than the reft, went back
a little, and come again in a few Minutes, running as faft as the heavy Sand would allow, and
by Signs gave them to know, that it was a great
Herd or Drove, or whatever it might be called,
of vaft monftrous Elephants.

As it was a Sight our Men had never feen, they
were defirous to fee it, and yet a little uneafy at
the Danger too; for tho' an Elephant is a heavy,
unwieldy Creature, yet in the deep Sand, which
was nothing at all to them, they marched at a
great Rate, and would foon have tired our People,
if they had had far to go, and had been purfued
by them.

Our Gunner was with them, and had a great
Mind to have gone clofe up to one of the outer-
moft of them, and to have clapt his Piece to his
Ear, and to have fired into him, becaufe he had
been told no Shot would penetrate them; but
they all diffwaded him, left, upon the Noife, they
fhould all turn upon, and purfue us; fo he was
reafoned out of it, and let them pafs, which in
our People's Circumftance was certainly the right
Way.

They were between 20 and 30 in Number, but
prodigious great ones; and tho' they often fhew'd
our Men that they faw them, yet they did not
turn out of their Way, or take any other Notice

of

of them, than, *as we might say*, juft to look at
them. We that were before, faw the Cloud of
Duft they raifed, but we thought it had been
our own Carravan, and fo took no Notice; but
as they bent their Courfe one Point of the Compafs, or thereabouts, to the Southward of the
Eaft, and we went due Eaft, they pafs'd by us
at fome little Diftance; fo that we did not fee
them, or know any thing of them till Evening,
when our Men came to us, and gave us this Account of them. However, this was a ufeful Experiment for our future Conduct in paffing the
Defart, as you fhall hear in its Place.

We were now upon our Work, and our Black
Prince was Head Surveyor, for he was an excellent Matt-Maker himfelf, and all his Men underftood it; fo that they foon made us near a Hundred Matts: And as every Man, I mean of the
Negroes, carried one, it was no Manner of Load,
and we did not carry an Ounce of Provifions the
lefs. The greateft Burthen was to carry fix long
Poles, befides fome fhorter Stakes; but the Negroes made an Advantage of that, for carrying
them between two, they made the Luggage of
Provifions which they had to carry, fo much the
lighter, binding it upon two Poles, and fo made
three Couple of them. As foon as we faw this,
we made a little Advantage of it too; for having
three or four of our Baggs called Bottles, (I mean
Skins or Bladders to carry Water) more than the
Men could carry, we got them fill'd, and carried
them this Way, which was a Day's Water and
more for our Journey.

Having now ended our Work, made our Matts,
and fully recruited our Stores of all things neceffary, and having made us Abundance of fmall
Ropes

Ropes of Matting for ordinary Use, as we might have Occasion, we set forward again, having interrupted our Journey eight Days in all, upon this Affair. To our great Comfort, the Night before we set out, there fell a very violent Shower of Rain, the Effects of which we found in the Sand; tho' the Heat of one Day dry'd the Surface as much as before, yet it was harder at Bottom, not so heavy, and was cooler to our Feet, by which Means we march'd, as we reckoned, about fourteen Miles instead of seven, and with much more Ease.

When we came to encamp, we had all things ready, for we had fitted our Tent, and set it up for Trial where we made it; so that in less than an Hour, we had a large Tent raised, with an Inner and Outer Apartment, and two Entrances. In one we lay our selves, in the other our Negroes, having light pleasant Matts over us, and others at the same time under us. Also we had a little Place without all for our Buffloes, for they deserved our Care, being very useful to us, besides carrying Forage and Water for themselves. Their Forage was a Root which our Black Prince directed us to find, not much unlike a Pasnip, very moist and nourishing, of which there was Plenty wherever we came, this horrid Desart excepted.

When we came the next Morning to decamp, our Negroes took down the Tent, and pull'd up the Stakes, and all was in Motion in as little time as it was set up. In this Posture we march'd eight Days, and yet could see no End, no Change of our Prospect, but all looking as wild and dismal as at the Beginning. If there was any Alteration, it was, that the Sand was no where so deep

and

and heavy as it was the firft three Days. This we thought might be, becaufe for fix Months of the Year the Winds blowing Weft, (as for the other fix, they blew conftantly Eaft) the Sand was driven violently to the Side of the Defart where we fet out, where the Mountains lying very high, the Eafterly *Monfoons,* when they blew, had not the fame Power to drive it back again; and this was confirm'd by our finding the like Depth of Sand on the fartheft Extent of the Defart to the Weft.

It was the ninth Day of our Travel in this Wildernefs, when we came to the View of a great Lake of Water, and you may be fure this was a particular Satisfaction to us, becaufe we had not Water left for above two or three Days more, at our fhorteft Allowance; I mean, allowing Water for our Return, if we had been driven to the Neceffity of it. Our Water had ferved us two Days longer than we expected, our Buffloes having found for two or three Days, a kind of Herb like a Broad flat Thiftle, tho' without any Prickle, fpreading on the Ground and growing in the Sand, which they eat freely of, and which fupplied them for Drink as well as Forage.

The next Day, which was the tenth from our fetting out, we came to the Edge of this Lake, and very happily for us, we came to it at the South Point of it, for to the North we could fee no End of it; fo we paffed by it, and travelled three Days by the Side of it, which was a great Comfort to us, becaufe it lightened our Burthen, there being no need to carry Water, when we had it in View; and yet, tho' here was fo much Water, we found but very little Alteration

tion in the Defart, no Trees, no Grafs or Herbage, except that Thiftle, as I call'd it, and two
or three more Plants, which we did not underftand, of which the Defart began to be pretty
full.

But as we were refrefhed with the Neighbourhood of this Lake of Water, fo we were now
gotten among a prodigious Number of ravenous
Inhabitants, the like whereof, tis moft certain
the Eye of Man never faw: For as I firmly believe,
that never Man, nor a Body of Men, paffed this
Defart fince the Flood, fo I believe there is not
the like Collection of fierce, ravenous, and de-
vouring Creatures in the World; I mean not in
any particular Place.

For a Day's Journey before we came to this
Lake, and all the three Days we were paffing
by it, and for fix or feven Days March after it,
the Ground was fcattered with Elephants Teeth,
in fuch a Number, as is incredible; and as fome
of them may have lain there for fome Hundreds
of Years, fo feeing the Subftance of them fcarce
ever decays, they may lye there for ought I
know to the End of Time. The Size of fome
of them is, it feems, to thofe to whom I have
reported it, as incredible as the Number, and I
can affure you, there were feveral fo heavy, as
the ftrongeft Man among us could not lift. As
to Number, I queftion not but there are enough
to load a thoufand Sail of the biggeft Ships in the
World, by which I may be underftood to mean,
that the Quantity is not to be conceived of;
feeing that as they lafted in View for above eighty
Miles Travelling, fo they might continue as far
to the right Hand, and to the left as far, and
many times as far, for ought we knew; for it

I

feems

feems the Number of Elephants hereabouts is
prodigious great. In one Place in particular, we
faw the Head of an Elephant, with feveral Teeth
in it, but one the biggeft that ever I faw: TheFlefh
was confumed to be fure many Hundred Years
before, and all the other Bones; but three of
our ftrongeft Men could not lift this Scull and
Teeth: The great Tooth, I believe, weighed at
leaft 300 Weight, and this was particularly remarkable to me, that I obferved the whole Scull
was as good Ivory as the Teeth, and I believe all
together weighed at leaft 600 Weight, and tho'
I do not know but, by the fame Rule, all the
Bones of the Elephant may be Ivory; yet I
think there is this juft Objection againft it
from the Example before me, that then all the
other Bones of this Elephant would have been
there as well as the Head.

I propofed to our Gunner, that feeing we had
travelled now 14 Days without Intermiffion, and
that we had Water here for our Refrefhment,
and no Want of Food yet, or any Fear of it;
we fhould reft our People a little, and fee at
the fame time, if perhaps we might kill fome
Creatures that were proper for Food. The Gunner, who had more Forecaft of that kind, than
I had, agreed to the Propofal, and added, why
might we not try to catch fome Fifh out of the
Lake? The firft thing we had before us, was
to try if we could make any Hooks, and this
indeed put our Artificer to his Trumps; however, with fome Labour and Difficulty he did it,
and we catched frefh Fifh of feveral kinds. How
they came there, none but he that made the
Lake, and all the World, knows; for to be fure
no

no human Hands ever put any in there, or pulled any out before.

We not only catched enough for our prefent Refrefhment, but we dried feveral large Fifhes of Kinds which I cannot defcribe, in the Sun, by which we lengthen'd out our Provifion confiderably; for the Heat of the Sun dried them fo effectually without Salt, that they were perfectly cured dry and hard in one Day's time.

We refted our felves here five Days, during which time we had Abundance of pleafant Adventures with the wild Creatures, too many to relate: One of them was very particular, which was a Chafe between a She Lion, or Lionefs, and a large Deer; and tho' the Deer is naturally a very nimble Creature, and fhe flew by us like the Wind, having perhaps about 300 Yards the Start of the Lion, yet we found the Lion by her Strength, and the Goodnefs of her Lungs, got Ground of her. They paft by us within about a Quarter of a Mile, and we had a View of them a great Way, when having given them over, we were furprized about an Hour after, to fee them come thundering back again on the other Side of us, and then the Lion was within 30 or 40 Yards of her, and both ftraining to the Extremity of their Speed, when the Deer coming to the Lake, plunged into the Water, and fwam for her Life, as fhe had before run for it.

The Lionefs plunged in after her, and fwam a little way, but came back again; and when fhe was got upon the Land, fhe fet up the moft hideous Roar that ever I heard in my Life, as if done in the Rage of having loft her Prey.

We walked out Morning and Evening conftantly; the Middle of the Day we refrefhed our felves under

I 2

our

our Tent; but one Morning early we faw another Chafe, which more nearly concern'd us than the other; for our Black Prince, walking by the Side of the Lake, was fet upon by a vaft great Crocodile, which came out of the Lake upon him; and tho' he was very light of Foot, yet it was as much as he could do to get away: He fled amain to us, and the Truth is, we did not know what to do, for we were told no Bullet would enter her; and we found it fo at firft, for tho' three of our Men fired at her, yet fhe did not mind them; but my Friend the Gunner, a ventrous Fellow, of a bold Heart, and great Prefence of Mind, went up fo near as to thruft the Muzzle of his Piece into her Mouth, and fired but let his Piece fall, and run for it the very Moment he had fired it: The Creature raged a great while, and fpent its Fury upon the Gun, making Marks upon the very Iron with her Teeth, but after fome time fainted and died.

Our Negroes fpread the Banks of the Lake all this while, for Game, and at length killed us three Deer, one of them very large, the other two very fmall. There was Water-Fowl alfo in the Lake, but we never came near enough to them to fhoot any; and, as for the Defart, we faw no Fowls any where in it, but at the Lake.

We likewife killed two or three Civet Cats, but their Flefh is the worft of Carrion; we faw Abundance of Elephants at a Diftance, and obferved, that they always go in very good Company, that is to fay, Abundance of them together, and always extended in a fair Line of Battle; and this, they fay, is the way they defend themfelves from their Enemies; for if Lions or Tygers, Wolves or any Creatures, attack

tack them, they being drawn up in a Line, sometimes reaching five or six Miles in Length, whatever comes in their Way is sure to be trod under Foot, or beaten in Pieces with their Trunks, or lifted up in the Air with their Trunks; so that if a hundred Lions or Tygers were coming along, if they meet a Line of Elephants, they will always fly back till they see Room to pass by to the Right Hand or to the Left; and if they did not, it would be impossible for one of them to escape; for the Elephant, tho' a heavy Creature, is yet so dexterous and nimble with his Trunk, that he will not fail to lift up the heaviest Lion, or any other wild Creature, and throw him up in the Air quite over his Back, and then trample him to Death with his Feet. We saw several Lines of Battle thus, we saw one so long, that indeed there was no End of it to be seen, and, I believe, their might be 2000 Elephants in a Row, or Line. They are not Beasts of Prey, but live upon the Herbage of the Field, as an Ox does, and, it is said, that tho' they are so great a Creature, yet that a smaller Quantity of Forage supplies one of them, than will suffice a Horse.

The Numbers of this kind of Creature that are in those Parts are inconceivable, as may be gather'd from the prodigious Quantity of Teeth, which as I said we saw in this vast Desart, and indeed we saw a 100 of them to one of any other Kinds.

One Evening we were very much surprized; we were most of us laid down upon our Matts to Sleep, when our Watch came running in among us, being frighted with the sudden Roaring of some Lions just by them, which it seems they

had

had not feen, the Night being dark, till they
were juft upon them. There was, as it proved,
an old Lion and his whole Family, for there was
the Lionefs and three young Lions, befides the
old King, who was a monftrous great one: One
of the young ones, who were good large well
grown ones too, leapt up upon one of our Negroes,
who ftood Centinel, before he faw him, at which
he was heartily frighted, cried out, and run
into the Tent: Our other Man, who had a
Gun, had not Prefence of Mind at firft to
fhoot him, but ftruck him with the But-End
of his Piece, which made him whine a little,
and then growl at him fearfully; but the Fellow
retired, and we being all alarmed, three of our
Men fnatched up their Guns, run to the Tent-
Door, where they faw the great old Lion by the
Fire of his Eyes, and firft fired at him, but,
we fuppofed, miffed him, or at leaft did not
kill him; for they went all off, but raifed a
moft hideous Roar, which, as if they had called
for Help, brought down a prodigious Number
of Lions, and other furious Creatures, we know
not what about them, for we could not fee them;
but their was a Noife and Yelling, and Howling,
and all fort of fuch Wildernefs Mufick on every
Side of us, as if all the Beafts of the Defart were
affembled to devour us.

We asked our Black Prince what we fhould
do with them? *Me go*, fays he, *fright them all*; fo
he fnatches up two or three of the worft of our
Matts, and, getting one of our Men to ftrike
fome Fire, he hangs the Matt up at the End of
a Pole, and fet it on Fire, and it blazed abroad
a good while; at which the Creatures all moved
off, for we heard them roar, and make their

bellow-

bellowing Noife at a great Diftance. Well, fays
our Gunner, if that will do, we need not burn
our Matts, which are our Beds to lay under us,
and our Tilting to cover us. Let me alone, fays
he, fo he comes back into our Tent, and falls to
making fome artificial Fire-Works, and the like;
and he gave our Centinels fome to be ready at
Hand, upon Occafion, and particularly he placed
a great Piece of Wild-fire upon the fame Pole
that the Matt had been tied to, and fet it on
Fire, and that burnt there fo long, that all the
Wild Creatures left us for that time.

However, we began to be weary of fuch Company, and, to be rid of them, we fet forward
again two Days fooner than we intended. We
found now, that tho' the Defart did not end,
nor could we fee any Appearance of it, yet that
the Earth was pretty full of green Stuff, of one
fort or another, fo that our Cattle had no Want.
And fecondly, that there were feveral little
Rivers which run into the Lake, and fo long
as the Country continued low, we found Water
fufficient, which eafed us very much in our
Carriage, and we went on yet fixteen Days more
without yet coming to any Appearance of better
Soil: After this we found the Country rife a little,
and by that we perceived, that the Water would
fail us, fo, for fear of the worft, we filled our
Bladder Bottles with Water; we found the Country rifing gradually thus for three Days continually, when, on the fudden, we perceived, that
tho' we had mounted up infenfibly, yet that
we were on the Top of a very high ridge of Hills,
tho' not fuch as at firft.

When we came to look down on the other Side
of the Hills we faw, to the great Joy of all our

Hearts,

Hearts, that the Defart was at an End; that the Country was clothed with Green, Abundance of Trees, and a large River, and we made no doubt but that we fhould find People and Cattel alfo; and here, by our Gunner's Account, who kept our Computations, we had marched above 400 Miles over this difmal Place of Horrour, having been four and thirty Days a-doing of it, and confequently were come about 1100 Miles of our Journey.

We would willingly have defcended the Hills that Night, but it was too late; the next Morning we faw every thing more plain, and refted our felves under the Shade of fome Trees; which were now the moft refrefhing things imaginable to us, who had been fcorched above a Month without a Tree to cover us. We found the Country here very pleafant, efpecially confidering that we came from, and we killed fome Deer here alfo, which we found very frequent under the Cover of the Woods; alfo we killed a creature like a Goat, whofe Flefh was very god to eat, but it was no Goat: We found alfo a great Number of Fowls like Partridge, but fomething fmaller, and were very tame, fo that we lived here very well, but found no People, at leaft none that would be feen, no not for feveral Days Journey; and, to allay our Joy, we were almoft every Night difturbed with Lions and Tygers; Elephants indeed we faw none here.

In three Days March we came to a River, which we faw from the Hills, and which we called the Golden River, and we found it run Northward, which was the firft Stream we had met with that did fo; it run with a very rapid Cur-

current, and our Gunner pulling out his Map, assured me that this was either the River *Nile*, or run into the great Lake; out of which the River *Nile* was said to take its Beginning; and he brought out his Carts and Maps, which by his Instruction, I began to understand very well; and told me, he would convince me of it, and indeed he seemed to make it so plain to me, that I was of the same Opinion.

But I did not enter into the Gunner's Reason for this Enquiry, not in the least, till he went on with it farther, and stated it thus; if this is the River *Nile*, why should not we build some more Canoes, and go down this Stream rather than to expose our selves to any more Desarts and scorching Sands, in Quest of the Sea, which when we are come to, we shall be as much at a Loss how to get home as we were at *Madagascar*.

The Argument was good, had there been no Objections in the Way, of a Kind which none of us were capable of answering; but upon the whole it was an Undertaking of such a Nature, that every one of us thought it impracticable, and that upon several Accounts; and our Surgeon, who was himself a good Scholar, and a Man of Reading, tho' not acquainted with the Business of Sailing, opposed it; and some of his Reasons, I remember, were such as these; first, the Length of the Way, which both he and the Gunner allowed by the Course of the Water and Turnings of the River, would be at least 4000 Miles. Secondly, The innumerable Crocodiles in the River, which we should never be able to escape. Thirdly, The dreadful Desarts in the Way; and lastly, the approaching rainy Season, in which
the

the Streams of the *Nile* would be fo furious, and
rife fo high, fpreading far and wide over all
the plain Country, that we fhould never be able
to know when we were in the Channel of the
River, and when not, and fhould certainly be caft
away, over-fet, or run a-ground fo often, that it
would be impoffible to proceed by a River fo
exceffively dangerous.

This laft Reafon he made fo plain to us, that
we began to be fo fenfible of it our felves; fo that
we agreed to lay that Thought afide, and proceed
in our firft Courfe Weftward towards the Sea:
But as if we had been loath to depart, we continued, by way of refrefhing our felves, to loy-
ter two Days upon this River, in which time
our Black Prince, who delighted much in wandering up and down, came one Evening and
brought us feveral little Bits of fomething, he
knew not what; but he found it felt heavy, and
looked well, and fhewed it to me, as what he
thought was fome Rarity. I took not much
Notice of it to him, but ftepping out, and calling the Gunner to me, I fhewed it him, and told
him what I thought, *viz.* that it was certainly Gold: He agreed with me in that, and alfo
in what follow'd, that we would take the Black
Prince out with us the next Day, and make him
fhew us where he found it, that if there was any
Quantity to be found, we would tell our Company of it, but if there was but little, we would
keep Counfel, and have it to our felves.

But we forgot to engage the Prince in the
Secret, who innocently told fo much to all the
reft, as that they gueffed what it was, and came
to us to fee; when we found it was publick, we
were more concerned to prevent their fufpeft-

ing

ing that we had any Design to conceal it, and
openly telling our Thoughts of it, we called our
Artificer, who agreed presently that it was Gold;
so I proposed, that we should all go with the
Prince to the Place where he found it, and if any
Quantity was to be had, we would lye here some
time, and see what we could make of it.

Accordingly, we went every Man of us, for no
Man was willing to be left behind in a Discovery of such a Nature. When we came to the
Place, we found it was on the West Side of the
River, not in the main River, but in another small
River or Stream which came from the West, and
run into the other River at that Place. We fell
to raking in the Sand, and washing it in our
Hands, and we seldom took up a Handful of Sand,
but we washed some little round Lumps as big as
a Pin's Head, or sometimes as big as a Grapestone,
into our Hands, and we found in two or three
Hours time, that every one had got some, so
we agreed to leave off, and go to Dinner.

While we were eating, it came into my
Thoughts, that while we work'd at this Rate in
a thing of such Nicety and Consequence, it was
ten to one if the Gold, which was the *Make-
bait* of the World, did not first or last set us
together by the Ears to break our good Articles and our Understanding one among another,
and perhaps cause us to part Companies, or
worse; I therefore told them, that I was indeed
the youngest Man of the Company, but as they
had always allowed me to give my Opinion in
things, and had sometimes been pleased to follow
my Advice, so I had something to propose now,
which I thought, would be for all our Advantages,
and I believed they would all like it very well. I

told

told them we were in a Country where we all
knew there was a great deal of Gold, and that
all the World sent Ships thither to get it; that
we did not indeed know where it was, and so we
might get a great deal, or a little, we did not
know whether; but I offered it to them to consider whether it would not be the best Way for
us, and to preserve the good Harmony and
Friendship that had been always kept among
us, and which was so absolutely necessary to our
Safety, that what we found should be brought
together to one common Stock, and be equally
divided at last, rather than to run the Hazard of
any Difference which might happen among us,
from any one's having found more or less than another. I told them, that if we were all upon one
Bottom, we should all apply our selves heartily to
the Work, and besides that, we might then set
our Negroes all to Work for us, and receive
equally the Fruit of their Labour, and of our own,
and being all exactly alike Sharers, there could
be no just Cause of Quarrel or Disgust among us.

They all approv'd the Proposal, and every one
jointly swore, and gave their Hands to one another, that they would not conceal the least Grain
of Gold from the rest; and consented, that if
any one or more should be found to conceal
any, all that he had should be taken from him,
and divided among the rest: And one thing
more was added to it by our Gunner, from Confiderations equally good and just; that if any one
of us, by any Play, Bett, Game, or Wager, won
any Money or Gold, or the Value of any from
another, during our whole Voyage till our Return
quite to *Portugal*, he should be obliged by us all
to restore it again on the Penalty of being dif-
arm'd,

arm'd, and turn'd out of the Company, and of having no Relief from us on any Account whatfoever. This was to prevent Wagering and Playing for Money, which our Men were apt to do by feveral Means, and at feveral Games, tho' they had neither Cards or Dice.

Having made this wholefom Agreement, we went chearfully to Work, and fhew'd our Negroes how to work for us; and working up the Stream on both Sides, and in the Bottom of the River, we fpent about three Weeks Time dabbling in the Water; by which time, as it lay all in our Way, we had gone about fix Miles, and not more; and ftill the higher we went, the more Gold we found; till at laft, having pafs'd by the Side of a Hill, we perceived on a fudden, that the Gold ftopp'd, and that there was not a Bit taken up beyond that Place; it prefently occurr'd to my Mind, that it muft then be from the Side of that little Hill that all the Gold we found was work'd down.

Upon this, we went back to the Hill, and fell to Work with that. We found the Earth loofe, and of a yellowifh loamy Colour, and in fome Places, a white hard Kind of Stone, which in defcribing fince to fome of our Artifts, they tell me was the Spar which is found by the Oar, and furrounds it in the Mine. However, if it had been all Gold, we had no Inftrument to force it out; fo we paffed that: But fcratching into the loofe Earth with our Fingers, we came to a furprizing Place, where the Earth for the Quantity of two Bufhels, I believe, or thereabouts, crumbled down with little more than touching it, and apparently fhewed us that there was a great deal of Gold in it. We took it all carefully up, and

washing

wafhing it in the Water, the loamy Earth wafh'd
away, and left the Gold Duft free in our Hands;
and that which was more remarkable, was, that
when this loofe Earth was all taken away, and we
came to the Rock or hard Stone, there was not
one Grain of Gold more to be found.

At Night we came all together to fee what we
had got, and it appeared we had found in that
Day's Heap of Earth, about Seven and Fifty
Pound Weight of Gold Duft, and about Thirty
Four Pound more in all the reft of our Works
in the River.

It was a happy Kind of Difappointment to us,
that we found a full Stop put to our Work;
for had the Quantity of Gold been ever fo fmall,
yet had any at all come, I do not know when we
fhould have given over; for having rummaged this
Place, and not finding the leaft Grain of Gold in
any other Place, or in any of the Earth there,
except in that loofe Parcel, we went quite back
down the fmall River again, working it over and
over again, as long as we could find any thing
how fmall foever; and we did get fix or feven
Pound more the fecond time. Then we went
into the firft River, and tried it up the Stream
and down the Stream, on the one Side and on the
other. Up the Stream we found nothing, no not
a Grain; down the Stream we found very little,
not above the Quantity of Half an Ounce in two
Miles working; fo back we came again to the
Golden River, as we juftly called it, and work'd
it up the Stream and down the Stream twice more
a-piece, and every time we found fome Gold, and
perhaps might have done fo, if we had ftay'd
there till this time; but the Quantity was at laft
fo fmall, and the Work fo much the harder,
that

that we agreed by Confent to give it over, left we fhould fatigue our felves and our Negroes fo, as to be quite unfit for our Journey. When we had brought all our Purchafe together, we had in the whole three Pound and a Half of Gold to a Man, Share and Share alike, according to fuch a Weight and Scale as our ingenious Cutler made for us to weigh it by, which he did indeed by guefs, but which, as he faid he was fure was rather more than lefs, and fo it prov'd at laft; for it was near two Ounces more than Weight in a Pound. Befides this, there was feven or eight Pound Weight left, which we agreed to leave in his Hands, to work it into fuch Shapes as we thought fit to give away to fuch People as we might yet meet with, from whom we might have Occafion to buy Provifions, or even to buy Friendfhip, or the like; and particularly we gave about a Pound to our Black Prince, which he hammer'd and work'd by his own indefatigable Hand, and fome Tools our Artificer lent him, into little round Bits, as round almoft as Beads, tho' not exact in Shape, and drilling Holes thro' them, put them all upon a String, and wore them about his black Neck, and they look'd very well there I affure you; but he was many Months a-doing it. And thus ended our firft Golden Adventure.

We now began to difcover what we had not troubled our Heads much about before; and that was, that let the Country be good or bad that we were in, we could not travel much farther, for a confiderable time. We had been now five Months and upwards in our Journey, and the Seafon began to change; and Nature told us, that being in a Climate that had a Winter as well as a Summer, tho' of a differing Kind from what our own

Coun-

Country produced, we were to expect a wet Season, and such as we should not be able to travel in, as well by reason of the Rain it self, as of the Floods which it would occasion wherever we should come; and tho' we had been no Strangers to those wet Seasons in the Island of *Madagascar*, yet we had not thought much of them since we begun our Travels; for setting out when the Sun was about the Solstice, that is, when it was at the greatest Northern Distance from us, we had found the Benefit of it in our Travels. But now it drew near us apace, and we found it began to rain; upon which we called another General Council, in which we debated our present Circumstances, and in particular, whether we should go forward, or seek for a proper Place upon the Bank of our Golden River, which had been so lucky to us to fix our Camp for the Winter.

Upon the whole, it was resolved to abide where we were; and it was not the least Part of our Happiness that we did so, as shall appear in its Place.

Having resolved upon this, our first Measures were to set our Negroes to Work, to make Hutts or Houses for our Habitation; and this they did very dexterously; only that we changed the Ground where we had at first intended it, thinking, as indeed it happen'd, that the river might reach it upon any sudden Rain. Our Camp was like a little Town, in which our Hutts were in the Center, having one large one in the Center of them also, into which all our particular Lodgings opened; so that none of us went into our Apartments, but thro' a publick Tent where we all eat and drank together, and kept our Councils and
Socie-

Society, and our Carpenters made us Tables,
Benches, and Stools in Abundance, as many as
we could make ufe of.

We had no Need of Chimneys, it was hot
enough without Fire; but yet we found our felves
at laft oblig'd to keep a Fire every Night upon
a particular Occafion: For tho' we had in all
other Refpects a very pleafant and agreeable Scituation, yet we were rather worfe troubled with
the unwelcome Vifits of wild Beafts here, than in
the Wildernefs it felf; for as the Deer, and other
gentle Creatures came hither for Shelter and
Food, fo the Lions, and Tigers, and Leopards,
haunted thefe Places continually for Prey.

When firft we difcovered this, we were fo
uneafy at it, that we thought of removing our
Scituation; but after many Debates about it, we
refolved to fortify our felves in fuch a Manner, as
not to be in any Danger from it; and this our
Carpenters undertook, who firft palifadoed our
Camp quite round with long Stakes (for we had
Wood enough) which Stakes were not ftuck in
one by another like Pales, but in an irregular
Manner; a great Multitude of them fo placed,
that they took up near two Yards in Thicknefs,
fome higher, fome lower, all fharpened at the
Top, and about a Foot afunder; fo that had
any Creature jump'd at them, unlefs he had gone
clean over, which it was very hard to do, he
would be hung upon twenty or thirty Spikes.

The Entrance into this, had larger Stakes than
the reft, placed fo before one another, as to make
three or four fhort Turnings, which no four-
footed Beaft bigger than a Dog could poffibly
come in at; and that we might not be attack'd
by any Multitude together, and confequently be

K   alarm'd

alarm'd in our Sleep, as we had been, or be oblig'd to wafte our Ammunition, which we were very chary of, we kept a great Fire every Night without the Entrance of our Palifade, having a Hutt for our two Centinels to ftand in free from the Rain, juft within the Entrance, and right againft the Fire.

To maintain this Fire, we cut a prodigious deal of Wood, and piled it upon a Heap to dry, and with the green Boughs made a fecond Covering over our Hutts, fo high and thick, that it might caft the Rain off from the firft, and keep us effectually dry.

We had fcarce finifhed all thefe Works, but that the Rain came on fo fierce, and fo continued, that we had little time to ftir abroad for Food, except indeed that our Negroes, who wore no Clothes, feem'd to make nothing of the Rain, tho' to us *Europeans* in thofe hot Climates, nothing is more dangerous.

We continued in this Pofture for four Months, that is, from the Middle of *June* to the Middle of *October*; for tho' the Rains went off, at leaft the greateft Violence of them, about the *Equinox*, yet as the Sun was then juft over our Heads, we refolved to ftay a while till it was pafs'd us a little to the Southward.

During our Encampment here, we had feveral Adventures with the ravenous Creatures of that Country, and had not our Fire been always kept burning, I queftion much whether all our Fence, tho' we ftrengthen'd it afterwards with twelve or fourteen Rows of Stakes more, would have kept us fecure. It was always in the Night that we had the Difturbance of them, and fometimes they came in fuch Multitudes, that we
thought

thought all the Lions, and Tigers, and Leopards, and Wolves of *Africa* were come together to attack us. One Night being clear Moonſhine, one of our Men being upon the Watch, told us, he verily believed he ſaw Ten Thouſand wild Creatures of one Sort or another, paſs by our little Camp; and ever as they ſaw the Fire, they ſheer'd off, but were ſure to howl or roar, or whatever it was, when they were paſt.

The Muſick of their Voices was very far from being pleaſant to us, and ſometimes would be ſo very diſturbing, that we could not ſleep for it; and often our Centinels would call us, that were awake to come and look at them. It was one windy tempeſtuous Night after a very rainy Day, that we were indeed all called up; for ſuch innumerable Numbers of Deviliſh Creatures came about us, that our Watch really thought they would attack us. They would not come on the Side where the Fire was; and tho' we thought our ſelves ſecure every where elſe, yet we all got up, and took to our Arms. The Moon was near the Full, but the Air full of flying Clouds, and a ſtrange Hurricane of Wind to add to the Terror of the Night; when looking on the Back Part of our Camp, I thought I ſaw a Creature within our Fortification, and ſo indeed he was, except his Haunches; for he had taken a running Leap, I ſuppoſe, and with all his Might had thrown himſelf clear over our Paliſadoes, except one ſtrong Pile which ſtood higher than the reſt, and which had caught hold of him, and by his Weight he had hang'd himſelf upon it, the Spike of the Pile running into his Hinder-Haunch or Thigh, on the Inſide, and by that he hung growling and biting the Wood for Rage. I ſnatcht up a Lance

K 2   from

from one of the Negroes that ſtood juſt by me, and running to him, ſtruck it three or four Times into him, and diſpatch'd him; being unwilling to ſhoot, becauſe I had a Mind to have a Volley fired among the reſt, whom I could ſee ſtanding without as thick as a Drove of Bullocks going to a Fair. I immediately called our People out, and ſhewed them the Object of Terror which I had ſeen, and without any farther Conſultation, fired a full Volley among them, moſt of our Pieces being loaden with two or three Sluggs or Bullets a-piece. It made a horrible Clutter among them, and in general they all took to their Heels, only that we could obſerve, that ſome walk'd off with more Gravity and Majeſty than others, being not ſo much frighted at the Noiſe and Fire; and we could perceive that ſome were left upon the Ground ſtruggling as for Life, but we durſt not ſtir out to ſee what they were.

Indeed they ſtood ſo thick, and were ſo near us, that we could not well miſs killing or wounding ſome of them, and we believe they had certainly the Smell of us, and of our Victuals we had been killing; for we had killed a Deer, and three or four of thoſe Creatures like Goats, the Day before; and ſome of the Offal had been thrown out behind our Camp, and this we ſuppoſe drew them ſo much about us; but we avoided it for the future.

Tho' the Creatures fled, yet we heard a frightful Roaring all Night at the Place where they ſtood, which we ſuppoſed was from ſome that were wounded; and as ſoon as Day came, we went out to ſee what Execution we had done, and, indeed, it was a ſtrange Sight; there were three Tygers and two Wolves quite killed, beſides the

the Creature I had killed within our Palifado, which feem'd to be of an ill-gendered kind, between a Tyger and a Leopard. Befides this, there was a noble old Lion alive, but with both his Fore Legs broke, fo that he could not ftir away, and he had almoft beat himfelf to Death with ftruggling all Night; and we found, that this was the wounded Soldier that had roared fo loud, and given us fo much Difturbance: Our Surgeon, looking at him, fmiled; Now, fays he, if I could be fure this Lion would be as grateful to me, as one of his Majefty's Anceftors was to *Andronicus* the *Roman* Slave, I would certainly fet both his Legs again, and cure him. I had not heard the Story of *Andronicus*, fo he told it me at large; but as to the Surgeon, we told him, he had no Way to know whether the Lion would do fo or not, but to cure him firft, and truft to his Honour; but he had no Faith; fo, to difpatch him, and put him out of his Torment, he fhot him into the Head, and killed him, for which we called him the King-Killer ever after.

Our Negroes found no lefs than five of thefe ravenous Creatures wounded and dropt at a Diftance from our Quarters; whereof, one was a Wolf, one a fine fpotted young Leopard, and the other were Creatures that we knew not what to call them.

We had feveral more of thefe Gentle-folks about us after that, but no fuch general Rendezvous of them as that was, any more; but this ill Effect it had to us, that it frighted the Deer and other Creatures from our Neighbourhood, of whofe Company we were much more defirous, and who were neceffary for our Subfiftence: However, our Negroes went out every Day a-

Hunting

Hunting, as they called it, with Bow and Arrow, and they scarce ever failed of bringing us home some thing or other; and particularly we found in this Part of the Country, after the Rains had fallen some time, Abundance of Wild-fowl, such as we have in *England*; Duck, Teal, Widgeon, &c. some Geese, and some Kinds that we had never seen before, and we frequently killed them. Also we catched a great Deal of fresh Fish out of the River, so that we wanted no Provision; if we wanted any thing, it was Salt to eat with our fresh Meat, but we had a little left, and we used it sparingly; for, as to our Negroes, they would not taste it, nor did they care to eat any Meat that was seasoned with it.

The Weather began now to clear up, the Rains were down, and the Floods abated, and the Sun, which had passed our Zenith, was gone to the Southward a good Way, so we prepared to go on of our Way.

It was the 12th of *October* or thereabouts, that we began to set forward, and having an easy Country to travel in, as well as to supply us with Provisions, tho' still without Inhabitants, we made more Dispatch, travelling some times, as we calculated it 20 or 25 Miles a Day; nor did we halt any were in eleven Days March, one Day excepted, which was to make a Raft to carry us over a small River, which having swelled with the Rains was not yet quited own.

When we were past this River, which by the Way run to the Northward too, we found a great Row of Hills in our Way; we saw indeed the Country open to the Right at a great Distance, but as we kept true to our Course due West, we were not willing to go a great Way out of our

Way,

Way, only to fhun a few Hills; fo we advanced;
but we were furprized, when being not quite come
to the Top, one of our Company who with two
Negroes was got up before us, cry'd out the *Sea!*
the *Sea!* and fell a-dancing and jumping as Signs
of Joy.

The Gunner and I were moft furprized at it,
becaufe we had but that Morning been calcu-
lating, that we muft have yet above a 1000 Miles
to the Sea-fide, and that we could not expect to
reach it till an other rainy Seafon would be
upon us, fo that when our Man cry'd out the
Sea, the Gunner was angry, and faid he was
mad.

But we were both in the greateft Surprize imaginable, when coming to the Top of the Hill, and
tho' it was very high, we faw nothing but Water,
either before us, or to the right Hand or the
left, being a vaft Sea without any Bound but the
Horizon.

We went down the Hill full of Confufion of
Thought, not being able to conceive whereabouts we were, or what it muft be, feeing by
all our Charts the Sea was yet a vaft Way off.

It was not above three Miles from the Hills
before we came to the Shore, or Water-edge
of this Sea, and there, to our further Surprize,
we found the Water frefh and pleafant to drink;
fo that in fhort we knew not what Courfe to
take : The Sea, as we thought it to be, put a
full ftop to our Journey, (I mean Weftward) for
it lay juft in the Way. Our next Queftion was
which Hand to turn to, to the Right or the
Left, but this was foon refolved; for as we
knew not the Extent of it, we confidered that
our Way, if it had been the Sea really, muft be to

the North; and therefore, if we went to the South now, it muſt be juſt ſo much out of our Way at laſt : So having ſpent a good Part of the Day in our Surprize at the Thing, and conſulting what to do, we ſet forward to the North.

We travelled upon the Shore of this Sea full 23 Days, before we could come to any Reſolution about what it was; at the End of which, early one Morning, one of our Seamen cried out Land, and it was no falſe Alarm, for we ſaw plainly the Tops of ſome Hills at a very great Diſtance, on the further Side of the Water, due Weſt; but tho' this ſatisfied us that it was not the Sea, but an Inland Sea or Lake, yet we ſaw no Land to the Northward, that is ſo ſay, no End of it; but were obliged to travel eight Days more, and near a 100 Miles further, before we came to the End of it, and then we found this Lake or Sea ended in a very great River, which run N. or N. by E. as the other River had done, which I mention'd before.

My Friend the Gunner, upon examining, ſaid, that he believed that he was miſtaken before, and that this was the River *Nile*, but was ſtill of the Mind, that we were of before, that we ſhould not think of a Voyage into *Egypt* that Way; ſo we reſolved upon croſſing this River, which however was not ſo eaſy as before, the River being very rapid, and the Channel very broad.

It coſt us therefore a Week here to get Materials to waft our ſelves and Cattel over this River; for tho' here were Store of Trees, yet there were none of any conſiderable Growth, ſufficient to make a Canoe.

During our March on the Edge of this Bank, we met with great Fatigue, and therefore travell'd vell'd fewer Miles in a Day than before, there being fuch a prodigious Number of little Rivers that came down from the Hills on the Eaft Side, emptying themfelves into this Gulph, all which Waters were pretty high, the Rains having been but newly over.

In the laft three Days of our Travel we met with fome Inhabitants, but we found they lived upon the little Hills, and not by the Water Side; nor were we a little put to it for Food in this March, having killed nothing for four or five Days, but fome Fifh we caught out of the Lake, and that not in fuch Plenty as we found before.

But to make us fome amends, we had no Difturbance upon all the Shore of this Lake, from any wild Beafts; the only Inconveniency of that Kind was, that we met an ugly, venemous, deformed kind of a Snake or Serpent in the wet Grounds near the Lake, that feveral times purfued us, as if it would attack us; and if we ftruck at, or threw any thing at it, would raife it felf up, and hifs as loud it might be heard a great Way; it had a hellifh, ugly, deformed Look and Voice, and our Men would not be perfwaded but it was the Devil, only that we did not know what Bufinefs Satan could have there, where there were no People.

It was very remarkable that we had now travelled a 1000 Miles without meeting with any People, in the Heart of the whole Continent of *Africa*, where to be fure never Man fet his Foot fince the Sons of *Noah* fpread themfelves over the Face of the whole Earth; here alfo our Gunner took an Obfervation with his Foreftaff to determine our Latitude, and he found now, that having marched about 33 Days

North-

Northward, we were in 6 Degrees 22 Minutes South Latitude.

After having with great Difficulty got over this River, we came into a ſtrange wild Country, that began a little to affright us; for tho' the Country was not a Deſart of dry ſcalding Sand, as that was we had paſſed before, yet it was mountainous, barren and infinitely full of moſt furious wild Beaſts, more than any Place we had paſt yet. There was indeed a kind of coarſe Herbage on the Surface, and now and then a few Trees or rather Shrubs; but People we could ſee none, and we began to be in great Suſpenſe about Victuals; for we had not killed a Deer a great while, but had lived chiefly upon Fiſh and Fowl alway by the Water Side, both which ſeemed to fail us now; and we were in the more Conſternation, becauſe we could not lay in a Stock here to proceed upon, as we did before, but were obliged to ſet out with Scarcity, and without any Certainty of a Supply.

We had however no Remedy but Patience; and having killed ſome Fowls, and dried ſome Fiſh, as much as with ſhort Allowance we reckoned would laſt us five Days, we reſolved to venture, and venture we did; nor was it without Cauſe that we were apprehenſive of the Danger, for we travelled the five Days, and met neither with Fiſh, or Fowl, or four-footed Beaſt whoſe Fleſh was fit to eat; and we were in a moſt dreadful Apprehenſion of being famiſhed to Death; on the ſixth Day we almoſt faſted, or, as we may ſay, we eat up all the Scraps of what we had left, and at Night lay down ſupperleſs upon our Matts with heavy Hearts, being obliged the eighth Day to kill one of our

poor

poor faithful Servants the Buffloes, that carry'd our Baggage; the flesh of this Creature was very good, and so sparingly did we eat of it, that it lasted us all three Days and a half, and was just spent; and we were upon the point of killing another, when we saw before us a Country that promised better, having high Trees and a large River in the middle of it.

This encouraged us, and we quicken'd our March for the River Side, tho' with empty Stomachs, and very faint and weak; but before we came to this River we had the good Hap to meet with some young Deer, a Thing we had long wished for. In a Word, having shot three of them, we came to a full Stop to fill our Bellies, and never gave the Flesh time to cool before we eat it; nay 'twas much we could stay to kill it, and had not eaten it alive, for we were in short almost famished.

Through all that unhospitable Country we saw continually Lions, Tygers, Leopards, Civet Cats, and Abundance of Kinds of Creatures that we did not understand; we saw no Elephants, but every now and then we met with an Elephant's Tooth lying on the Ground, and some of them lying as it were half buried by the Length of Time that they had lain there.

When we came to the Shore of this River, we found it run Northerly still, as all the rest had done, but with this Difference, that as the Course of the other Rivers were N. by E. or N. N. E. the Course of this lay N. N. W.

On the farther Bank of this River we saw some Sign of Inhabitants, but met with none for the first Day; but the next Day we came into an Inhabited Country, the People all Negroes

groes, and stark naked, without Shame, both
Men and Women.

We made Signs of Friendſhip to them, and
found them a very frank, civil, and friendly ſort
of People. They came to our Negroes without
any Suſpition, nor did they give us any Reaſon
to ſuſpect them of any Villainy, as the others
had done; we made Signs to them that we
were hungry, and immediately ſome naked
Women ran and fetched us great Quantities of
Roots, and of Things like Pumpkins, which
we made no Scruple to eat; and our Artificer
ſhewed them ſome of his Trinkets that he had
made, ſome of Iron, ſome of Silver, but none
of Gold: They had ſo much Judgment to chuſe
that of Silver before the Iron, but when we
ſhewed them ſome Gold, we found they did not
value it ſo much as either of the other.

For ſome of theſe Things they brought us
more Proviſions, and three living Creatures as
big as Calves, but not of that Kind; neither did
we ever ſee any of them before; their Fleſh was
very good; and after that they brought us
twelve more, and ſome ſmaller Creatures, like
Hares, all which were very welcome to us who
were indeed at a very great Loſs for Proviſions.

We grew very intimate with theſe People,
and indeed they were the civilleſt and moſt friendly People that we met with at all, and mightily
pleaſed with us; and which was very particular,
they were much eaſier to be made to underſtand
our Meaning, than any we had met with before.

At laſt, we began to enquire our Way, pointing to the Weſt, they made us underſtand eaſily
that we could not go that Way, but they
pointed to us, that we might go North-Weſt,

ſo

fo that we prefently underftood that there was
another Lake in our Way, which proved to be
true; for in two Days more we faw it plain, and
it held us till we paft the Equinoctial Line,
lying all the Way on our left Hand, tho' at
a great Diftance.

Travelling thus Northward, our Gunner
feemed very anxious about our Proceedings; for
he affured us, and made me fenfible of it by
the Maps, which he had been teaching me out
of, that when we came into the Latitude of fix
Degrees, or thereabouts, North of the Line, the
Land trended away to the Weft, to fuch a Length,
that we fhould not come at the Sea under a March
of above 1500 Miles farther Weftward than the
Country we defired to go to. I asked him if there
were no Navigable Rivers that we might meet
with, which running into the Weft Ocean, might
perhaps carry us down their Stream, and then if
it were 1500 Miles, or twice 1500 Miles, we might
do well enough, if we could but get Provifions.

Here he fhewed me the Maps again, and that
there appeared no River whofe Stream was of
any fuch Length as to do us any Kindnefs, till
we came perhaps within 2 or 300 Miles of the
Shore, except the *Rio Grande*, as they call it,
which lay farther Northward from us, at leaft
700 Miles; and that then he knew not what
kind of Country it might carry us through; for
he faid it was his Opinion, that the Heats on
the North of the Line, even in the fame Latitude,
were violent, and the Country more defolate,
barren, and barbarous than thofe of the South;
and that when we came among the Negroes in
the North Part of *Africa*, next the Sea, efpecially thofe who had feen and trafficked with

the

the *Europeans*, such as *Dutch*, *Englifh*, *Portuguefe*,
Spaniards, &c. that they had moft of them been fo
ill ufed at fome time or other, that they would
certainly put all the Spight they could upon
us in meer Revenge.

Upon thefe Confiderations, he advifed us, that
as foon as we had paffed this Lake, we fhould
proceed W. S. W. that is to fay, a little enclining
to the South, and that in Time we fhould meet
with the great River *Congo*, from whence the
Coaft is called *Congo*, being a little North of *Angola*, where we intended at firft to go.

I asked him, if ever he had been on the Coaft
of *Congo*; he faid yes he had, but was never on
Shore there: Then I asked him, how we fhould get
from thence to the Coaft where the *European*
Ships came, feeing if the Land trended away
Weft for 1500 Miles, we muft have all that Shore
to traverfe, before we could double the Weft
Point of it.

He told me, it was ten to one but we fhould
hear of fome *European* Ships to take us in, for
that they often vifited the Coaft of *Congo* and
Angola, in Trade with the Negroes; and that if
we could not, yet, if we could but find Provifions, we fhould make our Way as well along
the Sea-Shore, as along the River, till we came
to the Gold Coaft, which he faid was not above
4 or 500 Miles North of *Congo*, befides the turning of the Coaft Weft about 300 more; that
Shore being in the Latitude of fix or feven Degrees, and that there the *Englifh*, or *Dutch*, or
French, had Settlements or Factories, perpaps all
of them.

I confefs, I had more Mind all the while he argued, to have gone Northward, and Shipt our
felves

felves in the *Rio Grand*, or as the Traders call it, the River *Negro* or *Niger*, for I knew that at laſt it would bring us down to the *Cape de Verd*, where we were ſure of Relief; whereas at the Coaſt we were going to now, we had a prodigious Way ſtill to go, either by Sea or Land, and no Certainty which way to get Proviſions but by Force; but for the preſent I held my Tongue, becauſe it was my Tutor's Opinion.

But when, according to his Deſire, we came to turn Southward, having paſſed beyond the ſecond great Lake, our Men began all to be uneaſy, and ſaid, we were now out of our Way for certain, for that we were going farther from home, and that we were indeed far enough off already.

But we had not marched above twelve Days more, eight whereof was taken up in rounding the Lake, and four more Southweſt, in order to make for the River *Congo*, but we were put to another full Stop, by entring a Country ſo deſolate, ſo frightful, and ſo wild, that we knew not what to think or do; for beſides that it appeared as a terrible and boundleſs Deſart, having neither Woods, Trees, Rivers, or Inhabitants; ſo even the Place where we were, was deſolate of Inhabitants, nor had we any Way to gather in a Stock of Proviſions for the paſſing this Deſart, as we did before at our entring the firſt, unleſs we had marched back four Days to the Place where we turned the Head of the Lake.

Well, notwithſtanding this we ventured, for to Men that had paſſed ſuch wild Places as we had done, nothing could ſeem too deſperate to undertake : We ventured I ſay, and the rather becauſe we ſaw very high Mountains in our way at a

great

great Diftance, and we imagined, wherever there was Mountains, there would be Springs and Rivers, where Rivers, there would be Trees and Grafs, where Trees and Grafs, there would be Cattel, and where Cattel, fome Kind of Inhabitants.

At laft, in Confequence of this fpeculative Philofophy, we entered this Waft, having a great Heap of Roots and Plants for our Bread, fuch as the *Indians* gave us, a very little Flefh, or Salt, and but a little Water.

We travelled two Days towards thofe Hills, and ftill they feemed as far off as they did at firft, and it was the fifth Day before we got to them; indeed we travelled but foftly, for it was exceffive hot, and we were much about the very *Equinoctial* Line, we hardly knew whether to the South or the North of it.

As we had concluded that, where there were Hills there would be Springs, fo it happened; but we were not only furprized, but really frighted, to find the firft Spring we came to, and which looked admirably clear and beautiful, be falt as Brine: It was a terrible Difappointment to us, and put us under melancholy Apprehenfions at firft; but the Gunner who was of a Spirit never difcouraged, told us we fhould not be difturbed at that, but be very thankful, for Salt was a Bait we ftood in as much Need of as any thing, and there was no Queftion but we fhould find frefh Water as well as Salt; and here our Surgeon fteps in to encourage us, and told us, that if we did not know, he would fhew us a Way how to make that falt Water frefh, which indeed made us all more chearful, tho' we wondered what he meant.

Mean

Mean time our Men, without bidding, had been feeking about for other Springs, and found feveral, but ftill they were all falt ; from whence we concluded, that there was a falt Rock or Mineral Stone in thofe Mountains, and perhaps they might be all of fuch a Subftance: But ftill I wondered by what Witchcraft it was that our Artift the Surgeon would make this falt Water turn frefh, and I long'd to fee the Experiment, which was indeed a very odd one ; but he went to Work with as much Affurance, as if he had try'd it on the very Spot before.

He took two of our large Matts, and fow'd them together, and they made a kind of a Bag four Foot broad, three Foot and a Half high, and about a Foot and a Half thick when it was full.

He caufed us to fill this Bag with dry Sand, and tread it down as clofe as we could, not to burft the Matts. When thus the Bag was full within a Foot, he fought fome other Earth, and filled up the reft with it, and ftill trod it all in as hard as he could. When he had done, he made a Hole in the upper Earth, about as broad as the Crown of a large Hat, or fomething bigger about, but not fo deep, and bad a Negroe fill it with Water, and ftill as it fhrunk away, to fill it again, and keep it full. The Bag he had placed at firft crofs two Pieces of Wood, about a Foot from the Ground, and under it he ordered fome of our Skins to be fpread, that would hold Water. In about an Hour, and not fooner, the Water began to come dropping thro' the Bottom of the Bag, and to our great Surprize, was perfect frefh and fweet ; and this continued for feveral Hours: But in the End, the Water began to be a little

L   brackifh.

brackifh. When we told him that, Well then, *faid he*, turn the Sand out, and fill it again; whether he did this by way of Experiment from his own Fancy, or whether he had feen it done before, I do not remember.

The next Day we mounted the Tops of the Hills, where the Profpect was indeed aftonifhing; for as far as the Eye could look, South, or Weft, or North-Weft, there was nothing to be feen but a vaft howling Wildernefs, with neither Tree or River, or any green thing. The Surface we found, as the Part we paffed the Day before, had a kind of thick Mofs upon it, of a blackifh dead Colour, but nothing in it that look'd like Food, either for Man or Beaft.

Had we been ftored with Provifions to have entred for ten or twenty Days upon this Wildernefs, as we were formerly, and with frefh Water, we had Hearts good enough to have ventured; tho' we had been obliged to come back again; for if we went North, we did not know but we might meet with the fame; but we neither had Provifions, neither were we in any Place where it was poffible to get them. We killed fome wild ferine Creatures at the Foot of thefe Hills; but except two things like to nothing that we ever faw before, we met with nothing that was fit to eat. Thefe were Creatures that feemed to be between the Kind of a Buffloe and a Deer, but indeed refembled neither; for they had no Horns, and had great Legs like a Cow, with a fine Head, and the Neck like a Deer. We killed alfo at feveral times a Tiger, two young Lions, and a Wolf, but, God be thanked, we were not fo reduced as to eat Carrion.

Upon

Upon this terrible Prospect I renew'd my Motion of turning Northward, and making towards the River *Niger*, or *Rio Grand*, then to turn West towards the *English* Settlements on the Gold Coast, to which every one most readily consented, only our Gunner, who was indeed our best Guide, tho' he happen'd to be mistaken at this time. He moved, that as our Coast was *now* Northward, so we might slant away North West, that so by crossing the Country, we might perhaps meet with some other River that run into the *Rio Grand* Northward, or down to the Gold Coast Southward, and so both direct our Way, and shorten the Labour; as also, because, if any of the Country was inhabited and fruitful, we should probably find it upon the Shore of the Rivers, where alone we could be furnished with Provisions.

This was good Advice, and too rational not to be taken; but our present Business was, what to do to get out of this dreadful Place we were in; behind us was a Waste, which had already cost us five Days March, and we had not Provisions for five Days left to go back again the same Way. Before us was nothing but Horrour as above, so we resolv'd, seeing the Ridge of Hills we were upon had some Appearance of Fruitfulness, and that they seemed to lead away to the Northward a great Way, to keep under the Foot of them on the East Side, to go on as far as we could, and in the mean time to look diligently out for Food.

Accordingly we moved on the next Morning; for we had no time to lose, and to our great Comfort we came in our first Morning's March to very good Springs of fresh Water; and least we should have a Scarcity again, we filled all our

Blad-

Bladder Bottles, and carried it with us. I fhould alfo have obferved, that our Surgeon who made the falt Water frefh, took the Opportunity of thofe falt Springs, and made us the Quantity of three or four Pecks of very good Salt.

In our third March we found an unexpected Supply of Food, the Hills being full of Hares; they were of a kind fomething different from ours in *England*, larger, and not fo fwift of Foot, but very good Meat. We fhot feveral of them, and the little tame Leopard, which I told you we took at the Negroe Town that we plundered, hunted them like a Dog, and killed us feveral every Day; but fhe would eat nothing of them unlefs we gave it her, which indeed in our Circumftance was very obliging. We falted them a little, and dried them in the Sun whole, and carry'd a ftrange Parcel along with us, I think it was almoft three Hundred; for we did not know when we might find any more, either of thefe, or any other Food. We continued our Courfe under thefe Hills very comfortably eight or nine Days, when we found to our great Satisfaction, the Country beyond us began to look with fomething a better Countenance. As for the Weft Side of the Hills, we never examin'd it till this Day, when three of our Company, the reft halting for Refrefhment, mounted the Hills again to fatisfy their Curiofity, but found it all the fame ; nor could they fee any End of it, no not to the North, the Way we were going; fo the tenth Day finding the Hills made a Turn, and led as it were into the vaft Defart, we left them, and continued our Courfe North; the Country being very tolerably full of Woods, fome Waft, but not tedioufly long ; till we came, by our Gunner's Obfervation, into the

Lati-

Latitude of 8 Degrees, 5 Minutes, which we were nineteen Days more a performing.

All this Way we found no Inhabitants, Abundance of wild ravenous Creatures, with whom we became so well acquainted now, that really we did not much mind them. We saw Lions and Tigers, and Leopards every Night and Morning in Abundance; but as they seldom came near us, we let them go about their Busineſs; if they offer'd to come near us, we made falſe Fire with any Gun that was uncharged, and they would walk off as ſoon as they ſaw the Flaſh.

We made pretty good Shift for Food all this Way; for ſometimes we killed Hares, ſometimes ſome Fowls, but for my Life I cannot give Names to any of them, except a kind of Partridge, and another that was like our Turtles. Now and then we began to meet with Elephants again in great Numbers, thoſe Creatures delighting chiefly in the woody Part of the Country.

This long continued March fatigued us very much, and two of our Men fell ſick, indeed ſo very ſick, we thought they would have died; and one of our Negroes died ſuddenly. Our Surgeon ſaid it was an Apoplexy, but *he wondered at it, he ſaid,* for he could never complain of his high Feeding. Another of them was very ill, but our Surgeon with much ado perſwading him, indeed it was almoſt forcing him, to be let Blood, he recover'd.

We halted here twelve Days for the ſake of our ſick Men, and our Surgeon perſwaded me, and three or four more of us, to be let Blood during the time of Reſt, which with other things he gave us, contributed very much to our continued

nued Health, in fo tedious a March, and in fo hot a Climate.

In this March we pitched our matted Tents every Night, and they were very comfortable to us, tho' we had Trees and Woods to fhelter us alfo in moft Places. We thought it very ftrange, that in all this Part of the Country we yet met with no Inhabitants; but the principal Reafon as we found afterwards was, that we having kept a Weftern Courfe firft, and then a Northern Courfe, were gotten too much into the Middle of the Country, and among the Defarts: Whereas the Inhabitants are principally found among the Rivers, Lakes, and Low-Lands as well to the South-Weft, as to the North.

What little Rivulets we found here, were fo empty of Water, that except fome Pits, and little more than ordinary Pools, there was fcarce any Water to be feen in them; and they rather fhewed, that during the Rainy Months they had a Channel, than that they had really any running Water in them at that time: By which it was eafy for us to judge, that we had a great Way to go; but this was no Difcouragement fo long as we had but Provifions, and fome reafonable Shelter from the violent Heat, which indeed I thought was much greater now, than when the Sun was juft over our Heads.

Our Men being recovered, we fet forward again, very well ftored with Provifions and Water fufficient, and bending our Courfe a little to the Weftward of the North, travelled in Hopes of fome favourable Stream which might bear a Canoe; but we found none till after twenty Days Travel, including eight Days Reft, for our Men being weak we refted very often; efpecially when

when we came to Places which were proper for our Purpose; where we found Cattel, Fowl, or any thing to kill for our Food. In those twenty Days March, we advanced four Degrees to the Northward, besides some Meridian Distance Westward, and we met with Abundance of Elephants, and with a good Number of Elephants Teeth scatter'd up and down, here and there, in the Woody Grounds especially; some of which were very large. But they were no Booty to us; our Business was Provisions, and a good Passage out of the Country; and it had been much more to our Purpose, to have found a good fat Deer, and to have killed it for our Food, than a hundred Ton of Elephants Teeth; and yet as you shall presently hear, when we came to begin our Passage by Water, we once thought to have built a large Canoe on purpose to have loaded her with Ivory, but this was when we knew nothing of the Rivers, nor knew any thing how dangerous, and how difficult a Passage it was that we were like to have in them, nor had considered the Weight of Carriage to lug them to the Rivers where we might Embark.

At the End of twenty Days Travel, as above, in the Latitude of three Degrees, sixteen Minutes, we discovered in a Valley, at some Distance from us, a pretty tolerable Stream, which we thought deserved the Name of a River, and which run its Course N. N. W. which was just what we wanted. As we had fixt our Thoughts upon our Passage by Water, we took this for the Place to make the Experiment, and bent our March directly to the Valley.

There was a small Thicket of Trees just in our Way, which we went by, thinking no harm,

what

when on a sudden one of our Negroes was very
dangerously wounded with an Arrow, shot into
his back slanting between his Shoulders. This
put us to a full Stop, and three of our Men with
two Negroes spreading the Wood, for it was
but a small one, found a Negro with a Bow,
but no Arrow, who would have escaped; but our
Men that discovered him, shot him in Revenge of the Mischief he had done; so we lost the
Opportunity of taking him Prisoner, which if we
had done, and sent him home with good Usage,
it might have brought others to us in a friendly
Manner.

Going a little farther, we came to five Negro
Hutts or Houses, built after a differing Manner
from any we had seen yet; and at the Door of
one of them, lay seven Elephants Teeth piled
up against the Wall or Side of the Hutt, as if
they had been provided against a Market: Here
were no Men, but seven or eight Women, and
near twenty Children: We offered them no Uncivility of any kind, but gave them every one a
Bit of Silver beaten out thin, as I observed before, and cut Diamond fashion, or in the Shape
of a Bird; at which the Women were over-joy'd
and brought out to us several Sorts of Food,
which we did not understand, being Cakes of
a Meal made of Roots, which they bake in the
Sun, and which eat very well. We went a little
Way farther, and pitched our Camp for that
Night, not doubting but our Civility to the
Women would produce some good Effect, when
their Husbands might come Home.

Accordingly, the next Morning, the Women,
with eleven Men, five young Boys, and two good
big Girls, came to our Camp; before they came
quite

quite to us, the Women called aloud, and made
an odd fcreeking Noife, to bring us out, and
accordingly we came out, when two of the Wo-
men, fhewing us what we had given them, and
pointing to the Company behind, made fuch
Signs as we could eafily underftand fignified
Friendfhip. When the Men advanced, having
Bows and Arrows, they laid them down on the
Ground, fcraped, and threw Sand over their
Heads, and turned round three times with their
Hands laid up upon the Tops of their Heads.
This it feems, was a folemn Vow of Friendfhip.
Upon this we beckon'd them with our Hands to
come nearer ; then they fent the Boys and Girls
to us firft, which, it feems was to bring us more
Cakes of Bread, and fome green Herbs, to eat,
which we receiv'd, and took the Boys up and kiffed,
them, and the little Girls too ; then the Men came
up clofe to us, and fat them down on the Ground,
making Signs, that we fhould fit down by them,
which we did. They faid much to one another,
but we could not underftand them, nor could
we find any way to make them underftand us ;
much lefs whither we were going, or what we
wanted, only that we eafily made them underftand we wanted Victuals ; whereupon one of
the Men cafting his Eyes about him towards a
rifing Ground that was about half a Mile off,
ftarts up as if he was frighted, flies to the Place
where they had laid down their Bows and Arrows, fnatches up a Bow and two Arrows, and
run like a race Horfe to the Place : When he
came there, he let fly both his Arrows, and
comes back again to us with the fame Speed ;
we feeing he came with the Bow, but without the
Arrows, were the more inquifitive, but the Fellow
faying

saying nothing to us, beckons to one of our Negroes to come to him, and we bid him go; so he led
him back to the Place, where lay a kind of a Deer,
shot with two Arrows, but not quite dead; and,
between them, they brought it down to us. This
was for a Gift to us, and was very welcome, I
assure you, for our Stock was low. These People were all stark naked.

The next Day there came about a Hundred
Men to us, and Women, making the same aukward
Signals of Friendship; and dancing and shewing
themselves very well pleased, and any thing they
had they gave us. How the Man in the Wood
came to be so butcherly and rude, as to shoot at
our Men, without making any Breach first, we
could not imagine; for the People were simple,
plain, and inoffensive, in all our other Conversation with them.

From hence we went down the Bank of the
little River I mentioned, and where I found we
should see whole Nations of Negroes, but whether friendly to us, or not, that we could make
no Judgment of yet.

The River was of no Use to us, as to the Design
of making Canoes, a great while, and we tra-
versed the Country, on the Edge of it about
five Days more, when our Carpenters finding
the Stream encrease, proposed to pitch our
Tents, and fall to work to make Canoes; but
after we had begun the Work, and cut down
two or three Trees, and spent five Days in the
Labour, some of our Men wandring further
down the River, brought us Word, that the
Stream rather decreased than encreased, sinking
away into the Sands, or drying up by the Heat
of the Sun; so that the River appeared not able

to

to carry the leaft Canoe, that could be any way ufeful to us, fo we were obliged to give over our Enterprize, and move on.

In our further Profpect this Way, wemarch'd three Days full Weft the Country on the North Side, being extraordinary mountainous, and more parched and dry than any we had feen yet; whereas, in the Part which looks due Weft, we found a pleafant Valley, running a great way between two great Ridges of Mountains: The Hills look'd frightful, being entirely bare of Trees or Grafs, and even white with the Drinefs of the Sand; but in the Valley we had Trees, Grafs, and fome Creatures that were fit for Food, and fome Inhabitants.

We paft by fome of their Hutts or Houfes, and faw People about them, but they run up into the Hills as foon as they faw us; at the End of this Valley we met with a peopled Country, and at firft it put us to fome doubt, whether we fhould go among them, or keep up towards the Hills Northerly; and as our Aim was principally, as before, to make our Way to the River *Niger*, we enclined to the latter, purfuing our Courfe by the Compafs to the N. W. We march'd thus without Interruption feven Days more, when we met with a furprizing Circumftance, much more defolate and difconfolate than our own, and, which, in time to come, will fcarce feem credible.

We did not much feek the converfing, or acquainting our felves with the Natives of the Country, except where we found the Want of them for our Provifion, or their Direction for our Way; fo that whereas we found the Country here begin to be very populous, efpecially towards

wards our left Hand, that is, to the South, we
kept at the more Diftance Northerly, ftill ftretching towards the Weft.

In this Tract we found fomething or other to
kill and eat, which always fupplied our Neceffity,
tho' not fo well as we were provided in our firft
fetting out; being thus, as it were, pufhing to
avoid the peopled Country, we at laft came to a
very pleafant, agreeable Stream of Water, not
big enough to be called a River, but running to
the N. N. W. which was the very Courfe we
defired to go.

On the fartheft Bank of this Brook we perceiv'd
fome Hutts of Negroes not many, and in a little
low Spot of Ground fome *Maife* or *Indian* Corn
growing, which intimated prefently to us, that
there were fome Inhabitants on that Side, lefs barbarous than what we had met with in other
Places where we had been.

As we went forward our whole Carravan bein g
in a Body, our Negroes, who were in the Front,
cry'd out, that they faw a *White Man*; we were not
much furprized at firft, it being, as we thought, a
Miftake of the Fellows, and asked them what
they meant; when one of them ftept to me,
and pointing to a Hutt on the other Side of the
Hill, I was aftonifhed to fee a White Man
indeed, but ftark naked, very bufy near the
Door of his Hutt, and ftooping down to
the Ground w th f mething in his Hand, as if he
had been at fome Work, and his back being towards us, he did not fee us.

I gave Notice to our Negroes to make no Noife,
and waited till fome more of our Men were come
up, to fhew the Sight to them, that they might be
fure I was not miftaken, and we were foon fatisfied

fied of the Truth; for the Man having heard
fome Noife, ftarted up, and looked full at us,
as much furprized, to be fure, as we were,
but whether with Fear or Hope, we then
knew not.

As he difcovered us, fo did the reft of the Inhabitants belonging to the Hutts about him, and
all crouded together, looking at us at a Diftance:
A little Bottom, in which the Brook ran, lying
between us, the white Man, and all the reft,
as he told us afterwards, not knowing well whether they fhould ftay, or run away: However, it
prefently came into my Thoughts, that if there
were white Men among them, it would be much
eafier for us to make them underftand what we
meant, as to Peace or War, than we found it with
others; fo tying a Piece of white Rag to the End
of a Stick, we fent two Negroes with it to the
Bank of the Water, carrying the Pole up as
high as they could; it was prefently underftood,
and two of their Men, and the white Man, came
to the Shore on the other Side.

However, as the white Man fpoke no *Portuguefe*,
they could underftand nothing of one another,
but by Signs; but our Men made the white Man
underftand, that they had white Men with
them too, at which they faid the white Man
laught. However, to be fhort, our Men came
back, and told us they were all good Friends,
and in about an Hour four of our Men, two Negroes, and the Black Prince went to the River
Side, were the white Man came to them.

They had not been half a Quarter of an Hour,
but a Negro came running to me, and told me
the white Man was *Inglefe*, as he called him;
upon which I run back, eagerly enough you may
be

be sure with him, and found as he said, that he was an *Englishman*; upon which he embraced me very passionately, the Tears running down his Face. The first Surprize of his seeing us was over before we came, but any one may conceive of it, by the brief Account he gave us afterwards of his very unhappy Circumstance; and of so unexpected a Deliverance, such as perhaps never happened to any Man in the World; for it was a Million to one odds, that ever he could have been relieved; nothing but an Adventure that never was heard or read of before, could have suited his Case, unless Heaven by some Miracle that never was to be expected, had acted for him.

He appeared to be a Gentleman, not an ordinary bred Fellow, Seaman, or labouring Man; this shewed it self in his Behaviour, in the first Moment of our conversing with him, and in spight of all the Disadvantages of his miserable Circumstance.

He was a middle-aged Man, not above 37 or 38, tho' his Beard was grown exceeding long, and the Hair of his Head and face strangely covered him to the Middle of his Back and Breast, he was white, and his Skin very fine, tho' discoloured, and in some Places blistered and covered with a brown blackish Substance, scurfy, scaly, and hard which was the Effect of the scorching Heat of the Sun; he was stark naked, and had been so, as he told us, upwards of two Years.

He was so exceedingly transported at our meeting with him, that he could scarce enter into any Discourse at all with us for that Day, and when he could get away from us for a little, we saw him walking alone, and shewing all the

most

moſt extravagant Tokens of an ungovernable Joy; and even afterwards he was never without Tears in his Eyes for ſeveral Days, upon the leaſt Word ſpoken by us of his Circumſtances, or by him of his Deliverance.

We found his Behaviour the moſt courteous and endearing I ever ſaw in any Man whatever, and moſt evident Tokens of a mannerly well-bred Perſon, appeared in all things he did or ſaid; and our People were exceedingly taken with him. He was a Scholar, and a Mathematician; he could not ſpeek *Portugueſe* indeed, but he ſpoke *Latin* to our Surgeon, *French* to another of our Men, and *Italian* to a Third.

He had no Leiſure in his Thoughts to ask us whence we came, whither we were going, or who we were; but would have it always as an Anſwer to himſelf, that to be ſure wherever we were a-going, we came from Heaven, and were ſent on purpoſe to ſave him from the moſt wretched Condition that ever Man was reduced to.

Our Men pitching their Camp on the Bank of a little River oppoſite to him, he began to enquire what Store of Proviſion we had, and how we propoſed to be ſupplied; when he found that our Store was but ſmall, he ſaid he would talk with the Natives, and we ſhould have Proviſions enough; for he ſaid they were the moſt courteous, good natured Part of the Inhabitants in all that Part of the Country, as, we might ſuppoſe by his living ſo ſafe among them.

The firſt things this Gentleman did for us were indeed of the greateſt Conſequence to us; for firſt he perfectly informed us where we were, and which was the propereſt Courſe for us to
steer :

fteer : fecondly, he put us in a Way how to furnifh our felves effectually with Provifions; and
Thirdly, he was our compleat Interpreter and
Peace-maker with all the Natives, who now
began to be very numerous about us; and who
were a more fierce and politick People than
thofe we had met with before; not fo eafily
terrified with our Arms as thofe, and not fo
ignorant, as to give their Provifions and Corn
forour little Toys, fuch as I faid before our
Artificer made; but as they had frequently traded
and converfed with the *Europeans* on the Coaft,
or with other Negro Nations that had traded
and been concerned with them, they were the lefs
ignorant, and the lefs fearful, and confequently
nothing was to be had from them but by Exchange for fuch things as they liked.

This I fay of the Negro Natives, which we
foon came among; but as to thefe poor People that he lived among, they were not much
acquainted with Things, being at the Diftance
of above 300 Miles from the Coaft, only that
they found Elephants Teeth upon the Hills to
the North, which they took and carried about
fixty or feventy Miles South, where other trading
Negroes ufually met them, and gave them Beads
Glafs, Shels, and Cowries for them, fuch as
the *Englifh* and *Dutch* and other Traders, furnifh
them with from *Europe*.

We now began to be more familiar with our new
Acquaintance; and firft, tho' we made but a forry
Figure as to Clothes our felves, having neither
Shoe, or Stocking, or Glove or Hat among us,
and but very few Shirts, yet as well as we could
we clothed him; and firft our Surgeon having
Sciffers and Razors, fhaved him, and cut his
Hair;

Hair; a Hat, as I say, we had not in all our Stores, but he supply'd himself by making himself a Cap of a Piece of a Leopard Skin, most artificially. As for Shoes or Stockings, he had gone so long without them, that he cared not even for the Buskins and Foot-Gloves we wore, which I described above.

As he had been curious to hear the whole Story of our Travels, and was exceedingly delighted with the Relation; so we were no less to know, and pleased with the Account of his Circumstance, and the History of his coming to that strange Place alone, and in that Condition, which we found him in, as above.

This Account of his would indeed be in it self the Subject of an agreeable History, and would be as long and as diverting as our own, having in it many strange and extraordinary Incidents, but we cannot have Room here to launch out into so long a Digression; the Sum of his History was this.

He had been a Factor for the *English Guiney* Company at *Siera Leon*, or some other of their Settlements which had been taken by the *French*, where he had been plundered of all his own Effects, as well as of what was intrusted to him by the Company. Whether it was, that the Company did not do him Justice in restoring his Circumstances, or in further employing him, he quitted their Service, and was employed by those they called Separate Traders; and being afterwards out of Employ there also, traded on his own Account; when passing unwarily into one of the Company's Settlements, he was either betray'd into the Hands of some of the Natives, or some how or other was surprized by them. Howe-

ver,

ver, as they did not kill him, he found Means to
escape from them at that time, and fled to another
Nation of the Natives, who being Enemies to the
other, entertained him friendly, and with them
he lived some time; but not liking his Quarters,
or his Company, he fled again, and several times
changed his Landlords; sometimes was carry'd
by Force, sometimes hurried by Fear, as Circumstances altered with him (the Variety of
which deserves a History by it self) till at last
he had wandred beyond all Possibility of Return,
and had taken up his Abode where we found him,
where he was well received by the petty King of
the Tribe he lived with; and he, in Return, in-
structed them how to value the Product of their
Labour, and on what Terms to trade with those
Negroes who came up to them for Teeth.

As he was naked, and had no Clothes, so he
was naked of Arms for his Defence, having neither Gun, Sword, Staff, or any Instrument of
War about him, no not to guard himself against
the Attacks of a wild Beast, of which the Country was very full. We asked him how he came
to be so entirely abandoned of all Concern for his
Safety? He answered, That to him that had so
often wish'd for Death, Life was not worth defending; and that as he was entirely at the Mercy of the Negroes, they had much the more Confidence in him, seeing he had no Weapons to hurt
them. As for wild Beasts, he was not much concerned about that; for he scarce ever went from
his Hutt; but if he did, the Negroe King and
his Men went all with him, and they were all armed with Bows and Arrows, and Lances, with
which they would kill any of the ravenous Creatures, Lions as well as others; but that they seldom

dom came abroad in the Day; and if the Negroes wander any where in the Night, they always build a Hutt for themselves, and make a Fire at the Door of it, which is Guard enough.

We enquired of him, what we should next do towards getting to the Sea-side; he told us we were about 120 *English* Leagues from the Coast, where almost all the *European* Settlements and Factories were, and which is called the Gold Coast; but that there were so many different Nations of Negroes in the Way, that it was ten to one if we were not either fought with continually, or starv'd for Want of Provisions: But that there were two other Ways to go, which, if he had had any Company to go with him, he had often contrived to make his Escape by. The one was to travel full West, which, tho' it was farther to go, yet was not so full of People; and the People we should find, would be so much the civiller to us, or be so much the easier to fight with: Or, that the other Way was, if possible, to get to the *Rio Grand*, and go down the Stream in Canoes. We told him, that was the Way we had resolved on before we met with him; but then he told us, there was a prodigious Desart to go over, and as prodigious Woods to go thro,' before we came to it, and that both together were at least twenty Days March for us, travel as hard as we could.

We ask'd him, if there were no Horses in the Country, or Asses, or even Bullocks or Buffloes to make use of in such a Journey, and we shewed him ours, of which we had but three left; he said No, all the Country did not afford any thing of that kind.

He

He told us, that in this great Wood there were innumerable Numbers of Elephants, and upon the Defart, great Multitudes of Lions, Linxes, Tygers, and Leopards, &c. and that it was to that Wood, and to that Defart that the Negroes went to get Elephants Teeth, where they never failed to find a great Number.

We enquired ftill more, and particularly the Way to the Gold Coaft, and if there were no Rivers to eafe us in our Carriage; and told him, as to the Negroes fighting with us, we were not much concern'd at that; nor were we afraid of ftarving; for if they had any Victuals among them, we would have our Share of it: And therefore, if he would venture to fhew us the Way, we would venture to go; and as for himfelf, we told him we would live and dye together, there fhould not a Man of us ftir from him.

He told us, with all his Heart, if we refolv'd it, and would venture, we might be affured he would take his Fate with us, and he would endeavour to guide us fuch a Way, as we fhould meet with fome friendly Savages who would ufe us well, and perhaps ftand by us againft fome others who were lefs tractable: So, in a Word, we all refolved to go full South for the Gold Coaft.

The next Morning he came to us again, and being all met in Council, as we may call it, he began to talk very ferioufly with us, that fince we were now come after a long Journey to a View of the End of our Troubles, and had been fo obliging to him, as to offer Carrying him with us, he had been all Night revolving in his Mind what he and we all might do to make

our

our felves fome Amends for all our Sorrows;
and firft he faid, he was to let me know, that
we were juft then in one of the richeft Parts of
the World, tho' it was really otherwife, but a
defolate, difconfolate Wildernefs; for fays he,
there's not a River here but runs Gold, not a
Defart but without Plowing bears a Crop of Ivory. What Mines of Gold, what immenfe Stores
of Gold thofe Mountains may contain, from
whence thefe Rivers come, or the Shores which
thefe Waters run by, we know not, but may
imagine that they muft be inconceivably rich, feeing fo much is wafhed down the Stream by the
Water wafhing the Sides of the Land, that the
Quantity fuffices all the Traders which the *European* World fend thither. We ask'd him how
far they went for it, feeing the Ships only trade
upon the Coaft. He told us, that the Negroes
on the Coaft fearch the Rivers up for the Length
of 150 or 200 Miles, and would be out a Month
or two or three at a Time, and always come
Home fufficiently rewarded; but, fays he, they
never come thus far, and yet hereabouts is as
much Gold as there. Upon this he told us,
that he believed he might have gotten a Hundred Pound Weight of Gold, fince he came thither, if he had employed himfelf to look and
work for it, but as he knew not what to do
with it, and had long fince defpaired of being
ever delivered from the Mifery he was in, he
had entirely omitted it. For what Advantage
had it been to me, faid he, or what richer had
I been, if I had a Ton of Gold Duft, and lay and
wallowed in it; the Richnefs of it, *faid he,* would not
give me one Moment's Felicity, or relieve me in
the prefent Exigency. Nay, fays he, as you all fee,

it

It would not buy me Clothes to cover me, or a Drop of Drink to save me from perishing. 'Tis of no Value here, says he; there are several People among these Hutts that would weigh Gold against a few Glass Beads, or a Cockle-Shell, and give you a Handful of Gold Dust for a Handful of Cowries. *N. B.* These are little Shells which our Children call Blackamores Teeth.

When he had said thus, he pulled out a Piece of an earthen Pot baked hard in the Sun: Here *says he,* is some of the Dirt of this Country, and if I would, I could have got a great deal more; and shewing it to us, I believe there was between two and three Pound Weight of Gold Dust, of the same Kind and Colour with that we had gotten already, as before. After we had look'd at it a while, he told us smiling, we were his Deliverers, and all he had, as well as his Life, was ours; and therefore, as this would be of Value to us when we came to our own Country, so he desired we would accept of it among us, and that this was the only time that he had repented that he had pickt up no more of it.

I spoke for him as his Interpreter to my Comrades, and in their Names thank'd him; but speaking to them in *Portuguese,* I desired them to refer the Accepting his Kindness to the next Morning, and so I did, telling him we would farther talk of this Part in the Morning; so we parted for that time.

When he was gone, I found they were all wonderfully affected with his Discourse, and with the Generosity of his Temper, as well as the Magnificence of his Present, which in another Place had been extraordinary. Upon the whole, not to detain you with Circumstances, we agreed, that
seeing

feeing he was now one of our Number, and that as we were a Relief to him in carrying him out of the difmal Condition he was in, fo he was equally a Relief to us, in being our Guide thro' the reft of the Country, our Interpreter with the Natives, and our Director how to manage with the Savages, and how to enrich our felves with the Wealth of the Country ; that therefore we would put his Gold among our common Stock, and every one fhould give him as much as would make his up juft as much as any fingle Share of our own, and for the future we would take our Lot together, taking his folemn Engagement to us, as we had before one to another, that we would not conceal the leaft Grain of Gold we found, one from another.

In the next Conference we acquainted him with the Adventures of the Golden River, and how we had fhared what we got there ; fo that every Man had a larger Stock than he for his Share; that therefore inftead of taking any from him, we had refolved every one to add a little to him. He appeared very glad that we had met with fuch good Succefs, but would not take a Grain from us, till at laft preffing him very hard, he told us, that then he would take it thus: That when we came to get any more, he would have fo much out of the firft as fhould make him even, and then we would go on as equal Adventurers; and thus we agreed.

He then told us, he thought it would not be an unprofitable Adventure, if before we fet forward, and after we had got a Stock of Provifions, we fhould make a Journey North to the Edge of the Defart he had told us of, from whence our Negroes might bring every one a

M 4   large

large Elephant's Tooth, and that he would get
some more to assist; and that after a certain
Length of Carriage, they might be conveyed by
Canoes to the Coast, where they would yield a
very great Profit.

I objected against this, on Account of our other
Design we had of getting Gold Dust; and that
our Negroes, who, we knew would be faithful
to us, would get much more by searching the
Rivers for Gold for us, than by lugging a great
Tooth of an Hundred and fifty Pound Weight, a
Hundred Mile, or more, which would be an
unsufferable Labour to them after so hard a Journey, and would certainly kill them.

He acquiesced in the Justice of this Answer,
but fain would have had us gone to see the
woody Part of the Hills, and the Edge of the
Desart, that we might see how the Elephants
Teeth lay scattered up and down there; but
when we told him the Story of what we had seen
before, as is said above, he said no more.

We stay'd here twelve Days, during which
Time the Natives were very obliging to us, and
brought us Fruits, Pompions, and a Root like
Carrots, tho' of quite another Taste, but not
unpleasant neither, and some *Guiney* Fowls whose
Names we did not know. In short, they brought
us Plenty of what they had, and we lived very
well, and we gave them all such little Things as
our Cutler had made, for he had now a whole
Bag full of them.

On the thirteenth Day we set forward, taking
our new Gentleman with us. At Parting, the
Negroe King sent two Savages with a Present
to him, of some dried Flesh, but I do not remember what it was, and he gave him again three
Silver

Silver Birds which our Cutler help'd him to, which I affure you was a Prefent for a King.

We travelled now South, a little Weft, and here we found the firft River for above 2000 Miles March, whofe Water run South, all the reft running North or Weft. We followed this River, which was no bigger than a good large Brook in *England*, till it began to encreafe its Water. Every now and then we found our *Englifhman* went down as it were privately to the Water, which was to try the Land. At Length, after a Day's March upon this River, he came running up to us with his Hands full Sand, and faying *Look here*. Upon looking, we found that a good deal of Gold lay fpangled among the Sand of the River. Now, fays he, I think we may begin to work; fo he divided our Negroes into Couples, and fet them to Work, to fearch and wafh the Sand and Ooze in the Bottom of the Water where it was not deep.

In the firft Day and a Quarter, our Men all together had gathered a Pound and two Ounces of Gold, or thereabouts; and as we found the Quantity encreafed, the farther we went, we followed it about three Days, till another fmall Rivulet join'd the firft, and then fearching up the Stream, we found Gold there too; fo we pitch'd our Camp in the Angle where the Rivers join'd, and we diverted our felves, as I may call it, in wafhing the Gold out of the Sand of the River, and in getting Provifions.

Here we ftay'd thirteen Days more, in which time we had many pleafant Adventures with the Savages, too long to mention here, and fome of them too homely to tell off; for fome of our Men had made fomething free with their Women, which,

which, had not our new Guide made Peace for us with one of their Men, at the Price of seven fine Bits of Silver, which our Artificer had cut out into the Shapes of Lions, and Fishes, and Birds, and had punch'd Holes to hang them up by (an inestimable Treasure!) we must have gone to War with them and all their People.

All the while we were busy washing Gold Dust out of the Rivers, and our Negroes the like, our ingenious Cutler was hammering and cutting, and he was grown so dexterous by Use, that he formed all Manner of Images. He cut out Elephants, Tygers, Civet Cats, Ostriches, Eagles, Cranes, Fowls, Fishes, and indeed whatever he pleased, in thin Plates of hammer'd Gold, for his Silver and Iron was almost all gone.

At one of the Towns of these Savage Nations we were very friendly received by their King; and as he was very much taken with our Workman's Toys, he sold him an Elephant cut out of a Gold Plate as thin as a Six-pence, at an extravagant Rate. He was so much taken with it, that he would not be quiet till he had given him almost a Handful of Gold Dust, as they call it. I suppose it might weigh three Quarters of a Pound; the Piece of Gold that the Elephant was made of, might be about the Weight of a Pistole, rather less than more. Our Artist was so honest, tho' the Labour and Art was all his own, that he brought all the Gold, and put it into our common Stock: But we had indeed no Manner of Reason in the least to be covetous; for, as our new Guide told us, we that were strong enough to defend our selves, and had Time enough to stay (for we were none of us in Haste) might in time get together what

Quan-

Quantity of Gold we pleafed, even to an Hundred Pound Weight a Man, if we thought fit; and therefore he told us, tho' he had as much Reafon to be fick of the Country as any of us, yet if we thought to turn our March a little to the South-Eaft, and pitch upon a Place proper for our Head Quarters, we might find Provifions plenty enough, and extend our felves over the Country among the Rivers for two or three Year to the Right and Left, and we fhould foon find the Advantage of it.

The Propofal, however good as to the profitable Part of it, fuited none of us; for we were all more defirous to get Home, than to be rich, being tired of the exceffive Fatigue of above a Year's continual Wandring among Defarts and wild Beafts.

However, the Tongue of our new Acquaintance had a Kind of Charm in it, and ufed fuch Arguments, and had fo much the Power of Perfwafion, that there was no refifting him. He told us, it was prepofterous not to take the Fruit of all our Labours, now we were come to the Harveft; that we might fee the Hazard the *Europeans* run, with Ships and Men, and at great Expence, to fetch a little Gold; and that we that were in the Center of it, to go away empty handed, was unaccountable; that we were ftrong enough to fight our Way thro' whole Nations, and might make our Journey afterward to what Part of the Coaft we pleafed; and we fhould never forgive our felves when we came to our own Country, to fee we had 500 Piftoles in Gold, and might as eafily have had 5000, or 10000, or what we pleafed; that he was no more covetous than we, but feeing it was in all our

Powers

Powers to retrieve our Misfortunes at once, and to make our felves eafy for all our Lives, he could not be faithful to us, or grateful for the Good we had done him, if he did not let us fee the Advantage we had in our Hands; and he affured us, he would make it clear to our own Underftanding, that we might in two Years time, by good Management, and by the Help of our Negroes, gather every Man a Hundred Pound Weight of Gold, and get together perhaps two Hundred Ton of Teeth: Whereas, if once we pufh'd on to the Coaft, and feparated, we fhould never be able to fee that Place again with our Eyes, or do any more than Sinners did with Heaven, wifh themfelves there, but know they can never come at it.

Our Surgeon was the firft Man that yielded to his Reafoning, and after him the Gunner; and they two indeed had a great Influence over us, but none of the reft had any Mind to ftay, nor I neither, I muft confefs; for I had no Notion of a great deal of Money, or what to do with my felf, or what to do with it if I had it. I thought I had enough already, and all the Thoughts I had about difpofing of it, if I came to *Europe*, was only how to fpend it as faft as I could, buy me fome Clothes, and go to Sea again to be a Drudge for more.

However, he prevailed with us by his good Words at laft, to ftay but for fix Months in the Country, and then, if we did refolve to go, he would fubmit: So at length we yielded to that, and he carry'd us about fifty *Englifh* Miles South-Eaft, where we found feveral Rivulets of Water, which feem'd to come all from a great Ridge of Mountains, which lay to the North-Eaft, and which, by our Calculation, muft be the Beginning
that

that Way of the great Waft, which we had been forc'd Northward to avoid.

Here we found the Country barren enough, but yet we had, by his Direction, Plenty of Food; for the Savages round us, upon giving them some of our Toys, as I have so often mentioned, brought us in whatever they had: And here we found some Maife, or *Indian* Wheat, which the Negroe Women planted, as we sow Seeds in a Garden, and immediately our new Proveditor ordered some of our Negroes to plant it, and it grew up presently, and by watering it often, we had a Crop in less than three Months Growth.

As soon as we were settled, and our Camp fix'd, we fell to the old Trade of Fishing for Gold in the Rivers mentioned above; and our *English* Gentleman so well knew how to direct our Search, that we scarce ever lost our Labour.

One time, having set us to Work, he asked, if we would give him Leave, with four or five Negroes, to go out for six or seven Days, to seek his Fortune, and see what he could discover in the Country, assuring us, whatever he got should be for the publick Stock. We all gave him our Consent, lent him a Gun; and two of our Men desiring to go with him, they took then six Negroes with them, and two of our Buffloes that came with us the whole Journey; they took about eight Days Provision of Bread with them, but no Flesh, except about as much dried Flesh as would serve them two Days.

They travelled up to the Top of the Mountains I mentioned just now, where they saw, (as our Men afterwards vouch'd it to be) the same Desart which we were so justly terrified at, when we were on the further Side, and which, by our

Calcu-

Calculation, could not be lefs than 300 Miles broad, and above 600 Miles in Length, without knowing where it ended.

The Journal of their Travels is too long to enter upon here ; they ftayed out two and fifty Days, when they brought us feventeen Pound, and fomething more (for we had no exact Weight) of Gold Duft, fome of it in much larger Pieces than any we found before ; befides about fifteen Ton of Elephants Teeth, which he had, partly by good Ufage, and partly by bad, obliged the Savages of the Country to fetch, and bring down to him from the Mountains, and which he made others bring with him quite down to our Camp. Indeed we wondered what was coming to us, when we faw him attended with above 200 Negroes ; but he foon undeceived us, when he made them all throw down their Burthens on a Heap, at the Entrance of our Camp.

Befides this, they brought two Lions Skins, and five Leopards Skins, very large and very fine. He asked our Pardon for his long Stay, and that he had made no greater a Booty, but told us, he had one Excurfion more to make, which he hop'd fhould turn to a better Account.

So having refted himfelf, and rewarded the Savages that brought the Teeth for him, with fome Bits of Silver and Iron cut out Diamond Fafhion, and with two fhap'd like little Dogs, he fent them away mightily pleafed.

The fecond Journey he went, fome more of our Men defired to go with him, and they made a Troop of ten white Men, and ten Savages, and the two Buffloes to carry their Provifions and Ammunition. They took the fame Courfe, only not exactly the fame Tract, and they ftay'd
thirty

thirty two Days only, in which time they killed
no lefs than fifteen Leopards, three Lions, and
feveral other Creatures, and brought us Home
four and twenty Pound, fome Ounces of Gold
Duft, and only fix Elephants Teeth, but they
were very great ones.

Our Friend the *Englifhman* fhewed us now, that
our Time was well beftow'd; for in five Months
which we had ftayed here, we had gathered fo
much Gold Duft, that when we came to fhare it,
we had five Pound and a Quarter to a Man, befides what we had before, and befides fix or feven
Pound Weight which we had at feveral times given our Artificer to make Baubles with; and now
we talk'd of going forward to the Coaft, to put
an End to our Journey; but our Guide laught at
us then: Nay you can't go now, *fays he*; for the
rainy Seafon begins next Month, and there will
be no ftirring then. This we found indeed reafonable, fo we refolved to furnifh our felves with
Provifions that we might not be obliged to go
abroad too much in the Rain, and we fpread our
felves fome one Way, fome another, as far as
we cared to venture, to get Provifions, and our
Negroes killed us fome Deer which we cured
as well as we could, in the Sun, for we had now
no Salt.

By this time the rainy Months were fet in,
and we could fcarce, for above two Months,
look out of our Hutts. But that was not all, for
the Rivers were fo fwelled with the Land Floods
that we fcarce knew the little Brooks and Rivulets from the great navigable Rivers. This had
been a very good Opportunity for to have convey'd by Water, upon Rafts, our Elephants
Teeth, of which we had a very great Pile; for

as

as we always gave the Savages fome Reward for
their Labour, the very Women would bring us
Teeth upon every Opportunity, and fometimes a
great Tooth carried between two; fo that our
Quantity was encreafed to about two and twenty
Ton of Teeth.

As foon as the Weather proved fair again, he
told us he would not prefs us to any further Stay,
fince we did not care whether we got any more
Gold or no; that we were indeed the firft Men
ever he met with in his Life, that faid they had
Gold enough, and of whom it might be truly faid,
that when it lay under our Feet, we would
not ftoop to take it up. But fince he had made
us a Promife, he would not break it, nor prefs
us to make any farther Stay, only he thought
he ought to tell us, that now was the Time,
after the Land Flood, when the greateft Quantity of Gold was found; and that if we ftayed
but one Month, we fhould fee Thoufands of Savages fpread themfelves over the whole Country,
to wafh the Gold out of the Sand, for the *Euro-*
pean Ships who would come on the Coaft; that they
do it then, becaufe the Rage of the Floods always
works down a great deal of Gold out of the
Hills; and if we took the Advantage to be there
before them, we did not know what extraordinary things we might find.

This was fo forcible, and fo well argued, that
it appeared in all our Faces we were prevailed
upon; fo we told him we would all ftay: For
tho' it was true we were all eager to be gone, yet
the evident Profpect of fo much Advantage,
could not well be refifted: That he was greatly
miftaken when he fuggefted, that we did not defire to encreafe our Store of Gold, and in that
we

we were refolved to make the utmoft Ufe of the
Advantage that was in our Hands, and would
ftay as long as any Gold was to be had, if it was
another Year.

He could hardly exprefs the Joy he was in on
this Occafion, and the fair Weather coming on,
we began juft as he directed, to fearch about
the Rivers for more Gold; at firft we had but
little Encouragement, and began to be doubtful,
but it was very plain that the Reafon was the
Water was not fully fallen, or the Rivers reduced
to there ufual Channel; but in a few Days we
were fully requited, and found much more Gold
than at firft, and in bigger Lumps; and one of
our Men wafhed out of the Sand a Piece of Gold
as big as a fmall Nut, which weighed by our Eftimation, for we had no fmall Weights, almoft an
Ounce and a half.

This Succefs made us extreamly diligent, and
in little more than a Month, we had all together
gotten near fixty Pound Weight of Gold;
but after this, as he told us, we found Abundance of the Savages, both Men, Women and
Children, hunting every River and Brook, and
even the dry Land of the Hills for Gold, fo that
we could do nothing like then, compared to what
we had done before.

But our Artificer found a Way to make other
People find us in Gold without our own Labour;
for when thefe People began to appear, he had a
confiderable Quantity of his Toys, Birds, Beafts,
&c. fuch as before, ready for them, and the *Englifh*
Gentleman being the Interpreter, he brought the
Savages to admire them; fo our Cutler had Trade
enough; and to be fure fold his Goods at a monftrous Rate; for he would get an Ounce of Gold,

N   fome-

fometimes two, for a Bit of Silver, perhaps of
the Value of a Groat, nay if it were Iron; and if
it was of Gold, they would not give the more
for it; and it was incredible almoft to think
what a Quantity of Gold he got that Way.

In a Word, to bring this happy Journey to a
Conclufion, we encreafed our Stock of Gold here
in three Months Stay more, to fuch a Degree,
that bringing it all to a common Stock, in order
to Share it, we divided almoft four Pound Weight
again to every Man, and then we fet forward
for the Gold Coaft, to fee what Method we
could find out for our Paffage into *Europe*.

There happened feveral very remarkable Incidents in this Part of our Journey, as to how we
were, or were not, received friendly, by the feveral
Nations of Savages through whom we paft; how
we delivered one Negroe King from Captivity,
who had been a Benefactor to our new Guide;
and how our Guide in Gratitude, by our Affiftance, reftored him to his Kingdom, which perhaps
might contain about 300 Subjects; how he entertained us; and how he made his Subjects go with
our *Englifhman*, and fetch all our Elephants
Teeth, which we had been obliged to leave behind us, and to carry them for us to the River,
the Name of which I forgot, where we made
Rafts, and in eleven Days more came down to
one of the *Dutch* Settlements on the Gold Coaft,
where we arrived in perfect Health, and to our
great Satisfaction. As for our Cargo of Teeth,
we fold it to the *Dutch* Factory, and received
Clothes and other Neceffaries for our felves, and
fuch of our Negroes as we thought fit to keep
with us; and it is to be obferved, that we had
four Pound of Gunpowder left when we ended

our

Journey. The *Negro Prince* we made perfectly
free, clothed him out of our common Stock,
and gave him a Pound and a half of Gold for
himself, which he knew very well how to manage, and here we all parted after the most friendly
Manner possible. Our *Englishman* remained in the
Dutch Factory some time, and, as I heard afterwards, died there of Grief; for he having sent a
Thousand Pound Sterling over to *England* by the
Way of *Holland*, for his Refuge, at his Return
to his Friends, the Ship was taken by the *French*,
and the Effects all lost.

The rest of my Comrades went away in a
small Bark, to the two *Portuguese* Factories, near
Gambia, in the Latitude of fourteen; and I with
two Negroes which I kept with me, went away
to *Cape Coast Castle*, where I got Passage for *England*, and arrived there in *September*; and thus
ended my first Harvest of *Wild Oats*, the rest
were not sowed to so much Advantage.

I had neither Friend, Relation, nor Acquaintance in *England*, tho' it was my Native Country, I had consequently no Person to trust with
what I had, or to counsel me to secure or save
it; but falling into ill Company, and trusting the
Keeper of a Publick House in *Rotherhith* with a
great Part of my Money, and hastily squander-
ing away the rest, all that great Sum, which I
got with so much Pains and Hazard, was gone
in little more than two Years Time; and as I even
rage in my own Thoughts to reflect upon the
Manner how it was wasted, so I need record no
more; the rest Merits to be conceal'd with Blushes,
for that it was spent in all Kinds of Folly and
Wickedness; so this Scene of my Life may be said

to

to have begun in Theft, and ended in Luxury; a fad Setting out, and a worfe Coming home.

About the Year   I began to fee the Bottom of my Stock, and that it was Time to think of farther Adventures, for my Spoilers, as I call them, began to let me know, that as my Money declined, their Refpect would ebb with it, and that I had nothing to expect of them farther than as I might command it by the Force of my Money, which in fhort would not go an Inch the farther, for all that had been fpent in their Favour before.

This fhocked me very much, and I conceived a juft Abhorrence of their Ingratitude; but it wore off; nor had I with it any Regret at the wafting fo glorious a Sum of Money, as I brought to *England* with me.

I next fhipped my felf, in an evil Hour to be fure, on a Voyage to *Cadiz*, in a Ship called the   and in the Courfe of our Voyage, being on the Coaft of *Spain*, was obliged to put in to the *Groyn*, by a ftrong South Weft Wind.

Here I fell into Company with fome Mafters of Mifchief, and among them, one forwarder than the reft, began an intimate Confidence with me, fo that we called one another Brothers, and communicated all our Circumftances to one another; his Name was *Harris*. This Fellow came to me one Morning, asking me if I would go on Shore, and I agreed; fo we got the Captain's Leave for the Boat, and went together. When we were together, he asked me if I had a Mind for an Adventure that might make amends for all paft Misfortunes; I told him yes, with all my Heart; for I did not care where I went, having nothing to lofe, and no Body to leave behind me.

He

He then asked me if I would fwear to be fecret, and that if I did not agree to what he propofed, I would neverthelefs never betray him;
I readily bound my felf to that, upon the moft
folemn Imprecations and Curfes that the Devil
and both of us could invent.

He told me then, there was a brave Fellow in
the other Ship, pointing to another *Englifh*
Ship which rode in the Harbour, who in Concert with fome of the Men had refolved to mutiny the next Morning, and run away with the
Ship; and that if we could get Strength enough
among our Ship's Company we might do the fame.
I liked the Propofal very well, and he got eight
of us to join with him, and he told us, that as
foon as his Friend had begun the Work, and was
Mafter of the Ship, we fhould be ready to do
the like; this was his Plot, and I without the
leaft Hefitation, either at the Villainy of the Faĉt,
or the Difficulty of performing it, came immediately into the wicked Confpiracy, and fo it
went on among us; but we could not bring our
Part to Perfeĉtion.

Accordingly on the Day appointed, his Cor-
refpondent in the other Ship, whofe Name was
Wilmot, began the Work, and having feized the
Captain's Mate, and other Officers, fecured the
Ship, and gave the Signal to us; we were but
eleven in our Ship, who were in the Confpiracy,
nor could we get any more that we could truft,
fo that leaving the Ship, we all took the Boat
and went off to join the other.

Having thus left the Ship I was in, we were
entertained with a great deal of Joy by Captain
Wilmot and his new Gang; and being well prepared for all manner of Roguery, bold, defpe-

rate,

rate, I mean my felf, without the leaft Checks
of Confcience, for what I was entred upon, or
for any Thing I might do, much lefs with any
Apprehenfion of what might be the Confequence of it; I fay, having thus embarked with
this Crew, which at laft brought me to confort
with the moft famous Pyrates of the Age, fome of
whom have ended their Journals at the Gallows:
I think the giving an Account of fome of my
other Adventures may be an agreeable Piece
of Story; and this I may venture to fay before
Hand, upon the Word of a P Y R A T E, that I
fhall not be able to recollect the full, no not by
far, of the great Variety which has formed one
of the moft reprobate Schemes that ever Man was
capable to prefent to the World.

I that was, as I have hinted before, an original
Thief, and a Pyrate even by Inclination before,
was now in my Element, and never undertook
any Thing in my Life with more particular Satisfaction.

Captain *Wilmot*, for fo we are now to call him,
being thus poffeffed of a Ship, and in the Manner
as you have heard, it may be eafily concluded
he had nothing to do to ftay in the Port, or to
wait either the Attempts which might be made
from the Shore, or any Change which might
happen among his Men. On the Contrary, we
weighed Anchor the fame Tide, and ftood out to
Sea, fteering away for the *Canaries*. Our Ship
had Twenty Two Guns, but was able to carry
Thirty; and befides, as fhe was fitted out for a
Merchant Ship only, fhe was not furnifhed either
with Ammunition or fmall Arms fufficient for
our Defign, or for the Occafion we might have
in Cafe of a Fight; fo we put into *Cadiz*, that is
to

to fay, we came to an Anchor in the Bay ; and the
Captain and one whom we call'd young Captain
Kid, who was the Gunner, and fome of the Men
who could beft be trufted, among whom was my
Comrade *Harris*, who was made fecond Mate,
and my felf who was made a Lieutenant ; fome
Bales of *Englifh* Goods were propofed to be carried on Shore with us for Sale ; but my Comrade,
who was a compleat Fellow at his Bufinefs, propofed a better Way for it ; and having been in
the Town before, told us in fhort, that he would
buy what Powder and Bullet, fmall Arms, or
any thing elfe we wanted, on his own Word, to
be paid for when they came on Board, in fuch
Englifh Goods as we had there. This was by much
the beft Way, and accordingly he and the Captain went on Shore by themfelves, and having made
fuch a Bargain as they found for their Turn, came
away again in two Hours time, and bringing only a Butt of Wine, and five Casks of Brandy with
them, we all went on Board again.

The next Morning two Barco Longo's came
off to us deep loaden, with five *Spaniards* on board
them, for Traffick. Our Captain fold them good
Pennyworths, and they delivered us fixteen Barrels of Powder, twelve fmall Runlets of fine Powder for our fmall Arms, fixty Mufquets, and
twelve Fuzees for the Officers ; feventeen Ton of
Cannon Ball, fifteen Barrels of MufquetBullets,
with fome Swords, and twenty good Pair of Piftols. Befides this, they brought thirteen Butts
of Wine (for we that were now all become Gen-
tlemen fcorn'd to drink the Ship's Beer) alfo fixteen Puncheons of Brandy, with twelve Barrels
of Raifins, and twenty Chefts of Lemons : All
which were paid for in *Englifh* Goods ; and over

and

and above, the Captain received 600 Pieces of Eight in Money. They would have come again, but we would stay no longer.

From hence we sailed to the *Canaries*, and from thence onward to the *West-Indies*, where we committed some Depredation upon the *Spaniards* for Provision, and took some Prizes, but none of any great Value, while I remained with them, which was not long at that Time; for having taken a *Spanish* Sloop on the Coast of *Cartagena*, my Friend made a Motion to me, that we should desire Captain *Wilmot* to put us into the Sloop, with a Proportion of Arms and Ammunition, and let us try what we could do; she being much fitter for our Business than the great Ship, and a better Sailer. This he consented to, and we appointed our Rendezvous at *Tobago*, making an Agreement, that whatever was taken by either of our Ships, should be shared among the Ship's Company of both; all which we very punctually observed, and join'd our Ships again about fifteen Months after, at the Island of *Tobago*, as above.

We cruised near two Years in those Seas, chiefly upon the *Spaniards*; not that we made any Difficulty of taking *English* Ships, or *Dutch*, or *French*, if they came in our Way; and particularly Captain *Wilmot* attack'd a *New-England* Ship bound from the *Maderas* to *Jamaica*; and another bound from *New-York* to *Berbadoes*, with Provisions; which last was a very happy Supply to us. But the Reason why we meddled as little with *English* Vessels as we could, was, first, because, if they were Ships of any Force, we were sure of more Resistance from them; and secondly, because we found the *English* Ships had less Booty when taken; for the *Spaniards* generally had Money on board, and

and that was what we beſt knew what to do with. Captain *Wilmot* was indeed more particularly cruel when he took any *Engliſh* Veſſel, that they might not too ſoon have Advice of him in *England*, and ſo the Men of War have Orders to look out for him. But this Part I bury in Silence for the preſent.

We encreaſed our Stock in theſe two Years conſiderably, having taken 60000 Pieces of Eight in one Veſſel, and 100000 in another ; and being thus firſt grown rich, we reſolved to be ſtrong too ; for we had taken a Brigantine built at *Virginia*, an excellent Sea Boat, and a good Sailer, and able to carry twelve Guns ; and a large *Spaniſh* Frigat-built Ship, that ſailed incomparably well alſo, and which afterwards, by the Help of good Carpenters, we fitted up to carry twenty eight Guns. And now we wanted more Hands, ſo we put away for the Bay of *Campeachy*, not doubting we ſhould ſhip as many Men there as we pleaſed, and ſo we did.

Here we ſold the Sloop that I was in ; and Captain *Wilmot* keeping his own Ship, I took the Command of the *Spaniſh* Frigat, as Captain, and my Comrade *Harris* as eldeſt Lieutenant, and a bold enterprizing Fellow he was as any the World afforded. One *Culverdine* was put into the Brigantine, ſo that we were now three ſtout Ships, weil Mann'd, and Victualled for twelve Months ; for we had taken two or three Sloops from *New-England* and *New-York*, loaden with Flour , Peaſe, and Barrell'd Beef, and Pork, going for *Jamaica* and *Berbadoes* ; and for more Beef we went on Shore on the Iſle of *Cuba*, where we killed as many black Cattel as we pleaſed, tho' we had very little Salt to cure them.

Out

Out of all the Prizes we took here, we took their Powder and Bullet, their small Arms and Cutlasses; and as for their Men, we always took the Surgeon and the Carpenter, as Persons who were of particular Use to us upon many Occasions; nor were they always unwilling to go with us, tho' for their own Security, in Case of Accidents, they might easily pretend they were carried away by Force, of which I shall give a pleasant Account in the Course of my other Expeditions.

We had one very merry Fellow here, a Quaker, whose Name was *William Walters*, whom we took out of a Sloop bound from *Penfilvania* to *Berbadoes*. He was a Surgeon, and they called him Doctor; but he was not employed in the Sloop as a Surgeon, but was going to *Berbadoes* to get a *Birth*, as the Sailors call it. However, he had all his Surgeon's Chest on board, and we made him go with us, and take all his Implements with him. He was a comick Fellow indeed, a Man of very good solid Sense, and an excellent Surgeon; but what was worth all, very good humour'd and pleasant in his Conversation, and a bold, stout, brave Fellow too, as any we had among us.

I found *William*, as I thought, not very averse to go along with us, and yet resolved to do it so, that it might be apparent he was taken away by Force; and to this Purpose he comes to me, Friend, says he, thou sayest I must go with thee, and it is not in my Power to resist thee, if I would; but I desire thou wilt oblige the Master of the Sloop which I am on board, to certify under his Hand that I was taken away by Force, and against my Will; and this he said with so

much

much Satisfaction in his Face, that I could not but understand him. Ay, ay, *says I*, whether it be against your Will, or no, I'll make him and all the Men give you a Certificate of it, or I'll take them all along with us, and keep them till they do: So I drew up the Certificate my self, wherein I wrote that he was taken away by main Force, as a Prisoner, by a Pyrate Ship; that they carried away his Chest and Instruments first, and then bound his Hands behind him, and forced him into their Boat; and this was signed by the Master and all his Men.

Accordingly I fell a swearing at him, and called to my Men to tye his Hands behind him, and so we put him into our Boat, and carry'd him away. When I had him on board, I called him to me: Now, Friend, says I, I have brought you away by Force, it is true, but I am not of the Opinion I have brought you away so much against your Will as they imagine: Come, says I, you will be a useful Man to us, and you shall have very good Usage among us; so I unbound his Hands, and first ordered all things that belonged to him to be restored to him, and our Captain gave him a Dram.

Thou hast dealt friendly by me, says he, and I'll be plain with thee, whether I came willingly to thee, or not: I shall make my self as useful to thee as I can; but thou knowest it is not my Business to meddle when thou art to fight. No, no, says the Captain, but you may meddle a little when we share the Money. Those things are useful to furnish a Surgeon's Chest, says *William*, and smiled; but I shall be moderate.

In short, *William* was a most agreeable Companion, but he had the better of us in this Part,
that

that, if we were taken, we were fure to be hang'd, and he was fure to efcape; and he knew it well enough: But in fhort he was a fprightly Fellow, and fitter to be Captain than any of us. I fhall have often an Occafion to fpeak of him in the reft of the Story.

Our Cruifing fo long in thefe Seas began now to be fo well known, that not in *England* only, but in *France* and *Spain*, Accounts had been made publick of our Adventures, and many Stories told how we murthered the People in cold Blood, tying them Back to Back, and throwing them into the Sea; one Half of which however was not true, tho' more was done than it is fit to fpeak of here.

The Confequence of this however was, that feveral *Englifh* Men of War were fent to the *Weft Indies*, and were particularly inftructed to cruize in the Bay of *Mexico*, and the Gulph of *Florida*, and among the *Bahama* Iflands, if poffible, to attack us.

We were not fo ignorant of things, as not to expect this, after fo long a Stay in that Part of the World; but the firft certain Account we had of them, was at the *Honduras*, when a Veffel coming in from *Jamaica*, told us, that two *Englifh* Men of War were coming directly from *Jamaica* thither, in Queft of us. We were indeed as it were embay'd, and could not have made the leaft Shift to have got off, if they had come directly to us; but as it happen'd, fome body had informed them that we were in the Bay of *Campeachy*, and they went directly thither, by which we were not only free of them, but were fo much to the Windward of them, that they could not make

any

any Attempt upon us, tho' they had known we were there.

We took this Advantage, and ftood away for *Carthagena*, and from thence with great Difficulty beat it up at a Diftance from under the Shore for St. *Martha*, till we came to the *Dutch* Ifland of *Curafoe*, and from thence to the Ifland of *Tobago*; which, as before, was our Rendezvous; which being a deferted uninhabited Ifland, we at the fame time made ufe of for a Retreat: Here the Captain of the *Brigantine* died, and Captain *Harris* at that time my Lieutenant, took the Command of the *Brigantine*.

Here we came to a Refolution, to go away to the Coaft of *Brafil*, and from thence to the Cape of *Good Hope*, and fo for the *Eaft-Indies*: But Captain *Harris*, as I have faid, being now Captain of the *Brigantine*, alledged that his Ship was too fmall for fo long a Voyage; but that if Captain *Wilmot* would confent, he would take the Hazard of another Cruize, and he would follow us in the firft Ship he could take: So we appointed our Rendezvous to be at *Madagafcar*, which was done by my Recommendation of the Place, and the Plenty of Provifions to be had there.

Accordingly he went away from us *in an evil Hour*, for inftead of taking a Ship to follow us, he was taken, as I heard afterwards, by an *Englifh* Man of War, and being laid in Irons, died of meer Grief and Anger before he came to *England*: His Lieutenant, I have heard, was afterwards executed in *England* for a Pyrate, and this was the End of the Man who firft brought me into this unhappy Trade.

We

We parted from *Tobago* three Days after, bending our Courſe for the Coaſt of *Braſil*, but had not been at Sea above Twenty Four Hours, when we were ſeparated by a terrible Storm, which held three Days, with very little Abatement or Intermiſſion. In this Juncture, Captain *Wilmot* happen'd unluckily to be on board my Ship, very much to his Mortification; for we not only loſt Sight of his Ship, but never ſaw her more, till we came to *Madagaſcar*, where ſhe was caſt away. In ſhort, after having in this Tempeſt loſt our Fore-Top Maſt, we were forced to put back to the Iſle of *Tobago* for Shelter, and to repair our Damage, which brought us all very near our Deſtruction.

We were no ſooner on Shore here, and all very buſy looking out for a Piece of Timber for a Top-Maſt, but we perceived ſtanding in for the Shore, an *Engliſh* Man of War of Thirty ſix Guns: It was a great Surprize to us indeed, becauſe we were diſabled ſo much, but to our great good Fortune we lay pretty ſnug and cloſe among the high Rocks, and the Man of War did not ſee us, but ſtood off again upon his Cruiſe; ſo we only obſerved which Way ſhe went, and at Night leaving our Work, reſolved to ſtand off to Sea, ſteering contrary Way from that which we obſerved ſhe went. And this we found had the deſired Succeſs, for we ſaw him no more: We had gotten an old Mizen Top-Maſt on board, which made us a Jury Fore-Top-Maſt for the preſent, and ſo we ſtood away for the Iſle *Trinidad*, where, though there were *Spaniards* on Shore, yet we landed ſome Men with our Boat, and cut a very good Piece of Fir to make us a

new

new Top-Maſt, which we got fitted up effectually, and alſo we got ſome Cattle here to eke out our Proviſions, and calling a Council of War among our ſelves, we reſolved to quit thoſe Seas for the preſent, and ſteer away for the Coaſt of *Braſil*.

The firſt thing we attempted here, was only getting freſh Water; but we learnt, that there lay the *Portugueſe* Fleet at the Bay of *All-Saints*, bound for *Lisbon*, ready to ſail, and only waited for a fair Wind; this made us lye by, wiſhing to ſee them put to Sea, and accordingly as they were, with, or without Convoy, to attack or avoid them.

It ſprung up a freſh Gale in the Evening, at S. W. by W. which being fair for the *Portugal* Fleet, and the Weather pleaſant and agreeable, we heard the Signal given to unmore, and running in under the Iſland of *Si*—— we hauled our Main-Sail and Fore-Sail up in the Brails, lower'd the Top-Sail upon the Cap, and clewed them up that we might lye as ſnug as we could, expecting their coming out; and the next Morning ſaw the whole Fleet come out accordingly, but not at all to our Satisfaction, for they conſiſted of Twenty ſix Sail, and moſt of them Ships of Force, as well as Burthen, both Merchant Men and Men of War; ſo ſeeing there was no meddling, we lay ſtill where we was alſo, till the Fleet was out of Sight, and then ſtood off and on, in hopes of meeting with further Purchaſe.

It was not long before we ſaw a Sail, and immediately gave her Chaſe, but ſhe proved an excellent Sailer, and ſtanding out to Sea, we ſaw plainly ſhe truſted to her Heels, that is to ſay, to her Sails; however, as we were a clean Ship we gained upon her, tho' ſlowly, and had we had a

Day

Day before us, we fhould certainly have come up with her, but it grew dark apace, and in that Cafe we knew we fhould lofe Sight of her.

Our merry Quaker perceiving us to crowd ftill after her in the Dark, wherein we could not fee which way fhe went, come very drily to me; *Friend* Singleton, fays he, *doeft thee know what we are a doing?* Says I, *yes, why we are chafing yon Ship, are we not?* And *how doft thou know that,* fays he very gravely ftill? *Nay, that is true,* fays I again, *we cannot be fure. Yes Friend,* fays he, *I think we may be fure that we are running away from her, not chafing her. I am afraid,* adds he, *thou art turned Quaker, and haft refolved not to ufe the Hand of Power, or art a Coward, and art flying from thy Enemy.*

What do you mean, fays I, I think I fwore at him; *what do ye fneer at now? you have always one dry Rub or another to give us.*

Nay, fays he, *it's plain enough, the Ship ftood off to Sea, due Eaft on purpofe to lofe us, and thou may'ft be fure her Bufinefs does not lie that Way; for what fhould fhe do at the Coaft of* Africa *in this Latitude, which would be as far South as* Congo *or* Angola; *but as foon as it is dark, that we fhall lofe Sight of her, fhe will tack and ftand away Weft again for the* Brafil *Coaft, and for the Bay, where thou knoweft fhe was going before; and are not we then a running away from her?* I am greately in hopes, Friend, *fays the dry gibing Creature,* Thou wilt turn Quaker, for I fee thou art not for Fighting.

Very well WILLIAM, fays I, *then I fhall make an excellent Pyrate.* However, *William* was in the right, and I apprehended what he meant immediately, and Captain *Wilmot,* who lay very fick in his Cabin, overhearing us, underftood him as well as
I, and

I, and called out to me, that *William* was right, and it was our beſt Way to change our Courſe, and ſtand away for the Bay, where it was Ten to one but we ſhould ſnap her in the Morning.

Accordingly, we went about ſnip, got our Larboard Tacks on board, ſet the Top-gallant Sails, and crowded for the Bay of *All-Saints*, where we came to an Anchor, early in the Morning juſt out of Gun Shot of the Forts; we furl'd our Sails with Rope-Yarns, that we might haul home the Sheets without going up to looſe them, and lowering our Main and Fore-Yards, looked juſt as if we had lain there a good while.

In two Hours after, we ſaw our Game, ſtanding in for the Bay with all the Sail ſhe could make, and ſhe came innocently into our very Mouths, for we lay ſtill, till we ſaw her almoſt within Gun Shot; when our Fore Maſt Geers being ſtretched fore and aft, we firſt run up our Yards, and then hauled home the Top-Sail Sheets; the Rope-Yarns that furled them giving Way of themſelves, the Sails were ſet in a few Minutes; at the ſame time ſlipping our Cable, we came upon her before ſhe could get under Way upon 'tother Tack: They were ſo ſurprized, that they made little or no Reſiſtance, but ſtruck after the firſt Broad-Side.

We were conſidering what to do with her, when *William* came to me. *Hark thee Friend,* ſays he, *thou haſt made a fine Spot of Work of it now, haſt thou not? To borrow thy Neighbour's Ship here, juſt at thy Neighbour's Door, and never ask him Leave; now doſt thou not think there are ſome Men of War in the Port, thou haſt given them the Alarm ſufficiently; thou will have them upon thy Back before Night, depend upon it, to ask thee, wherefore, Thou diſt ſo?*

O   *Truly*

Truly William, said I, *for ought I know, that may be true : What then shall we do next ?* Says he, *thou hast but two Things to do, either go in and take all the rest, or else get thee gone before they come out, and take thee ; for I see they are hoisting a Top-Mast to yon great Ship, in order to put to Sea immediately, and they won't be long before they come to talk with thee ; and what wilt thou say to them, when they ask thee why thou borrowedst their Ship without Leave ?*

As *William* said, so it was, we could see by our Glasses that they were all in a Hurry, manning and fitting some Sloops they had there, and a large Man of War, and it was plain they would soon be with us; but we were not at a Loss what to do; we found the Ship we had taken was loaden with nothing considerable for our Purpose, except some Cocoa, some Sugar, and Twenty Barrels of Flower; the rest of her Loading was Hides; so we took out all we thought for our Turn, and among the rest all her Ammunition, great Shot, and small Arms, and turned her off; we also took a Cable and three Anchors she had, which were for our Purpose, and some of her Sails; she had enough left just to carry her into Port, and that was all.

Having done this, we stood on upon the *Brasil* Coast, Southward, till we came to the Mouth of the River *Janiero* : But as we had two Days the Wind blowing hard at S. E. and S. S. E. we were obliged to come to an Anchor under a little Island, and wait for a Wind. In this time the *Portuguese* had it seems given Notice over Land to the Governour there, that a Pyrate was upon the Coast ; so that when we came in View of the Port, we saw two Men of War riding just without the Bar, whereof one we found was

get-

getting under Sail with all poffible Speed, having
flipt her Cable, on purpofe to fpeak with us;
the other was not fo forward, but was preparing
to follow: In lefs than an Hour they ftood both
fair after us, with all the Sail they could make.

Had not the Night come on, *William*'s Words
had been made good; they would certainly
have asked us the Queftion what we did there?
for we found the foremoft Ship gained upon us,
efpecially upon one Tack; for we plied away
from them to Windward, but in the Dark lofing
Sight of them, we refolved to change our Courfe,
and ftand away directly to Sea, not doubting but
we fhould lofe them in the Night.

Whether the *Portuguéfe* Commander gueffed
we would do fo or no, I know not; but in the
Morning when the Day-light appeared, inftead
of having loft him, we found him in Chafe of us,
about a League a-Stern; only to our great good
Fortune we could fee but one of the two; however this one was a great Ship, carried fix and
forty Guns, and an admirable Sailer, as appeared
by her out-failing us; for our Ship was an excellent Sailer too, as I have faid before.

When I found this, I eafily faw there was no
Remedy, but we muft engage; and as we knew
we could expect no Quarters from thofe Scoun-
drels the *Portuguefe*, a Nation I had an original
Averfion to, I let Captain *Wilmot* know how
it was. The Captain, fick as he was, jumped
up in the Cabin, and would be led out upon the
Deck, for he was very weak, to fee how it was;
well, *fays he*, we'll fight them.

Our Men were all in good heart before, but to
fee the Captain fo brisk who had lain ill of a Ca-
lenture Ten or Eleven Days, gave them double

Cou-

Courage, and they went all Hands to work to make a clear Ship and be ready. *William* the Quaker comes to me with a kind of a Smile; Friend, fays he, what does yon Ship follow us for? Why fays I, to fight us you may be fure; Well, fays he, and will he come up with us doft thou think? Yes, faid I, you fee fhe will. Why then, Friend, fays the dry Wretch, why doft thou run from her ftill, when thou feeft fhe will over-take thee? Will it be better for us to be over-taken further off than here? Much at one for that, fays I; why what would you have us do? Do! fays he, let us not give the poor Man more Trouble than needs muft; let us ftay for him, and hear what he has to fay to us; he will talk to us in Powder and Ball faid I : Very well then, fays he if that be his Country Language, we muft talk to him in the fame, muft we not? Or elfe how fhall he underftand us? Very well *William*, fays I, we underftand you; and the Captain as ill as he was, called to me, *William*'s right again, fays he, as good here as a League further; fo he gives a Word of Command, *Haul up the Main-Sail*, we'll fhorten Sail for him.

Accordingly we fhortened Sail; and as we expected her upon our Lee Side, we being then upon our Starboard Tack, brought 18 of our Guns to the Larboard Side, refolving to give him a Broad-Side that fhould warm him ; it was about half an Hour before he came up with us, all which time we luffed up, that we might keep the Wind of him, by which he was obliged to run up under our Lee, as we defigned him; when we got him upon our Quarter we edg'd down, and received the Fire of five or fix of his Guns; by this time you may be fure all our Hands were at their

their Quarters, so we clapt our Helm hard *a Weather*, let go the Lee Braces of the Main Top-sail, and laid it a-back, and so our Ship fell athwart the *Portuguese* Ship's Hawse; then we immediately poured in our Broad-Side, raking them fore and aft, and killed them a great many Men.

The *Portuguese*, we could see were in the utmost Confusion; and not being aware of our Design, their Ship having fresh Way, run their Boltsprit into the fore Part of our main Shrouds, as that they could not easily get clear of us, and so we lay locked after that Manner, the Enemy could not bring above five or six Guns, besides their Small-Arms, to bear upon us, while we played our whole Broadside upon him.

In the middle of the Heat of this Fight, as I was very busy upon the Quarter Deck, the Captain calls to me, for he never stirred from us, what the Devil is Friend *William* a-doing yonder, says the Captain, has he any Business upon Deck? I stept forward, and there was Friend *William* with two or three stout Fellows lashing the Ships Bolt-sprit fast to our Main-Mast, for fear they should get away from us; and every now and then he pulled a Bottle out of his Pocket and gave the Men a Dram to encourage them. The Shot flew about his Ears as thick as may be supposed in such an Action, where the *Portuguese*, to give them their due, fought very briskly, believing at first they were sure of their Game, and trusting to their Superiority; but there was *William*, as composed, and in as perfect Tranquillity as to Danger, as if he had been over a Bowl of Punch, only very busy securing the Matter, that a Ship of Fourty six Guns should not run away from a Ship of Eight and Twenty.

The

This Work was too hot to hold long; our Men behaved bravely; our Gunner, a gallant Man, shouted below, pouring in his Shot at such a Rate, that the *Portuguese* began to slacken their Fire; we had dismounted several of their Guns by firing in at their Forecastle, and raking them, as I said, fore and aft; and presently comes *William* up to me; *Friend* says he, very calmly, *What doest thou mean? Why dost thou not visit thy Neighbour in the Ship, the Door being open for thee?* I understood him immediately, for our Guns had so tore their Hull, that we had beat two Port Holes into one, and the Bulk Head of their Steerage was split to Pieces, that they could not retire to their close Quarters; so I gave the Word immediately to board them. Our Second Lieutenant, with about Thirty Men, entered in an Instant over the Forecastle, followed by some more, with the Boatswain, and cutting in Pieces about Twenty five Men that they found upon the Deck, and then throwing some Grenadoes into the Steerage, they entered there also; upon which the *Portuguese* cried Quarter presently, and we mastered the Ship, contrary indeed to our own Expectation; for we would have compounded with them, if if they would have sheered off, but laying them athwart the Hawse at first, and following our Fire furiously, without giving them any time to get clear of us, and work their Ship, by this means, tho' they had six and forty Guns, they were not able to Fight above five or six, as I said above, for we beat them immediately from their Guns in the Forecastle, and killed them Abundance of Men between Decks, so that when we entered they had hardly found Men enough to fight us Hand to Hand upon their Deck.

The

The Surprize of Joy, to hear the *Portuguese*
cry Quarter, and fee their Antient ftruck, was
fo great to our Captain, who as I have faid, was
reduced very weak with a high Fever, that it
gave him new Life ; Nature conquered the Di-
ftemper, and the Fever abated that very Night:
So that in two or three Days he was fenfibly better, his Strength began to come, and he was able
to give his Orders effectually in every thing that
was material, and in about ten Days was entirely
well, and about the Ship.

In the mean time, I took Poffeffion of the *Portuguefe* Man of War, and Captain *Wilmot* made me,
or rather I made my felf, Captain of her for the
prefent; about Thirty of their Seamen took Service with us, fome of which were *French*, fome
Genoefes, and we fet the reft on Shore the next
Day, on a little Ifland on the Coaft of *Brafil*, except fome wounded Men who were not in a Condition to be removed; and whom we were bound to
keep on board, but we had an Occafion afterwards
to difpofe of them at the Cape, where at their
own Requeft we fet them on Shore.

Captain *Wilmot*, as foon as the Ship was taken,
and the Prifoners ftowed, was for ftanding in
for the River *Janiero* again, not doubting but we
fhould meet with the other Man of War, who
not having been able to find us, and having loft
the Company of her Comrade, would certainly
be returned, and might be furprized by the Ship
we had taken, if we carryed *Portuguefe* Colours,
and our Men were all for it.

But our Friend *William* gave us better Counfel;
for he came to me, Friend, fays he, I underftand
the Captain is for failing back to the *Rio Janiero*,

in

in Hopes to meet with the other Ship that was
in Chafe of thee yefterday; is it true, doft thou
intend it? Why, yes, fays I, *William*, pray why
not? Nay, *fays he*, thou mayft do fo if thou
wilt. Well, I know that too, *William*, faid I;
but the Captain is a Man will be ruled by Reafon; what have you to fay to it? Why, fays
William gravely, I only ask what is thy Bufinefs,
and the Bufinefs of all the People thou haft with
thee? Is it not to get Money? Yes, *William*, it is
fo, in our honeft Way: And wouldft thou, fays
he, rather have Money without Fighting, or
Fighting without Money? I mean, which wouldft
thou have by Choice, fuppofe it to be left to
thee? O *William*, fays I, the firft of the two, to
be fure. Why then, *fays he*, what great Gain
haft thou made of the Prize thou haft taken now,
tho' it has coft the Lives of thirteen of thy
Men, befides fome hurt? It is true, thou haft
got the Ship and fome Prifoners, but thou wouldft
have had twice the Booty in a Merchant Ship,
with not one Quarter of the Fighting; and how
doft thou know either what Force, or what Number of Men may be in the other Ship, and what
Lofs thou mayft fuffer, and what Gain it fhall be
to thee, if thou take her? I think indeed thou
mayft much better let her alone.

Why, *William*, it is true faid I, and I'll go tell
the Captain what your Opinion is, and bring
you Word what he fays. Accordingly I went
to the Captain, and told him *William*'s Reafons,
and the Captain was of his Mind, that our Bufinefs was indeed Fighting when we could not help
it, but that our main Affair was Money, and
that with as few Blows as we could; fo that Adventure was laid afide, and we ftood along Shore
again

again South, for the River *de la Plata*, expecting
some Purchase thereabouts; especially we had
our Eyes upon some of the *Spanish* Ships from the
Bruenos Ayres, which are generally very rich in
Silver, and one such Prize would have done our
Business. We ply'd about here in the Latitude
of   South for near a Month, and nothing offer'd; and here we began to consult what
we should do next, for we had come to no Resolution yet. Indeed my Design was always for the
Cape de Bona Speranza, and so to the *East Indies*.
I had heard some flaming Stories of Captain *Avery*,
and the fine things he had done in the *Indies*,
which were doubled and doubled even Ten Thou-
sand-fold, and from taking a great Prize in the
Bay of *Bengal*, where he took a Lady said to be
the *Great Mogul*'s Daughter, with a great Quantity of Jewels about her. We had a Story told
us, that he took a *Mogul* Ship, so the foolish Sailors called it, loaden with Diamonds.

I would fain have had Friend *William*'s Advice,
whither we should go, but he always put it off
with some *Quaking* Quibble or other. In short,
he did not care for directing us neither; whether
he made a Piece of Conscience of it, or whether
he did not care to venture having it come against
him afterwards, or no, this I know not; but we
concluded at last without him.

We were however pretty long in resolving,
and hanker'd about the *Rio de la Plata* a long
time; at last we spy'd a Sail to Windward, and
it was such a Sail as I believe had not been seen in
that Part of the World a great while; it wanted
not that we should give it Chase, for it stood directly towards us, as well as they that steer'd
could make it; and even that was more Accident

of

of Weather than any thing elſe : For if the Wind
had chopt about any where, they muſt have gone
with it. I leave any Man that is a Sailor, or un-
derſtands any thing of a Ship, to judge what a
Figure this Ship made when we firſt ſaw her,
and what we could imagine was the Matter with
her. Her Main Top-Maſt was come by the Board,
about ſix Foot above the Cap, and fell forward,
the Head of the Top-gallant Maſt, hanging in
the Fore Shrouds by the Stay ; at the ſame time
the Pareil of the Mizen Topſail Yard, by
ſome Accident giving Way, the Mizen Topſail Braces (the ſtanding Part of which being
faſt to the Main Topſail Shrouds) brought the
Mizen Topſail, Yard and all, down with it,
which ſpread over Part of the Quarter Deck like
an Awning : The Fore-Topſail was hoiſted up
two Thirds of the Maſt, but the Sheets were
flown. The Fore Yard was lower'd down upon
the Forecaſtle, the Sail looſe, and Part of it
hanging over-board. In this Manner ſhe came
down upon us with the Wind quartering : In a
Word, the Figure the whole Ship made, was the
moſt confounding to Men that underſtood the Sea,
that ever was ſeen ; ſhe had no Boat, neither had
ſhe any Colours out.

When we came near to her, we fired a Gun to
bring her to. She took no Notice of it, nor of
us, but came on juſt as ſhe did before. We fired
again, but 'twas all one : At length we came within Piſtol Shot of one another, but no body anſwered nor appeared ; ſo we began to think that
it was a Ship gone aſhore ſomewhere in Diſtreſs,
and the Men having forſaken her, the high Tide
had floated her off to Sea. Coming nearer to her,
we run up along Side of her ſo cloſe, that we
could

could hear a Noise within her, and fee the Motion of feveral People thro' her Ports.

Upon this we Mann'd our two Boats full of Men, and very well armed, and ordered them to board her at the fame Minute, as near as they could, and to enter one at her Fore-chains on one Side, and the other a Mid-fhip on the other Side. As foon as they came to the Ship's Side, a furprizing Multitude of black Sailors, *fuch as they were*, appeared upon Deck, and in fhort, terrify'd our Men fo much, that the Boat which was to enter her Men in the Wafte, ftood off again, and durft not board her; and the Men that enter'd out of the other Boat, finding the firft Boat, as they thought, beaten off, and feeing the Ship full of Men, jump'd all back again into their Boat, and put off, not knowing what the Matter was. Upon this we prepared to pour in a Broadfide upon her. But our Friend *William* fet us to Rights again here; for it feems he guefs'd how it was fooner than we did, and coming up to me (for it was our Ship that came with her) Friend, fays he, I am of Opinion thou art wrong in this Matter, and thy Men have been wrong alfo in their Conduct: I'll tell thee how thou fhalt take this Ship, without making ufe of thofe things call'd Guns. How can that be, *William*, faid I? Why, faid he, thou mayft take her with thy Helm; thou feeft they keep no Steerage, and thou feeft the Condition they are in; board her with thy Ship upon her Lee Quarter, and fo enter her from the Ship: I am perfwaded thou wilt take her without Fighting, for there is fome Mifchief has befallen the Ship, which we know nothing of,

In

In a Word, it being a smooth Sea, and little
Wind, I took his Advice, and lay'd her aboard.
Immediately our Men entred the Ship, where
we found a large Ship with upwards of 600 Negroes, Men and Women, Boys and Girls, and not
one Christian, or white Man, on board.

I was struck with Horror at the Sight, for
immediately I concluded, as was partly the Case,
that these black Devils had got loose, had murthered all the white Men, and thrown them into the Sea; and I had no sooner told my Mind
to the Men, but the Thought of it so enraged
them, that I had much ado to keep my Men
from cutting them all in Pieces. But *William*,
with many Perswasions prevailed upon them,
by telling of them, that it was nothing but what,
if they were in the Negroes Condition, they
would do, if they could; and that the Negroes
had really the highest Injustice done them, to be
sold for Slaves without their Consent; and that
the Law of Nature dictated it to them; that they
ought not to kill them, and that it would be
wilful Murder to do it.

This prevailed with them, and cooled their
first Heat; so they only knock'd down twenty
or thirty of them, and the rest run all down
between Decks, to their first Places, believing,
as we fancy'd, that we were their first Masters
come again.

It was a most unaccountable Difficulty we had
next, for we could not make them understand
one Word we said, nor could we understand one
Word our selves that they said. We endeavoured by Signs to ask them whence they came,
but they could make nothing of it; we pointed
to the Great Cabin, to the Round-house, to the
Cook-

Cook-room, then to our Faces, to ask if they had no white Men on board, and where they were gone? But they could not underſtand what we meant: On the other Hand, they pointed to our Boat, and to their Ship, asking Queſtions as well as they could, and ſaid a Thouſand things, and expreſſed themſelves with great Earneſtneſs, but we could not underſtand a Word of it all, or know what they meant by any of their Signs.

We knew very well they muſt have been taken on board the Ship as Slaves, and that it muſt be by ſome *European* People too. We could eaſily ſee that the Ship was a *Dutch*-built Ship, but very much alter'd, having been built upon, and as we ſuppoſe, in *France*; for we found two or three *French* Books on board, and afterwards we found Clothes, Linnen, Lace, ſome old Shoes, and ſeveral other things: We found among the Proviſions, ſome Barrels of *Iriſh* Beef, ſome *New-foundland* Fiſh, and ſeveral other Evidences that there had been Chriſtians on board, but ſaw no Remains of them. We found not a Sword, Gun, Piſtol, or Weapon of any kind, except ſome Cutlaſſes; and the Negroes had hid them below where they lay. We ask'd them what was become of all the ſmall Arms, pointing to our own, and to the Places where thoſe belonging to the Ship had hung: One of the Negroes underſtood me preſently, and beckon'd to me to come up upon the Deck, where taking my Fuzee, which I never let go out of my Hand for ſome time after we had maſter'd the Ship; I ſay, offering to take hold of it, he made the proper Motion of throwing it into the Sea, by which I underſtood, as I did afterwards, that they had thrown all the ſmall Arms, Powder, Shot, Swords, &c. in-

to

to the Sea, believing, as I fuppofed, thofe things
would kill them, tho' the Men were gone.

After we underftood this, we made no Queftion but that the Ship's Crew having been furprized by thefe defperate Rogues, had gone the fame
Way, and had been thrown over-board alfo. We
look'd all over the Ship, to fee if we could find
any Blood, and we thought we did perceive fome
in feveral Places; but the Heat of the Sun melt-
ing the Pitch and Tar upon the Decks, made it
impoffible for us to difcern it exactly, except in
the Round-houfe, where we plainly faw that
there had been much Blood. We found the
Skuttle open, by which we fuppofed the Captain
and thofe that were with him had made their
Retreat into the Great Cabin, or thofe in the
Cabin had made their Efcape up into the Round-
houfe.

But that which confirmed us moft of all in
what had happen'd, was, that upon farther Enquiry we found that there were feven or eight
of the Negroes very much wounded, two or
three of them with Shot; whereof one had his
Leg broke, and lay in a miferable Condition, the
Flefh being mortified, and, as our Friend *William*
faid, in two Days more he would have died.
William was a moft dexterous Surgeon, and he
fhew'd it in this Cure; for tho' all the Surgeons
we had on board both our Ships (and we had no
lefs than five that called themfelves bred Surgeons, befides two or three who were Pretenders or
Affiftants) and all thefe gave their Opinion that
the Negroe's Leg muft be cut off, and that his
Life could not be faved without it; that the
Mortification had touch'd the Marrow in the
Bone, that the Tendons were mortified, and that
he

he could never have the Use of his Leg, if it
should be cured. *William* said nothing in general, but that his Opinion was otherwise, and that
he desired the Wound might be search'd, and
that he would then tell them farther. Accordingly he went to Work with the Leg, and, as
he desired he might have some of the Surgeons
to assist him, we appointed him two of the ablest
of them to help, and all of them to look on, if
they thought fit.

William went to Work his own Way, and some
of them pretended to find Fault at first. However, he proceeded, and search'd every Part of
the Leg where he suspected the Mortification had
touch'd it : In a Word, he cut off a great deal
of mortified Flesh ; in all which the poor Fellow
felt no Pain. *William* proceeded till he brought
the Vessels which he had cut to bleed, and the
Man to cry out : Then he reduced the Splinters
of the Bone, and calling for Help, *set it, as we call
it,* and bound it up, and laid the Man to Rest,
who found himself much easier than before.

At the first Opening, the Surgeons began to
triumph, the Mortification seem'd to spread, and
a long red Streak of Blood appeared from the
Wound upwards to the Middle of the Man's
Thigh, and the Surgeons told me the Man would
die in a few Hours. I went to look at it, and
found *William* himself under some Surprize ; but
when I ask'd him how long he thought the poor
Fellow could live, he look'd gravely up at me,
and said, *As long as thou canst :* I am not at all
apprehensive of his Life, said he, but I would
cure him if I could, without making a Cripple of
him. I found he was not just then upon the Ope-
ration, as to his Leg, but was mixing up something

thing to give the poor Creature, to repel, as I thought, the spreading Contagion, and to abate or prevent any feverish Temper that might happen in the Blood: After which he went to Work again, and open'd the Leg in two Places above the Wound, cutting out a great deal of mortified Flesh, which it seems was occasioned by the Bandage which had press'd the Parts too much, and withal, the Blood being at that time in a more than common Disposition to mortify, might assist to spread it.

Well, our Friend *William* conquer'd all this, clear'd the spreading Mortification, that the red Streak went off again, the Flesh began to heal, and Matter to run; and in a few Days the Man's Spirits began to recover, his Pulse beat regular, he had no Fever, and gathered Strength daily; and in a Word he was a perfect sound Man in about ten Weeks, and we kept him amongst us, and made him an able Seaman. But to return to the Ship, we never could come at a certain Information about it, till some of the Negroes which we kept on board, and whom we taught to speak *English*, gave the Account of it afterwards, and this maim'd Man in particular.

We enquired by all the Signs and Motions we could imagine, what was become of the People, and yet we could get nothing from them. Our Lieutenant was for torturing some of them to make them confess; but *William* opposed that vehemently; and when he heard it was under Consideration, he came to me, Friend, says he, I make a Request to thee, not to put any of these poor Wretches to Torment. Why, *William*, said I, why not? You see they will not give any Account of what is become of the white
Men.

Men. Nay, says *William*, do not say so; I suppose they have given thee a full Account of every Particular of it. How so, says I, pray what are we the wiser for all their Jabbering? Nay, says *William*, that may be thy Fault, for ought I know; thou wilt not punish the poor Men because they cannot speak *English*, and perhaps they never heard a Word of *English* before. Now I may very well suppose, that they have given thee a large Account of every thing; for thou seest with what Earnestness, and how long some of them have talk'd to thee, and if thou canst not understand their Language, nor they thine, how can they help that; at the best thou doest but suppose that they have not told thee the whole Truth of the Story, and on the contrary I suppose they have, and how wilt thou decide the Question, whether thou art right, or whether I am right? Besides, what can they say to thee, when thou askest them a Question upon the Torture, and at the same time they do not understand the Question, and thou doest not know whether they say *Ay* or *No*?

It is no Complement to my Moderation, to say I was convinc'd by these Reasons; and yet we had all much ado to keep our second Lieutenant from murthering some of them to make them tell. What if they had told, he did not understand one Word of it; but he would not be perswaded but that the Negroes must needs understand him, when he ask'd them, whether the Ship had any Boat or no, like ours, and what was become of it?

But there was no Remedy but to wait till we made these People understand *English*; and to adjourn the Story till that time. The Case was

P   thus.

thus. Where they were taken on board the Ship, that we could never underſtand, becauſe they never knew the *Engliſh* Names which we give to thoſe Coaſts, or what Nation they were who belong'd to the Ship, becauſe they knew not one Tongue from another ; but thus far the Negroe I examin'd, who was the ſame whoſe Leg *William* had cured, told us, that they did not ſpeak the ſame Language we ſpoke, nor the ſame our *Portugueze* ſpoke ; ſo that in all Probability they muſt be *French* or *Dutch*.

Then he told us, that the white Men uſed them barbarouſly ; that they beat them unmercifully ; that one of the Negroe Men had a Wife, and two Negroe Children, one a Daughter about ſixteen Years old ; that a White Man abuſed the Negroe Man's Wife, and afterwards his Daughter, which, as he ſaid, made all the Negroe Men mad; and that the Woman's Husband was in a great Rage, at which the White Man was ſo provoked, that he threaten'd to kill him ; but in the Night, the Negroe Man being looſe, got a great Club, by which he made us underſtand he meant a Handſpike, and that when the ſame *Frenchman* (*if it was a* Frenchman) came among them again, he began again to abuſe the Negroe Man's Wife ; at which the Negroe taking up the Handſpike, knock'd his Brains out at one Blow; and then taking the Key from him with which he uſually unlock'd the Hand-cuffs which the Negroes were fetter'd with, he ſet about a Hundred of them at Liberty, who getting up upon the Deck by the ſame Skuttle that the White Man came down ; and taking the Man's Cutlaſs who was killed, and laying hold of what came next them, they fell upon the Men that were

were upon the Deck, and killed them all, and afterwards thofe they found upon the Forecaftle; that the Captain and his other Men, who were in the Cabin and the Round-houfe, defended themfelves with great Courage, and fhot out at the Loopholes at them, by which he and feveral other Men were wounded, and fome killed; but that they broke into the Round-houfe after a long Difpute, where they killed two of the white Men, but own'd that the two white Men killed eleven of their Men before they could break in; and then the reft having got down the Skuttle into the Great Cabin, wounded three more of them.

That after this, the Gunner of the Ship having fecured himfelf in the Gun-room, one of his Men haul'd up the Long-Boat clofe under the Stern, and putting into her all the Arms and Ammunition they could come at, got all into the Boat, and afterwards took in the Captain, and thofe that were with him, out of the Great Cabin. When they were all thus embark'd, they refolved to lay the Ship aboard again, and try to recover it; that they boarded the Ship in a defperate Manner, and killed at firft all that ftood in their Way; but the Negroes being by this time all loofe, and having gotten fome Arms, tho' they underftood nothing of Powder and Bullet, or Guns; yet the Men could never mafter them. However, they lay under the Ship's Bow, and got out all the Men they had left in the Cook-room, who had maintained themfelves there, notwithftanding all the Negroes could do, and with their fmall Arms killed between thirty and forty of the Negroes, but were at laft forc'd to leave them.

They

They could give me no Account whereabouts this was, whether near the Coast of *Africk,* or far off, or how long it was before the Ship fell into our Hands; only in general, it was a great while ago, *as they called it,* and by all we could learn, it was within two or three Days after they had set Sail from the Coast. They told us, that they had killed about thirty of the white Men, having knock'd them on the Head with Crows and Hand-spikes, and such things as they could get; and one strong Negroe killed three of them with an Iron Crow, after he was shot twice thro' the Body, and that he was afterwards shot thro' the Head by the Captain himself at the Door of the Round-house, which he had split open with the Crow ; and this we suppose was the Occasion of the great Quantity of Blood which we saw at the Round-house Door.

The same Negroe told us, that they threw all the Powder and Shot they could find, into the Sea, and they would have thrown the great Guns into the Sea, if they could have lifted them. Being ask'd how they came to have their Sails in such a Condition, his Answer was, *they no understand, they no know what the Sails do* ; that was, they did not so much as know that it was the Sails that made the Ship go ; or understand what they meant, or what to do with them. When we asked him whither they were going, he said, they did not know, but believed they should go Home to their own Country again. I asked him in particular, what he thought we were, when we came first up with them ? He said, they were terribly frighted, believing we were the same white Men that had gone away in their Boats, and were come again in a great Ship, with
the

the two Boats with them, and expected they
would kill them all.

This was the Account we got out of them,
after we had taught them to speak *English*, and
to understand the Names and Use of the things
belonging to the Ship, which they had Occasion to speak of, and we observed that the Fellows were too innocent to dissemble in their
Relation, and that they all agreed in the Particulars, and were always in the same Story,
which confirm'd very much the Truth of what
they said.

Having taken this Ship, our next Difficulty
was, what to do with the Negroes. The *Portugueze* in the *Brasils* would have bought them all of
us, and been glad of the Purchase, if we had
not shew'd our selves Enemies there, and been
known for Pyrates; but as it was, we durst not
go on Shore any where thereabouts, or treat with
any of the Planters, because we should raise the
whole Country upon us; and if there were any
such things as Men of War in any of their
Ports, we should be assured to be attack'd by
them, and by all the Force they had by Land
or Sea.

Nor could we think of any better Success,
if we went Northward to our own Plantations.
One while we determined to carry them all away
to the *Buenos Ayres*, and sell them there to the
Spaniards; but they were really too many for
them to make Use of; and to carry them round
to the South-Seas, which was the only Remedy
that was left, was so far, that we should be
no Way able to subsist them for so long a
Voyage.

At laſt, our old never-failing Friend *William* help'd us out again, as he had often done, at a Dead-lift. His Propoſal was this, that he ſhould go as Maſter of the Ship, and about twenty Men ſuch as we could beſt truſt, and attempt to trade privately upon the Coaſt of *Braſil*, with the Planters, not at the principal Ports, becauſe that would not be admitted.

We all agreed to this, and appointed to go away our ſelves towards the *Rio de la Plata*, where we had Thought of going before, and to wait for him not there, but at *Port St. Pedro*, as the *Spaniards* call it, lying at the Mouth of the River which they call *Rio Grande*, and where the *Spaniards* had a ſmall Fort, and a few People, but we believe there was no Body in it.

Here we took up our Station, cruiſing off and on, to ſee if we could meet any Ships going to, or coming from the *Buenos Ayres*, or the *Rio de la Plata*; but we met with nothing worth Notice. However, we employed our ſelves in things neceſſary for our going off to Sea; for we filled all our Water Casks, and got ſome Fiſh for our preſent Uſe, to ſpare as much as poſſible our Ship's Stores.

William in the mean time went away to the North, and made the Land about the *Cape de St. Thomas*, and betwixt that and the Iſles *de Tuberon*, he found Means to trade with the Planters for all his Negroes, as well the Women as the Men, and at a very good Price too; for *William*, who ſpoke *Portugueſe* pretty well, told them a fair Story enough, that the Ship was in Scarcity of Proviſions, that they were driven a great Way out of their Way, and indeed, *as we ſay,* out of their Knowledge, and that they muſt go

up

up to the Northward as far as *Jamaica*, or fell
there upon the Coaft. This was a very plau-
fible Tale, and was eafily believed; and if you
obferve the Manner of the Negroes Sailing, and
what happened in their Voyage, was every Word
of it true.

By this Method, and being true to one another, *William* paft for what he was; I mean, for
a very honeft Fellow, and by Affiftance of one
Planter, who fent to fome of his Neighbour
Planters, and managed the Trade among themfelves, he got a quick Market; for in lefs than
five Weeks, *William* fold all his Negroes, and at
laft fold the Ship it felf, and fhipp'd himfelf and
his twenty Men, and two Negroe Boys whom he
had left, in a Sloop, one of thofe which the Planters ufed to fend on board for the Negroes.
With this Sloop Captain *William*, as we then called him, came away, and found us at *Port St. Pedro*, in the Latitude of 32 Degrees, 30 Minutes
South.

Nothing was more furprizing to us, than to
fee a Sloop come along the Coaft, carrying *Portugueze* Colours, and come in directly to us, after
we were affured he had difcovered both our
Ships. We fired a Gun upon her nearer Ap-
proach, to bring her to an Anchor, but immediately fhe fired five Guns by Way of Salute,
and fpread her *English* Antient : Then we began
to guefs it was Friend *William*, but wondered
what was the Meaning of his being in a Sloop,
whereas we fent him away in a Ship of near
300 Tuns; but he foon let us into the whole
Hiftory of his Management, with which we had
a great deal of Reafon to be very well fatisfy'd.
As foon as he had brought the Sloop to an An-

P 4   chor,

chor, he came aboard of my Ship, and there
he gave us an Account how he began to
trade, by the Help of a *Portugueze* Planter,
who lived near the Sea-fide; how he went
on Shore, and went up to the firft Houfe he
could fee, and asked the Man of the Houfe to
fell him fome Hoggs, pretending at firft he only ftood in upon the Coaft to take in frefh Water, and buy fome Provifions; and the Man not
only fold him feven fat Hoggs, but invited him
in, and gave him and five Men he had with him,
a very good Dinner, and he invited the Planter
on board his Ship, and in Return for his Kindnefs, gave him a Negroe Girl for his Wife.

This fo obliged the Planter, that the next
Morning he fent him on board, in a great
Luggage Boat, a Cow and two Sheep, with a
Cheft of Sweet-meats, and fome Sugar, and a
great Bag of Tobacco, and invited Captain *William*
on Shore again: That after this, they grew from
one Kindnefs to another, that they began to talk
about Trading for fome Negroes; and *William*
pretending it was to do him Service, confented
to fell him thirty Negroes for his private Ufe
in his Plantation, for which he gave *William*
ready Money in Gold, at the Rate of five and
thirty Moydores *per* Head; but the Planter was
obliged to ufe great Caution in the bringing them
on Shore: For which Purpofe, he made *William*
weigh and ftand out to Sea, and put in again,
above fifty Miles farther North, where at a
little Creek he took the Negroes on Shore at
another Plantation, being a Friend's of his whom
it feems he could truft.

This Remove brought *William* into a farther In-
timacy, not only with the firft Planter, but alfo
with

with his Friends, who defired to have fome of the Negroes alfo ; fo that from one to another, they bought fo many, till one over-grown Planter took 100 Negroes, which was all *William* had left, and fharing them with another Planter, that other Planter chaffer'd with *William* for Ship and all, giving him in Exchange a very clean, large, well-built Sloop of near fixty Tons, very well furnifh'd, carrying fix Guns, but we made her afterwards carry twelve Guns. *William* had 300 Moydores of Gold, befides the Sloop, in Payment for the Ship, and with this Money, he ftored the Sloop as full as fhe could hold with Provifions, efpecially Bread, fome Pork, and about fixty Hoggs alive : Among the reft, *William* got eighty Barrels of good Gunpowder, which was very much for our Purpofe, and all the Provifions which were in the *French* Ship he took out alfo.

This was a very agreeable Account to us, efpecially when we faw, that *William* had received in Gold coin'd, or by Weight, and fome *Spanifh* Silver, 60000 Pieces of Eight, befides a new Sloop, and a vaft Quantity of Provifions.

We were very glad of the Sloop in particular, and began to confult what we fhould do, whether we had not beft turn off our great *Portuguefe* Ship, and ftick to our firft Ship and the Sloop, feeing we had fcarce Men enough for all three, and that the biggeft Ship was thought too big for our Bufinefs ; however, another Difpute which was now decided, brought the firft to a Conclufion. The firft Difpute was, whither we fhould go ? My Comrade, as I called him now, that is to fay, he that was my Captain before we took this *Portuguefe* Man of War, was for going to the South Seas, and coafting up the Weft Side of *America*, where

where we could not fail of making several good Prizes upon the *Spaniards* and that then if Occasion required, we might come home by the South-Seas to the *Eaſt-Indies* and ſo go round the Globe as others had done before us.

But my Head lay another Way, I had been in the *Eaſt-Indies*, and had entertained a Notion ever ſince that, that if we went thither we could not fail of making good Work of it, and that we might have a ſafe Retreat, and good Beef to Victual our Ship, among my old Friends the Natives of *Zamguebar*, on the Coaſt of *Mozambique*, or the Iſland of St. *Laurence*: I ſay, my Thoughts lay this Way and I read ſo many Lectures to them all, of the Advantages they would certainly make of their Strength, by the Prizes they would take in the Gulph of *Mocha* or the *Red-Sea*, and on the Coaſt of *Malabar* or the Bay of *Bengal*, that I amaz'd them.

With theſe Arguments I prevailed on them, and we all reſolved to ſteer away S. E. for the Cape of *Good Hope* ; and in Conſequence of this Reſolution, we concluded to keep the Sloop, and ſail with all three, not doubting, as I aſſured them, but we ſhould find Men there to make up the Number wanting, and if not, we might caſt any of them off when we pleaſed.

We could do no leſs than make our Friend *William* Captain of the Sloop, which with ſuch good Management he had brought us. He told us, tho' with much good Manners, he would not command her as a Fregat, but if we would give her to him for his Share of the *Guinea* Ship, which we came very honeſtly by, he would keep us Company as a Victualler, if we commanded him, as long as he was under the ſame Force that took him away.

We

We underftood him, fo we gave him the Sloop, but upon Condition that he fhould not go from us, and fhould be entirely under our Command: However, *William* was not fo eafy as before; and indeed, as we afterwards wanted the Sloop, to cruife for Purchafe, and a Right thorow-paced Pyrate in her; fo I was in fuch Pain for *William*, that I could not be without him, for he was my Privy-Counfellour and Companion upon all Occafions; fo I put a *Scotfman*, a bold enterprizing gallant Fellow into her, named *Gordon*, and made her carry 12 Guns, and four Paterero's, though indeed we wanted Men, for we were none of us Mann'd in Proportion to our Force.

We failed away for the Cape of *Good Hope*, the Beginning of *October* 1706, and paffed by in Sight of the Cape, the 12 of *November* following, having met with a great deal of bad Weather: We faw feveral Merchant Ships in the Road there, as well *English* as *Dutch*, whether outward bound or homeward we could not tell; *be it what it would*, we did not think fit to come to an Anchor, not knowing what they might be, or what they might attempt againft us, when they knew what we were: However, as we wanted frefh Water, we fent the two Boats belonging to the *Portuguefe* Man of War, with all *Portuguefe* Seamen or *Negroes* in them, to the Watering Place, to take in Water: And in the mean time we hung out a *Portuguefe* Antient at Sea, and lay by all that Night. They knew not what we was, but it feems we paft for any thing but really what we was.

Our Boats returning the third time loaden, about five a Clock next Morning, we thought our felves fufficiently water'd, and ftood away

to

to the Eaftward; but before our Men returned
the laft time, the Wind blowing an eafy Gale at
Weft, we perceived a Boat in the Grey of the
Morning, under Sail, crowding to come up with
us, as if they were afraid we fhould be gone.
We foon found it was an *Englifh* Long-Boat, and
that it was pretty full of Men; we could not
imagine what the Meaning of it fhould be; but
as it was but a Boat, we thought there could
be no great Harm in it to let them come on
board: And if it appeared they came only to
enquire who we were, we would give them a full
Account of our Bufinefs, by taking them along
with us, feeing we wanted Men as much as any
thing; but they faved us the Labour of being in
doubt how to difpofe of them, for it feems our
Portuguefe Seamen who went for Water, had not
been fo filent at the Watering Place, as we
thought they would have been. But the Cafe,
in fhort was this. Captain   , *I forbear
his Name at prefent, for a particular Reafon,* Captain
of an *Eaft India* Merchant Ship, bound afterwards for *China,* had found fome Reafon to be
very fevere with his Men, and had handled fome
of them very roughly at St. *Helena*; infomuch,
that they threaten'd among themfelves to leave
the Ship the firft Opportunity, and had long
wifh'd for that Opportunity: Some of thefe
Men, it feems, had met with our Boat at the Watering Place, and enquiring of one another who
we were, and upon what Account; whether the
Portuguefe Seamen, by faultring in their Account,
made them fufpect that we were out upon the
Cruife, or whether they told it in plain *Englifh,*
or no (for they all fpoke *Englifh* enough to be underftood) but fo it was, that as foon as ever the

Men

Men carried the News on board, that the Ships which lay by to the Eaftward were *Englifh*, and that they were going upon *the Account*, which by the Way was a Sea Term for a Pyrate; I fay, as foon as ever they heard it, they went to work, and getting all things ready in the Night, their Chefts and Clothes, and whatever elfe they could, they came away before it was Day, and came up with us about feven a Clock.

When they came by the Ship's Side which I commanded, we hailed them in the ufual Manner, to know what and who they were, and what their Bufinefs? They anfwered, they were *Englifhmen*, and defired to come aboard : We told them they might lay the Ship on board, but ordered they fhould let only one Man enter the Ship, till the Captain knew their Bufinefs, and that he fhould come without any Arms: They faid Ay, with all their Hearts.

We prefently found their Bufinefs, and that they defired to go with us; and as for their Arms, they defired we would fend Men on board the Boat, and that they would deliver them all to us, which was done. The Fellow that came up to me, told me how they had been ufed by their Captain, how he had ftarved the Men, and ufed them like Dogs; and that if the reft of the Men knew they fhould be admitted, he was fatisfied two Thirds of them would leave the Ship. We found the Fellows were very hearty in their Refolution, and jolly brisk Sailors they were; fo I told them I would do nothing without our Admiral, that was, the Captain of the other Ship: So I fent my Pinnace on board Captain *Wilmot*, to defire him to come on board; but he was indifpofed, and being to Leeward, excufed his coming,

but

but left it all to me: But before my Boat was returned, Captain *Wilmot* called to me by his Speaking Trumpet, which all the Men might hear as well as I, thus, calling me by my Name, *I hear they are honest Fellows, pray tell them they are all welcome, and make them a Bowl of Punch.*

As the Men heard it as well as I, there was no need to tell them what the Captain said; and as soon as the Trumpet had done, they set up a Huzza that shewed us they were very hearty in their coming to us; but we bound them to us by a stronger Obligation still, after this: For when we came to *Madagascar*, Captain *Wilmot*, with Consent of all the Ship's Company, ordered that these Men should have as much Money given them out of the Stock, as was due to them for their Pay in the Ship they had left; and after that, we allowed them Twenty Pieces of Eight a Man Bounty Money: And thus we entred them upon Shares, as we were all, and brave stout Fellows they were, being Eighteen in Number, whereof two were Midship-Men, and one a Carpenter.

It was the 28th of *November*, when having had some bad Weather, we came to an Anchor in the Road off of St. *Augustine* Bay, at the South West End of my old Acquaintance the Isle of *Madagascar*: We lay here a while, and traffick'd with the Natives for some good Beef, tho' the Weather was so hot, that we could not promise our selves to salt any of it up to keep; but I shewed them the Way which we practised before, to salt it first with *Salt-Petre*, then cure it, by drying it in the Sun, which made it eat very agreeably, tho' not so wholesome for our Men, that not agreeing with our Way of Cooking, *viz.* Boiling with Pudding,

ding, Brewes, &c. and particularly this Way would be too falt, and the Fat of the Meat be refty, or dry'd away, fo as not to be eaten.

This however we could not help, and made our felves amends by feeding heartily on the frefh Beef while we were there, which was excellent good and fat, every Way as tender, and as well relifhed as in *England*, and thought to be much better to us who had not tafted any in *England* for fo long a Time.

Having now for fome time remained here, we began to confider that this was not a Place for our Bufinefs; and I that had fome Views, a particular Way of my own, told them, that this was not a Station for thofe that look'd for Purchafe; that there were two Parts of the Ifland which were particularly proper for our Purpofes; firft the Bay on the Eaft Side of the Ifland, and from thence to the Ifland *Mauritius*, which was the ufual Way which Ships that came from the *Malabar* Coaft, or the Coaft of *Coromandel*, Fort *St. George*, &c. ufed to take, and where, if we waited for them, we ought to take our Station.

But on the other Hand, as we did not refolve to fall upon the *European* Traders, who were generally Ships of Force, and well Manned, and where Blows muft be looked for; fo I had another Profpect, which I promifed my felf would yield equal Profit, or perhaps greater, without any of the Hazard and Difficulty of the former, and this was the Gulph of *Mocha* or the *Red Sea*.

I told them that the Trade here was great, the Ships rich, and the Streight of *Babelmandel* narrow; fo that there was no doubt but we might cruife fo as to let nothing flip our Hands, having the

Seas

Seas open from the *Red Sea* along the Coaſt of *Arabia,* to the *Perſian* Gulph, and the *Malabar* Side of the *Indies.*

I told them, what I had obſerved when I ſailed round the Iſland, in my former Progreſs, how that on the Northmoſt Point of the Iſland were ſeveral very good Harbours, and Roads for our Ships: That the Natives were even more civil, and traƈtable, if poſſible, than thoſe where we were, not having been ſo often ill treated by *European* Sailors, as thoſe had in the South and Eaſt Sides; and that we might always be ſure of a Retreat, if we were driven to put in by any Neceſſity, either of Enemies or of Weather.

They were eaſily convinced of the Reaſonableneſs of my Scheme, and Captain *Wilmot,* whom I now called our Admiral, tho' he was at firſt of the Mind to go and lye at the Iſland *Mauritius,* and wait for ſome of the *European* Merchant Ships from the Road of *Coromandel,* or the Bay of *Bengal,* was now of my Mind. It is true, we were ſtrong enough to have attacked an *Engliſh Eaſt India* Ship of the greateſt Force, though ſome of them were ſaid to carry fifty Guns; but I repreſented to him, that we were ſure to have Blows, and Blood if we took them, and after we had done, their Loading was not of equal Value to us, becauſe we had no room to diſpoſe of their Merchandize: And as our Circumſtances ſtood, we had rather have taken one outward bound *Eaſt India* Ship, with her ready Caſh on board, perhaps to the Vallue of forty or fifty Thouſand Pound, than three homeward bound, though their Loading would at *London* be worth three times the Money; becauſe, we knew not whither to go to diſpoſe of the Cargo; whereas
the

the Ships from *London* had Abundance of things
we knew how to make ufe of, befides their Money; fuch as their Stores of Provifions, and Liquors, and great Quantities of the like fent to
the Governours and Factories at the *Englifh* Settlements, for their Ufe: So that if we refolved to
look for our own Country Ships, it fhould be
thofe that were outward bound, not the *London*
Ships homeward.

All thefe things confidered, brought the
Admiral to be of my Mind entirely; fo after taking in Water, and fome frefh Provifions where we lay, which was near *Cape St. Mary*,
on the South-Weft Corner of the Ifland, we
weighed, and ftood away South, and afterwards
S. S. E. to round the Ifland, and in about fix Days
Sail, got out of the Wake of the Ifland, and
fteer'd away North, till we came off of *Port
Dauphin*, and then North by Eaft, to the Latitude
of 13 Degrees, 40 Minutes, which was, in fhort,
juft at the fartheft Part of the Ifland; and the
Admiral keeping a-head, made the open Sea fair
to the Weft, clear of the whole Ifland; upon
which he brought to, and we fent the Sloop to
ftand in round the fartheft Point North, and
coaft along the Shore, and fee for a Harbour
to put into, which they did, and foon brought
us an Account, that there was a deep Bay, with
a very good Road, and feveral little Iflands under
which they found good Riding, in 10 to 17 Fathom Water, and accordingly there we put in.

However, we afterwards found Occafion to
remove our Station, as you fhall hear prefently.
We had now nothing to do, but go on Shore,
and acquaint our felves a little with the Natives,
take in frefh Water, and fome frefh Provifions,

Q   and

and then to Sea again. We found the People very eafy to deal with, and fome Cattel they had;
but it being at the Extremity of the Ifland,
they had not fuch Quantities of Cattel here.
However, for the prefent, we refolved to appoint this for our Place of Rendezvous, and go
and look out. This was about the latter End
of *April.*

Accordingly we put to Sea, and cruifed away
to the Northward, for the *Arabian* Coaft: It was
a long Run; but as the Winds generally blow
Trade from the South, and S. S. E. from *May*
to *September,* we had good Weather, and in about
twenty Days we made the Ifland of *Saccatia,*
lying South from the *Arabian* Coaft, and E. S. E.
from the Mouth of the Gulph of *Mocha,* or the
Red Sea.

Here we took in Water, and ftood off and on
upon the *Arabian* Shore. We had not cruifed
here above three Days, or thereabouts, but I
fpy'd a Sail, and gave her Chafe; but when we
came up with her, never was fuch a poor Prize
chafed by Pyrates that look'd for Booty; for we
found nothing in her, but poor, half-naked *Turks*
going a Pilgrimage to *Mecca,* to the Tomb of
their Prophet *Mahomet*; the Jonk that carry'd
them had no one thing worth taking away, but
a little Rice, and fome Coffee, which was all the
poor Wretches had for their Subfiftence; fo we
let them go, for indeed we knew not what to do
with them.

The fame Evening we chafed another Jonk
with two Mafts, and in fomething better Plight
to look at than the former. When we came
on board, we found them upon the fame Errand,
but only that they were People of fome better

Fafhion

Fashion than the other ; and here we got fome
Plunder, fome *Turkifh* Stores, a few Diamonds in
the Ear-drops of five or fix Perfons, fome fine
Perfian Carpets, of which they made their Saffra's
to lye upon, and fome Money ; fo we let them go
alfo.

We continued here eleven Days longer, and
faw nothing but now and then a Fifhing-Boat ;
but the twelfth Day of our Cruife, we fpy'd a
Ship : Indeed I thought at firft it had been an
Englifh Ship, but it appeared to be an *European*
freighted for a Voyage from *Goa*, on the Coaft of
Malabar, to the Red Sea, and was very rich. We
chafed her, and took her, without any Fight,
tho' they had fome Guns on board too, but not
many. We found her Manned with *Portuguefe*
Seamen, but under the Direction of five Merchant *Turks*, who had hired her on the Coaft of
Malabar, of fome *Portugal* Merchants, and had
loaden her with Pepper, Salt-petre, fome Spices,
and the reft of the Loading was chiefly Callicoes
and wrought Silks, fome of them very rich.

We took her, and carried her to *Saccatia*, but
we really knew not what to do with her, for the
fame Reafons as before ; for all their Goods were
of little or no Value to us. After fome Days we
found Means to let one of the *Turkifh* Merchants
know, that if he would ranfom the Ship, we
would take a Sum of Money, and let them go.
He told me, if I would let one of them go on
Shore for the Money, they would do it : So we
adjufted the Value of the Cargo at 30000 Du-
cats. Upon this Agreement we allowed the Sloop
to carry him on Shore at *Dofar* in *Arabia*, where
a rich Merchant laid down the Money for them,
and came off with our Sloop ; and on Payment

of

of the Money, we very fairly and honeftly let
them go.

Some Days after this, we took an *Arabian* Jonk
going from the Gulph of *Perfia* to *Mocha*, with a
good Quantity of Pearl on board; we gutted
him of the Pearl, which, it feems, was belonging to fome Merchants at *Mocha*, and let him go,
for there was nothing elfe worth our taking.

We continued cruifing up and down here, till
we began to find our Provifions grow low, when
Captain *Wilmot* our Admiral told us, 'twas time
to think of going back to the Rendezvous, and
the reft of the Men faid the fame, being a little
weary of beating about for above three Months
together, and meeting with little or nothing com-
par'd to our great Expectations. But I was very
loath to part with the Red Sea at fo cheap a Rate,
and prefs'd them to tarry a little longer, which
at my Inftance we did; but three Days afterwards, to our great Misfortune, underftood, that
by Landing the *Turkifh* Merchants at *Dofar*, we
had alarmed the Coaft as far as the Gulph of
Perfia, fo that no Veffel would ftir that Way, and
confequently nothing was to be expected on that
Side.

I was greatly mortify'd at this News, and
could no longer withftand the Importunities of
the Men, to return to *Madagafcar*. However, as
the Winds continued ftill to blow at S. S. E. to
E. by S. we were obliged to ftand away towards
the Coaft of *Africa*, and the *Cape Guarde Foy*, the
Winds being more variable under the Shore, than
in the open Sea.

Here we chopp'd upon a Booty which we did
not look for, and which made Amends for all our
Waiting; for the very fame Hour that we made

Land,

Land, we fpy'd a large Veffel failing along the Shore, to the Southward. The Ship was of *Bengal*, belonging to the Great *Mogul*'s Country, but had on board a *Dutch* Pilot, whofe Name, if I remember right, was *Vanderdieft*, and feveral *European* Seamen, whereof three were *Englifh*. She was in no Condition to refift us ; the reft of her Seamen were *Indians* of the *Mogul*'s Subjects, fome *Malabars*, and fome others. There were five *Indian* Merchants on board, and fome *Armenian:* It feems they had been at *Mocha* with Spices, Silks, Diamonds, Pearls, Callicoe, &c. fuch Goods as the Country afforded, and had little on board now but Money in Pieces of Eight, which, by the Way, was juft what we wanted ; and the three *Englifh* Seamen came along with us, and the *Dutch* Pilot would have done fo too ; but the two *Armenian* Merchants entreated us not to take him ; for that he being their Pilot, there was none of the Men knew how to guide the Ship: So, at their Requeft, we refufed him ; but we made them promife he fhould not be ufed ill for being willing to go with us.

We got near 200000 Pieces of Eight in this Veffel ; and if they faid true, there was a *Jew* of *Goa* who intended to have embark'd with them, who had 200000 Pieces of Eight with him, all his own ; but his good Fortune fpringing out of his ill Fortune, hinder'd him, for he fell 'fick at *Mocha*, and could not be ready to travel, which was the Saving of his Money.

There was none with me at the Taking this Prize, but the Sloop ; for Captain *Wilmot*'s Ship proving leaky, he went away for the Rendezvous before us, and arrived there the Middle of *December* ; but not liking the Port, he left a great Crofs

on

on Shore, with Directions written on a Plate of
Lead fixt to it, for us to come after him to the
great Bay of *Mangahelly*, where he found a very good Harbour ; but we learnt a Piece of News
here, that kept us from him a great while, which
the Admiral took Offence at; but we ftopt his
Mouth with his Share of 200000 Pieces of Eight
to him and his Ship's Crew. But the Story which
interrupted our coming to him was this. Between
Mangahelly and another Point called *Cape St. Seba-
ftian*, there came on Shore in the Night, an
European Ship ; and whether by Strefs of Weather, or Want of a Pilot, I know not, but the
Ship ftranded, and could not be got off.

We lay in the Cove, or Harbour, where, as
I have faid, our Rendezvous was appointed, and
had not yet been on Shore, fo we had not feen
the Directions our Admiral had left for us.

Our Friend *William*, of whom I have faid nothing a great while, had a great Mind one Day
to go on Shore, and importuned me to let him
have a little Troop to go with him, for Safety,
that they might fee the Country. I was mightily againft it for many Reafons ; but particularly
I told him, he knew the Natives were but Savages, and they were very treacherous, and I defired him that he would not go; and had he gone
on much farther, I believe I fhould have downright refufed him, and commanded him not to
go.

But in order to perfwade me to let him go,
he told me, he would give me an Account of the
Reafon why he was fo importunate. He told
me, the laft Night he had a Dream, which was
fo forcible, and made fuch an Impreffion upon
his Mind, that he could not be quiet till he had
made

made the Propofal to me to go, and if I refufed him, then he thought his Dream was figni-
ficant, and if not, then his Dream was at an
End.

His Dream was, he faid, that he went on Shore
with 30 Men, of which the Cockfwain he faid
was one, upon the Ifland, and that they found a
Mine of Gold, and enrich'd them all; but this
was not the main thing he faid, but that the
fame Morning he had dreamt fo, the Cockfwain
came to him juft then, and told him, that he
dreamt he went on Shore on the Ifland of *Madagafcar*, and that fome Men came to him and
told him, they would fhew him where he fhould
get a Prize would make them all rich.

Thefe two things put together began to weigh
with me a little, tho' I was never inclined to
give any Heed to Dreams ; but *William*'s Importunity turn'd me effectually, for I always put
a great deal of Strefs upon his Judgment : So
that in fhort, I gave them Leave to go; but I
charged them not to go far off from the Sea Coaft,
that if they were forced down to the Sea-Side
upon any Occafion, we might perhaps fee them,
and fetch them off with our Boats.

They went away early in the Morning, one and
thirty Men of them in Number, very well arm'd,
and very ftout Fellows; they travell'd all the Day,
and at Night made us a Signal that all was well,
from the Top of a Hill, which we had agreed on,
by making a great Fire.

Next Day they march'd down the Hill on the
other Side, inclining towards the Sea-Side, as
they had promifed, and faw a very pleafant Valley
before them with a River in the Middle of it,
which a little farther below them feemed to be

Q 4   big

big enough to bear small Ships: They marched
a-pace towards this River, and were surprized
with the Noise of a Piece going off, which by
the Sound could not be far off; they listened
long, but could hear no more, so they went
on to the River Side, which was a very fine
fresh Stream, but widened a-pace, and they
kept on by the Banks of it, till almost at once
it opened or widened into a good large Creek,
or Harbour, about five Miles from the Sea;
and that which was still more surprizing, as
they marched forward, they plainly saw in
the Mouth of the Harbour, or Creek, the Wreck
of a Ship.

The Tide was up, as we call it, that did not
appear very much above the Water, but as they
made downwards, they found it grew bigger,
and bigger, and the Tide soon after ebbing out,
they found it lay dry upon the Sands, and appeared to be the Wreck of a considerable
Vessel, larger than could be expected in that
Country.

After some time, *William* taking out his Glass
to look at it more nearly, was surprized with
hearing a Musquet Shot whistle by him, and
immediately after that, he heard the Gun, and
saw the Smoke from the other Side; upon which
our Men immediately fired three Musquets to
discover, if possible, what or who they were.
Upon the Noise of these Guns, Abundance of Men
came running down to the Shore, from among
some Trees, and our Men could easily perceive
that they were *Europeans*, tho' they knew not of
what Nation: However, our Men halloo'd to
them, as loud as they could, and by and by
they got a long Pole, and set it up, and hung a
white

white Shirt upon it for a Flag of Truce. They
on the other Side faw it, by the help of their
Glaſſes too, and quickly after, our Men fee
a Boat launch off from the Shore, as they
thought, but it was from another Creek it feems,
and immediately they came rowing over the
Creek to our Men, carrying alſo a white Flag as
a Token of Truce.

It is not eaſy to defcribe the Surprize of Joy
and Satisfaction that appeared on both Sides, to
fee not only white Men, but *Engliſh* Men, in a
Place ſo remote; but what then muſt it be, when
they came to know one another, and to find that
they were not only Country Men, but Comrades,
and that this was the very Ship that Captain
Wilmot, our Admiral, commanded, and whoſe
Company we had loſt in the Storm at *Tobago*,
after making an Agreement to Rendezvous at
Madagaſcar?

They had, it feems, got Intelligence of us, when
they came to the South Part of the Iſland, and
had been a roving as far as the Gulph of *Bengal*,
when they met Captain *Avery*, with whom they
joined, took feveral rich Prizes, and amongſt the
reſt, one Ship with the great *Mogul*'s Daughter,
and an immenſe Treaſure in Money and Jewels,
and from thence they came about the Coaſt of
Coromandel, and afterwards that of *Malabar*, into
the Gulph of *Perſia*, where they alſo took
ſome Prize, and then defigned for the South Part
of *Madagaſcar*; but the Winds blowing hard at
S. E. and S. E. by E. they came to the Northward of the Iſle, and being after that feparated
by a furious Tempeſt from the N. W. they were
forced into the Mouth of that Creek, where they
loſt their Ship. And they told us alſo, that they
heard

heard that Captain *Avery* himfelf had loft his Ship alfo, not far off.

When they had thus acquainted one another with their Fortunes, the poor over-joyed Men were in Hafte to go back to communicate their Joy to their Comrades; and leaving fome of their Men with ours, the reft went back; and *William* was fo earneft to fee them, that he and two more went back with them, and there he came to their little Camp where they lived. There were about a hundred and fixty Men of them in all; they had got their Guns on Shore, and fome Ammunition, but a good deal of their Powder was fpoil'd. However they had raifed a fair Platform, and mounted twelve Pieces of Cannon upon it, which was a fufficient Defence to them on that Side of the Sea; and juft at the End of the Platform they had made a Launch, and a little Yard, and were all hard at Work building another little Ship, as I may call it, to go to Sea in, but they put a Stop to this Work upon the News they had of our being come in.

When our Men went into their Hutts, it was furprizing indeed to fee the vaft Stock of Wealth they had got, in Gold, and Silver, and Jewels, which however they told was a Trifle to what Captain *Avery*, had wherever he was gone.

It was five Days we had waited for our Men, and no News of them, and indeed, I gave them over for loft; but was furprized, after five Days waiting, to fee a Ship's Boat come rowing towards us along Shore; what to make of it, I could not tell, but was at laft better fatisfied, when our Men told me they heard them halloo, and faw them wave their Caps to us.

In

In a little time they came quite up to us, and
I faw Friend *William* ftand up in the Boat and
make Signs to us; fo they came on Board: But
when I faw there was but fifteen of our one and
thirty Men, I asked him what was become of
their Fellows? *O!* fays William, *they are all very
well, and my Dream is fully made good, and the Cockfwain's too.*

This made me very impatient to know how
the Cafe ftood; fo he told us the whole Story,
which indeed furprized us all. The next Day
we weighed, and ftood away Southerly to join
Captain *Wilmot* and his Ship at *Mangahelly,* where
we found him, as I faid, a little chagrin at our
Stay; but we pacified him afterwards with telling him the Hiftory of *William's* Dream, and the
Confequence of it.

In the mean time, the Camp of our Comrades
was fo near *Mangahelly,* that our Admiral, and I,
Friend *William,* and fome of the Men, refolved
to take the Sloop, and go and fee them, and
fetch them all, and their Goods, Bag and
Baggage, on board our Ship, which accordingly we did; and found their Camp, their For-
tifications, the Battery of Guns they had erected,
their Treafure, and all the Men, juft as *William*
had related it; fo after fome Stay, we took all the
Men into the Sloop, and brought them away
with us.

It was fome time before we knew what was
become of Captain *Avery;* but after about a
Month, by the Direction of the Men who had
loft their Ship, we fent the Sloop to cruife along
the Shore, to find out, if poffible, where they
were, and in about a Week's Cruife our Men
found them; and particularly, that they had loft
their Ship, as well as our Men had loft theirs,

and

and that they were every Way in as bad a Condition as ours.

It was about ten Days before the Sloop returned, and Captain *Avery* with them; and this was the whole Force that, as I remember, Captain *Avery* ever had with him; for now we joined all our Companies together, and it stood thus: We had two Ships and a Sloop, in which, we had three Hundred and twenty Men, but much too few to Man them as they ought to be, the great *Portuguese* Ship requiring of her self near 400 Men to Man her compleatly: As for our loft, *but now found* Comrade, her Compliment of Men was 180, or there abouts, and Captain *Avery* had about three Hundred Men with him, whereof, he had ten Carpenters with him, most of which were taken aboard the Prize they had taken; so that, in a Word, all the Force *Avery* had at *Madagascar* in the Year 1699, or thereabouts, amounted to our three Ships, for his own was loft, as you have heard, and never had any more than about twelve Hundred Men in all.

It was about a Month after this, that all our Crews got together, and as *Avery* was unshipt, we all agreed to bring our own Company into the *Portuguese* Man of War and the Sloop, and give Captain *Avery* the *Spanish* Frigate, with all the Tackles, and Furniture Guns, and Ammunition for his Crew by themselves; for which they being full of Wealth, agreed to give us Forty Thousand Pieces of Eight.

It was next considered, what Course we should take: Captain *Avery*, to give him his due, proposed our building a little City here, establishing our selves on Shore, with a good Fortification.

tion, and Works proper to defend our felves, and that, as we had Wealth enough, and could encreafe it to what Degree we pleafed, we fhould content our felves to retire here, and bid Defiance to the World. But I foon convinc'd him that this Place would be no Security to us, if we pretended to carry on our cruifing Trade: For that then all the Nations of *Europe*, and indeed of that Part of the World, would be engaged to root us out. But if we refolved to live there, as in a Retirement, and plant in the Country, as private Men, and give over our Trade of Pyrating, then indeed we might Plant, and fettle our felves where we pleafed; but then I told him, the beft Way would be to treat with the Natives, and buy a Tract of Land of them, farther up the Country, feated upon fome navigable River, where Boats might go up and down for Pleafure, but not Ships to endanger us: That thus Planting the high Ground with Cattle, fuch as Cows and Goats, of which the Country alfo was full, to be fure we might live here as well as any Men in the World; and I owned to him, I thought it was a good Retreat for thofe that were willing to leave off, and lay down, and yet did not care to venture home and be hanged; that is to fay, to run the Rifque of it.

Captain *Avery*, however he made no pofitive Difcovery of his Intentions, feemed to me to decline my Notion of going up into the Country to Plant; on the contrary, it was apparent he was of Captain *Wilmot*'s Opinion, that they might maintain themfelves on Shore, and yet carry on their cruifing Trade too; and upon this they refolved: But as I afterwards underftood, about fifty of their Men went up the Country, and

fet-

fettled themfelves in an Inland Place, as a Co-
lony; whether they are there ftill or not, I cannot
tell, or how many of them are left alive; but it's
my Opinion, they are there ftill, and that they
are confiderably encreafed, for as I hear, they
have got fome Women among them, tho' not
many; for it feems five *Dutch* Women, and three
or four little Girls were taken by them in a
Dutch Ship which they afterwards took going to
Mocha, and three of thofe Women marrying
fome of thefe Men, went with them to live in
their new Plantation; but of this I only fpeak
by Hear-fay.

As we lay here fome time, I found our People mightily divided in their Notions; fome were
for going this Way, and fome that, till at laft I
began to forefee they would part Company, and
perhaps we fhould not have Men enough to keep
together, to Man the great Ship, fo I took Captain *Wilmot* afide, and began to talk to him
about it; but foon perceived that he enclined
himfelf to ftay at *Madagafcar,* and having got a
vaft Wealth for his own Share, had fecret Defigns
of getting Home fome Way or other.

I argued the Impoffibility of it, and the Hazard
he would run, either of falling into the Hands
of Thieves and Murtherers in the *Red Sea,* who
would never let fuch a Treafure as his was
pafs their Hands, or of his falling into the
Hands of the *Englifh, Dutch,* or *French,* who would
certainly hang him for a Pyrate. I gave him an
Account of the Voyage I had made from this
very Place to the Continent of *Africk,* and what
a Journey it was to travel on Foot.

In fhort, nothing could perfwade him, but he
would go into the *Red Sea* with the Sloop, and
where

where the Children of *Ifrael* paft through the Sea dry-fhod, and landing there, would travel to *Grand Cairo* by Land, which is not above eighty Miles, and from thence he faid he could Ship himfelf by the Way of *Alexandria,* to any Part of the World.

I reprefented the Hazard, and indeed the Impoffibility of his paffing by *Mocha,* and *Judda,* without being attack'd, if he offered it by Force; or plundered, if he went to get Leave, and explained the Reafons of it fo much, and fo effectually, that tho' at laft he would not hearken to it himfelf, none of his Men would go with him. They told him, they would go any where with him, to ferve him, but that this was running himfelf and them into certain Deftruction, without any Poffibility of avoiding it, or Probability of anfwering his End. The Captain took what I faid to him quite wrong, and pretended to refent it, and gave me fome Buccanier Words upon it; but I gave him no Return to it, but this, that I advifed him for his Advantage, that if he did not underftand it fo, it was his Fault, not mine; that I did not forbid him to go, nor had I offered to perfwade any of the Men not to go with him, tho' it was to their apparent Deftruction.

However, warm Heads are not eafily cooled; the Captain was fo eager, that he quitted our Company, and with moft Part of his Crew, went over to Captain *Avery,* and forted with his People, taking all the Treafure with him, which, by the Way, was not very fair in him, we having agreed to fhare all our Gains, whether more or lefs, whether abfent or prefent.

Our Men mutter'd a little at it, but I pacified them as well as I could, and told them, it

was

was eafy for us to get as much, if we minded our Hits; and Captain *Wilmot* had fet us a very good Example: For by the fame Rule, the Agreement of any farther Sharing of Profits with them, was at an End. I took this Occafion to put into their Heads, fome Part of my farther Defigns, which were, to range over the Eaftern Sea, and fee if we could not make our felves as rich as Mr. *Avery*, who, it was true, had gotten a prodigious deal of Money, tho' not one Half of what was faid of it in *Europe.*

Our Men were fo pleafed with my forward, enterprizing Temper, that they affured me that they would go with me, one and all, over the whole Globe, wherever I would carry them; and as for Captain *Wilmot*, they would have nothing more to do with him. This came to his Ears, and put him into a great Rage; fo that he threaten'd, if I came on Shore, he would cut my Throat.

I had Information of it privately, but took no Notice of it at all, only I took Care not to go unprovided for him, and feldom walked about but in very good Company. However, at laft Captain *Wilmot* and I met, and talked over the Matter very ferioufly, and I offered him the Sloop to go where he pleafed: Or, if he was not fatisfied with that, I offered to take the Sloop, and leave him the great Ship. But he declined both, and only defired that I would leave him fix Carpenters, which I had in our Ship, more than I had need of, to help his Men to finifh the Sloop that was begun before we came thither, by the Men that loft his Ship. This I confented readily to, and lent him feveral other Hands that were ufeful to them, and in a little time they
built

built a ſtout Brigantine able to carry fourteen Guns, and two Hundred Men.

What Meaſures they took, and how Captain *Avery* managed afterwards, is too long a Story to meddle with here; nor is it any of my Buſineſs, having my own Story ſtill upon my Hands.

We lay here about theſe ſeveral ſimple Diſputes almoſt five Months, when about the latter End of *March* I ſet Sail with the great Ship, having in her forty four Guns, and four hundred Men, and the Sloop, carrying eighty Men. We did not ſteer to the *Malabar* Coaſt, and ſo to the Gulph of *Perſia*, as was at firſt intended, the Eaſt Monſoons blowing yet too ſtrong, but we kept more under the *African* Coaſt, where we had the Wind variable till we paſs'd the Line, and made the Cape *Baſſa* in the Latitude of four Degrees 10 Minutes; from thence, the Monſoons beginning to change to the N. E. and N. N. E. we led it away, with the Wind large, to the *Maldivies*, a famous Ledge of Iſlands, well known by all the Sailors who have gone into thoſe Parts of the World ; and, leaving theſe Iſlands a little to the South, we made Cape *Comerin*, the Southermoſt Land of the Coaſt of *Malabar*, and went round the Iſle of *Ceylon*. Here we lay by a while, to wait for Purchaſe; and here we ſaw three large *Engliſh Eaſt-India* Ships going from *Bengal*, or from Fort St. *George*, home ward for *England*, or rather for *Bombay* and *Surat*, till the Trade ſet in.

We brought to, and hoiſting an *Engliſh* Ancient and Pendant, lay by for them, as if we intended to attack them. They could not tell what to make of us a good while, though they ſaw our Colours; and, I believe, at firſt they

R thought

thought us to be *French*; but as they came nearer to us, we let them soon see what we were, for we hoifted a black Flag with two crofs Daggers in it, on our Main Top-maft Head, which let them fee what they were to expect.

We foon found the Effect of this; for, at firft they fpread their Antients, and made up to us in a Line as if they would fight us, having the Wind off Shore fair enough, to have brought them on board us; but when they faw what Force we were of, and found we were Cruifers of another kind, they ftood away from us again, with all the Sail they could make. If they had come up, we fhould have given them an unexpect Welcome, but as it was, we had no Mind to follow them, fo we let them go for the fame Reafons which I mentioned before.

But though we let them pafs, we did not defign to let others go, at fo eafy a Price: It was but the next Morning that we faw a Sail, ftanding round Cape *Comeriw*, and fteering, as we thought, the fame Courfe with us. We knew not at firft what to do with her, becaufe fhe had the Shore on her Larboard Quarter, and if we offered to chafe her, fhe might put into any Port or Creek, and efcape us; but to prevent this, we fent the Sloop, to get in between her and the Land; as foon as fhe faw that, fhe haled in to keep the Land aboard, and when the Sloop ftood towards her, fhe made right afhore with all the Canvas fhe could fpread.

The Sloop however came up with her, and engaged her, and found fhe was a Veffel of ten Guns, *Portuguefe* built, but in the *Dutch* Traders Hands, and manned by *Dutchmen*, who were bound from the Gulph of *Perfia*, to *Batavia*, to fetch

Spices

Spices and other Goods from thence. The Sloop's
Men took her, and had the Rummaging of her
before we came up: She had in her some *European*
Goods, and a good round Sum of Money, and
some Pearl; so that tho' we did not go to the
Gulph for the Pearl, the Pearl came to us out
of the Gulph, and we had our Share of it. This
was a rich Ship, and the Goods were of very
considerable Value, besides the Money and the
Pearl.

We had a long Consultation here, what we
should do with the Men; for, to give them the
Ship, and let them pursue their Voyage to *Java*,
would be to alarm the *Dutch* Factory there, who
are by far the strongest in the *Indies*, and to
make our Passage that Way impracticable; whereas we resolved to visit that Part of the World,
in our Way, but were not willing to pass the
great Bay of *Bengal*, where we hoped for a great
deal of Purchase; and therefore it behoved us not
to be Way-laid before we came there, because they
knew we must pass by the Streights of *Malacca*,
or those of *Sundy*, and either Way it was very
easy to prevent us.

While we were consulting this in the great
Cabin, the Men had had the same Debate before the Mast, and it seems the Majority there
were for pickling up the poor *Dutchmen* among
the Herrings; in a Word, they were for throwing them all into the Sea. Poor *William* the
Quaker was in great Concern about this, and
comes directly to me, to talk about it. *Hark
thee*, says William, *what wilt thou do with these*
Dutchmen *thou haft on board, thou wilt not let them
go I suppose*, says he? *Why* says I, William, *would
you advise me to let them go? No*, says William, *I can-*

not

not *fay it is fit for thee to let them go*; *that is to fay,
to go on with their Voyage to* Batavia, *becaufe it is not
for thy Turn, that the* Dutch *at* Batavia *fhould have
any Knowledge of thy being in thefe Seas. Well then*, fays
I, *to him, I know no Remedy but to throw them Over-
board. You know* William, fays I, *a Dutchman fwims
like a Fifh, and all our People here are of the fame Opinion as well as I*; *at the fame time I refolved it fhould not
be done, but wanted to hear what* William *would fay*:
*But he gravely replyed, if all the Men in the Ship were
of that Mind, I will never believe that thou wilt be of
that Mind thy felf*; *for I have heard thee proteft a-
gainft Cruelty in all other Cafes. Well* William fays I,
*that is true, but what then fhall we do with them?
Why*, fays William, *is there no way but to murther
them? I am perfwaded thou canft not be in earneft*; *no
indeed* William, fays I, *I am not in earneft, but
they fhall not go* Iava, *no nor to* Ceylon, *that is certain.
But*, fays William, *the Men have done thee no Injury
at all, Thou haft taken a great Treafure from them,
what canft thou pretend to hurt them for? Nay*, William,
fays I, *do not talk of that, I have Pretence enough if
that be all: My Pretence is to prevent doing me hurt,
and that is as neceffary a Piece of the Law of Self-Pre-
fervation as any you can name*; *but the main Thing is,
I know not what to do with them to prevent their
prating.*

While *William* and I was talking, the poor
Dutchmen were openly condemned to die as it
maybe called, by the whole Ship's Company ; and
fo warm were the Men upon it, that they grew
very clamorous; and when they heard that *William* was againft it, fome of them fwore they
fhould die, and if *William* oppofed it, he fhould
drown along with them.

But

But, as I was refolved to put an End to their cruel Project, fo I found it was time to take upon me a little, or the bloody Humour might grow too ftrong; fo I called the *Dutchmen* up, and talked a little with them. Firft, I asked them if they were willing to go with us; two of them offered it prefently, but the reft, which were fourteen, declined it. Well then, faid I, where would you go? They defired they fhould go to *Ceylon*. No, I told them, I could not allow them to go to any *Dutch* Factory, and told them very plainly the Reafons of it, which they could not deny to be juft. I let them know alfo the cruel bloody Meafures of our Men, but that I had refolved to fave them, if poffible, and therefore I told them, I would fet them on Shore at fome *Englifh* factory in the Bay of *Bengal*, or put them on board any *Englifh* Ship I met, after I was paft the Streights of *Sundy* or of *Malacca*, but not before; for as to my coming back again, I told them, I would run the venture of their *Dutch* Power from *Batavia*, but I would not have the News come there before me, becaufe it would make all their Merchant Ships lay up, and keep out of our Way.

It come next into our Confideration, what we fhould do with their Ship? but this was not long refolving; for there were but two Ways, either to fet her on Fire, or to run her on Shore, and we chofe the laft; fo we fet her Fore-Sail with the Tack at the Cat-head, and leafht her Helm a little to Starboard, to anfwer her Head-Sail, and fo fet her a-going, with neither Cat or Dog in her, and it was not above two Hours before we faw her run right afhore upon the Coaft, a little beyond

R 3   the

the Cape *Comerin*, and away we went round about *Ceylon*, for the Coaft of *Coromandel*.

We failed along there, not in Sight of the Shore, only, but fo near, as to fee the Ships in the Road at *Fort St. David*, *Fort St. George*, and at the other Factories along that Shore, as well as along the Coaft of *Galconda*, carying our *Englifh* Antient, when we came near the *Dutch* Factories, and *Dutch* Colours when we paft by the *Englifh* Factories. We met with little Purchafe upon this Coaft, except two fmall Veffels of *Golconda*, bound crofs the Bay with Bales of Callicoe's and Muflins, and wrought Silks, and fifteen Bales of Romalls, from the Bottom of the Bay, which were going, on whofe Account we knew not, to *Achin*, and to other Ports on the Coaft of *Malacca*; we did not enquire to what Place in particular, but we let the Veffels go, having none but *Indians* on board.

In the Bottom of the Bay, we met with a great *Jonk* belonging to the *Mogul*'s Court, with a great many People, Paffengers as we fuppofed them to be; it feems they were bound for the River *Hugely*, or *Ganges* and came from *Sumatra*; this was a Prize worth taking indeed, and we got fo much Gold in her, befides other Goods which we did not meddle with, Peper in particular, that it had like to have put an End to our Cruife; for almoft all my Men faid we were rich enough, and defired to go back again to *Madagafcar*; but I had other things in my Head ftill, and when I came to talk to them, and fet Friend *William* to talk with them, we put fuch further Golden Hopes into their Heads, that we foon prevailed with them to let us go on.

My

My next Defign was, to leave all the dangerous Streights of *Malacca*, *Sincapore*, and *Sundy*, where we could expect no great Booty, but what we might light on in *European* Ships, which we must fight for ; and tho' we were able to fight, and wanted no Courage, even to Defperation; yet we were rich too, and refolved to be richer, and took this for our Maxim : That while we were fure the Wealth we fought was to be had without fighting, we had no Occafion to put our felves to the Neceffity of fighting for that which would come upon eafy Terms.

We left therefore the Bay of *Bengal*, and coming to the Coaft of *Sumatra*, we put in at a fmall Port, where there was a Town, inhabited only by *Mallayans*, and here we took in frefh Water, and a large Quantity of good Pork pickled up, and well falted, notwithftanding the Heat of the Climate, being in the very Middle of the *Torrid Zone*, viz. In three Degrees, fifteen Minutes North Latitude. We alfo took on board both our Veffels, forty Hogs alive, which ferved us for frefh Provifions, having Abundance of Food for them fuch as the Country produced ; fuch as Guams, Potatoes, and a fort of coarfe Rice good for nothing elfe, but to feed the Swine. We killed one of thefe Hogs every Day, and found them to be excellent Meat. We took in alfo a monftrous Quantity of Ducks, and Cocks and Hens, the fame kind as we have in *England*, which we kept for Change of Provifions, and if I remember right, we had no lefs than two Thoufand of them ; fo that at firft we were peftered with them very much, but we foon leffened them by boiling, roafting, ftewing, &c. for we never wanted while we had them.

My

My long projected Design now lay open to me, which was, to fall in amongst the *Dutch* Spice Islands, and see what Mischief I could do there ; accordingly we put out to Sea, the 12th of *August*, and passing the Line the 17th, we stood away due South leaving the Straits of *Sunda*, and the Isle of *Iava* on the East, till we came to the Latitude of eleven Degrees, twenty Minutes, when we steered East and E. N. E. having easy Gales from the W. S. W. till we came among the *Moluccas*, or Spice Islands.

We passed those Seas with less Difficulty than in other Places, the Winds to the South of *Iava*, being more variable, and the Weather good, tho' sometimes we met with Squally Weather, and short Storms ; but when we came in among the Spice Islands themselves, we had a Share of the Monsoones, or Trade Winds, and made use of them accordingly.

The infinite Number of Islands which lye in these Seas, embarraft us strangely, and it was with great Difficulty that we worked our Way thro' them ; then we steered for the North Side of the *Phillipines*, where we had a double Chance for Purchase, *viz.* either to meet with the *Spanish* Ships from *Acapulco* on the Coast of *New-Spain*, or we were certain not to fail of finding some Ships or Jonks of *China*, who, if they came from *China*, would have a great Quantity of Goods of Value on Board, as well as Money ; or if we took them going back, we should find them loaden with Nutmegs and Cloves from *Banda* and *Ternate*, or from some of the other Islands.

We were right in our Guesses here to a tittle, and we steered directly through a large Out-let, which

which they call a Streight, tho' it be fifteen Miles
broad, and to an Iſland they call *Daurma*, and
from thence N. N. E. to *Banda*; between theſe
Iſlands we met with a *Dutch* Jonque, or Veſſel
going to *Amboyna*. We took her without much
Trouble, and I had much ado to prevent our
Men murthering all the Men, as ſoon as they
heard them ſay, they belonged to *Amboyna*, the
Reaſon I ſuppoſe any one will gueſs.

We took out of her about ſixteen Ton of Nut-
megs, ſome Proviſions, and their ſmall Arms,
for they had no great Guns, and let the Ship go:
From thence we ſailed directly to the *Banda*
Iſland or Iſlands, where we were ſure to get
more Nutmegs, if we thought fit; for my Part
I would willingly have got more Nutmegs, tho'
I had paid for them, but our People abhorred
paying for any thing; ſo we got about twelve
Ton more at ſeveral times, moſt of them from
Shore, and only a few in a ſmall Boat of the Natives, which was going to *Gilolo*. We would have
traded openly, but the *Dutch*, who have made
themſelves Maſters of all thoſe Iſlands, forbid
the People dealing with us, or any Strangers
whatever, and keep them ſo in Awe, that they
durſt not do it; ſo we could indeed have made
nothing of it, if we had ſtay'd longer, and therefore reſolved to be gone for *Ternate*, and ſee if we
could make up our Loading with Cloves.

Accordingly we ſtood away North, but found
our ſelves ſo intangled among innumerable Iſlands,
and without any Pilot that underſtood the Channel and Races between them, that we were obliged to give it over, and reſolved to go back again
to *Banda*, and ſee what we could get among the
other Iſlands thereabouts.

The

The firſt Adventure we made here, had like to have been fatal to us all, for the Sloop being a-head, made the Signal to us for ſeeing a Sail, and afterwards another, and a third, by which we underſtood ſhe ſaw three Sail, whereupon we made more Sail to come up with her, but on a ſudden was gotten among ſome Rocks, falling foul upon them in ſuch a Manner as frighted us all very heartily; for having it ſeems but juſt Water enough as it were to an Inch, our Rudder ſtruck upon the Top of a Rock, which gave us a terrible Shock, and ſplit a great Piece off of the Rudder, and indeed diſabled it ſo, that our Ship would not ſteer at all; at leaſt not ſo as to be de-pended upon, and we were glad to Hand all our Sails, except our Fore-ſail and Main-top-ſail, and with them we ſtood away to the Eaſt, to ſee if we could find any Creek or Harbour, where we might lay the Ship on Shore, and repair our Rud-der; beſides, we found the Ship her ſelf had re-ceived ſome Damage, for ſhe had ſome little Leak near her Stern Poſt, but a great Way under Water.

By this Miſchance we loſt the Advantages, whatever they were, of the three Sail of Ships which we afterward came to hear, were ſmall *Dutch* Ships from *Batavia*, going to *Banda* and *Amboyna*, to load Spice, and no doubt had a good Quantity of Money on board.

Upon the Diſaſter I have been ſpeaking of, you may very well ſuppoſe that we came to an An-chor as ſoon as we could, which was upon a ſmall Iſland not far from *Banda*, where tho' the *Dutch* keep no Factory, yet they come at the Seaſon to buy Nutmegs and Mace. We ſtay'd there thir-teen Days; but there being no Place where we

could

could lay the Ship on Shore, we fent the Sloop to cruife among the Iflands, to look out for a Place fit for us. In the mean time we got very good Water here, fome Provifions, Roots, and Fruits, and a good Quantity of Nutmegs and Mace, which we found Ways to trade with the Natives for, without the Knowledge of their Mafters the *Dutch.*

At length our Sloop return'd, having found another Ifland where there was a very good Harbour, we run in, and came to an Anchor. We immediately unbent all our Sails, fent them afhore upon the Ifland, and fet up feven or eight Tents with them: Then we unrigged our Topmafts, and cut them down, hoifted all our Guns out, our Provifions and Loading, and put them afhore in the Tents. With the Guns we made two fmall Batteries, for fear of a Surprize, and kept a Look out upon the Hill. When we were all ready, we laid the Ship a-ground upon a hard Sand, the upper End of the Harbour, and fhor'd her up on each Side. At low Water fhe lay almoft dry, fo we mended her Bottom, and ftopt the Leak which was occafioned by ftraining fome of the Rudder Irons with the Shock which the Ship had againft the Rock.

Having done this, we alfo took Occafion to clean her Bottom, which, having been at Sea fo long, was very foul. The Sloop Wafh'd and Tallow'd alfo, but was ready before us, and cruifed eight or ten Days among the Iflands, but met with no Purchafe; fo that we began to be tired of the Place, having little to divert us, but the moft furious Claps of Thunder that ever were read or heard of in the World.

We

We were in Hopes to have met with some Purchase here among the *Chinese*, who we had been
told came to *Ternate* to trade for Cloves, and to
the *Banda* Isles, for Nutmegs, and we could have
been very glad to have loaded our Galleon, or
great Ship, with these two Sorts of Spice, and
have thought it a glorious Voyage; but we found
nothing stirring more than what I have said, except *Dutchmen*, who by what Means we could not
imagine, had either a Jealousy of us, or Intelligence of us, and kept themselves close in their
Ports.

I was once resolved to have made a Descent at
the Island of *Dumas*, the Place most famous for
the best Nutmegs; but Friend *William*, who was
always for doing our Business without Fighting,
disswaded me from it, and gave such Reasons for
it, that we could not resist; particularly the great
Heats of the Season, and of the Place, for we
were now in the Latitude of just half a Degree
South; but while we were disputing this Point,
we were soon determined by the following Accident. We had a strong Gale of Wind at S. W.
by W. and the Ship had fresh Way, but a great
Sea rolling in upon us from the N. E. which we
afterwards found was the Pouring in of the Great
Ocean East of *New Guinea*. However, as I said,
we stood away large, and made fresh Way, when
on the sudden, from a dark Cloud which hover'd
over our Heads, came a Flash, or rather Blast of
Lightning, which was so terrible, and quiver'd
so long among us, that not I only, but all our
Men thought the Ship was on Fire. The Heat
of the Flash or Fire was so sensibly felt in our Faces, that some of our Men had Blisters raised by
it

it on their Skins, not immediately perhaps by the Heat, but by the poifonous or noxious Particles, which mix'd themfelves with the Matter inflam'd. But this was not all; the Shock of the Air which the Fracture in the Clouds made, was fuch, that our Ship fhook as when a Broadfide is fired, and her Motion being check'd as it were at once by a Repulfe fuperior to the Force that gave her Way before, the Sails all flew back in a Moment, and the Ship lay, as we might truly fay, Thunder-ftruck. As the Blaft from the Cloud was fo very near us, it was but a few Moments after the Flafh, that the terribleft Clap of Thunder followed that was ever heard by Mortals. I firmly believe a Blaft of a Hundred Thoufand Barrels of Gunpowder could not have been greater to our Hearing; nay indeed, to fome of our Men it took away their Hearing.

It is not poffible for me to defcribe, or any one to conceive the Terrour of that Minute. Our Men were in fuch a Confternation, that not a Man on board the Ship had Prefence of Mind to apply to the proper Duty of a Sailor, except Friend *William*; and had not he run very nimbly, and with a Compofure that I am fure I was not Mafter of, to let go the Fore-fheet, fet in the Weather Brace of the Fore-yard, and haul'd down the Topfails, we had certainly brought all our Mafts by the Board, and perhaps have been overwhelm'd in the Sea.

As for my felf, I muft confefs my Eyes were open to my Danger, tho' not the leaft to any thing of Application for Remedy. I was all Amazement and Confufion, and this was the firft Time that I can fay I began to feel the Effects of
that

that Horrour which I know since much more of, upon the just Reflection on my former Life. I thought my self doom'd by Heaven to sink that Moment into eternal Destruction; and with this peculiar Mark of Terror, *viz.* That the Vengeance was not executed in the ordinary Way of human Justice, but that God had taken me into his immediate Disposing, and had resolved to be the Executer of his own Vengeance.

Let them alone describe the Confusion I was in, who know what was the Case of ——— *Child* of *Shadwell*, or *Francis Spira*. It is impossible to describe. My Soul was all Amazement and Surprize; I thought my self just sinking into Eternity, owning the divine Justice of my Punishment, but not at all feeling any of the moving, softning Tokens of a sincere Penitent, afflicted at the Punishment, but not at the Crime, alarmed at the Vengeance, but not terrify'd at the Guilt, having the same Gust to the Crime, tho' terrified to the last Degree at the Thought of the Punishment, which I concluded I was just now going to receive.

But perhaps many that read this will be sensible of the Thunder and Lightning, that may think nothing of the rest, or rather may make a Jest of it all, so I say no more of it at this time, but proceed to the Story of the Voyage. When the Amazement was over, and the Men began to come to themselves, they fell a calling for one another, every one for his Friend, or for those he had most Respect for; and it was a singular Satisfaction to find that no body was hurt. The next thing was to enquire if the Ship had received no Damage, when the Boatswain stepping

ping

ping forward, found that Part of the Head was gone, but not fo as as to endanger the Bolt-fprit; fo we hoifted our Topfails again, haul'd aft the Fore-fheet, brac'd the Yards, and went went our Courfe as before : Nor can I deny but that we were all fomewhat like the Ship, our firft Aftonifhment being a little over, and that we found the Ship fwim again, we were foon the fame irreligious hardned Crew that we were before, and I among the reft.

As we now fteer'd, our Courfe lay N. N. E. and we paffed thus with a fair Wind, thro' the Streight or Channel between the Ifland of *Gilolo*, and the Land of *Nova Guinea*, when we were foon in the open Sea or Ocean on the South Eaft of the *Philippines*, being the great Pacifick, or South Sea, where it may be faid to join it felf with the vaft *Indian* Ocean.

As we paffed into thefe Seas fteering due North, fo we foon crofs'd the Line to the North Side, and fo failed on towards *Mindanoa* and *Manilla*, the chief of the *Philippine* Iflands, without meeting with any Purchafe, till we came to the Northward of *Manilla*, and then our Trade began ; for here we took three *Japonefe* Veffels, tho' at fome Diftance from *Manilla*. Two of them had made their Market, and were going Home with Nutmegs, Cinnamon, Cloves, &c. befides all Sorts of *European* Goods brought with the *Spanifh* Ships from *Acapulco*. They had together eight and thirty Ton of Cloves, and five or fix Ton of Nutmegs, and as much Cinnamon. We took the Spice, but meddled with very little of the *European* Goods, they being, as we thought, not worth our while, but we were very forry for it

foon

soon after, and therefore grew wiser upon the next Occasion.

The third *Japonese* was the best Prize to us, for he came with Money, and a great deal of Gold uncoin'd, to buy such Goods as we mentioned above: We eased him of his Gold, and did him no other Harm, and having no Intention to stay long here, we stood away for *China.*

We were at Sea above two Months upon this Voyage, beating it up against the Wind, which blew steadily from the North East, and within 2 Point or two one Way or other; and this indeed was the Reason why we met with the more Prizes in our Voyage.

We were just gotten clear of the *Philippines,* and as we purposed to go to the Isle of *Formosa,* when the Wind blew so fresh at N. N. E. that there was no making any thing of it, and we were forced to put back to *Laconia,* the most Northerly of those Islands. We rode here very secure, and shifted our Situation not in View of any Danger, for there was none, but for a better Supply of Provisions, which we found the People very willing to supply us with.

There lay while we remained here, three very great Galleons or *Spanish* Ships, from the South Seas, whether newly come in, or ready to sail, we could not understand at first; but as we found the *China* Traders began to load and set forward to the North, we concluded the *Spanish* Ships had newly unloaded their Cargo, and these had been buying; so we doubted not but we should meet with Purchase in the rest of our Voyage, neither indeed could we well miss of it.

We stay'd here till the beginning of *May,* when we were told the *Chinese* Traders would
set

set forward, for the Northern Monsoons end about the latter End of *March*, or the Beginning of *April*; so that they are sure of fair Winds Home. Accordingly we hired some of the Country Boats, which are very swift Sailers, to go and bring us Word how Affairs stood at *Manilla*, and when the *China* Jonks would sail, and by this Intelligence we ordered our Matters so well, that three Days after we set Sail, we fell in with no less than eleven of them, out of which however having by Misfortune of discovering our selves, taken but three, we contented our selves, and pursued our Voyage to *Formosa*. In these three Vessels we took in short such a Quantity of Cloves, Nutmegs, Cinnamon, and Mace, besides Silver, that our Men began to be of my Opinion, *That we were rich enough*; and in short, we had nothing to do now, but to consider by what Methods to secure the immense Treasure we had got.

I was secretly glad to hear, that they were of this Opinion; for I had long before resolved, if it was possible, to perswade them to think of returning, having fully perfected my first projected Design, of Rummaging among the Spice Islands, and all those Prizes, which were exceeding rich at *Manilla*, was quite beyond my Design.

But now I had heard what the Men said, and h they thought we were very well. I let them k by Friend *William*, that I intended only to sa: the Island *Formosa*, where I should find Opport nity to turn our Spices and *European* Goods int ready Money, and that then I would tack about for the South, the Northern Monsoons being per - haps by that time also ready to set in. They all approved of my Design, and willingly went for-

S ward,

ward, becaufe, befides the Winds, which would
not permit until October, to go to the South : I
fay, befides this, we were now a very deep Ship,
having near two Hundred Ton of Goods on board,
and particularly fome very valuable. The Sloop
alfo had a Proportion.

With this Refolution we went on chearfully,
when within about twelve Days Sail more, we
made the Ifland *Formofa*, at a great Diftance, but
were our felves fhot beyond the Southermoft
Part of the Ifland, being to Leeward, and almoft
upon the Coaft of *China*. Here we were a little
at a Lofs ; for the *Englifh* Factories were not far
off, and we might be obliged to fight fome of
their Ships, if we met with them ; which tho'
we were able enough to do, yet we did not
defire it on many Accounts ; and particularly
becaufe we did not think it was our Bufinefs to
have it known who we were, or that fuch a kind
of People as we had been feen on the Coaft.
However, we were obliged to keep up to the
Northward, keeping as good an Offing as we could,
with refpect to the Coaft of *China*. We had not
failed long, but we chafed a fmall *Chinefe* Jonk ;
and having taken her, we found fhe was bound
to the Ifland of *Formofa*, having no Goods on
board but fome Rice, and a fmall Quantity of
a ; but fhe had three *Chinefe* Merchants in her,
they told us they were going to meet a
ge Veffel of their Conntry, which came from
nquin, and lay in a River in *Formofa* whofe Name
forget, and they were going to the *Philippine*
Iflands, with Silks, Muflins, Callicoes, and fuch
Goods as are the Product of *China*, and fome Gold ;
that their Bufinefs was to fell their Cargo, and
buy Spices and *European* Goods.

This

This fuited very well with our Purpofe; fo I
refolved now that we would leave off being Pyrates, and turn Merchants; fo we told them
what Goods we had on board, and that if they
would bring their Super-Cargoes or Merchants
on board, we would trade with them. They
were very willing to trade with us, but terribly
afraid to truft us; nor was it an unjuft Fear,
for we had plundered them already of what they
had. On the other Hand, we were as diffident
as they, and very uncertain what to do; but
William the Quaker put this Matter into a Way
of Barter. He came to me, and told me he really thought the Merchants look'd like fair Men,
that meant honeftly; and befides, fays *William*,
it is their Intereft to be honeft now; for as they
know upon what Terms we got the Goods we
are to truck with them, fo they know we can
afford good Pennyworths; and in the next Place,
it faves them going the whole Voyage: So that
the Southerly Monfoons yet holding, if they
traded with us, they could immediately return
with their Cargo to *China, tho' by the Way we afterwards found they intended for* Japan. But that
was all one, for by this Means they fav'd at
leaft eight Months Voyage. Upon thefe Foun-
dations *William* faid he was fatisfied we might
truft them: For, fays *William*, I would as foon
truft a Man whofe Intereft binds him to be juft
to me, as a Man whofe Principle binds himfelf.
Upon the whole, *William* propofed that two of
the Merchants fhould be left on board our Ship
as Hoftages, and that Part of our Goods fhould
be loaded in their Veffel, and let the third go
with it into the Port where their Ship lay; and
when he had delivered the Spices, he fhould

bring

b:ing back such things as it was agreed should be exchanged. This was concluded on, and *William* the Quaker ventured to go along with them, which upon my Word I should not have cared to have done, nor was I willing that he should; but he went still upon the Notion, that it was their Interest to treat him friendly.

In the mean time we came to an Anchor under a little Island, in the Latitude of 23 Degrees, 28 Minutes, being just under the Northern Tropick, and about twenty Leagues from the Island. Here we lay thirteen Days, and I began to be very uneasy for my Friend *William*, for they had promised to be back again in four Days, which they might very easily have done. However, at the End of thirteen Days we saw three Sail coming directly to us, which a little surprized us all at first, not knowing what might be the Case, and we began to put our selves in a Posture of Defence; but as they came nearer us, we were soon satisfy'd: For the first Vessel was that which *William* went in, who carried a Flag of Truce, and in a few Hours they all came to an Anchor, and *William* came on board us with a little Boat, with the *Chinese* Merchant in his Company, and two other Merchants, which seem'd to be a kind of Brokers for the rest.

Here he gave us an Account, how civilly he had been used, how they had treated him with all imaginable Frankness and Openness, that they had not only given him the full Value of his Spices and other Goods which he carry'd, in Gold, by good Weight, but had loaded the Vessel again with such Goods as he knew we were willing to trade for; and that afterwards they had resolved to bring the great Ship out of the Harbour, to lye

lye where we were, that so we might make what Bargain we thought fit; only *William* said he had promised in our Name, that we should use no Violence with them, nor detain any of the Vessels after we had done trading with them. I told him, we would strive to outdo them in Civility, and that we would make good every Part of his Agreement. In Token whereof I caused a white Flag likewise to be spread at the Poop of our great Ship, which was the Signal agreed on.

As to the third Vessel which came with them, it was a kind of Bark of the Country, who having Intelligence of our Design to traffick, came off to deal with us, bringing a great deal of Gold, and some Provisions, which at that time we were very glad of.

In short, we traded upon the high Seas with these Men, and indeed we made a very good Market, and yet sold Thieves Pennyworths too. We sold here above sixty Ton of Spice, chiefly Cloves and Nutmegs, and above two Hundred Bales of *European* Goods; such as Linnen and Wollen Manufactures. We considered we should have Occasion for some such things our selves, and so we kept a good Quantity of *English* Stuffs, Cloaths, Bays, &c. for our selves. I shall not take up any of the little Room I have left here, with the further Particulars of our Trade; 'tis enough to mention, that except a Parcel of Tea, and twelve Bales of fine *China* wrought Silks, we took nothing in Exchange for our Goods but Gold: So that the Sum we took here in that glittering Commodity, amounted to above Fifty Thousand Ounces good Weight.

When we had finished our Barter, we restored the Hostages, and gave the three Merchants about

the

the Quantity of Twelve Hundred Weight of Nutmegs, and as many of Cloves, with a handsom Present of *European* Linnen and Stuff for themselves, as a Recompence for what we had taken from them; and so we sent them away exceedingly well satisfy'd.

Here it was that *William* gave me an Account, that while he was on board the *Japonese* Vessel, he met with a kind of Religious, or *Japan* Priest, who spoke some Words of *English* to him; and being very inquisitive to know how he came to learn any of those Words, he told him, that there was in his Country *thirteen Englishmen*; he called them *Englishmen* very articulately and distinctly, for he had conversed with them very frequently and freely : He said they were all that were left of two and thirty Men, who came on Shore on the North Side of *Japan*, being driven upon a great Rock in a stormy Night, where they lost their Ship, and the rest of their Men were drowned : That he had perswaded the King of his Country to send Boats off to the Rock or Island, where the Ship was lost, to save the rest of the Men, and to bring them on Shore; which was done, and they were used very kindly, and had Houses built for them, and Land given them to plant for Provision, and that they lived by themselves.

He said he went frequently among them, to perswade them to worship their God, an Idol, I suppose, of their own making, which he said they ungratefully refused; and that therefore the King had once or twice ordered them to be all put to Death; but that, *as he said*, he had prevailed upon the King to spare them, and let them live their own Way, as long as they were quiet and peace-

peaceable, and did not go about to withdraw others from the Worſhip of the Country.

I ask'd *William*, why he did not enquire from whence they came? I did, *ſaid William*, for how could I but think it ſtrange, ſaid he, to hear him talk of *Engliſh* Men on the North Side of *Japan*. Well, ſaid I, what Account did he give of it? An Account, ſaid *William*, that will ſurprize thee, and all the World after thee, that ſhall hear of it, and which makes me wiſh thou wouldſt go up to *Japan*, and find them out. What do ye mean, ſaid I? Whence could they come? Why, ſays *William*, he pull'd out a little Book, and in it a Piece of Paper, where it was written in an *Engliſh* Man's Hand, and in plain *Engliſh* Words, thus; and ſays *William*, I read it my ſelf: *We came from Greenland*, and from the *North Pole*. This indeed was amazing to us all, and more to thoſe Seamen among us who knew any thing of the infinite Attempts which had been made from *Europe*, as well by the *Engliſh* as the *Dutch*, to diſcover a Paſſage that Way into thoſe Parts of the World; and as *William* preſs'd us earneſtly to go on to the North, to reſcue thoſe poor Men, ſo the Ship's Company began to incline to it; and in a Word, we all came to this, that we would ſtand in to the Shore of *Formoſa*, to find this Prieſt again, and have a farther Account of it all from him. Accordingly the Sloop went over, but when they came there, the Veſſels were very unhappily ſail'd, and this put an End to our Enquiry after them, and perhaps may have diſappointed Mankind of one of the moſt noble Diſcoveries that ever was made, or will again be made in the World, for the Good of Mankind in general: But ſo much for that.

Willi⌐

William was so uneasy at losing this Opportunity, that he press'd us earnestly to go up to *Japan,* to find out these Men. He told us, that if it was nothing but to recover Thirteen honest poor Men from a kind of Captivity, which they would otherwise never be redeemed from, and where perhaps they might some time or other be murdered by the barbarous People, in Defence of their Idolatry; it were very well worth our while, and it would be in some Measure making amends for the Mischiefs we had done in the World: But we that had no Concern upon us for the Mischiefs we had done, had much less about any Satisfaction to be made for it; so he found that kind of Discourse would weigh very little with us. Then he press'd us very earnestly to let him have the Sloop to go by himself, and I told him I would not oppose it; but when he came to the Sloop, none of the Men would go with him; for the Case was plain, they had all a Share in the Cargo of the great Ship, as well as in that of the Sloop, and the Richness of the Cargo was such, that they would not leave it by any means: So poor *William,* much to his Mortification, was obliged to give it over. What became of those thirteen Men, or whether they are not there still, I can give no Account of.

We were now at the End of our Cruise; what we had taken was indeed so considerable, that it was not only enough to satisfy the most covetous and the most ambitious Minds in the World, but it did indeed satisfy us; and our Men declared they did not desire any more. The next Motion therefore was about going back, and the Way by which we should perform the Voyage, so as not to be attack'd by the *Dutch* in the Straits of *Sunda.*

We

We had pretty well ftored our felves here with Provifions, and it being now near the Return of the Monfoons, we refolved to ftand away to the Southward; and not only to keep without the *Philippine* Iflands, that is to fay, to the Eaft-ward of them, but to keep on to the Southward, and fee if we could not leave, not only the *Molucco's*, or Spice Iflands, behind us, but even *Nova Guinea* and *Nova Hollandia* alfo; and fo getting into the variable Winds, to the South of the Tropick of *Capricorn*, fteer away to the Weft, over the great *Indian* Ocean.

This was indeed at firft a monftrous Voyage in its Appearance, and the Want of Provifions threaten'd us. *William* told us in fo many Words, that it was impoffible we could carry Provifions enough to fubfift us for fuch a Voyage, and efpe-cially frefh Water; and that as there would be no Land for us to touch at, where we could get any Supply, it was a Madnefs to undertake it.

But I undertook to remedy this Evil, and therefore defired them not to be uneafy at that, for I knew we might fupply our felves at *Mindanao*, the moft Southerly Ifland of the *Philippines*. Accordingly, we fet Sail, having taken all the Provifions here that we could get, the 28th of *September*, the Wind veering a little at firft from the N. N. W. to the N. E. by E. but afterwards fettled about the N. E. and the E. N. E. We were nine Weeks in this Voyage, having met with feveral Interruptions by the Weather, and put in under the Lee of a fmall Ifland in the La-titude of 16 Degrees, 12 Minutes, of which we never knew the Name, none of our Charts ha-ving given any Account of it: I fay, we put in here, by reafon of a ftrange *Tornado* or Hurricane,

which

which brought us into a great deal of Danger. Here we rode about fixteen Days, the Winds being very tempeftuous, and the Weather uncertain. However, we got fome Provifions on Shore, fuch as Plants and Roots, and a few Hoggs. We believed there were Inhabitants on the Ifland, but we faw none of them.

From hence, the Weather fettling again, we went on, and came to the Southmoft Part of *Mindanao*, where we took in frefh Water, and fome Cows; but the Climate was fo hot, that we did not attempt to falt up any more, than fo as to keep a Fortnight or three Weeks, and away we ftood South ward croffing the Line, and leaving *Gillolo* on the Starboard Side, we coafted the Country they call *New Guiney*, where, in the Latitude of eight Degrees South, we put in again for Provifions and Water, and where we found Inhabitants, but they fled from us, and were altogether inconverfable. From thence, failing ftill Southward, we left all behind us that any of our Charts or Maps take any Notice of, and went on till we came to the Latitude of 17 Degrees, the Wind continuing ftill N. E.

Here we made Land to the Weftward, which when we had kept in Sight for three Days, coafting along the Shore, for the Diftance of about four Leagues, we began to fear we fhould find no Outlet Weft, and fo fhould be obliged to go back again, and put in among the *Molucco's* at laft; but at length we found the Land break off, and go trending away to the Weft Sea, feeming to be all open to the South and S. W. and a great Sea came rowling out of the South, which gave us to underftand, that there was no Land that Way for a great Way.

In

In a Word, we kept on our Courſe to the South, a little Weſterly, till we paſs'd the South Tropick, where we found the Winds variable; and now we ſtood away fair Weſt, and held it out for about twenty Days, when we diſcovered Land right a-head, and on our Larboard Bow, we made directly to the Shore, being willing to take all Advantages now for ſupplying our ſelves with freſh Proviſions and Water, knowing we were now entring on that vaſt unknown *Indian* Ocean, perhaps the greateſt Sea on the Globe, having with very little Interruption of Iſlands, a continued Sea quite round the Globe.

We found a good Road here, and ſome People on Shore; but when we landed, they fled up the Country, nor would they hold any Correſpondence with us, or come near us, but ſhot at us ſeveral Times with Arrows as long as Launces. We ſet up white Flags for a Truce, but they either did not, or would not, underſtand it: On the contrary, they ſhot our Flag of Truce thro' ſeveral times with their Arrows; ſo that, in a Word, we never came near any of them.

We found good Water here, tho' it was ſomething difficult to get at it, but for living Creatures we could ſee none; for the People, if they had any Cattle, drove them all away, and ſhew'd us nothing but themſelves, and that ſometimes in a threatning Poſture, and in Number ſo great, that made us ſuppoſe the Iſland to be greater than we at firſt imagined. It is true, they would not come near enough for us to engage with them, at leaſt, not openly; but they came near enough for us to ſee them, and by the Help of our Glaſſes, to ſee that they were clothed and arm'd, but their Clothes were only about their lower

and

and middle Parts; that they had long Launces,
like Half Pikes, in their Hands, besides Bows and
Arrows; that they had great high Things on
their Heads, made, as we believed, of Feathers,
and which look'd something like our Grenadi-
ers Caps in *England*.

When we saw them so shye, that they would
not come near us, our Men began to range over
the Island, *if it was such, for we never surrounded
it*, to search for Cattel, and for any of the *Indians* Plantations, for Fruits or Plants; but they
soon found, to their Cost, that they were to use
more Caution than that came to, and that they
were to discover perfectly every Bush and every
Tree, before they ventured abroad in the Country; for, about fourteen of our Men going further than the rest, into a Part of the Country
which seemed to be planted, as they thought,
for it did but seem so, only I think it was over-
grown with Canes, such as we make our Cane
Chairs with : I say, venturing too far, they were
suddenly attack'd with a Shower of Arrows from
almost every Side of them, as they thought,
out of the Tops of the Trees.

They had nothing to do, but to fly for it,
which however they could not resolve on, till
five of them were wounded; nor had they escaped so, if one of them had not been so much
wiser, or thoughtfuller than the rest, as to consider, that tho' they could not see the Enemy,
so as to shoot at them, yet perhaps the Noise
of their Shot might terrify them, and that they
should rather fire at a Venture. Accordingly
Ten of them faced about, and fired at random
any where among the Canes.

The

The Noife and the Fire not only terrify'd
the Enemy, but, as they believed, their Shot had
luckily hit fome of them ; for they found not only that the Arrows which came thick among
them before, ceafed, but they heard the *Indians*
halloo, after their Way, to one another, and make
a ftrange Noife more uncouth and inimitably
ftrange, than any they had ever heard, more like
the Howling and Barking of wild Creatures in
the Woods, than like the Voice of Men, only
that fometimes they feemed to fpeak Words.

They obferv'd alfo, that this Noife of the *Indians* went farther and farther off, fo that they were
fatisfied the *Indians* fled away, except on one Side,
where they heard a doleful Groaning and Howling, and where it continued a good while, which
they fuppofed was from fome or other of them
being wounded, and howling by reafon of their
Wounds ; or kill'd, and others howling over
them : But our Men had enough of making Dif-
coveries ; fo they did not trouble themfelves to
look farther, but refolved to take this Opportunity to retreat. But the worft of their Adventure
was to come ; for as they came back, they pafs'd
by a prodigious great Trunk of an old Tree,
what Tree it was they faid they did not know, but
it ftood like an old decay'd Oak in a Park, where
the Keepers in *England* take *a Stand*, as they call
it, to fhoot a Deer, and it ftood juft under the
fteep Side of a great Rock or Hill, that our People could not fee what was beyond it.

As they came by this Tree, they were of a fudden fhot at from the Top of the Tree, with feven
Arrows and three Launces, which, to our great
Grief, kill'd two of our Men, and wounded three
more. This was the more furprizing, becaufe
being

being without any Defence, and so near the Trees, they expected more Launces and Arrows every Moment; nor would flying do them any Service, the *Indians* being, as appeared, very good Marks-men. In this Extremity they had happily this Presence of Mind, *viz.* to run close to the Tree, and stand, as it were under it; so that those above could not come at, or see them, to throw their Launces at them. This succeeded, and gave them Time to consider what to do: They knew their Enemies and Murtherers were above, for they heard them talk, and those above knew those were below; but they below were obliged to keep close for fear of their Launces from above. At length, one of our Men looking a little more strictly than the rest, thought he saw the Head of one of the *Indians*, just over a dead Limb of the Tree, which, it seems, the Creature sat upon. One Man immediately fired, and levell'd his Piece so true, that the Shot went thro' the Fellow's Head, and down he fell out of the Tree immediately, and came upon the Ground with such Force, with the Height of his Fall, that if he had not been killed with the Shot, he would certainly have been killed with dashing his Body against the Ground.

This so frighted themselves, that besides the howling Noise they made in the Tree, our Men heard a strange Clutter of them in the Body of the Tree, from whence they concluded they had made the Tree hollow, and were got to hide themselves there. Now, had this been the Case, they were secure enough from our Men; for it was impossible any of our Men could get up the Tree on the Out-side, there being no Branches to climb by; and, to shoot at the Tree, that
they

they tried several times to no Purpose, for the Tree was so thick, that no Shot would enter it. They made no Doubt however, but that they had their Enemies in a Trap, and that a small Siege would either bring them down Tree and all, or starve them out: So they resolved to keep their Post, and send to us for Help. Accordingly two of them came away to us for more Hands, and particularly desired, that some of our Carpenters might come with Tools, to help cut down the Tree, or at least to cut down other Wood, and set Fire to it; and That they concluded would not fail to bring them out.

Accordingly our Men went like a little Army, and with mighty Preparations for an Enterprize, the like of which has scarce been ever heard, to form the Siege of a great Tree. However, when they came there, they found the Task difficult enough, for the old Trunk was indeed a very great one, and very tall, being at least Two and Twenty Foot high, with seven old Limbs standing out every Way on the Top, but decay'd, and very few Leaves, if any, left on it.

William the Quaker, whose Curiosity led him to go among the rest, proposed, that they should make a Ladder, and get up upon the Top, and then throw Wild-fire into the Tree, and smoke them out. Others proposed going back, and getting a great Gun out of the Ship, which should split the Tree in Pieces with the Iron Bullets: Others, that they should cut down a great deal of Wood, and pile it up round the Tree, and set it on Fire, and to burn the Tree, and the *Indians* in it.

These Consultations took up our People no less than two or three Days, in all which Time
they

they heard nothing of the fuppofed Garrifon
within this wooden Caftle, nor any Noife within. *William*'s Projeƈt was firft gone about, and
a large ftrong Ladder was made, to fcale this
wooden Tower ; and in two or three Hours time,
it would have been ready to mount: When, on
a fudden, they heard the Noife of the *Indians* in
the Body of the Tree again, and a little after, feveral of them appeared in the Top of the Tree,
and threw fome Launces down at our Men ; one
of which ftruck one of our Seamen a-top of the
Shoulder, and gave him fuch a defperate Wound,
that the Surgeons not only had a great deal of
Difficulty to cure him, but the poor Man endu-
red fuch horrible Tortures, that we all faid they
had better have killed him outright. However,
he was cured at laft, tho' he never recover'd the
perfeƈt Ufe of his Arm, the Launce having cut
fome of the Tendons on the Top of the Arm,
near the Shoulder, which, as I fuppofe, performed the Office of Motion to the Limb before ;
fo that the poor Man was a Criple all the Days of
his Life. But to return to the defperate Rogues
in the Tree ; our Men fhot at them, but did not
find they had hit them, or any of them ; but as
foon as ever they fhot at them, they could hear
them huddle down into the Trunk of the Tree
again, and there to be fure they were fafe.

Well, however, it was this which put by the
Projeƈt of *William*'s Ladder ; for when it was done,
who would venture up among fuch a Troop of
bold Creatures as were there? And who, they
fuppofed, were defperate by their Circumftances ?
And as but one Man at a time could go up, they
began to think that it would not do ; and indeed I was of the Opinion, *for about this time I*
was

was come to their Affiftance, that the going up the Ladder would not do, unlefs it was thus, that a Man fhould, as it were run juft up to the Top, and throw fome Fire-works into the Tree, and fo come down again; and this we did two or three Times, but found no Effect of it. At laft, one of our Gunners made a Stink-pot, as we called it, being a Compofition which only fmokes, but does not flame or burn; but withal the Smoke of it is fo thick, and the Smell of it fo intolerably naufeous, that it is not to be fuffered. This he threw into the Tree himfelf, and we waited for the Effect of it, but heard or faw nothing all that Night, or the next Day; fo we concluded the Men within were all fmother'd: When, on a fudden, the next Night, we heard them upon the Top of the Tree again, fhouting and hallooing like Madmen.

We concluded, as any body would, that this was to call for Help, and we refolved to continue our Siege; for we were all enraged to fee our felves fo baulk'd by a few wild People whom we thought we had fafe in our Clutches; and indeed never was there fo many concurring Circumftances to delude Men, in any Cafe we had met with. We refolved however to try another Stink-pot the next Night, and our Engineer and Gunner had got it ready, when hearing a Noife of the Enemy, on the Top of the Tree, and in the Body of the Tree, I was not willing to let the Gunner go up the Ladder, which, I faid, would be but to be certain of being murthered. However, he found a *Medium* for it, and that was to go up a few Steps, and with a long Pole in his Hand, to throw it in upon the Top of the Tree, the Ladder being ftanding all this while

T   againft

againſt the Top of the Tree; but when the Gunner, with his Machine at the Top of his Pole,
came to the Tree with three other Men to help
him, behold the Ladder was gone.

This perfectly confounded us, and we now concluded the *Indians* in the Tree had by this Piece
of Negligence taken the Opportunity, and come
all down the Ladder, made their Eſcape, and had
carried away the Ladder with them. I laugh'd
moſt heartily at my Friend *William*, who, as I
ſaid, had the Direction of the Siege, and had ſet
up a Ladder, for the Garriſon, *as we called them,*
to get down upon, and run away. But when
Day-Light came, we were all ſet to rights again;
for there ſtood our Ladder haul'd up on the Top
of the Tree, with about Half of it in the Hollow of the Tree, and the other Half upright in
the Air. Then we began to laugh at the *Indians* for Fools, that they could not as well have
found their Way down by the Ladder, and have
made their Eſcape, as to have pull'd it up by main
Strength into the Tree.

We then reſolved upon Fire, and ſo to put an
End to the Work at once, and burn the Tree
and its Inhabitants together; and accordingly
we went to Work to cut Wood, and in a few
Hours time we got enough, as we thought,
together; and piling it up round the Bottom
of the Tree, we ſet it on Fire: So waiting at a
Diſtance, to ſee when the Gentlemens Quarters
being too hot for them, they would come flying
out at the Top. But we were quite confounded,
when, on a ſudden, we found the Fire all put
out by a great Quantity of Water thrown upon
it. We then thought the Devil muſt be in them
to be ſure. Says *William*, this is certainly the

cunningeft Piece of *Indian* Engineering that ever
was heard of, and there can be but one thing more
to guefs at, befides Witchcraft and Dealing with
the Devil, *which I believe not one Word of, fays he*;
and that muft be, that this is an artificial Tree,
or a natural Tree artificially made hollow down
into the Earth, thro' Root and all; and that thefe
Creatures have an artificial Cavity underneath it,
quite into the Hill, or a Way to go thro', and
under the Hill, to fome other Place, and where
that other Place is, we know not; but if it be
not our own Fault, I'll find the Place, and follow them into it, before I am two Days older.
He then called the Carpenters to know of them,
if they had any large Saws that would cut thro'
the Body, and they told him they had not any
Saws that were long enough, nor could Men
work into fuch a monftrous old Stump in a great
while; but that they would go to Work with
it with their Axes, and undertake to cut it down
in two Days, and ftock up the Root of it in two
more. But *William* was for another Way, which
proved much better than all this; for he was
for filent Work, that, if poffible, he might catch
fome of the Fellows in it; fo he fets twelve
Men to it with large Augurs, to bore great Holes
into the Side of the Tree, to go almoft thro', but
not quite thro'; which Holes were bored without Noife, and when they were done, he filled
them all with Gun-Powder, ftopping ftrong Plugs
bolted crofs-ways into the Holes, and then boring
a flanting Hole of a lefs Size down into the greater
Hole, all which were fill'd with Powder, and at
once blown up. When they took Fire, they
made fuch a Noife, and tore and fplit the Tree
in fo many Places, and in fuch a Manner, that

we

we could fee plainly, fuch another Blaft would demolifh it, and fo it did. Thus at the fecond time we could at two or three Places put our Hands into them, and difcovered the Cheat, namely, that there was a Cave or Hole dug into the Earth, from, or thro' the Bottom of the Hollow, and that it had Communication with another Cave further in, where we heard the Voices of feveral of the wild Folks calling and talking to one another.

When we came thus far we had a great Mind to get at them, and *William* defired, that three Men might be given him with Hand-Grenadoes, and he promifed to go down firft, and boldly he did fo; for *William*, give him his due, had the Heart of a Lion.

They had Piftols in their Hands, and Swords by their Sides; but, as they had taught the *Indians* before, by their Stink-Pots, the *Indians* returned them in their own Kind, for they made fuch a Smoke come up out of the Entrance into the Cave or Hollow, that *William* and his three Men, were glad to come running out of the Cave, and out of the Tree too, for mere want of Breath, and indeed they were almoft ftifled.

Never was a Fortification fo well defended, or Affailants fo many ways defeated; we were now for giving it over, and particularly I called *William*, and told him, I could not but laugh to fee us fpinning out our Time here for nothing; that I could not imagine what we were doing, that it was certain the Rogues that were in it were cunning to the laft Degree, and it would vex any Body to be fo baulked by a few naked ignorant Fellows; but ftill it was not worth our while to pufh it any further, nor was there any

thing

thing that I knew of to be got by the Conquest
when it was made, so that I thought it high time
to give it over.

William acknowledged, that, what I said was
just, and that there was nothing but our Curiosity to be gratified in this Attempt; and tho',
as *he said*, he was very desirous to have
searched into the Thing, yet he would not insist
upon it, so we resolved to quit it, and come
away, which we did. However, *William* said,
before we went, he would have this Satisfaction
of them, *viz.* that he burnt down the Tree and
stopt up the Entrance into the Cave. While he
was doing this, the Gunner told him, he would
have one-Satisfaction of the Rogues, and this
was, that he would make a Mine of it, and see
which way it had Vent : Upon this he fetches
two Barrels of Powder out of the Ships, and
placed them in the Inside of the hollow Cave, as
far in as he durst go to carry them, and then
filling up the Mouth of the Cave where the Tree
stood, and ramming it sufficiently hard, leaving
only a Pipe or Touch-hole, he gave Fire to it,
and stood at a Distance to see which way it
would operate, when, on the sudden, he found
the Force of the Powder burst its way out among
some Bushes on the other Side the little Hill I
mentioned, and that it came roaring out there
as out of the Mouth of a Cannon; immediately running thither we saw the Effects of the
Powder.

First, We saw that *there* was the other Mouth
of the Cave, which the Powder had so torn and
open'd, that the loose Earth was so fallen in
again, that nothing of Shape could be discerned ;
but there we saw what was become of the Garri-

son

ſon of *Indians* too, who had given us all this
Trouble; for ſome of them had no Arms, ſome
no Legs, ſome no Head, ſome lay half buried
in the Kubbiſh of the Mine, that is to ſay, in
the looſe Earth that fell in; and, in ſhort,
there was a miſerable Havock made of them
all, for we had good Reaſon to believe, not one
of them that were in the Inſide could eſcape,
but rather were ſhot out of the Mouth of the
Cave like a Bullet out of a Gun.

We had now our full Satisfaction of the *Indians*, but, in ſhort, this was a loſing Voyage, for
we had two Men killed, one quite crippled,
five more wounded; we ſpent two Barrels of
Powder, and eleven Days Time, and all to get
the Underſtanding how to make an *Indian* Mine,
or how to keep Garriſon in a hollow Tree, and
with this Wit bought at this dear Price, we
came away, having taken in ſome freſh Water,
but got no freſh Proviſions.

We then conſidered what we ſhould do to get
back again to *Madagaſcar*; we were much about
the Latitude of the *Cape of Good Hope*, but had
ſuch a very long Run, and were neither ſure
of meeting with fair Winds, or with any
Land in the Way, that we knew not what to
think of it. *William* was our laſt Reſort in this
Caſe again, and he was very plain with us.
Friend, *ſaid he*, to *CAPT. WILMOT*, what Occaſion haſt thou to run the Venture of ſtarving,
merely for the Pleaſure of ſaying, thou haſt
been where no Body ever was before; there are
a great many Places nearer home, of which thou
mayeſt ſay the ſame thing, at a leſs Expence; I
ſee no Occaſion thou haſt of keeping thus far
South, any longer than till you are ſure you are

to

to the Weſt End of *Iæva* and *Sumatra,* and then
thou may'ſt ſtand away North towards *Ceylon,*
and the Coaſt of *Coromandel* and *Maderas,* where
thou may'ſt get both. freſh Water, and freſh
Proviſions, and to that Part it's likely we may
hold out well enough with the Stores that we have
already.

This was wholeſome Advice, and ſuch as was
not to be ſlighted, ſo we ſtood away to the Weſt,
keeping between the Latitude of 31, and 35, and
had very good Weather and fair Winds for about
ten Days Sail, by which Time, by our Reckoning,
we were clear of the Iſles, and might run away
to the North; and, if we did not fall in with
Ceylon, we ſhould at leaſt go into the great deep
Bay of *Bengal.*

But we were out in our Reckoning a great
deal, for when we had ſtood due North for
about fifteen or ſixteen Degrees, we met with
Land again on our Star-board Bow, about three
Leagues Diſtance, ſo we came to an Anchor
about half a League from it, and Manned out
our Boats to ſee what ſort of a Country it was:
We found it a very good one, freſh Water eaſy
to come at, but no Cattle, that we could ſee, or
Inhabitants, and we were very ſhye of ſearching
too far after them, leſt we ſhould make ſuch
another Journey as we did laſt; ſo that we let
rambling alone, and choſe rather to take what
we could find, which was only a few wild Mangoes, and ſome Plants of ſeveral Kinds, which
we knew not the Names of.

We made no Stay here, but put to Sea again,
N. W. by N. but had little Wind for a Fortnight
more, when we made Land again, and ſtanding
in with the Shore, we were ſurprized to find

ouſ

our felves on the South Shore of *Iava*; and juft
as we were coming to an Anchor, we faw a Boat
carrying *Dutch* Colours, failing along Shore. We
were not follicitous to fpeak with them, or any
other of their Nation, but left it indifferent to
our People, when they went on Shore, to fee
the *Dutchmen*, or not to fee them; our Bufinefs
was to get Provifions, which indeed by this time
were very fhort with us.

We refolved to go on Shore with our Boats in
the moft convenient Place we could find, and to
look out a proper Harbour to bring the Ship
into, leaving it to our Fate, whether we fhould
meet with Friends or Enemies, refolving however, not to ftay any confiderable Time, at leaft,
not long enough to have Expreffes fent crofs the
Ifland to *Batavia*, and for Ships to come round
from thence to attack us.

We found, according to our Defire, a very
good Harbour, where we rode in feven Fathom
Water, well defended from the Weather, whatever might happen, and here we got frefh Provifions, fuch as good Hogs, and fome Cows; and
that we might lay in a little Store, we kill'd
fixteen Cows, and pickled and barrelled up the
Flefh as well as we could be fuppofed to do in the
Latitude of eight Degrees from the Line.

We did all this in about five Days, and filled
our Casks with Water, and the laft Boat was
coming off with Herbs and Roots, we being un-
moor'd, and our Fore Top-Sail loofe for failing,
when we fpy'd a large Ship to the Northward,
bearing down directly upon us; we knew not what
fhe might be, but concluded the worft, and made
all poffible Hafte to get our Anchor up, and get
under Sail, that we might be in a Readinefs to
fee

see what she had to say to us, for we were under no great Concern for one Ship; but our Notion was, that we should be attack'd by three or
four together.

By the time we had got up our Anchor, and
the Boat was stow'd, the Ship was within a League
of us, and, as we thought, bore down to engage
us; so we spread our black Flag or Ancient on
the Poop, and the bloody Flag at the Top-mast
Head, and having made a clear Ship, we stretcht
away to the Westward, to get the Wind of him.

They had, it seems, quite mistaken us before,
expecting nothing of an Enemy or a Pyrate in
those Seas, and not doubting but we had been
one of their own Ships, they seem'd to be in
some Confusion when they found their Mistake; so
they immediately haul'd up on a-Wind on t'other
Tack, and stood edging in for the Shore, towards
the Eastermost Part of the Island. Upon this we
tack'd, and stood after him with all the Sail we
could, and in two Hours came almost within Gun
Shot. Tho' they crowded all the Sail they could
lay on, there was no Remedy but to engage us,
and they soon saw their Inequality of Force.
We fired a Gun for them to bring to, so they
Mann'd out their Boat, and sent to us with a
Flag of Truce. We sent back the Boat, but
with this Answer to the Captain, that he had
nothing to do, but to strike, and bring his Ship
to an Anchor under our Stern, and come on board
us himself, when he should know our Demands;
but that however, since he had not yet put us
to the Trouble of forcing him, which we saw we
were able to do, we assured them, that the Captain should return again in Safety, and all his
Men; and that supplying us with such things as
we

we fhould demand, his Ship fhould not be plundered. They went back with this Meffage, and it was fome time after they were on board, before they ftruck, which made us begin to think they refufed it; fo we fired a Shot, and in a few Minutes more we perceived their Boat put off; and as foon as the Boat put off, the Ship ftruck, and came to an Anchor, as was directed.

When the Captain came on board, we demanded an Account of their Cargo, which was chiefly Bales of Goods from *Bengal* for *Bantam*. We told them our prefent Want was Provifions, which they had no need of, being juft at the End of their Voyage; and that if they would fend their Boat on Shore with ours, and procure us fix and twenty Head of black Cattel, threefcore Hogs, a Quantity of Brandy and Arrack, and three Hundred Bufhels of Rice, we would let them go free.

As to the Rice, they gave us fix Hundred Bufhels, which they had actually on board, together with a Parcel Shipt upon Freight. Alfo they gave us thirty middling Casks of very good Arrack, but Beef and Pork they had none. However, they went on Shore with our Men, and bought eleven Bullocks and fifty Hogs, which were pickled up for our Occafion, and upon the Supplies of Provifion from Shore, we difmifs'd them and their Ship.

We lay here feven Days before we could furnifh our felves with the Provifions agreed for, and fome of the Men fancied the *Dutchmen* were contriving our Deftruction; but they were very honeft, and did what they could to furnifh the Black Cattel, but found it impoffible to fupply fo many. So they came and told us ingenuoufly,

that

that unlefs we could ftay a while longer, they could get no more Oxen or Cows than thofe Eleven, with which we were obliged to be fatif-fied, taking the Value of them in other things, rather than ftay longer there. On our Side we were punctual with them in obferving the Conditions we had agreed on, nor would we let any of our Men fo much as go on board them, or fuffer any of their Men to come on board us; for had any of our Men gone on board, no body could have anfwer'd for their Behaviour, any more than if they had been on Shore in an Enemy's Country.

We were now Victualled for our Voyage, and as we matter'd not Purchafe, we went merrily on for the Coaft of *Ceylon*, where we intended to touch to get frefh Water again, and more Provifions; and we had nothing material offer'd in this Part of the Voyage, only that we met with contrary Winds, and were above a Month in the Paffage.

We put in upon the South Coaft of the Ifland, defiring to have as little to do with the *Dutch* as we could; and as the *Dutch* were Lords of the Country as to Commerce, fo they are more fo of the Sea Coaft, where they have feveral Forts, and in particular, have all the Cinnamon, which is the Trade of that Ifland.

We took in frefh Water here, and fome Provifions, but did not much trouble our felves about laying in any Stores, our Beef and Hogs which we got at *Iava* being not yet all gone by a good deal. We had a little Skirmifh on Shore here with fome of the People of the Ifland, fome of our Men having been a little too familiar with the *Homely Ladies* of the Country; for Homely
indeed

indeed they were, to fuch a Degree, that if our
Men had not had good Stomachs that Way, they
would fcarce have touch'd any of them.

I could never fully get it out of our Men what
they did, they were fo true to one another in
their Wickednefs; but I underftood in the main,
that it was fome barbarous thing they had done,
and that they had like to have paid dear for
it; for the Men refented it to the laft Degree,
and gathered in fuch Numbers about them, that
had not fixteen more of our Men, in another
Boat, ccme all in the Nick of Time, juft to re-
fcue our firft Men, who were but Eleven, and
fo fetch them off by main Force, they had been
all cut off, the Inhabitants being no lefs than two
or three Hundred, armed with Darts and Launces, the ufual Weapons of the Country, and
which they are very dexterous at the throwing,
even fo dexterous, that it was fcarce credible:
And had our Men ftood to fight them, as fome
of them were bold enough to talk of, they had
been all overwhelmed and kill'd. As it was,
feventeen of our Men were wounded, and fome
of them very dangeroufly. But they were more
frighted than hurt too; for every one of them
gave themfelves over for dead Men, believing
the Launces were poifoned. But *William* was our
Comfort here too; for when two of our Surgeons were of the fame Opinion, and told the Men
foolifhly enough, that they would die, *William*
chearfully went to Work with them, and cured
them all but one, who rather died by drinking
fome Arrack Punch, than of his Wound, the
Excefs of Drinking throwing him into a Fever.

We had enough of *Ceylon*, tho' fome of our
People were for going afhore again, fixty or
seventy

feventy Men together, to be revenged; but *William* perfwaded them againft it, and his Reputation was fo great among the Men, as well as with us that were Commanders, that he could influence them more than any of us.

They were mighty warm upcn their Revenge, and they would go on Shore, and deftroy five Hundred of them. Well, fays *William*, and fuppofe you do, what are you the better? Why then, fays one of them, fpeaking for the reft, we fhall have our Satisfaction. Well, and what will you be the better for that, fays *William*? They could then fay nothing to that. Then, fays *William*, if I miftake not, your Bufinefs is Money: Now I defire to know, if you conquer and kill two or three Thoufand of thefe poor Creatures, they have no Money, pray what will you get? They are poor naked Wretches, what fhall you gain by them? But then faid *William*, perhaps, in doing this, you may chance to lofe Half a Score of your own Company, as 'tis very probable you may, pray, what Gain is in it, and what Account can you give the Captain for his loft Men? In fhort, *William* argued fo effectually, that he convinc'd them that it was mere Murther, to do fo; and that the Men had a Right to their own, and that they had no Right to take them away: That it was deftroying innocent Men, who had acted no otherwife than as the Laws of Nature dictated; and that it would be as much Murther to do fo, as to meet a Man on the High-way, and kill him, for the mere fake of it, in cold Blood, not regarding whether he had done any Wrong to us or no.

Thefe Reafons prevailed with them at laft, and they were content to go away, and leave them

as

as they found them. In the firſt Skirmiſh they
killed between ſixty and ſeventy Men, and
wounded a great many more, but they had nothing, and our People got nothing by it, but the
Loſs of one Man's Life, and the Wounding ſixteen
more, as above.

But another Accident brought us to a Neceſſity
of further Buſineſs with theſe People, and indeed
we had like to have put an End to our Lives and Adventures all at once among them; for, about three
Days after our Putting out to Sea, from the Place
where we had that Skirmiſh, we were attack'd
by a violent Storm of Wind from the South, or
rather a Hurricane of Wind from all the Points
Southward, for it blew in a moſt deſperate and
furious Manner, from the S. E. to the S. W.
one Minute at one Point, and then inſtantly turning about again to another Point, but with the
ſame Violence; nor were we able to work the
Ship in that Condition: So that the Ship I was
in ſplit three Topſails, and at laſt brought the
Main Top-maſt by the Board; and in a Word,
we were once or twice driven right aſhore; and
one time, had not the Wind ſhifted the very
Moment it did, we had been daſh'd in a Thouſand Pieces upon a great Ledge of Rocks, which
lay off about Half a League from the Shore; but,
as I have ſaid, the Wind ſhifting very often, and
at that time coming to the E. S. E. we ſtretcht
off, and got above a League more Sea-room in
Half an Hour. After that, it blew with ſome
Fury S. W. by S. then S. W. by W. and put us
back again a great Way to the Eaſtward of the
Ledge of Rocks, where we found a fair Opening
between the Rocks and the Land, and endeavoured to come to an Anchor there; but we
found

found there was no Ground fit to Anchor in, and that we fhould lofe our Anchors, there being nothing but Rocks. We ftood thro' the Opening, which held about four Leagues; the Storm continued, and now we found a dreadful foul Shore, and knew not what Courfe to take. We look'd out very narrowly for fome River, or Creek, or Bay, where we might run in, and come to an Anchor, but found none a great while. At length we faw a great Head-Land lye out far South into the Sea, and that to fuch a Length, that, in fhort, we faw plainly, that if the Wind held where it was, we could not Weather it; fo we run in as much under the Lee of the Point as we could, and came to an Anchor in about twelve Fathom Water.

But the Wind veering again in the Night, and blowing exceeding hard, our Anchors came home, and the Ship drove till the Rudder ftruck againft the Ground; and had the Ship gone Half her Length further, fhe had been loft, and every one of us with her. But our Sheet Anchor held its own, and we heaved in fome of the Cable, to get clear of the Ground we had ftruck upon. It was by this only Cable that we rode it out all Night, and towards Morning we thought the Wind abated a little, and it was well for us that it was fo; for in fpite of what our Sheet Anchor did for us, we found the Ship faft a-ground in the Morning, to our very great Surprize and Amazement.

When the Tide was out, tho' the Water here ebb'd away, the Ship lay almoft dry upon a Bank of hard Sand, which never, I fuppofe, had any Ship upon it before; the People of the Country came down in great Numbers, to look at us, and gaze, not knowing what we were, but gaping

at

at us as at a great Sight or Wonder, at which
they were furpriz'd, and knew not what to do.

I have Reafon to believe, that upon the Sight
they immediately fent an Account of a Ship being
there, and of the Condition we were in ; for the
next Day there appeared a great Man, whether
it was their King or no, I knew not, but he had
Abundance of Men with him, and fome with long
Javelins in their Hands, as long as Half Pikes ;
and thefe came all down to the Water's Edge, and
drew up in very good Order juft in our View.
They ftood near an Hour without making any
Motion, and then there came near twenty of
them with a Man before them, carrying a white
Flag before them. They came forward into the
Water as high as their Waftes, the Sea not going
fo high as before, for the Wind was abated, and
blew off Shore.

The Man made a long Oration to us, as we
could fee by his Geftures, and we fometimes heard
his Voice, but knew not a Word he'faid. *William*,
who was always ufeful to us, I believe, was here
again the Saving of all our Lives. The Cafe was
this. The Fellow, or what I might call him,
when his Speech was done, gave three great
Screams, for I know not what elfe to fay they
were, then lower'd his white Flag three times,
and then made three Motions to us with his Arm,
to come to him.

I acknowledge, that I was for Manning out the
Boat, and going to them ; but *William* would
by no means allow me : He told me, we ought
to truft no Body ; that if they were the Barbarians, and under their own Government, we might
be fure to be all murthered ; and if they were
Chriftians, we fhould not fare much better, if
they

they knew who we were ; that it was the Custom
of the *Malabars*, to betray all People that they
could get into their Hands ; and that these were
some of the same People ; and that if we had
any Regard to our own Safety, we should not
go to them by any means. I opposed him a great
while, and told him, I thought he used to be
always right, but that now I thought he was not ;
that I was no more for running needless Risques,
than he, or any one else ; but I thought all Nations in the World, even the most savage People,
when they held out a Flag of Peace, kept the
Offer of Peace made by that Signal, very sacred-
ly, and I gave him several Examples of it in my
History of my *African* Travels, which I have here
gone thro' in the Beginning of this Work ; and
that I could not think these People worse than
some of them. And besides, I told him, our
Case seem'd to be such, that we must fall into
some body's Hands or other, and that we had
better fall into their Hands by a friendly Treaty,
than by a forced Submission ; nay, tho' they had
indeed a treacherous Design ; and therefore I was
for a Parley with them.

Well, Friend, says *William* very gravely, if thou
wilt go, I cannot help it ; I shall only desire to
take my last Leave of thee at Parting, for depend
upon it, thou wilt never see us again : Whether
we in the Ship may come off any better at last, I
cannot resolve thee ; but this I will answer for, that
we will not give up our Lives idly, and in cool
Blood, as thou art going to do ; we will at least
preserve our selves as long as we can, and die at
last like Men, not like Fools trapann'd by the
Wiles of a few Barbarians.

William

William fpoke this with fo much Warmth, and
yet with fo much Affurance of our Fate, that I
began to think a little of the Rifque I was going to run. I had no more Mind to be murthered than he; and yet I could not for my Life be
fo faint-hearted in the thing, as he. Upon which
I asked him, if he had any Knowledge of the
Place, or had ever been here? He faid, *No*. Then
I asked him, if he had heard or read any thing
about the People of this Ifland, and of their Way
of treating any Chriftians that had fallen into
their Hands? And he told me, he had heard of
one, and he would tell me the Story afterward.
His Name, he faid, was *Knox*, Commander of an
Eaft India Ship, who was driven on Shore, juft as
we were, upon this Ifland of *Ceylon*, tho' he could
not fay it was at the fame Place, or whereabouts:
That he was beguiled by the Barbarians, and in-
ticed to come on Shore, juft as we were invited to
do at that time; and that when they had him,
they furrounded him and eighteen or twenty of
his Men, and never fuffered them to return, but
kept them Prifoners, or murthered them, he
could not well tell which; but they were carried
away up into the Country, feparated from one
another, and never heard of afterwards, except
the Captain's Son, who miraculoufly made his
Efcape after twenty Years Slavery.

I had no Time then to ask him to give the
full Story of this *Knox*, much lefs to hear him
tell it me; but as it is ufual in fuch Cafes, when
one begins to be a little touch'd, I turn'd fhort
with him, Why then, Friend *William*, faid I,
what would you have us do? You fee what
Condition we are in, and what is before us; fomething muft be done, and that immediately. Why,
                                                  fays

fays *William*, I'll tell thee what thou fhalt do: Firſt cauſe a white Flag to be hang'd out, as they do to us, and Man out the Long-Boat and Pinnace with as many Men as they can well ſtow, to handle their Arms, and let me go with them, and thou ſhalt fee what we will do. If I miſcarry, thou may'ſt be ſafe; and I will alſo tell thee, that if I do miſcarry, it fhall be my own Fault, and thou ſhalt learn Wit by my Folly.

I knew not what to reply to him at firſt; but after ſome Pauſe, I ſaid, *William*, *William*, I am as loath you ſhould be loſt, as you are that I ſhould; and if there be any Danger, I deſire you may no more fall into it than I. Therefore, if you will, let us all keep in the Ship, fare alike, and take our Fate together.

No, no, ſays *William*, there's no Danger in the Method I propoſe; thou ſhalt go with me, if thou thinkeſt fit. If thou pleaſeſt but to follow the Meaſures that I ſhall reſolve on, depend upon it, tho' we will go off from the Ships, we will not a Man of us go any nearer them than within Call to talk with them. Thou feeſt they have no Boats to come off to us; but, ſays he, I rather deſire thou wouldſt take my Advice, and manage the Ship, as I ſhall give the Signal from the Boat, and let us concert that Matter together before we go off.

Well, I found *William* had his Meaſures in his Head all laid before-hand, and was not at a Loſs what to do at all; ſo I told him he ſhould be Captain for this Voyage, and we would be all of us under his Orders, which I would ſee obſerved to a Tittle.

Upon this Concluſion of our Debates, he ordered four and Twenty Men into the Long-Boat,

and

and twelve Men into the Pinnace, and the Sea being now pretty smooth, they went off, being all very well arm'd. Also he ordered, that all the Guns of the great Ship, on the Side which lay next the Shore, should be loaded with Musquet Balls, old Nails, Stubbs, and such like Pieces of old Iron, Lead, and any thing that came to Hand; and that we should prepare to fire as soon as ever he saw us lower the white Flag, and hoist up a red one in the Pinnace.

With these Measures fix'd 'between us, they went off towards the Shore, *William* in the Pinnace with twelve Men, and the Long-Boat coming after him with four and twenty more, all stout, resolute Fellows, and very well arm'd. They row'd so near the Shore, as that they might speak to one another, carrying a white Flag as the other did, and offerring a *Parle*. The Brutes, for such they were, shewed themselves very courteous, but finding we could not understand them, they fetch'd an old *Dutchman*, who had been their Prisoner many Years, and set him to speak to us. The Sum and Substance of his Speech was, That the King of the Country had sent his General down to know who we were, and what our Business was? *William* stood up in the Stern of the Pinnace, and told him, That as to that, he that was an *European* by his Language and Voice, might easily know what we were, and our Condition; the Ship being a-ground upon the Sand, would also tell him, that our Business there was that of a Ship in Distress; so *William* desired to know what they came down for with such a Multitude, and with Arms and Weapons, as if they came to War with us.

He

He anfwered, they might have good Reafon to come down to the Shore, the Country being alarmed with the Appearance of Ships of Strangers upon the Coaft; and as our Veffels were full of Men, and that we had Guns and Weapons, the King had fent Part of his military Men, that, in Cafe of any Invafion upon the Country, they might be ready to defend themfelves, whatfoe-'ver might be the Occafion.

But, fays he, as you are Men in Diftrefs, the King has ordered his General who is here alfo, to give you all the Affiftance he can, and to invite you on Shore, to receive you with all poffible Courtefy. Says *William* very quick upon him, before I give thee an Anfwer to that, I defire thee to tell me what thou art; for by thy Speech thou art an *European.* He anfwered prefently, he was a *Dutchman.* That I know well, fays *William,* by thy Speech; but art thou a Native *Dutchman* of *Holland,* or a Native of this Country, that has learnt *Dutch* by converfing among the *Hollanders,* who we know are fettled upon this Ifland.

No, *fays the Old Man,* I am a Native of *Delft* in the Province of *Holland* in *Europe.*

Well, fays *William* immediately, but art thou a Chriftian or a Heathen, or what we call a Renegado?

I am, *fays he,* a Chriftan, and fo they went on in a fhort Dialogue, as follows.

Will. Thou art a *Dutchman,* and a Chriftian, thou fayeft; pray, art thou a Freeman or a Servant?

Dutchm. I am a Servant to the King here, and in his Army.

Will. But art thou a Voluntier, or a Prifoner?

U 3   *Dutchm.*

Dutchm. Indeed I was a Prifoner at firft, but am at Liberty now, and fo am a Voluntier.

Will. That is to fay, being firft a Prifoner thou haft Liberty to ferve them ; but art thou fo at Liberty, that thou mayeft go away, if thou plea-feft, to thine own Countrymen ?

Dutchm. No, I do not fay fo ; my Country-men l've a great Way off, on the North and Eaft Parts of the Ifland, and there is no going to them, without the King's exprefs Licence.

Will. Well, and why doft not thou get a Li-cence to go away ?

Dutchm. I have never ask'd for it.

Will. And I fuppofe, if thou didft, thou knowft thou couldft not obtain it.

Dutchm. I cannot fay much as to that, but why do you ask me all thefe Queftions ?

Will. Why, my Reafon is good ; if thou art a Chriftian and a Prifoner, how canft thou confent to be made an Inftrument to thefe Barbarians, to betray us into their Hands, who are thy Country-men and Fellow-Chriftians ? Is it not a barbarous thing in thee to do fo ?

Dutchm. How do I go about to betray you ? Do I not give you an Account, how the King invites you to come on Shore, and has ordered you to be treated courteoufly, and affifted ?

Will. As thou art a Chriftian, tho' I doubt it much, doft thou believe the King or the General, as thou calleft it, means one Word of what he fays ?

Dutchm. He promifes you by the Mouth of his Great General.

Will. I don't ask thee what he promifes, or by whom ; but I ask thee this: Canft thou fay, that thou believeft he intends to perform it ?

Dutchm.

Dutchm. How can I anſwer that ? How can I tell what he intends?

Will. Thou canſt tell what thou believeſt.

Dutchm. I cannot ſay but he will perform it ; I believe he may.

Will. Thou art but a double-tongu'd Chriſtian, I doubt: Come, I'll ask thee another Queſtion : Wilt thou ſay, that thou believeſt it ; and that thou wouldſt adviſe me to believe it, and put our Lives into their Hands upon theſe Promiſes ?

Dutchm. I am not to be your Adviſer.

Will. Thou art perhaps afraid to ſpeak thy Mind, becauſe thou art in their Power : Pray, do any of them underſtand what thou and I ſay ? Can they ſpeak *Dutch ?*

Dutchm. No, not one of them, I have no Apprehenſions upon that Account at all.

Will. Why then anſwer me plainly, if thou art a Chriſtian : Is it ſafe for us to venture upon their Words, to put our ſelves into their Hands, and come on Shore?

Dutchm. You put it very home to me : Pray let me ask you another Queſtion : Are you in any Likelihood of getting your Ship off, if you refuſe it ?

Will. Yes, yes, we ſhall get off the Ship, now the Storm is over, we don't fear it.

Dutchm. Then I cannot ſay it is beſt for you to truſt them.

Will. Well, it is honeſtly ſaid.

Dutchm. But what ſhall I ſay to them ?

Will. Give them good Words, as they give us.

Dutchm. What good Words?

Will. Why let them tell the King, that we are Strangers, who were driven on his Coaſt by a great Storm ; that we thank him very kindly for

U 4   **his**

his Offer of Civility to us, which, if we are farther diftrefs'd, we will accept thankfully ; but
that at prefent we have no Occafion to come on
Shore : And befides, that we cannot fafely leave
the Ship in the prefent Condition fhe is in, but
that we are obliged to take Care of her, in order
to get her off, and expect in a Tide or two more,
to get her quite clear, and at an Anchor.

Dutchm. But he will expect you to come on
Shore then to vifit him, and make him fome
Prefent for his Civility.

Will. When we have got our Ship clear, and
ftopp'd the Leaks, we will pay our Refpects to
him.

Dutchm. Nay, you may as well come to him
now as then.

Will. Nay, hold Friend, I did not fay we would
come to him then : You talk'd of making him a
Prefent ; that is, to pay our Refpects to him, is
it not ?

Dutchm. Well, but I will tell him, that you
will come on Shore to him when your Ship is got
off ?

Will. I have nothing to fay to that, you may
tell him what you think fit.

Dutchm. But he will be in a great Rage, if I
do not.

Will. Who will he be in a great Rage at ?

Dutchm. At you.

Will. What Occafion have we to value that ?

Dutchm. Why, he will fend all his Army down
againft you.

Will. And what if they were all here juft now ?
What doft thou fuppofe they could do to us ?

Dutchm. He would expect they fhould burn
your Ships, and bring you all to him.

Will.

Will. Tell him, if he try, he may catch a *Tartar.*

Dutchm. He has a World of Men.

Will. Has he any Ships?

Dutchm. No, he has no Ships.

Will. Nor Boats?

Dutchm. No, nor Boats.

Will. Why, what then do you think we care for his Men? What canſt thou do now to us, if thou hadſt a Hundred Thouſand with thee?

Dutchm. O! they might ſet you on Fire.

Will. Set *us a Firing* thou mean'ſt: That they might indeed; but *Set us on Fire,* they ſhall not; they may try at their Peril, and we ſhall make mad Work with your Hundred Thouſand Men, if they come within Reach of our Guns, I aſſure thee.

Dutchm. But what if the King give you Hoſtages for your Safety?

Will. Whom can he give but mere Slaves and Servants like thy ſelf, whoſe Lives he no more values, than we an *Engliſh* Hound?

Dutchm. Whom do you demand for Hoſtages?

Will. Himſelf and your Worſhip.

Dutchm. What would you do with him?

Will. Do with him, as he would do with us, cut his Head off.

Dutchm. And what would you do to me?

Will. Do with thee? We would carry thee home into thine own Country; and tho' thou deſerveſt the Gallows, we would make a Man and a Chriſtian of thee again, and not do by thee as thou wouldſt have done by us, betray thee to a Parcel of mercileſs, ſavage Pagans, that know no God, nor how to ſhew Mercy to Man.

Dutchm.

Dutchm. You put a Thought in my Head that I will fpeak to you about to Morrow.

Thus they went away, and *William* came on board, and gave us a full Account of his Parley with the old *Dutchman,* which was very diverting, and to me inftructing, for I had Abundance of Reafon to acknowledge *William* had made a better Judgment of things than I.

It was our good Fortune to get our Ship off that very Night, and to bring her to an Anchor at about a Mile and a Half further out, and in deep Water, to our great Satisfaction; fo that we had no need to fear the *Dutchman*'s King with his Hundred Thoufand Men; and indeed we had fome Sport with them the next Day, when they came down, a vaft prodigious Multitude of them, very few lefs in Number, in our Imagination, than a Hundred Thoufand, with fome Elephants; tho' if it had been an Army of Elephants, they could have done us no Harm, for we were fairly at our Anchor now, and out of their Reach; and indeed we thought our felves more out of their Reach, than we really were; and it was ten Thoufand to One, that we had not been faft a-ground again; for the Wind blowing off Shore, tho' it made the Water fmooth where we lay, yet it blew the Ebb further out than ufual, and we could eafily perceive the Sand which we touch'd upon before, lay in the Shape of a Half Moon, and furrounded us with two Horns of it; fo that we lay in the Middle or Center of it, as in a round Bay, fafe juft as we were, and in deep Water; but prefent Death, as it were, on the right Hand, and on the left, for the two Horns,

or

or Points of the Sand, reach'd out beyond where our Ship lay near two Miles.

On that Part of the Sand which lay on our East Side, this misguided Multitude extended themselves; and being most of them not above their Knees, or most of them not above Ancle deep in the Water, they, as it were, surrounded us on that Side, and on the Side of the main Land, and a little Way on the other Side of the Sand, standing in a Half Circle, or rather three Fifths of a Circle, for about six Miles in Length; the other Horn, or Point of the Sand which lay on our West Side being not quite so shallow, they could not extend themselves upon it so far.

They little thought what Service they had done us, and how unwillingly, and by the greatest Ignorance, they had made themselves Pilots to us, while we having not sounded the Place, might have been lost, before we were aware. It is true, we might have sounded our new Harbour, before we had ventured out; but I cannot say for certain, whether we should or not; for I, for my Part, had not the least Suspicion of what our real Case was. However, I say, perhaps before we had weigh'd, we should have look'd about us a little. I am sure we ought to have done it; for besides these Armies of human Furies, we had a very leaky Ship, and all our Pumps could hardly keep the Water from growing upon us, and our Carpenters were over-board working to find out, and stop the Wounds we had received, heeling her first on one Side, and then on the other; and it was very diverting to see how, when our Men heel'd the Ship over to the Side next the wild Army that stood on the East Horn of the Sand, they were so amazed between Fright and Joy,

that

that it put them into a kind of Confusion, calling to one another, hallooing and skreeking in a Manner as it is impoſſible to deſcribe.

While we were doing this, for we were in a great Hurry, you may be ſure, and all Hands at Work, as well at the ſtopping our Leaks, as repairing our Rigging and Sails, which had receiv'd a great deal of Damage, and alſo in rigging a new Main-Top-Maſt, and the like: I ſay, while we were doing all this, we perceived a Body of Men, of near a Thouſand, move from that Part of the Army of the Barbarians, that lay at the Bottom of the ſandy Bay, and came all along the Water's Edge, round the Sand, till they ſtood juſt on our Broadſide *Eaſt*, and were within about Half a Mile of us. Then we ſaw the *Dutchman* come forward nearer to us, and all alone, with his white Flag and all his Motions, juſt as before, and there he ſtood.

Our Men had but juſt brought the Ship to Rights again, as they came up to our Broadſide, and we had very happily found out and ſtopp'd the worſt and moſt dangerous Leak that we had, to our very great Satisfaction; ſo I ordered the Boats to be haul'd up, and Mann'd as they were the Day before, and *William* to go as Plenipotentiary. I would have gone my ſelf, if I had underſtood *Dutch*; but as I did not, it was to no Purpoſe, for I ſhould be able to know nothing of what was ſaid, but from him at ſecond Hand, which might be done as well afterwards. All the Inſtructions I pretended to give *William*, was, if poſſible, to get the old *Dutchman* away, and, if he could, to make him come on board.

Well, *William* went juſt as before; and when he came within about ſixty or ſeventy Yards of
the

the Shore, he held up his white Flag, as the
Dutchman did, and turning the Boat's Broadside to
the Shore, and his Men lying upon their Oars,
the Parley or Dialogue began again thus.

Will. Well, Friend, what do'ft thou fay tou s
now ?

Dutchm. I come of the fame mild Errand as I
did yefterday.

Will. What do'ft thou pretend to come of a
mild Errand, with all thefe People at thy Back,
and all the foolifh Weapons of War they bring
with them ? Prithee, what doft thou mean ?

Dutchm. The King haftens us to invite the Captain and all his Men, to come on Shore, and has
ordered all his Men to fhew them all the Civility
they can.

Will. Well, and are all thofe Men come to
invite us afhore ?

Dutchm. They will do you no Hurt, if you
will come on Shore peaceably.

Will. Well, and what doft thou think they can
o to us, if we will not ?

Dutchm. I would not have them do you any
Hurt then neither.

Will. But prithee, Friend, do not make thy
felf Fool and Knave too : Do'ft not thou know
that we are out of Fear of all thy Army, and
out of Danger of all that they can do ? What
makes thee act fo fimply as well as fo knavifhly ?

Dutchm. Why you may think your felves fafer
than you are : You do not know what they
may do to you. I can affure you they are able to
do you a great deal of Harm, and perhaps burn
your Ship.

Will.

Will. Suppose that were true, as I am sure it is false, you see we have more Ships to carry us off, * *pointing to the Sloop.*

* *N. B.* Just at this Time we discovered the Sloop standing towards us from the East, along the Shore, at about the Distance of two Leagues, which was to our particular Satisfaction, she having been missing thirteen Days.

Dutchm. We do not value that, if you had ten Ships, you dare not come on Shore with all the Men you have, in a hostile Way; we are too many for you.

Will. Thou dost not even in that speak as thou meanest; and we may give thee a Tryal of our Hands, when our Friends come up to us; for thou hearest they have discovered us †.

† Just then the Sloop fired five Guns, which was to get News of us, for they did not see us.

Dutchm. Yes, I hear they fire, but I hope your Ship will not fire again; for if they do, our General will take it for breaking the Truce, and will make the Army let fly a Shower of Arrows at you in the Boat.

Will. Thou mayest be sure the Ship will fire, that the other Ship may hear them, but not with Ball, If thy General knows no better, he may begin when he will; but thou mayest be sure we will return it to his Cost.

Dutchm. What must I do then?

Will. Do, why go to him, and tell him of it before-hand then; and let him know, that the Ship firing is not at him, or his Men, and then come again, and tell us what he says.

Dutchm. No, I will send to him, which will do as well.

Will. Do as thou wilt; but I believe thou hadst better go thy self; for if our Men fire first, I suppose he will be in a great Wrath, and it

may

may be, at thee ; for, as for his Wrath at us, we tell thee before-hand, we value it not.

Dutchm. You flight them too much, you know not what they may do.

Will. Thou makeft as if thofe poor favage Wretches could do mighty things; prithee let us fee what you can all do, we value it not ; thou mayeft fet down thy Flag of Truce when thou pleafeft, and begin.

Dutchm. I had rather make a Truce, and have you all part Friends.

Will. Thou art a deceitful Rogue thy felf; for 'tis plain thou knoweft thefe People would only perfwade us on Shore, to entrap and furprize us; and yet thou that art a Chriftian, as thou calleft thy felf, would have us come on Shore, and put our Lives into their Hands who know nothing that belongs to Compaffion, good Ufage, or good Manners: How canft thou be fuch a Villain!

Dutchm. How can you call me fo? What have I done to you, and what would you have me do?

Will. Not act like a Traytor, but like one that was once a Chriftian, and would have been fo ftill, if you had not been a *Dutchman.*

Dutchm. I know not what to do not I, I wifh I were from them, they are a bloody People.

Will. Prithee make no Difficulty of what thou fhouldft do; Canft thou fwim ?

Dutchm. Yes, I can fwim; but if I fhould attempt to fwim off to you, I fhould have a Thoufand Arrows and Javelins fticking in me, before I fhould get to your Boat.

Will. I'll bring the Boat clofe to thee, and take thee on board, in fpite of them all. We will give them but one Volley, and I'll engage they will all run away from thee.

Dutchm.

Dutchm. You are miſtaken in them, I aſſure you; they would immediately come all running down to the Shore, and ſhoot Fire-Arrows at you, and ſet your Boat and Ship and all on Fire, about your Ears.

Will. We will venture that, if thou wilt come off.

Dutchm. Will you uſe me honourably when I am among you?

Will. I'll give thee my Word for it, if thou proveſt honeſt.

Dutchm. Will you not make me a Priſoner?

Will. I will be thy Surety Body for Body, that thou ſhalt be a Freeman, and go whither thou wilt, tho' I own to thee thou doſt not deſerve it.

Juſt at this time our Ship fired three Guns, to anſwer the Sloop, and let her know we ſaw her, who immediately, we perceived, underſtood it, and ſtood directly for the Place; but it is impoſſible to expreſs the Confuſion and filthy vile Noiſe, the Hurry and univerſal Diſorder, that was among that vaſt Multitude of People, upon our Firing of three Guns. They immediately all repaired to their Arms, as I may call it; for, to ſay they put themſelves into Order, would be ſaying nothing.

Upon the Word of Command then they advanced all in a Body to the Sea-ſide, and reſolving to give us one Volley of their Fire Arms, for ſuch they were, immediately they ſaluted us with a Hundred Thouſand of their Fire-Arrows, every one carrying a little Bag of Cloath dipt in Brimſtone, or ſome ſuch thing; which flying thro' the Air, had nothing to hinder it taking Fire as it flew, and it generally did ſo.

I can-

I cannot fay but this Method of attacking us,
by a Way we had no Notion of, might give us at
firft fome little Surprize; for the Number was fo
great at firft, that we were not altogether without Apprehenfions that they might unluckily fet
our Ship on Fire; fo that he refolved immediately
to row on Board, and perfwade us all to weigh,
and ftand out to Sea; but there was no time for
it, for they immediately let fly a Volley at the
Boat, and at the Ship from all Parts of the vaft
Crowd of People which ftood near the Shore.

Nor did they fire, as I may call it, all at once,
and fo leave off; but their Arrows being foon
notch'd upon their Bows, they kept continually
fhooting, fo that the Air was full of Flame.

I could not fay whether they fet their Cotton
Rag on Fire before they fhot the Arrow, for I
did not perceive they had Fire with them, which
however it feems they had. The Arrow, befides
the Fire it carried with it, had a Head, or a Peg,
as we call it, of a Bone, and fome of fharp Flint
Stone; and fome few of a Metal, too foft in itfelf
for Metal, but hard enough to caufe it to enter,
if it were a Plank, fo as to ftick where it fell.

William and his Men had Notice fufficient to lye
clofe behind their Wafte-boards, which for this
very Purpofe they had made fo high, that they
could eafily fink themfelves behind them, fo as to
defend themfelves from any thing that came Point
blank, *as we call it*, or upon a Line; but for what
might fall perpendicular out of the Air, they had
no Guard, but took the Hazard of that. At firft
they made as if they would row away, but before they went, they gave a Volley of their
fmall Arms, firing at thofe which ftood with the
Dutchman; but *William* ordered them to be fure

X

to take their Aim at others so as to miss him,
and they did so.

There was no Calling to them now, for the
Noise was so great among them, that they could
hear no Body; but our Men boldly row'd in nearer
to them, for they were at first driven a little off,
and when they came nearer, they fired a second
Volley, which put the Fellows into a great Confusion, and we could see from the Ship, that several of them were killed or wounded.

We thought this was a very unequal Fight,
and therefore we made a Signal to our Men, to
row away, that we might have a little of the
Sport as well as they; but the Arrows flew so
thick upon them, being so near the Shore, that
they could not sit to their Oars; so they spread
a little of their Sail, thinking they might sail
along the Shore, and lye behind their Waste-
boards: But the Sail had not been spread six
Minutes, but it had five Hundred Fire-Arrows
shot into it, and thro' it, and at length set it
fairly on Fire; nor were our Men quite out of
the Danger of its setting the Boat on Fire, and
this made them paddle and shove the Boat away
as well as they could, as they lay, to get further
off.

By this time they had left us a fair Mark at the
whole Savage Army; and as we had sheer'd the
Ship as near to them as we could, we fired among
the thickest of them six or seven times, five Guns
at a time, which shot old Iron, Musquet Bullets &c.

We could easily see that we made Havock of
them, and killed and wounded Abundance of
them, and that they were in a great Surprize at
it; but yet they never offered to stir, and all this
while their Fire-Arrows flew as thick as before.

At

At laſt, on a ſudden their Arrows ſtopt, and the old *Dutchman* came running down to the Water Side, all alone, with his white Flag as before, waving it as high as he could, and making Signals to our Boat to come to him again.

William did not care at firſt to go near him, but the Man continuing to make Signals to him to come, at laſt *William* went, and the *Dutchman* told him, that he had been with the General, who was much mollified by the Slaughter of his Men, and that now he could have any thing of him.

Any thing, ſays *William*, what have we to do with him? Let him go about his Buſineſs, and carry his Men out of Gun-Shot: Can't he?

Why, ſays the *Dutchman*, but he dares not ſtir, nor ſee the King's Face; unleſs ſome of your Men come on Shore, he will certainly put him to Death.

Why then, ſays *William*, he is a dead Man; for if it were to ſave his Life, and the Lives of all the Crowd that is with him, he ſhall never have one of us in his Power.

But I'll tell thee, ſaid *William*, how thou ſhalt cheat him, and gain thy own Liberty too, if thou haſt any Mind to ſee thy own Country again, and art not turn'd Savage, and grown fond of living all thy Days among Heathens and Savages.

I would be glad to do it with all my Heart, ſays he; but if I ſhould offer to ſwim off to you now, tho' they are ſo far from me, they ſhoot ſo true, that they would kill me before I got half Way.

But, ſays *William*, I'll tell thee how thou ſhalt come with his Conſent; go to him, and tell him, I have offer'd to carry you on board, to try if you could perſwade the Captain to come on Shore,

and

and that I would not hinder him, if he was willing to venture.

The *Dutchman* seem'd in a Rapture at the very first Word: I'll do it, says he, I am perswaded he will give me Leave to come.

Away he runs, as if he had a glad Message to carry, and tells the General, that *William* had promised, if he would go on board the Ship with me, he would perswade the Captain to return with him. The General was Fool enough to give him Order to go, and charg'd him not to come back without the Captain, which he readily promised, and very honestly might.

So they took him in, and brought him on board, and he was as good as his Word to them, for he never went back to them any more; and the Sloop being come to the Mouth of the Inlet where we lay, we weighed, and set Sail. But as we went out, being pretty near the Shore, we fired three Guns as it were among them, but without any Shot, for it was of no Use to us, to hurt any more of them. After we had fired, we gave them a Chear, as the Seamen call it; *that is to say*, we halloo'd at them by way of Triumph, and so carried off their Ambassador; how it fared with their General, we know nothing of that.

This Passage, when I related it to a Friend of mine, after my Return from those Rambles, agreed so well with his Relation of what happened to one Mr. *Knox*, an *English* Captain, who some time ago was decoyed on Shore by those People, that it could not but be very much to my Satisfaction to think what Mischief we had all escaped; and I think it cannot but be very profitable to record the other Story, *which is but short*, with my own, to shew, whoever reads this, what it was I avoided,
and

and prevent their falling into the like, if they have to do with the perfidious People of *Ceylon*. The Relation is as follows.

The Ifland of *Ceylon* being inhabited for the greateft Part by Barbarians, which will not allow any Trade or Commerce with any *European* Nation, and inacceffible by any Travellers, it will be convenient to relate the Occafion how the Author of this Story happen'd to go into this Ifland, and what Opportunities he had of being fully acquainted with the People, their Laws and Cuftoms, that fo we may the better depend upon the Account, and value it as it deferves, for the Rarity as well as the Truth of it; and both thefe the Author gives us a brief Relation of, in this Manner. His Words are as follows.

In the Year 1657, the *Anne* Fregat, of *London*, Captain *Robert Knox* Commander, on the 21ft of *January*, fet Sail out of the *Downes*, in the Service of the Honourable the *Eaft India* Company of *England*, bound for *Fort St. George* upon the Coaft of *Coromandel*, to trade for one Year from Port to Port in *India*; which having performed, as he was lading his Goods to return for *England*, being in the Road of *Matlipatam*, on the 19th of *November* 1659, there happen'd fuch a mighty Storm, that in it feveral Ships were caft away, and he was forc'd to cut his Main Maft by the Board, which fo difabled the Ship, that he could not proceed in his Voyage; whereupon, *Cotiar*, in the Ifland of *Ceylon* being a very commodious Bay fit for her prefent Diftrefs, *Thomas Chambers*, Efq; fince Sir *Thomas Chambers*, the Agent at *Fort St. George*, ordered that the Ship fhould take

in

in fome Cloath and *Indian* Merchants belonging
to *Porta Nova*, who might trade there while fhe
lay to fet her Maft, and repair the other Dama-
ges fuftained by the Storm. At her firft coming
thither, after the *Indian* Merchants were fet on
Shore, the Captain and his Men were very jea-
lous of the People of the Place, by reafon the
Englifh never had any Commerce or Dealing with
them; but after they had been there twenty Days,
going afhore and returning again at Pleafure,
without any Moleftation, they began to lay afide
all fufpicious Thoughts of the People that dwelt
thereabouts, who had kindly entertained them
for their Money.

By this time the King of the Country had Notice of their Arrival, and not being acquainted
with their Intents, he fent down a *Diffuava,* or
General, with an Army to them, who immediately fent a Meffenger to the Captain on board,
to defire him to come afhore to him, pretending
a Letter from the King. The Captain faluted
the Meffage with Firing of Guns, and ordered
his Son *Robert Knox*, and Mr. *John Loveland*, Merchant of the Ship, to go afhore and wait on him.
When they were come before him, he demanded
Who they were, and how long they fhould ftay? They
told him, *They were* Englifhmen, *and not to ftay
above twenty or thirty Days, and defired Permiffion to
trade in his Majefty's Port.* His Anfwer was, *That
the King was glad to hear that the* Englifh *were come
into his Country, and had commanded him to affift them,
as they fhould defire, and had fent a Letter to be delivered to none but the Captain himfelf.* They were
then twelve Miles from the Sea-Side, and therefore replied, *That the Captain could not leave his Ship
to come fo far; but if he pleafed to go down to the*

Sea-

Sea-Side, the Captain would wait on him to receive the Letter. Whereupon the *Diſſuava* deſired them to ſtay that Day, and on the Morrow he would go with them ; which, rather than diſpleaſe him in ſo ſmall a Matter, they conſented to. In the Evening, the *Diſſuava* ſent a Preſent to the Captain of Cattle and Fruits, &c. which being carried all Night by the Meſſengers, was delivered to him in the Morning, who told him withal, that his Men were coming down with the *Diſſuava,* and deſired his Company on Shore againſt his coming, having a Letter from the King to deliver into his own Hand. The Captain miſtruſting nothing, came on Shore with his Boat, and ſitting under .a Tamarind Tree, waited for the *Diſſuava.* In the mean time, the Native Soldiers privately ſurrounded him and the ſeven Men he had with him, and ſeizing them, carrried them to meet the *Diſſuava,* bearing the Captain on a Hammock on their Shoulders.

The nextDay the Long-Boat's Crew, not knowing what had happen'd, came on Shore to cut down a Tree to make Cheeks for the Main-Maſt, and were made Priſoners after the ſame Manner, tho' with more Violence, becauſe they were more rough with them, and made Reſiſtance, yet they were not brought to the Captain and his Company, but quarter'd in another Houſe in the ſame Town.

The *Diſſuava* having thus gotten two Boats, and eighteen Men, his next Care was to gain the Ship, and, to that End, telling the Captain that he and his Men were only detained becauſe the King intended to ſend Letters and a Preſent to the *Engliſh* Nation by him, deſired he would ſend ſome Men on board his Ship to order her

Stay ;

Stay; and because the Ship was in Danger of being fired by the *Dutch*, if she stay'd long in the Bay, to bring her up the River. The Captain did not approve of the Advice, but did not dare own his Dislike; and so sent his Son with the Order, but with a solemn Conjuration to return again, which he accordingly did, bringing a Letter from the Company in the Ship, *That they would not obey the Captain, nor any other in this Matter, but were resolved to stand on their own Defence.* This Letter satisfied the *Dissaava*, who thereupon gave the Captain Leave to write for what he would have brought him from the Ship, pretending, that he had not the King's Order to release them, though it would suddenly come.

The Captain seeing he was held in Suspense, and the Season of the Year spending for the Ship to proceed on her Voyage to some Place, sent Order to Mr. *John Burford* the chief Mate, to take Charge of the Ship, and set Sail to *Porta Nova*, from whence they came, and there to follow the Agent's Order.

And now began that long and sad Captivity they all along feared; the Ship being gone, the *Dissaava* was called up to the King, and they were kept under Guards a while, till a special Order came from the King to part them, and put one in a Town, for the Conveniency of their Maintenance, which the King ordered to be at the Charge of the Country. On *September*, 16, 1660, the Captain and his Son were placed in a Town called *Bonder Coostwat*, in the Country of *Hotcurly*, distant from the City of *Candi* Northward thirty Miles, and, from the rest of the *English*, a full Day's Journey. Here they had
their

their Provisions brought them twice a Day, without Money, so much as they could eat, and as good as the Country yielded. The Situation of the Place was very pleasant and commodious, but that Year that Part of the Land was very sickly by Agues and Fevers, of which many died. The Captain and his Son, after some time, were visited with the common Distemper, and the Captain being also loaded with Grief for his deplorable Condition, languish'd more than three Months, and then died, *February* the 9th 1660.

Robert Knox his Son being now left desolate, sick, and in Captivity, having none to comfort him but God, who is the Father of the fatherless, and hears the Groans of such as are in Captivity, being alone to enter upon a long Scene of Misery and Calamity, oppress'd with Weakness of Body and Grief of Soul, for the Loss of his Father, and his remediless Trouble that he was like to endure; and the first Instance of it was in the Burial of his Father: For he sent his Black Boy to the People of the Town, to desire their Assistance, because they understood not their Language; but they sent him only a Rope to drag him by the Neck into the Woods, and told him, *that they would offer him no other Help unless he would pay for it.* This barbarous Answer increased his Trouble, for his Father's Death, that now he was like to lye unburied, and be made a Prey to the wild Beasts in the Woods; for the Ground was very hard, and they had not Tools to dig with, and so it was impossible for them to bury him; but having a small Matter of Money left him, *viz.* a *Pagoda,* and a Gold Ring, he hired a Man, and so buried

him

him in as decent a Manner as their Condition would permit.

His dead Father being thus removed out of his Sight, but his Ague continuing, he was reduced very low, partly by Sorrow, and partly by his Difeafe; all the Comfort he had, was to go into the Wood, and Fields with a Book, either the *Practice of Piety*, or Mr. *Rogers*'s *Seven Treatifes*, which were the only two Books he had, and meditate and read, and fometimes pray, in which, his Anguifh made him often invert *Elijah*'s Petition, *That he might die*, becaufe his Life was a burthen to him. God, tho' he was pleafed to prolong his Life, yet he found a Way to lighten his Grief, by removing his Ague, and granting him a Defire, which above all things, was acceptable to him. He had read his two Books over fo often, that he had both almoft by Heart, and tho' they were both pious and good Writings, yet he long'd for the Truth from the original Fountain, and thought it his greateft Unhappinefs, that he had not a Bible, and did believe, that he fhould never fee one again : But, contrary to his Expectation, God brought him one after this Manner. As he was fifhing one Day, with his Black Boy, to catch fome Fifh to relieve his Hunger, an old Man pafs'd by them, and asked his Boy, whether his Mafter could read; and when the Boy had anfwered, *Yes*; he told him, *that he had gotten a Book from the* Portuguefe *when they left* Columbo; *and, if his Mafter pleafed, he would fell it him.* The Boy told his Mafter, who bad him go and fee what Book it was. The Boy having ferved the *Englifh* fome time, knew the Book, and, as foon

as

as he had got it into his Hand, came running to him, calling out before he came to him, *'Tis the Bible.* The Words ſtartled him, and he flung down his Angle to meet him, and, finding it true, was mightily rejoyc'd to ſee it; but he was a-fraid he ſhould not have enough to purchaſe it, tho' he was reſolved to part with all the Money he had, which was but one *Pagoda,* to buy it; but, his Black Boy perſwading him to ſlight it; and leave it to him to buy it, he at length, obtained it for a knit Cap.

This Accident he could not but look upon as a great Miracle, that God ſhould beſtow upon him ſuch an extraordinary Bleſſing, and bring him a Bible in his own native Language, in ſuch a remote Part of the World, where his Name was not known, and where it was never heard of, that an *Engliſhman* had ever been before. The Enjoyment of this Mercy was a great Comfort to him in his Captivity, and tho' he wanted no bodily Convenience that the Country did afford, for the King immediately after his Father's Death had ſent an expreſs Order to the Peo-ple of the Town, that they ſhould be kind to him, and give him good Victuals; and, after he had been ſome time in the Country, and un-derſtood the Language, he got him good Conve-niencies, as, a Horſe and Gardens, and falling to Husbandry, God ſo proſpered him, that he had Plenty, not only for himſelf, but to lend others; which being according to the Cuſtom of the Country, at 50 *per Cent.* a Year, much enriched him. He had alſo Goats, which ſerved him for Mutton, and Hogs and Hens: Notwith-ſtanding this, I ſay, for he lived as fine as any of their Noblemen, he could not ſo far forget

his

his native Country, as to be contented to dwell in a ſtrange Land, where there was to him a Famine of God's Word and Sacraments, the Want of which made all other things to be of little Value to him ; therefore, as he made it his daily and fervent Prayer to God, in his good time, to reſtore him to both, ſo at length he, with one *Stephen Rutland*, who had lived with him two Years before, reſolved to make their Eſcape, and, about the Year 1673, meditated all ſecret Ways to compaſs it. They had before taken up a Way of Peddling about the Country, and buying Tobacco, Pepper, Garlick, Combs, and all ſorts of Iron-Ware, and carried them into thoſe Parts of the Country where they wanted them ; and now, to promote their Deſign, as they went with their Commodities from Place to Place, they diſcourſed with the Country People, *for they could now ſpeak their Language well*, concerning the Ways and Inhabitants where the Iſle was thinneſt and fulleſt inhabited; where and how the Watches lay from one Country to another ; and what Commodities were proper for them to carry into all Parts; pretending, that they would furniſh themſelves with ſuch Wares as the reſpective Places wanted. None doubted but what they did was upon the Account of Trade, becauſe Mr. *Knox* was ſo well ſeated, and could not be ſuppoſed to leave ſuch an Eſtate, was by travelling Northward, becauſe that Part of the Land was leaſt inhabited; and ſo furniſhing themſelves with ſuch Wares as were vendible in thoſe Parts, they ſet forth, and ſteered their Courſe towards the North Part of the Iſland, knowing very little of the Ways, which were generally intricate and perplex'd, plexed, becaufe they have no publick Roads, but a Multitude of little Paths from one Town to another, and thofe often changing; and for White Men to enquire about the Ways, was very dangerous, becaufe the People would prefently fufpect their Defign.

At this Time they travelled from *Canda Uda*, as far as the Country of *Neurecalava*, which is in the furthermoft Parts of the King's Dominions, and about three Days Journey from their Dwelling. They were very thankful to Providence that they had paffed all Difficulties fo far; but yet durft not go any further, becaufe they had no Wares left to Traffick with; and it being the firft time they had been abfent fo long from home, they feared the Townfmen would come after them to feek for them, and fo they returned home, and went eight or ten times into thofe Parts with their Wares, till they became well acquainted both with the People and the Paths.

In thefe Parts Mr. *Knox* met his black Boy, whom he had turned away divers Years before. He had now got a Wife and Children, and was very poor; but being acquainted with thefe Quarters, he not only took Directions of him, but agreed with him for a good Reward, to conduct him and his Companion to the *Dutch*. He gladly undertook it, and a Time was appointed between them; but Mr. *Knox* being difabled by a grievous Pain which feized him on his right Side, and held him five Days, that he could not travel, this Appointment proved in vain; for tho' he went as foon as he was well, his Guide was gone into another Country about his Bufinefs, and they durft not at that time venture to run away with-

out

out him. These Attempts took up eight or nine
Years, various Accidents hindring their Designs,
but moſt commonly the dry Weather, becauſe
they fear'd, in the Woods, they ſhould be ſtarv'd
with Thirſt, all the Country being in ſuch a Condition almoſt four or five Years together for Lack
of Rain.

On *September* 22. 1679, they ſet forth again,
furniſhed with Knives and ſmall Axes, for their
Defence, becauſe they could carry them privately, and ſend all Sorts of Wares to ſell, as formerly, and all neceſſary Proviſions, the Moon
being twenty ſeven Days old, that they might have
Light to run away by, to try what Succeſs God
Almighty would now give them, in ſeeking their
Liberty. Their firſt Stage was to *Anarodgburro,*
in the Way to which lay a Wilderneſs, called
Parraoth Mocolane, full of wild Elephants, Tygers, and Bears; and becauſe 'tis the utmoſt
Confines of the King's Dominions, there is always a Watch kept.

In the Middle of the Way, they heard that
the Governour's Officers of theſe Parts were out
to gather up the King's Revenues and Duties,
to ſend them up to the City ; which put them
into no ſmall Fear, leſt finding them, they ſhould
ſend them back again: Whereupon they with-
drew to the Weſtern Parts of *Ecpoulpot,* and ſat
down to Knitting, till they heard they Officers
were gone. As ſoon as they were departed, they
went onwards of their Journey, having got a
good Parcel of Cotton Yarn to knit Caps with,
and having kept their Wares, as they pretended,
to exchange for dried Fiſh, which was ſold only
in thoſe lower Parts. Their Way lay neceſſari-
ly thro' the Governour's Yard at *Collinilla,* who
dwells

dwells there on Purpose to examine all that go and come. This greatly diftrefs'd them, becaufe he would eafily fufpect they were out of their Bounds, being Captives; however, they went refolutely to his Houfe, and meeting him, prefented him with a fmall Parcel of Tobacco and Betel; and fhewing him their Wares, told him, they came to get dried Flefh to carry back with them. The Governour did not fufpect them, but told them, he was forry they came in fo dry a Time, when no Deer could be catched, but if fome Rain fell, he would foon fupply them. This Anfwer pleafed them, and they feemed contented to ftay; and accordingly abiding with him two or three Days, and no Rain falling, they prefented the Governour with five or fix Charges of Gunpowder, which is a Rarity among them; and leaving a Bundle at his Houfe, they defired him to fhoot them fome Deer, while they made a Step to *Anarodgburro*. Here alfo they were put in a great Fright, by the coming of certain Soldiers from the King to the Governour, to give him Orders to fet a fecure Guard at the Watches, that no fufpicious Perfons might pafs; which, tho' it was only intended to prevent the Flight of the Relations of certain Nobles whom the King had clapt up; yet they feared they might wonder to fee white Men here, and fo fend them back again: But God fo ordered it, that they were very kind to them, and left them to their Bufinefs, and fo they got fafe to *Anarodgburro*. Their Pretence was dried Flefh, tho' they knew there was none to be had; but their real Bufinefs was to fearch the Way down to the *Dutch*, which they ftaid three Days to do: But finding, that in the Way to *Jafnapatan*, which is one of the *Dutch* Ports, there was a Watch which

could

could hardly be pass'd, and other Inconveniencies not surmountable, they resolved to go back, and take the River *Malwatogah,* which they had before judged would be a probable Guide to lead them to the Sea ; and that they might not be pursued, left *Anarodgburro* just at Night, when the People never travel for fear of wild Beasts. On *Sunday, Oct.* 12. being stored with all things needful for their Journey, *viz.* Ten Days Provision, a Basin to boil their Provision in, two Calabashes to fetch Water in, and two great Tallipat Leaves for Tents, with Jaggory, Sweet-meats, Tobacco, Betell, Tinder-Boxes, and a Deer-Skin for Shoes, to keep their Feet from Thorns, because to them they chiefly trusted. Being come to the River, they struck into the Woods, and kept by the Side of it ; yet not going on the Sand, left their Footsteps should be discerned, unless forced, and then going backwards.

Being gotten a good Way into the Wood, it began to rain ; wherefore they erected their Tents, made a Fire, and refresh'd themselves against the Rising of the Moon, which was then eighteen Days old ; and having tied Deer-Skins about their Feet, and eased themselves of their Wares, they proceeded in their Journey. When they had travelled three or four Hours with Difficulty, because the Moon gave but little Light among the thick Trees, they found an Elephant in their Way before them, and because they could not scare him away, they were forced to stay till Morning ; and so they kindled a Fire, and took a Pipe of Tobacco. By the Light they could not discern that ever any Body had been there, nothing being to be seen but Woods, and so they were in great Hopes that they were past all Danger, being beyond all Inhabitants ;

bitants; but they were miftaken; for the River winding Northward, brought them into the midft of a Parcel of Towns, called *Tiffea Wava*, where being in Danger of being feen, they were under a mighty Terror for had the People found them, they would have beat them, and fent them up to the King) and to avoid it, they crept into an hollow Tree, and fat there in Mud and Wet, till it began to grow dark, and then betaking themfelves to their Legs, travell'd till the Darknefs of Night ftopt them. They heard Voices behind them, and feared 'twas fomebody in Purfuit of them; but at length difcerning it was only an Hallooing to keep the wild Beafts out of the Corn, they pitched their Tents by the River, and having boiled Rice, and roafted Meat for their Suppers, and fatisfied their Hungers, they committed themfelves to God's Keeping, and laid them down to Sleep.

The next Morning, to prevent the worft, they got up early, and haften'd on their Journey; and tho' they were now got out of all Danger of the tame *Chiangulays*, they were in great Danger of the wild ones, of whom thofe Woods were full; and though they faw their Tents, yet they were all gone, fince the Rains had fallen, from the River into the Woods; and fo God kept them from that Danger, for had they met the wild Men, they had been fhot.

Thus they travelled from Morning to Night feveral Days, thro' Bufhes and Thorns, which made their Arms and Shoulders, which were naked, all of a Gore Blood. They often met with Bears, Hogs, Deer, and wild Buffloes, but they all run away as foon as they faw them. The River was exceeding full of Alligators. In the

Evening

Evening they used to pitch their Tents, and make great Fires both before and behind them, to affright the wild Beasts, and tho' they heard the Voices of all sorts, they saw none.

On *Thursday* at Noon they cross'd the River *Coronda Oya*, which parts the Country of the *Malabars* from the King's, and on *Friday* about Nine or Ten in the Morning, came among the Inhabitants, of whom they were as much afraid as of the *Chiangulays* before ; for tho' the *Wanniounay*, or Prince of this People, payeth Tribute to the *Dutch* out of Fear, yet he is better affected to the King of *Candi*, and if he had took them, would have sent them up to their old Master; but not knowing any Way to escape, they kept on their Journey by the River Side by Day, because the Woods were not to be travell'd by Night, for Thorns and wild Beasts, who came down then to the River to drink. In all the *Malabars* Country they met with only two Bramans, who treated them civilly, and for their Money one of them conducted them till they came into the Territories of the *Dutch*, and out of all Danger from the King of *Candi*, which did not a little rejoice them.; but yet they were in no small Trouble how to find the Way out of the Woods, till a *Malabar* for the Lucre of a Knife, conducted them to a *Dutch* Town, where they found Guides to conduct them from Town to Town, till they came to the Fort called *Arepa*, where they arrived *Saturday*, *October* 18. 1679, and there thankfully ador'd God's wonderful Providence, in thus compleating their Deliverance from a long Captivity of Nineteen Years and six Months.

I come

I come now back to my own History, which draws near a Conclusion, as to the Travels I took in this Part of the World. We were now at Sea, and we stood away to the North for a while, to try if we could get a Market for our Spice, for we were very rich in Nutmegs, but we ill knew what to do with them; we durst not go upon the *English* Coast, or, to speak more properly, among the *English* Factories to Trade; not that we were afraid to fight any two Ships they had; and besides that, we knew, that as they had no Letters of Mart or of Reprisals from the Government, so it was none of their Business to act offensively, no not tho' we were Pyrates. Indeed if we had made any Attempt upon them, they might have justify'd themselves in joining together to resist, and assisting one another to defend themselves; but to go out of their Business to attack a Pyrate Ship of almost fifty Guns, as we were, it was plain, that it was none of their Business, and consequently it was none of our Concern, so we did not trouble our selves about it; but, on the other Hand, it was none of our Business to be seen among them, and to have the News of us carried from one Factory to another: So that whatever Design we might be upon at another Time, we should be sure to be prevented and discovered: Much less had we any Occasion to be seen among the *Dutch* Factories, upon the Coast of *Malabar*; for, being fully loaden with the Spices which we had in the Sense of their Trade plundered them of, it would soon have told them what we were, and all that we had been doing, and they would, no doubt, have concerned themselves all manner of Ways to have fallen upon us.

The

The only Way we had for it was to stand away for
Goa, and Trade, if we could, for our Spices with the
Portuguese Factory there. Accordingly we sailed
almost thither, for we had made Land two Days
before, and, being in the Latitude of *Goa*, were
standing in fair for *Marmagoon*, on the Head of *Sal-
sat*, at the going up to *Goa*, when I called to the Man
at the Helm to bring the Ship to, and bid the Pilot
go away N. N. W. till we came out of Sight of the
Shore ; when *William* and I called a Council as we
used to do upon Emergences, what Course we
should take to trade there, and not be discovered ;
and we concluded, at length, that we would not
go thither at all ; but that *William*, with such
trusty Fellows only as could be depended upon,
should go in the Sloop to *Surat*, which was still
farther Northward, and trade there as Merchants, with such of the *English* Factory as they
could find to be for their Turn.

To carry this with the more Caution, and so
as not to be suspected, we agreed to take out all
her Guns, and to put such Men into her, and
no other, as would promise us not to desire or
offer to go on Shore, or to enter into any Talk
or Conversation with any that might come on
board : And to finish the Disguise to our Mind,
William documented two of our Men, one a Surgeon, as he himself was, and the other a ready-
witted Fellow, an old Sailor, that had been a
Pilot upon the Coast of *New-England*, and was
an excellent Mimick ; these two *William* dressed
up like two Quakers, and made them talk like
such. The old Pilot he made go Captain of the
Sloop, and the Surgeon for Doctor, as he was,
and himself Super-Cargo : In this Figure, and
the Sloop all plain, no curled Work upon her,
indeed

indeed fhe had not much before, and no Guns
to be feen, away he went for *Surat*.

I fhould indeed have obferved, that we went,
fome Days before we parted, to a fmall fandy
Ifland, clofe under the Shore, where there was
a good Cove of deep Water, like a Road, and
out of Sight of any of the Factories, which are
here very thick upon the Coaft. Here we fhift-
ed the Loading of the Sloop, and put into her
fuch Things only as we had a mind to difpofe of there, which was indeed little but Nutmegs and Cloves, but chiefly the former; and
from thence *William* and his two Quakers, with
about eighteen Men in the Sloop, went away to
Surat, and came to an Anchor at a Diftance from
the Factory.

William ufed fuch Caution, that he found
Means to go on Shore himfelf, and the Doctor, as
he called him, in a Boat, which came on board
them to fell Fifh, rowed with only *Indians* of the
Country, which Boat he afterwards hired to
carry him on board again. It was not long
that they were on Shore, but that they found
Means to get Acquaintance with fome *Englifhmen*, who, though they lived there, and perhaps, were the Company's Servants at firft,
yet appeared then to be Traders for themfelves,
in whatever Coaft-Bufinefs efpecially came in
their Way, and the Doctor was made the firft
to pick Acquaintance; fo he recommended his
Friend, the Super-Cargo, till, by Degrees, the
Merchants were as fond of the Bargain as our
Men were of the Merchants, only that the Cargo
was a little too much for them.

However, this did not prove a Difficulty long
with them; for the next Day they brought two

more

more Merchants, *English* also, into their Bargain; and, as *William* could perceive by their Difcourfe, they refolved, if they bought them, to carry them to the Gulph of *Perfia*, upon their own Accounts; *William* took the Hint, and, as he told me afterwards, concluded we might carry them there as well as they; but this was not *William*'s prefent Bufinefs; he had here no lefs than three and thirty Ton of Nuts, and eighteen Ton of Cloves. There was a good Quantity of Mace among the Nutmegs; but we did not ftand to make much Allowance. In fhort, they bargained, and the Merchants, who would gladly have bought Sloop and all, gave *William* Directions, and two Men for Pilots, to go to a Creek about fix Leagues from the Factory, where they brought Boats, and unloaded the whole Cargo, and paid *William* very honeftly for it. The whole Parcel amounting, in Money, to about thirty five thoufand Pieces of Eight, befides fome Goods of Value, which *William* was content to take, and two large Diamonds worth about three Hundred Pounds Sterling.

When they paid the Money, *William* invited them on board the Sloop, where they came, and the merry old Quaker diverted them exceedingly with his Talk, and *Thee'd* 'em, and *Thou'd* 'em, till he made 'em fo drunk, that they could not go on Shore for that Night.

They would fain have known who our People were, and whence they came, but not a Man in the Sloop would anfwer them to any Queftion they ask'd, but in fuch a Manner as let them think themfelves banter'd and jefted with. However, in Difcourfe, *William* faid, they were able Men for any Cargo we could have brought them,

and

and that they would have bought twice as much
Spice if we had had it. He ordered the merry
Captain to tell them, that they had another
Sloop that lay at *Marmagoon*, and that had a great
Quantity of Spice on board alſo ; and that if it
was not ſold when he went back, for that thither
he was bound, he would bring her up.

Their new Chaps were ſo eager, that they
would have bargain'd with the old Captain before-hand : Nay Friend, *ſaid he*, I will not trade
with thee unſight and unſeen ; neither do I know
whether the Maſter of the Sloop may not have
ſold his Loading already to ſome Merchants of
Salſet ; but if he has not, when I come to him, I
think to bring him up to thee.

The Doctor had his Employment all this
while, as well as *William* and the old Captain ; for
he went on ſhore ſeveral Times a Day in the *Indian* Boat, and brought freſh Proviſions for the
Sloop, which the Men had need enough of ; he
brought in particularly ſeventeen large Casks of
Arrack, as big as Buts, beſides ſmaller Quantities,
a Quantity of Rice, and Abundance of Fruits,
Mangoes, Pompions, and ſuch Things, with
Fowls and Fiſh. He never came on board but
he was deep laden ; for, in ſhort, he bought for
the Ship, as well as for themſelves ; and particu-
ly, they half loaded the Ship with Rice and Arrack, with ſome Hogs, and ſix or ſeven Cows, a-
live ; and thus being well victualled, and having
Directions for coming again, they returned
to us.

William was always the lucky welcome Meſſen-
ger to us, but never more welcome to us than
now ; for where we had thruſt in the Ship we could
get nothing, except a few Mangoes and Roots,

being

being not willing to make any Steps into the Country, or make our selves known, till we had News of our Sloop; and indeed our Mens Patience was almost tired, for it was seventeen Days that *William* spent upon this Enterprize, and well bestow'd too.

When he came back, we had another Conference upon the Subject of Trade, namely, whether we should send the rest of our Spices, and other Goods we had in the Ship, to *Surat*; or, whether we should go up to the Gulph of *Persia* our selves, where it was probable we might sell them as well as the *English* Merchants of *Surat*. *William* was for going our selves, which, by the Way, was from the good frugal Merchant-like Temper of the Man, who was for the best of every Thing: But here I over-ruled *William*, which I very seldom took upon me to do; but I told him, that, considering our Circumstances, it was much better for us to sell all our Cargoe here, though we made but half Price of them, than to go with them to the Gulph of *Persia*, where we should run a greater Risque, and where People would be much more curious and inquisitive into Things than they were here, and where it would not be so easy to manage them, seeing they traded freely and openly there, not by Stealth, as those Men seemed to do; and besides, if they suspected any Thing, it would be much more difficult for us to retreat, except by meer Force, than here, where we were upon the high Sea, as it were, and could be gone whenever we pleased, without any Disguise, or indeed without the least Appearance of being pursued, none knowing where to look for us.

My

My Apprehenfions prevailed with *William*, whether my Reafons did or no, and he fubmitted ; and we refolved to try another Ship's Loading to the fame Merchants ; the main Bufinefs was to confider how to get off of that Circumftance had expofed them with the *Englifh* Merchants ; namely, that it was our other Sloop ; but this the old Quaker Pilot undertook ; for being, as I faid, an excellent Mimick himfelf, it was the eafier for him to drefs up the Sloop in new Clothes ; and firft he put on all the carved Work he had taken off before ; her Stern, which was painted of a dumb white, or dun Colour, before all flat, was now all lacquer'd, and blue, and I know not how many gay Figures in it ; as to her Quarter, the Carpenters made her a neat little Gallery on either Side ; fhe had 12 Guns put into her, and fome Patereroes upon her Gunnel, none of which were there before ; and to finifh her new Habit or Appearance, and make her Change compleat, he ordered her Sails to be alter'd ; and as fhe failed before with a Half-Sprit, like a Yacht, fhe failed now with fquare Sail and Mizen Maft, like a Ketch ; fo that, in a Word, fhe was a perfect Cheat, difguifed in every Thing that a Stranger could be fuppofed to take any Notice of, that had never had but one View ; for they had been but once on board.

In this mean Figure the Sloop returned ; fhe had a new Man put into her for Captain, one we knew how to truft ; and the old Pilot appearing only as a Paffenger, the Doctor and *William* acting as the Super-Cargoes, by a formal Procuration from one Captain *Singleton*, and all Things ordered in Form.

We

We had a compleat Loading for the Sloop; for besides a very great Quantity of Nutmegs and Cloves, Mace, and some Cinnamon, she had on board some Goods, which we took in as we lay about the *Philippine* Islands, while we waited as looking for Purchase.

William made no Difficulty of selling this Cargoe also, and in about twenty Days returned again, freighted with all necessary Provisions for our Voyage, and for a long Time; and, as I say, we had a great deal of other Goods, he brought us back about three and thirty thousand Pieces of Eight, and some Diamonds; which, tho' *William* did not pretend to much Skill in, yet he made shift to act, so as not to be imposed upon, the Merchants he had to deal with too being very fair Men.

They had no Difficulty at all with these Merchants; for the Prospect they had of Gain made them not at all inquisitive; nor did they make the least Discovery of the Sloop; and as to the Selling them Spices which were fetch'd so far from thence, it seems it was not so much a Novelty there as we believed; for the *Portugueze* had frequently Vessels which came from *Macao* in *China*, who brought Spices, which they bought of the *Chinese* Traders, who again frequently dealt among the *Dutch* Spice Islands, and received Spices in Exchange for such Goods as they carried from *China*.

This might be called indeed the only trading Voyage we had made; and now we were really very rich; and it came now naturally before us to consider whither we should go next; our proper Delivery Port, as we ought to have called it, was at *Madagascar*, in the Bay of *Mangahelly*: But

William

William took me by my felf into the Cabbin of the Sloop one Day, and told me, he wanted to talk ferioufly with me a little ; fo we fhut our felves in, and *William* began with me.

Wilt thou give me Leave, *fays William*, to talk plainly with thee upon thy prefent Circumftan-ces, and the future Profpect of living, and wilt thou promife on thy Word to take nothing ill of me.

With all my Heart, *faid I*, *William*, I have al-ways found your Advice good, and your Defigns have not only been well laid, but your Counfel has been very lucky to us; and therefore fay what you will, I promife you I will not take it ill.

But that is not all my Demand, *fays William*, if thou doft not like what I am going to propofe to thee, thou fhalt promife me not to make it pub-lick among the Men.

I will not, *William*, *fays I*, upon my Word, and fwore to him too very heartily.

Why then, *fays William*, I have but one Thing more to article with thee about, and that is, that thou wilt confent, that if thou doft not ap-prove of it for thy felf, thou wilt yet confent that I fhall put fo much of it in Practice as re-lates to my felf, and my new Comrade *Doctor*, fo that it be in nothing to thy Detriment and Lofs.

In any Thing, *fays I*, *William*, but leaving me, I will; but I cannot part with you upon any Terms whatever.

Well, *fays William*, I am not defigning to part from thee, unlefs it is thy own Doing ; but affure me in all thefe Points ; and I will tell my Mind freely.

So

So I promiſed him every Thing he deſired of me in the ſolemneſt Manner poſſible, and ſo ſeriouſly and frankly withal, that *William* made no Scruple to open his Mind to me.

Why then, in the firſt Place, ſays *William*, ſhall I ask thee if thou doſt not think thou and all thy Men are rich enough, and have really gotten as much Wealth together (by whatſoever Way it has been gotten, that is not the Queſtion) as ye all know what to do with?

Why truly *William*, ſaid I, thou art pretty right, I think we have had pretty good Luck.

Well then, ſays *William*, I would ask, whether, if thou haſt gotten enough, thou haſt any Thought of leaving off this Trade; for moſt People leave off Trading when they are ſatisfied with getting, and are rich enough; for no body trades for the ſake of Trading, much leſs do any Men rob for the ſake of Thieving.

Well, *William*, ſays I, now I perceive what it is thou art driving at; I warrant you, ſays I, you begin to hanker after Home.

Why truly, ſays *William*, thou haſt ſaid it, and ſo I hope thou doſt too; it is natural for moſt Men that are abroad to deſire to come Home again at laſt, eſpecially when they are grown rich, and when they are (as thou owneſt thy ſelf to be) rich enough, and ſo rich, as they know not what to do with more if they had it.

Well, *William*, ſaid I, but now you think you have laid your Preliminary at firſt ſo home, that I ſhould have nothing to ſay; that is, that when I had got Money enough, it would be natural to think of going Home; but you have not explained what you mean by Home,

and

and there you and I shall differ. Why, Man, I am at Home, here is my Habitation, I never had any other in my Life time; I was a kind of Charity School-Boy, so that I can have no Desire of going any where for being rich or poor, for I have no where to go.

Why, *says William*, looking a little confused, art not thou an *Englishman?* Yes, *says I*, I think so, you see I speak *English*; but I came out of *England* a Child, and never was in it but once since I was a Man, and then I was cheated and imposed upon, and used so ill, that I care not if I never see it more.

Why hast thou no Relations or Friends there, *says he*, no Acquaintance, none that thou hast any Kindness for, or any remains of Respect for?

Not I, *William, said I*, not one, no more than I have in the Court of the Great *Mogul*.

Nor any Kindness for the Country, where thou wast born, *says William*.

Not I, any more than for the Island of *Madagascar*, nor so much neither; for that has been a fortunate Island to me more than once, as thou knowest, *William, said I*.

William was quite stunn'd at my Discourse, and held his Peace; and *I said to him*, go on, *William*, what hast thou to say farther? For I hear you have some Project in your Head, *says he*, come, let's have it out.

Nay, *says William*, thou hast put me to Silence, and all I had to say is over-thrown; all my Projects are come to nothing, and gone.

Well, but *William, said I*, let me hear what they were, for tho' it is so that what I have to aim at does not look your Way; and tho' I have
no

no Relation, no Friend, no Acquaintance in *England*, yet I do not say I like this roving, cruising Life, so well as never to give it over: Let me hear if thou canst propose to me any thing beyond it.

Certainly Friend, *says William*, very gravely, there is something beyond it, and lifting up his Hands, he seemed very much affected, and I thought I see Tears stand in his Eyes, but I, that was too hardned a Wretch to be moved with these Things, laughed at him; what, *says I*, you mean *Death*, I warrant you, don't you, that is beyond this Trade; why, when it comes, it comes, then we are all provided for.

Ay, *says William*, that is true; but it wou'd be better that some Things were thought on before that came.

Thought on, *says I*, what signifies thinking of it; to think of Death, is to dye; and to be always thinking of it, is to be all one's Life-long a dying; 'tis Time enough to think of it when it comes.

You will easily believe I was well qualified for a Pirate that could talk thus; but let me leave it upon Record for the Remark of other hardned Rogues like my self. My Conscience gave me a Pang that I had never felt before, when I said, *What signifies thinking of it*, and told me, I shou'd one Day think of these Words with a sad Heart, but the Time of my Reflection was not yet come; so I went on.

Says William, very seriously, I must tell thee, Friend, I am sorry to hear thee talk so; they that never think of dying, often dye without thinking of it.

I car-

I carried on the jefting Way a while farther, *and faid*, prithee do not talk of dying; how do we know we fhall ever dye, and began to laugh?

I need not anfwer thee to that, *fays William*, it is not my Place to reprove thee who art Commander over me here, but I had rather thou wouldft talk otherwife of Death; 'tis a coarfe Thing.

Say any Thing to me, *William, faid I*, I will take it kindly: *I began now to be very much moved at his Difcourfe.*

Says William, Tears running down his Face, it is becaufe Men live as if they were never to dye, that fo many dye before they know how to live; but it was not Death that I meant, when I faid, *That there was fomething to be thought of beyond this Way of Living.*

Why, *William, faid I*, what was that?

It was *Repentance, fays he.*

Why, *fays I*, did you ever know a Pirate repent?

At this he ftarted a little, and return'd, at the Gallows, I have one before, and I hope thou wilt be the fecond.

He fpoke this very affectionately, and with an Appearance of Concern for me.

Well, *William, fays I*, I thank you, and I am not fo fenfelefs of thefe Things, perhaps, as I make my felf feem to be; but come, let me hear your Propofal.

My Propofal, *fays William*, is for thy Good, as well as my own; we may put an End to this kind of Life, and repent; and I think the faireft Occafion offers for both at this very Time that ever did, or ever will, or indeed, can happen again.

Look

Look you, *William*, *says I*, let me have your Proposal for putting an End to our prefent Way of Living firft, for that is the Cafe before us, and you and I will talk of the other afterward. I am not fo infenfible, *faid I*, as you may think me to be ; but let us get out of this hellifh Condition we are in firft.

Nay, *fays William*, thou art in the right there ; we muft never talk of repenting while we continue Pirates.

Well, *fays I*, *William*, that's what I meant, for if we muft not reform, as well as be forry for what's done, I have no Notion what Repentance means ; indeed, at beft I know little of the Matter ; but the Nature of the thing feems to tell me, that the firft Step we have to take, is to break off this wretched Courfe, and I'll begin there with you with all my Heart.

I could fee by his Countenance, that *William* was throughly pleafed with the Offer ; and if he had Tears in his Eyes before, he had more now, but it was from a quite differing Paffion, for he was fo fwallow'd up with Joy, he could not fpeak.

Come, *William*, *fays I*, thou fheweft me plain enough thou haft an honeft Meaning. Doft thou think 'tis practicable for us to put an End to our unhappy Way of Living here, and get off ?

Yes, *fays he*, I think 'tis very practicable for me, whether 'tis for thee or no, that will depend upon thy felf.

Well, *fays I*, I give you my Word, that as I have commanded you all along, from the Time I firft took you on Board, fo you fhall command me from this Hour ; and every thing you direct me, I'll do.

Wilt

Wilt thou leave it all to me? Doft thou fay this freely?

Yes, *William, fays I,* freely, and I'll perform it faithfully.

Why then, *fays William,* my Scheme is this, we are now at the Mouth of the Gulph of *Perfia,* we have fold fo much of our Cargo here at *Surat,* that we have Money enough; fend me away for *Baffora* with the Sloop, loaden with the *China* Goods we have on Board, which will make another good Cargo; and I'll warrant thee I'll find Means among the *Englifh* and the *Dutch* Merchants there, to lodge a Quantity of Goods and Money alfo *as a Merchant,* fo as we will be able to have Recourfe to it again upon any Occafion, and when I come Home we will contrive the reft; and in the mean Time do you bring the Ship's Crew to take a Refolution to go to *Madagafcar,* as foon as I return.

I told him, I thought he need not go fo far as *Baffora,* but might run into *Gombaroon,* or to *Ormus,* and pretend the fame Bufinefs.

No, *fays he,* I cannot act with the fame Freedom there, becaufe the Company's Factory are there, and I may be laid hold of there on Pretence of Interloping.

Well, but, *faid I,* you may go to *Ormus* then, for I am loath to part with you fo long as to go to the Bottom of the *Perfian* Gulph. He return'd that I fhould leave it to him to do as he fhould fee Caufe.

We had taken a large Sum of Money at *Surat;* fo that we had near a hundred thoufand Pounds in Money at our Command; but on board the great Ship we had ftill a great deal more.

I or-

I ordered him publickly to keep the Money on board which he had, and to buy up with it a Quantity of Ammunition if he could get it, and so to furnish us for new Exploits; and in the mean Time I refolved to get a Quantity of Gold and fome Jewels, which I had on board the great Ship, and place them fo, that I might carry them off without Notice, as foon as he came back; and fo according to *William*'s Directions, I left him to go the Voyage, and I went on board the great Ship, in which we had indeed an immenfe Treafure.

We waited no lefs than two Months, for *William*'s Return; and indeed I began to be very uneafy about *William*, fometimes thinking he had abandoned me, and that he might have ufed the fame Artifice to have engaged the other Men to comply with him, and fo they were gone away together; and it was but three Days before his Return, that I was juft upon the Point of refolving to go away to *Madagafcar*, and give him over; but the old Surgeon, who mimicked the Quaker, and paffed for the Mafter of the Sloop at *Surat*, perfwaded me againft that; for which good Advice, and his apparent Faithfulnefs in what he had been trufted with, I made him a Party to my Defign, and he proved very honeft.

At length *William* came back, to our inexpreffible Joy, and brought a great many neceffary Things with him; as particularly, he brought fixty Barrels of Powder, fome Iron Shot, and about thirty Ton of Lead; alfo he brought a great deal of Provifions; and in a Word, *William* gave me a publick Account of his Voyage, in the Hearing of whoever happened to be upon the

Quarter-

Quarter-Deck, that no Sufpicions might be
found about us.

After all was done, *William* moved, that he
might go up again, and that I would go with
him; named feveral Things which we had on
board that he could not fell there, and particularly told us, he had been obliged to leave feveral Things there, the Caravans being not come
in; and that he had ingaged to come back again
with Goods.

This was what I wanted; the Men were eager
for his Going, and particularly becaufe he told
them they might load the Sloop back with
Rice and Provifions: But I feemed backward to
going; when the old Surgeon ftood up, and perfwaded me to go, and with many Arguments
preffed me to it; as part'cularly, if I did not go,
there would be no Order, and feveral of the
Men might drop away, and perhaps betray all
the reft; and that they fhould not think it fafe
for the Sloop to go again, if I did not go; and
to urge me to it, he offered himfelf to go
with me.

Upon thefe Confiderations I feemed to be over-
perfwaded to go; and all the Company feemed
the better fatisfied when I had confented: And
accordingly we took all the Powder, Lead, and
Iron out of the Sloop into the great Ship, and
all the other Things that were for the Ship's
Ufe, and put in fome Bales of Spices, and Casks
or Frailes of Cloves, in all about feven Ton, and
fome other Goods, among the Bales of which I
had convey'd all my private Treafure, which, I
affure you, was of no fmall Value; and away
I went.

At

At going off, I called a Council of all the Officers in the Ship, to confider in what Place they
fhould wait for me, and how long, where we appointed the Ship to ftay eight and twenty Days,
at a little Ifland on the *Arabian* Side of the Gulph;
and that if the Sloop did not come in that Time,
they fhould fail to another Ifland to the Weft of
that Place, and wait there fifteen Days more;
and that then if the Sloop did not come, they
fhould conclude fome Accident muft have happened, and the Rendezvous fhould be at *Madagafcar.*

Being thus refolved, we left the Ship, which
both *William,* and I, and the Surgeon never intended to fee any more : We fteered directly
for the Gulph, and through to *Baffaro,* or *Balfara.*
This City of *Balfara* lies at fome Diftance from
the Place where our Sloop lay, and the River
not being very fafe, and we but ill acquainted
with it, having but an ordinary Pilot, we went
on Shore at a Village where fome Merchants live,
and which is very populous, for the fake of fmall
Veffels riding there.

Here we ftay'd, and traded three or four
Days, landing all our Bales and Spices, and indeed the whole Cargoe, that was of any confiderable Value; which we chofe to do rather than
go up immediately to *Balfara,* till the Project
we had laid was put in Execution.

After we had bought feveral Goods, and were
preparing to buy feveral others, the Boat being
on Shore with twelve Men, my felf, *William,* the
Surgeon, and one Fourth Man, whom we had
fingled out, we contrived to fend a *Turk,* juft at
the Dusk of the Evening, with a Letter to the
Boatfwain; and giving the Fellow a Charge to
run

run with all possible Speed, we stood at a small
Distance to observe the Event. The Contents
of the Letter were thus written by the old
Doctor.

‘ Boatswain *Thomas*,

‘ WE are all betray'd; for God's Sake
‘ make off with the Boat, and get on
‘ board, or you are all lost. The Captain, *Wil-*
‘ *liam* the Quaker, and *George* the Reformade are
‘ seized and carried away ; I am escaped and hid,
‘ but cannot stir out ; If I do I am a dead Man :
‘ As soon as you are on board, cut or slip, and
‘ make Sail for your Lives.

‘ Adieu.

R. S.

We stood undiscovered, as above, it being
the Dusk of the Evening, and saw the *Turk* deliver the Letters; and in three Minutes we saw
all the Men hurry into the Boat, and put off;
and no sooner were they on board, but they
took the Hint, as we supposed; for the next
Morning they were out of Sight; and we
never heard Tale or Tidings of them since.

We were now in a good Place, and in very
good Circumstances, for we past for Merchants of *Persia*.

It is not material to record here what a
Mass of ill-gotten Wealth we had got together :
It will be more to the Purpose to tell you, that I
began to be sensible of the Crime of getting of it
in such a Manner as I had done, that I had very
little Satisfaction in the Possession of it ; and, as
I told *William*, I had no Expectation of keeping it,

Z 3

nor

nor much Defire; but as I faid to him one Day
walking out into the Fields near the Town at
Baffaro, fo I depended upon it, that it would be
the Cafe, which you will hear prefently.

We were perfectly fecured at *Baffaro*, by having frighted away the Rogues, our Comrades;
and we had nothing to do but to confider how to
vert our Treafure in Things proper to make us
look like Merchants, as we were now to be,
and not like Free-booters, as we really had
been.

We happened very opportunely here upon
a *Dutchman*, who had travelled from *Bengal* to
Agra, the Capital City of the *Great Mogul*, and
from thence was come to the Coaft of *Malabar* by
Land, and got Shipping fome how or other up
the Gulph; and we found his Defign was to go
up the great River to *Bagdat* or *Babylon*; and fo
by the Caravan to *Aleppo* and *Scanderoon*. As *William* fpoke *Dutch*, and was of an agreeable infinua-
ting Behaviour, he foon got acquainted with this
Dutchman, and difcovering our Circumftances to
one another, we found he had confiderable Effects
with him; and that he had traded long in that
Country, and was making homeward to his own
Country; and that he had Servants with him,
one an *Armenian*, whom he had taught to fpeak
Dutch, and who had fomething of his own, but
had a Mind to travel into *Europe*; and the other
a *Dutch* Sailor, whom he had picked up by his Fancy, and repofed a great Truft in him, and a very
honeft Fellow he was.

This *Dutchman* was very glad of an Acquaintance, becaufe he foon found that we directed our Thoughts to *Europe* alfo, and as he
found we were encumber'd with Goods only,
for

for we let him know nothing of our Money, he readily offer'd us his Affiftance, to difpofe of as many of them as the Place we were in would put off, and his Advice what to do with the reft.

While this was doing, *William* and I confulted what to do with our felves, and what we had ; and firft we refolved we would never talk ferioufly of any of our Meafures, but in the open Fields, where we were fure no Body could hear ; fo every Evening, when the Sun began to decline, and the Air to be moderate, we walk'd out fometimes this Way, fometimes that, to confult of our Affairs.

I fhould have obferved, that we had new cloathed our felves here after the *Perfian* Manner, in long Vefts of Silk, a Gown or Robe of *Englifh* Crimfon Cloth, very fine and handfome, and had let our Beards grow fo after the *Perfian* Manner, that we paft for *Perfian* Merchants, in View only, tho', *by the Way*, we could not underftand or fpeak one Word of the Language of *Perfia*, or indeed of any other but *Englifh* and *Dutch*, and of the latter I underftood very little.

However, the *Dutchman* fupply'd all this for us, and as we had refolved to keep our felves as retired as we could, though there were feveral *Englifh* Merchants upon the Place, yet we never acquainted our felves with one of them, or exchanged a Word with them, by which Means we prevented their Enquiry of us now, or their giving any Intelligence of us, if any News of our Landing here fhould happen to come, which it was eafy for us to know, was poffible enough, if any of our Comrades fell into bad Hands, or by many Accidents which we could not forefee.

It

It was during my being here, for here we ſtay'd near two Months, that I grew very thoughtful about my Circumſtances, not as to the Danger, neither indeed were we in any, but were entirely conceal'd and unſuſpected; but I really began to have other Thoughts of my ſelf, and of the World, than ever I had before.

William had ſtruck ſo deep into my unthinking Temper, with hinting to me, that there was ſomething beyond all this, that the preſent Time was the Time of Enjoyment, but that the Time of Account approached; that the Work that remain'd was gentler than the Labour paſt, *viz.* *Repentance,* and that it was high Time to think of it; I ſay theſe, and ſuch Thoughts as theſe, engroſs'd my Hours, and in a Word, I grew very ſad.

As to the Wealth I had, which was immenſely great, it was all like Dirt under my Feet; I had no Value for it, no Peace in the Poſſeſſion of it, no great Concern about me for the leaving of it.

William had perceiv'd my Thoughts to be troubled, and my Mind heavy and oppreſt for ſome Time; and one Evening, in one of our cool Walks, I began with him about the leaving our Effects. *William* was a wiſe and wary Man, and indeed all the Prudentials of my Conduct, had for a long Time been owing to his Advice, and ſo now all the Methods for preſerving our Effects, and even our ſelves lay upon him; and he had been telling me of ſome of the Meaſures he had been taking for our making homeward, and for the Security of our Wealth, when I took him very ſhort: *Why, William,* ſays I, *doſt thou think we ſhall ever be able to reach* Europe *with all this Cargo that we have about us.*

Ay,

Ay, *says William,* without doubt, as well as other Merchants with theirs, as long as it is not publickly known what Quantity, or of what Value our Cargo confifts.

Why, *William, fays I,* fmiling, do you think that if there is a *God above,* as you have fo long been telling me there is, and that we muft give an Account to him? I fay, Do you think if he be a righteous Judge, he will let us efcape thus with the Plunder, as we may call it, of fo many innocent People, nay, I might fay Nations, and not call us to an Account for it before we can get to *Europe,* where we pretend to enjoy it?

William appeared ftruck and furprized at the Queftion, and made no Anfwer for a great while, and I repeated the Queftion, adding, that it was not to be expected.

After a little Paufe, *fays William,* Thou haft ftarted a very weighty Queftion, and I can make no pofitive Anfwer to it, but I will ftate it thus; firft, it is Time, that if we confider the Juftice of God, we have no Reafon to expect any Protection, but as the ordinary Ways of Providence are out of the common Road of human Affairs, fo we may hope for Mercy ftill upon our Repentance, and we know not how good he may be to us; fo we are to act as if we rather depended upon the laft, I mean the merciful Part, than claimed the firft, which muft produce nothing but Judgment and Vengeance.

But hark ye, *William, fays I,* the Nature of Repentance, as you hinted once to me, included Reformation, and we can never reform; how then can we repent?

Why, can we never reform, *fays William?*

Becaufe,

Becaufe, *faid I*, we cannot reftore what we have taken away by Rapine and Spoil.

'Tis true, *fays William*, we can never do that, for we can never come to the Knowledge of the Owners-

But what then muft be done with our Wealth, *faid I*, the Effects of Plunder and Rapine? If we keep it, we continue to be Robbers and Thieves, and if we quit it, we cannot do Juftice with it, for we cannot reftore it to the right Owners?

Nay, *fays William*, the Anfwer to it is fhort; to quit what we have, and do it here, is to throw it away to thofe who have no Claim to it, and to diveft our felves of it, but to do no Right with it; whereas we ought to keep it carefully toge-ther, with a Refolution to do what Right with it we are able; and who knows what Opportunity Providence may put into our Hands, to do Juftice at leaft to fome of thofe we have injured, fo we ought at leaft to leave it to him, and go on, as it is, without doubt, our prefent Bufinefs to do, to fome Place of Safety, where we may wait his Will.

This Refolution of *William* was very fatisfying to me indeed, as, the Truth is, all he faid, and at all Times, was folid and good; and had not *Wil-liam* thus, as it were, quieted my Mind, I think verily I was fo alarmed at the juft Reafon I had to expect Vengeance from Heaven upon me for my ill-gotten Wealth, that I fhould have run away from it as the Devil's Goods; that I had nothing to do with that did not belong to me, and that I had no Right to keep, and was in certain Danger of being deftroy'd for.

However, *William* fettled my Mind to more prudent Steps than thefe, and I concluded that I ought,

ought, however, to proceed to a Place of Safety, and leave the Event to God Almighty's Mercy; but this I muſt leave upon Record, that I had from this Time no Joy of the Wealth I had got; I look'd upon it all as a ſtolen, and ſo indeed the greateſt Part of it was; I look'd upon it as a Hoard of other Mens Goods, which I had robbed the innocent Owners of, and which I ought, in a Word, to be hanged for here, and damned for hereafter; and now indeed I began ſincerely to hate my ſelf for a Dog, a Wretch that had been a Thief, and a Murtherer; a Wretch, that was in a Condition which no Body was ever in; for I had robb'd, and tho' I had the Wealth by me, yet it was impoſſible I ſhould ever make any Reſtitution; and upon this Account it run in my Head, that I could never repent, for that Repentance could not be ſincere without Reſtitution, and therefore I muſt of Neceſſity be damned, there was no room for me to eſcape: I went about with my Heart full of theſe Thoughts, little better than a diſtracted Fellow; in ſhort, running headlong into the dreadfulleſt Deſpair, and premeditated nothing but how to rid my ſelf out of the World; and indeed the Devil, if ſuch Things are of the Devil's immediate doing, followed his Work very cloſe with me, and nothing lay upon my Mind for ſeveral Days, but to ſhoot my ſelf into the Head with my Piſtol.

I was all this while in a vagrant Life, among Infidels, Turks, Pagans, and ſuch Sort of People; I had no Miniſter, no Chriſtian, to converſe with, but poor *William*, he was my Ghoſtly Father, or Confeſſor, and he was all the Comfort I had. As for my Knowledge of Religion, you have heard my Hiſtory; you may ſuppoſe I had not much, and

and as for the Word of God, I don't remember
that I ever read a Chapter in the *Bible* in my Life-
time ; I was *little Bob* at *Buffelton*, and went to
School to learn my *Teftament*

However, it pleafed God to make *William* the
Quaker every thing to me ; upon this Occafion I
took him out one Evening as ufual, and hurried
him away into the Fields with me, in more Hafte
than ordinary, and there, in fhort, I told him
the Perplexity of my Mind, and under what terrible Temptations of the Devil I had been, that
I muft fhoot my felf, for I could not fupport the
Weight and Terror that was upon me.

Shoot your felf, *fays William*, why, what will
that do for you ?

Why, *fays I*, 'twill put an End to a miferable
Life.

Well, *fays William*, are you fatisfied the next
will be better ?

No, no, *fays I*, much worfe to be fure.

Why then, *fays he*, fhoot your felf is the Devil's Notion, no doubt, for 'tis the Devil of a
Reafon, that becaufe thou art in an ill Cafe, that
therefore thou muft put thy felf into a worfe.

This fhock'd my Reafon indeed : Well, but
fays I, there is no bearing the miferable Condition
I am in.

Very well, *fays William*, but it feems there is
fome bearing a worfe Condition, and fo you will
fhoot your felf, that you may be paft Remedy.

I am paft Remedy already, *fays I*.

How do you know that, *fays he* ?

I am fatisfied of it, *faid I*.

Well, *fays he*, but you are not fure, fo you will
fhoot your felf to make it certain; for tho' on this
fide Death you can't be fure you will be damned

at

at all, yet the Moment you ſtep on the other ſide of Time, you are ſure of it ; for when 'tis done, 'tis not to be ſaid then that you will, but that you are damned.

Well, but, ſays William, *as if he had been between Jeſt and Earneſt,* pray, what didſt thou dream of laſt Night ?

Why, *ſaid I,* I had frightful Dreams all Night, and particularly I dreamt that the Devil came for me, and asked me what my Name was? and I told him, then he askt me what Trade I was? Trade, *ſays I,* I am a Thief, a Rogue, by my Calling ; I am a Pirate, and a Murtherer, and ought to be hanged ; ay, ay, ſays the Devil, ſo you do, and you are the Man I look'd for, and therefore come along with me, at which I was moſt horribly frighted, and cried out, ſo that it waked me, and I have been in a horrible Agony ever ſince.

Very well, *ſays William,* come, give me the Piſtol thou talk'ſt of juſt now.

Why, *ſays I,* what will you do with it ?

Do with it, *ſays William,* why, thou needſt not ſhoot thy ſelf, I ſhall be obliged to do it for thee, why, thou wilt deſtroy us all.

What do you mean, *William, ſaid I ?*

Mean, *ſaid he,* nay, what diſt thou mean ? to cry out aloud in thy Sleep, *I am a Thief, a Pirate, a Murtherer, and ought to be hanged ;* why, thou wilt ruine us all, 'twas well the *Dutchman* did not underſtand *Engliſh* : In ſhort, I muſt ſhoot thee to ſave my own Life ; come, come, *ſays he,* give me thy Piſtol.

I confeſs, this terrified me again another Way, and I began to be ſenſible, that if any Body had been near me to underſtand *Engliſh,* I had been undone, and the Thought of ſhooting my ſelf
forſook

forfook me from that Time, and I turned to *William*; you diforder me extremely, *William, faid I*, why, I am never fafe, nor is it fafe to keep me Company, what fhall I do? I fhall betray you all.

Come, come, Friend *Bob, fays he*, I'll put an End to it all, if you will take my Advice.

How's that, *faid I*?

Why only, *fays he*, that *the next Time thou talkeft with the Devil, thou wilt talk a little foftlier*, or we fhall be all undone, and you too.

This frighted me, I muft confefs, and allay'd a great deal of the Trouble of Mind I was in; but *William*, after he had done jefting with me, entered upon a very long and ferious Difcourfe with me about the Nature of my Circumftances, and about Repentance, that it ought to be attended indeed with a deep Abhorrence of the Crime that I had to charge my felf with, but that to defpair of God's Mercy was no Part of Repentance, but putting my felf into the Condition of the Devil; indeed, that I muft apply my felf with a fincere humble Confeffion of my Crime, to ask Pardon of God whom I had offended, and caft my felf upon his Mercy, refolving to be willing to make Reftitution, if ever it fhould pleafe God to put it into my Power, even to the utmoft of what I had in the World; and this he told me was the Method which he had refolved upon himfelf, and in this he told me he had found Comfort.

I had a great deal of Satisfaction in *William*'s Difcourfe, and it quieted me very much; but *William* was very anxious ever after about my talking in my Sleep, and took care to lye with me always himfelf, and to keep me from Lodging in any Houfe, where fo much as a Word of *Englifh* was underftood.

However,

However, there was not the like Occasion afterward, for I was much more composed in my Mind, and resolved for the future to live a quite differing Life from what I had done: As to the Wealth I had, I look'd upon it as nothing; I resolved to set it apart to any such Opportunity of doing Justice, that God should put into my Hand, and the miraculous Opportunity I had afterwards of applying some Parts of it to preserve a ruined Family, whom I had plunder'd, may be worth reading, if I have Room for it in this Account.

With these Resolutions I began to be restored to some Degrees of Quiet in my Mind, and having after almost three Months Stay at *Bassora* disposed of some Goods; but having a great Quantity left, we hired Boats according to the *Dutchman*'s Direction, and went up to *Bugdat*, or *Babylon*, on the River *Tygris*, or rather *Euphrates*; we had a very considerable Cargo of Goods with us, and therefore made a great Figure there, and were receiv'd with Respect; we had in Particular, two and Forty Bales of *Indian* Stuffs of sundry Sorts, Silk, Muslins, and fine Chints; we had Fifteen Bales of very fine *China* Silks, and Seventy Packs or Bales of Spices, particularly Cloves and Nutmegs, with other Goods; we were bid Money here for our Cloves, but the *Dutchman* advised us not to part with them, and told us, we should get a better Price at *Aleppo*, or in the *Levant*, so we prepared for the Caravan.

We concealed our having any Gold, or Pearls, as much as we could, and therefore sold Three or Four Bales of *China* Silks, and *Indian* Callicoes, to raise Money to buy Camels, and to pay the Customs,

Customs, which are taken at several Places, and for our Provisions over the Desarts.

I travelled this Journey careless to the last Degree of my Goods or Wealth, believing, that as I came by it all by Rapine and Violence, God would direct, that it should be taken from me again in the same Manner; and indeed, I think I might say, I was very willing it should be so; but as I had a merciful Protector above me, so I had a most faithful Steward, Counsellor, Partner, or whatever I might call him, who was my Guide, my Pilot, my Governor, my every thing, and took care both of me, and of all we had; and tho' he had never been in any of these Parts of the World, yet he took the Care of all upon him; and in about Nine and Fifty Days we arriv'd from *Baffora*, at the Mouth of the River *Tygris* and *Euphrates*, thro' the Desart, and thro' *Aleppo* to *Alexandria*, or as we call it, *Scanderoon*, in the *Levant*.

Here *William* and I, and the other two, our faithful Comrades, debated what we should do; and here *William* and I resolved to separate from the other Two, they resolving to go with the *Dutchman* into *Holland*, and by the Means of some *Dutch* Ship which lay then in the Road: *William* and I told them, we resolved to go and settle in the *Morea*, which then belonged to the *Venetians*.

It is true, we acted wisely in it not to let them know whither we went, seeing we had resolved to separate, but we took our old Doctor's Directions how to write to him in *Holland*, and in *England*, that we might have Intelligence from him on Occasion, and promised to give him an Account how to write to us, which
we

we afterwards did, as may in Time be made out.

We ſtay'd here ſome Time after they were gone, till at length not being thoroughly reſolved whither to go till then, a *Venetian* Ship touch'd at *Cyprus*, and put in at *Scanderoon* to look for Freight Home: We took the Hint, and bargaining for our Paſſage, and the Freight of our Goods, we embark'd for *Venice*, where in two and Twenty Days we arrived ſafe with all our Treaſure, and with ſuch a Cargo, take our Goods, and our Money, and our Jewels together, as I believe was never brought into the City by Two ſingle Men, ſince the State of *Venice* had a Being.

We kept our ſelves here *incognito* for a great while, paſſing for Two *Armenian* Merchants ſtill, as we had done before ; and by this Time we had gotten ſo much of the *Perſian* and *Armenian* Jargon, which they talk'd at *Baſſora*, and *Bagdat*, and every where that we came in the Country, as was ſufficient to make us able to talk to one another, ſo as not to be underſtood by any Body, though ſometimes hardly by our ſelves.

Here we converted all our Effects into Money, ſettled our Abode as for a conſiderable Time, and *William* and I maintaining an inviolable Friendſhip and Fidelity to one another, lived like two Brothers ; we neither had or ſought any ſeparate Intereſt; we converſ'd ſeriouſly and gravely, and upon the Subject of our Repentance continually ; we never changed, that is to ſay, ſo as to leave off our *Armenian* Garbs, and we were called at *Venice* the two *Grecians*.

I have been two or three times going to give a Detail of our Wealth, but it will appear incredible, and we had the greateſt Difficulty in the

World

World how to conceal it, being juftly apprehen-
five left we might be affaffinated in that Country
for our Treafure; at length *William* told me, he
began to think now that he muft never fee *England* any more, and that indeed he did not much
concern himfelf about it; but feeing we had
gained fo great a Wealth, and he had fome poor
Relations in *England*, and, if I was willing, he would
write to know if they were living, and to know
what Condition they were in; and if he found
fuch of them were alive, as he had fome Thoughts
about, he would, with my Confent, fend them
fomething to better their Condition.

I confented moft willingly, and accordingly
William wrote to a Sifter, and an Uncle, and in
about five Weeks Time receiv'd an Anfwer from
them both, directed to himfelf, under Cover of a
hard *Armenian* Name that he had given himfelf,
viz. Seignior *Conftantine Alexion of Ifpahan* at *Venice*.

It was a very moving Letter he receiv'd from
his Sifter, who after the moft paffionate Expreffi-
ons of Joy to hear he was alive, feeing fhe had
long ago had an Account that he was murthered by
the Pirates in the *Weft Indies*; fhe intreats him to
let her know what Circumftances he was in; tells
him, fhe was not in any Capacity to do any thing
confiderable for him, but that he fhould be welcome to her with all her Heart; that fhe was left
a Widow with Four Children, but kept a little
Shop in the *Minories*, by which fhe made fhift to
maintain her Family; and that fhe had fent him
Five Pound, left he fhould want Money in a
ftrange Country, to bring him Home.

I could

I could see the Letter brought Tears out of his Eyes, as he read it, and indeed when he shewed it me, and the little Bill for Five Pounds upon an *English* Merchant in *Venice*, it brought Tears out of my Eyes too.

After we had been both affected sufficiently with the Tenderness and Kindness of this Letter, he turns to me, *says he*, what shall I do for this poor Woman? I mused a while, at last, *says I*, I will tell you what you shall do for her; she has sent you Five Pounds, and she has Four Children, and her self, that's Five; such a Sum from a poor Woman in her Circumstances, is as much as Five Thousand Pounds is to us: You shall send her a Bill of Exchange for Five Thousand Pounds *English* Money, and bid her conceal her Surprize at it, till she hears from you again, but bid her leave off her Shop, and go and take a House some where in the Country, not far off from *London*, and stay there in a moderate Figure, till she hears from you again.

Now, says *William*, I perceive by it that you have some Thoughts of venturing into *England*.

Indeed *William*, *said I*, you mistake me, but it presently occurred to me that you should venture; for what have you done that you may not be seen there? Why should I desire to keep you from your Relations purely to keep me Company?

William look'd very affectionately upon me; nay, *says he*, we have embarked together so long, and come together so far, I am resolved I'll never part with thee as long as I live, go where thou wilt, or stay where thou wilt; and as for my Sister, said *William*, I cannot send her such a Sum of Money; for whose is all this Money we have? 'tis most of it thine.

No, *William*, *said I*, there is not a Penny of it mine but what is yours too, and I won't have any thing but an equal Share with you, and therefore you shall send it to her, if not, I will send it.

Why, *says William*, it will make the poor Woman distracted, she will be so surprized, she will go out of her Wits; well, *said William*, you may do it prudently; send her a Bill back'd of a Hundred Pounds, and bid her expect more in a Post or two; and that you will send her enough to live on without keeping Shop, and then send her more.

Accordingly *William* sent her a very kind Letter, with a Bill upon a Merchant in *London* for a Hundred and Sixty Pound, and bid her comfort her self with the Hope, that he should be able in a little Time to send her more. About ten Days after he sent her another Bill of Five Hundred and Forty Pound, and a Post or two after another for Three Hundred Pound, making in all a Thousand Pound; and told her he would send her sufficient to leave off her Shop, and directed her to take a House, as above.

He waited then till he received an Answer to all the Three Letters, with an Account, that she had received the Money, and which I did not expect, that she had not let any other Acquaintance know that she had received a Shilling from any Body, or so much as that he was alive, and would not till she heard again.

When he shewed me this Letter, well, *William said I*, this Woman is fit to be trusted with Life or any thing, send her the rest of the Five Thousand Pound; and I'll venture to *England* with you, to this Woman's House, whenever you will.

In

In a Word, we sent her Five Thousand Pound in good Bills, and she receiv'd them punctually, and in a little Time sent her Brother Word, that she had pretended to her Uncle that she was sickly, and could not carry on the Trade any longer, and that she had taken a large House about Four Miles from *London*, under Pretence of letting Lodgings for her Livelihood; and, in short, intimated as if she understood that he intended to come over to be *Incognito*, assuring him he should be as retired as he pleased.

This was opening the very Door for us, that we thought had been effectually shut for this Life; and in a Word, we resolved to venture, but to keep our selves entirely concealed, both as to Name, and every other Circumstance; and accordingly *William* sent his Sister Word, how kindly he took her prudent Steps, and that she had guessed right, that he desired to be retired, and that he obliged her not to increase her Figure, but live private, till she might perhaps see him.

He was going to send the Letter away; come, *William*, *said I*, you shan't send her an empty Letter, tell her, you have a Friend coming with you, that must be as retired as your self, and I'll send her Five Thousand Pound more.

So in short we made this poor Woman's Family rich, and yet when it came to the Point, my Heart failed me, and I durst not venture, and for *William*, he would not stir without me, and so we stayed about two Year after this, considering what we should do.

You may think, perhaps, that I was very prodigal of my ill-gotten Goods, thus to load a Stranger with my Bounty, and give a Gift like a

Prince

Prince to one that had been able to merit nothing of me, or indeed know me: But my Condition ought to be confidered in this Cafe; though I had Money to Profufion, yet I was perfectly deftitute of a Friend in the World to have the leaft Obligation or Affiftance from, or knew not either where to difpofe or truft any Thing I had while I lived, or whom to give it to, if I died.

When I had reflected upon the Manner of my Getting of it, I was fometimes for giving of it all to charitable Ufes, as a Debt due to Mankind, though I was a Roman-Catholick, and not at all of the Opinion, that it would purchafe me any Repofe to my Soul; but I thought, as it was got by a general Plunder, and which I could make no Satisfaction for, it was due to the Community, and I ought to diftribute it for the general Good. But ftill I was at a Lofs how, and where, and by whom to fettle this Charity, not daring to go Home to my own Country, left fome of my Comrades ftroled Home fhould fee and detect me; and, for the very Spoil of my Money, or the Purchafe of his own Pardon, betray and expofe me to an untimely End.

Being thus deftitute, I fay, of a Friend, I pitch'd thus upon *William*'s Sifter; the kind Step of her's to her Brother, who fhe thought to be in Diftrefs, fignifying a generous Mind, and a charitable Difpofition; and having refolved to make her the Object of my firft Bounty, I did not doubt but I fhould purchafe fomething of a Refuge for my felf, and a kind of a Centre, to which I fhould tend in my future Actions; for really a Man that has a Subfiftance, and no Refidence, no Place that has a Magnetick Influence upon his Affections, is in one of the moft odd uneafy Conditions

ditions in the World; nor is it in the Power of all his Money to make it up to him.

It was, as I told you, two Year and upwards, that we remained at *Venice*, and thereabout, in the greateſt Heſitation imaginable, irreſolute and unfixed to the laſt Degree. *William*'s Siſter importuned us daily to come to *England*, and wondered we ſhould not dare to truſt her, whom we had to ſuch a Degree obliged to be faithful ; and in a Manner lamented her being ſuſpected by us.

At laſt I began to incline ; and I ſaid to *William*, Come, Brother *William*, ſaid I, *for ever ſince our Diſcourſe at* Balſara, *I called him Brother*, if you will agree to two or three Things with me, I'll go Home to *England* with all my Heart.

Says William, let me know what they are.

Why firſt, *ſays I*, you ſhall not diſcloſe your ſelf to any of your Relations in *England*, but your Siſter, no not to one.

Secondly, we will not ſhave off our Muſtachoes or Beards, (for we had all along worn our Beards after the *Grecian* Manner) nor leave off our long Veſts, that we may paſs for *Grecians* and Foreigners.

Thirdly, That we ſhall never ſpeak *Engliſh* in publick before any body, your Siſter excepted.

Fourthly, That we will always live together, and paſs for Brothers.

William ſaid, he would agree to them all with all his Heart; but that the not ſpeaking *Engliſh* would be the hardeſt ; but he would do his beſt for that too: So, in a Word, we agreed to go from *Venice* to *Naples*, where we verted a large Sum of Money in Bales of Silk, left a large Sum in a Merchant's Hands at *Venice*, and another conſiderable Sum at *Naples*, and took Bills of Exchange for a great deal too ; and yet we came

with

with such a Cargoe to *London*, as few *American* Merchants had done for some Years; for we loaded in two Ships seventy three Bales of thrown Silk, besides thirteen Bales of wrought Silks from the Dutchy of *Milan*, shipt at *Genoa*; with all which I arrived safely, and some time after married my faithful Protectress, *William*'s Sister, with whom I am much more happy than I deserve.

And now, having so plainly told you, that I am come to *England*, after I have so boldly own'd what Life I have led abroad, 'tis Time to leave off, and say no more for the present, left some should be willing to inquire too nicely after

Your Old Friend,

CAPTAIN BOB.

F I N I S.